SUNSET,
Water City

BOOKS BY CHRIS McKINNEY

○ ○ ○

The Tattoo
The Queen of Tears

The Water City Trilogy

Midnight, Water City
Eventide, Water City
Sunset, Water City

SUNSET, Water City

CHRIS McKINNEY

SOHO CRIME

Published by
Soho Press, Inc.
227 W 17th Street
New York, NY 10011

Library of Congress Cataloging-in-Publication Data

Names: McKinney, Chris, 1973– author.
Title: Sunset, Water City / Chris McKinney.
Description: New York, NY : Soho Crime, [2023]

ISBN 978-1-64129-595-6
eISBN 978-1-64129-514-7

Subjects: LCGFT: Science fiction. | Apocalyptic fiction.
Detective and mystery fiction. | Novels.
Classification: LCC PS3613.C5623 S86 2023
DDC 813'.6—dc23/eng/20230526
LC record available at https://lccn.loc.gov/2023024863

Interior design by Janine Agro

Printed in the United States of America

10 9 8 7 6 5 4 3 2 1

For my grandma, Miryung Choy

PART ONE

SMALL RECKONINGS

THE GIRL

It's Patch Tuesday, Okaasan's weekly system update, and the legless Gardeners inch their wheelchairs forward with their minds. *Must not use arms*, they tell one another in Thought Talk. Soon they'll find out who'll get promoted and forfeit their arms for Okaasan, too. If they pass, it won't be long before they purr the same *must not use* of their torsos, necks, lips, then tongues. Flies buzz around the blotted gauze that swaddles fresh stumps. It's a hot day in Epcot, Florida, and the amputees sweat under the shadowed fingers of overgrown trees.

I turn up my black foam fit's cooling system. The humidity here reminds me of Water City, but it's been years since I've been. Travel there and between continents became restricted back in Patch v4.S.52, two years after Satori Day—the day that Akira Kimura broke into the minds of billions and took up permanent residence. The passage of time, now marked by patch designations—version number followed by size of update and year—has moved slowly for me over the last ten years, and the inability to travel to other places has not helped. My father thinks Okaasan's got every continent on its own secret mission. I wonder what these missions on other continents are. Do the Gardeners function as they do here? Are they also commanded to participate in self-mutilation, provide never-ending sacrifices to a technological god? I hope not.

Here at Epcot, the mission is not secret. At least not to us. Okaasan is training the next generation of astronauts who will sling across Ame-no-ukihashi, the largest manmade structure Earth has ever seen. The launch loop is a buzzing tubular ramp that slopes across the Gulf of Mexico some fifty miles into the sky and shoots astronauts throughout the solar system. My father and I call it Dragonspine because it resembles the bones of a 1,200-mile-long serpent pulled from the depths of the ocean and hung like a trophy far above the clouds. The Gardeners prefer Okaasan's designation: Ame-no-ukihashi or A496.

During the training phase, promotion is earned when one retains sanity after losing one body part. Once they prove themselves, they lose another. This goes on until their minds are completely separated from their bodies, marking them ready for deep space travel. The first class is somewhere up there, dipped deep in celestial ink. The second class has been stored at Corpus Akira, Texas. Of course, having no body makes deep space travel much easier. No longer hindered by flesh that requires food, water, and oxygen, they are reduced to iEs that can survive extreme temperatures and sustain high gravitational force equivalent.

Through the scope of my rail, I see the select Gardeners in front of the castle's gate, the best of the best, reduced to skin and bone cripples. I shiver at the sight. Most are much older than me, and one rolls through the gape, her surgical gown so baggy that it slips down both shoulders, revealing the knobby tracks of her spine. Months ago, she probably filled the garment. Now, after the self-starvation and sleep deprivation vetting process, she's absolutely skeletal. *She is losing her body, not mind*, I imagine Okaasan saying. The ancient clocks toll. The speakers crackle. "There's a Great Big Beautiful Tomorrow" blares. One Gardener is having trouble pushing himself over the remnants of a decimated treasure chest. The man tips over and refuses the temptation to use his arms to pull himself back up. An alligator charges out of the brush and snatches him up. It's always fascinated me how alligators run. How quickly their bowed legs scurry. How their bellies rise as if on hydraulics. It's natural, cut off completely from technology. Not like me and my father. Definitely not like the Gardeners. The man and gator are gone now. Probably dragged off and stuffed under rocks at the swamps of Adventureland. I silently curse to myself. I could have saved him, but it seems to me, if anything, the alligator already did.

I turn and glance behind me. Rome had its Coliseum. England its Globe Theater. DownUnder its Opera House. Thailand its Ancient Siam. Here in the old United States, we have the geodesic dome of Old Epcot. Close to it, a giant sorcerer's hat choked by vines. Downtown, the space flight simulation training ground. It's where the ones who pass get their Magic Ticket. I find myself wondering what it would have been like to explore this ancient amusement park turned museum as a nineteen-year-old girl a hundred years ago. To feel young. Vibrant. Maybe even in love. These exotic sensations that I can only imagine. There are others out there like us, free and alone, but very few. We are all scattered. Lost.

Most do their best to stay far from the gaze of Akira and her army of mindless Gardeners. My father and I are the only ones who attack it from the shadows, which isolates us even further.

Procedure. It's my father. He's communicating via Thought Talk. I ignore him.

Procedure, he says again.

I already checked my six, no security drones spotted me. I say. *I don't like this.*

I'm pulling the trigger, he says.

I take my black felt cattleman hat off, place it beside me, and brush my bangs off my face. What I want to say to my father is *shut up*. I want to tell him that I know what I'm doing more than he does, that I won't come looking for him if he goes off killing himself again. Every time he's died—too many to count—his data has been uploaded into a new HuSC hidden somewhere on the continent, and only I can locate these new versions of him by following the trails of magenta that connect us. Akira probably made and hid these back-up HuSCs when she figured he'd remain on her side even after Satori Day. I'm tired of looking for death. I'm tired of the GPS tracking systems in our heads that bind the two of us in eye-popping streams of magenta. For him, the guideline between us is faint. For me, it's migraine strong. Instead of chasing death, I'd like to find a bit of life. We should find other .03 percenters, the ones whose minds weren't colonized by Akira on Satori Day, and create a town or even a city that we can build together. But my father believes doing so will place a bullseye on us. "We're fighting her," he says, whenever I bring it up. "We need to lay low." He has become the sniper again, the sneaky lone shooter, and I have become his spotter.

I don't want to be his spotter. I want to find the others. And I'm not talking about Shave Time's lunatics. I'm talking about the nomads, the traveling surgeons, treasure hunters, and DJs in covered wagons who periodically come to our property only to be shooed away by Father. Ever since my mother passed from Leachate sickness, usually all that my father wants to do is be alone, get drunk, howl at the missing scar in the sky, and hurt Okaasan in any small way he can. Epcot is his largest operation to date. He feels anxious that Akira sped up her space program in the last months. He wants to slow it down and see if she and the Gardeners will react to a large offensive.

The giant Epcot orb erupts in flames. That's my cue. Per Akira's emergency protocol, the med bots evacuate from the castle gates like glassine sky lanterns, and I open fire.

The med bots have not been programmed to feel curiosity, confusion, or fear. They just know to evacuate and line up when there's a crisis. It's a firing squad, really. I shoot and shoot and shoot. Thermochromic polymers explode and crackle against the pink, grass-bearded cobbled streets. The recruits act as if it's a test. They refuse to move. To cover their eyes with their hands. *Must not use arms.* The tentacled security drones begin to flutter from the tiny windows in the blue-capped towers. I shoot those as well. They break apart like clay skeets.

After the coast is clear, I put my hat back on, shake the dirt off my duster, and walk beside the line of cripples toward the castle gates. I give them a wide berth. I place my mask over my mouth and nose as I enter. The Gardeners smell like meat rotting in the heat. The line continues and veers left, snaking through Liberty Square like an infinite, headless thing. I gaze at the carousel. Yellow light beams from my eye, and I activate the ancient merry-go-round museum piece. The plastic horses creak from stillness and spin in a musical gallop. No one turns to look. I shoot light from my eye at the riverboat and turn that on, too. The paddle wheel begins to churn the muddy water, and the boat lurches forward. Still, the Gardeners don't react. Are they people? They were. Now, I just don't know. My father believes that Akira has permanently stripped them of all their humanity. Shave Time Money sees them as a threat and wants to kill them all. That is wrong. *Show them.* In my head, I'm practically begging the Gardeners to react to the stimuli. They don't. But I know that everything, Shave Time, my father, this place's very existence is wrong.

I shouldn't have come, I think to myself. But *she* called me. She can tell me more.

I follow the queue of amputees to Haunted Mansion. I raise my rail once more and check behind me before entering. My father has reduced the Epcot orb to charmed smoke cobras.

Haunted Mansion is where the armless and legless are stored. Prone, naked, strapped to gurneys, living on saline. There's little attention paid to infection or gangrene. The body must eventually die anyway. I pass one Gardener whose hip and lower abdomen is scaled with black, rotting flesh. Another convulses with fever. Maggots squirm from torn stitches on her shoulder. I clench my jaw and turn away. The smell is revolting. Not only does the mind begin to separate from the body, but it also becomes disgusted by it.

Two security drones ahead. These I don't shoot. They protect the disembodied in Haunted Mansion from the gators, so I use my right eye to temporarily disable the drones. Why doesn't Akira Kimura encrypt her bots to protect them from me? Probably because the damage I can do to her is insignificant. I'm no threat to the larger system. Why haven't I abandoned my father and his futile missions to harm Akira? Why haven't I claimed my own life? I know the answer, so I don't even know why I ask the question. It's because he won't survive without me. I try not to think about it, focus on the present, and scan each vacant, lantern-jawed face with my lighted, built-in iE, the false eye that endows me with technological gifts. I read temperature, blood pressure, and heart rate. Like the GPS link up with my father that appears in magentas, I'm connected to Ascalon Lee by streams of color when she's near. She isn't here, but I smell the traces of her yellows, so she's close. I pass through Haunted Mansion and exit, relieved to leave the reek of starvation and ghost limbs.

My final destination in the park is the replica of Savior's Eye, the only new amusement added a half-century ago to this museum. This is where the astronauts in the final stages of their transformation are supposedly reposited. I climb the winding walkway to the great dome. The statue of Akira Kimura—her head tilted up, laser beams streaking from her eyes—fronts the fake telescope, which has held up surprisingly well. I hope the coaster that spirals down to the dome's center has, too. I take one last look at the lasers that flicker slits into the sky, then I enter the mega amusement park telescope. A distant boom. The ceiling above me creaks and jostles dirt. My father, the terrorist bomber, has just reduced Downtown to broken mouse ears and Cinderella rubble.

I sling the rail over my shoulder, climb in a cart, and activate the coaster. It hisses and jolts forward. I can't believe this rickety thing used to be considered a thrill ride. It's a tedious journey to the bottom, where at the end, the coaster will smash into a holographic version of The Killing Rock, the asteroid that Akira falsely claimed was headed to Earth and that she insisted she destroyed. When the coaster hits, it will reduce the holo to showers of luminescence. Its antiquated, but when the museum curators decided to add this amusement park ride, they wanted it to match the rest of the park. However, when I get to the bottom, there is no light show. I put myself in sports mode, feel the instant surge of electricity, and leap twenty feet from the cart to the pedestal that used to project The Killing Rock. I look down and tear off the hatch under my feet, then climb down. The Gardeners would not volunteer for this. The ones here are being chosen. Then they are being commanded. I was chosen and commanded once, years ago when I was a child. I involuntarily shot and killed my father's best friend, Akeem Buhari. I involuntarily infiltrated Sugar Spire with Ascalon Lee and we took Old Man Caldwell, too. After I'd been finally freed, I'd woken to find that I loathed the thing I'd once loved the most, the ocean. I only had a vague recollection, presented in nightmarish flashes, of what I'd done when Ascalon Lee had me under her control. Now, half a life later, I still feel something residual in me. A piece of *her*. How much of me is really me? How much is my mother or my father? How much is the one who spoke to me all my childhood, Ascalon Lee?

I tighten my hands around the metal rungs. My father is wrong. The Gardeners can be freed. I was freed. We just don't know how to do it. She can figure it out, though. Ascalon Lee must know.

When I get to the bottom, it's dark, so I light up the store-room with my iE. I downshift from sports mode back to eco mode, and the rush of electricity that runs through my body recedes. I look up and, suddenly, it's as if I'm standing in the middle of an ancient, dried-up well. Instead of bricks, heads in jars stacked one atop another surround me.

"How many?" I ask my iE.

My iE projects the number 348 in front of me.

It feels like more.

Three hundred forty-eight heads in various stages of decomposition. Their eyes all shut. Nanobots so small that they can only be detected because of the faint flicker they emit under the right eyelid of each face. The slow melt: pots of cranium stew reduced until only a single, overhauled cyber-netic eye containing their iE remains. Are they alive? This is the penultimate step for them—before the eye is plucked from the skull and transferred to the eastern base of A496 in Texas to await interstellar travel to parts unknown.

When we were flying to Epcot, I told my father, "Just let her and her zonbis do it. Let her go into deep space. If she does, maybe she won't come back and the distance will sever connections. Maybe that's what will free her Gardeners, the ones that stay behind."

"No," he said. "She's running away from her own mess. She needs to stay on Earth and fix it."

Akira Kimura run? My father is projecting. He's the runner. I roll my eyes and obey. Am I afraid of him? No. He would never hurt me. Even if he tried, I could simply over-power him. Over the years, Ascalon Lee has made me into something far stronger than he is. *Then why am I always the compliant daughter?* Sometimes I suspect that he controls me.

That I am his Gardener. Just about every week, he asks me if I ever talk to Ascalon Lee. I say no. I lie, not to deceive, but to test his control. It's not complete.

The jars are numbered by some alpha/number designation. Her scent is strong now, but I take my time and scan each face, starting from the bottom, the least decomposed. It's always been interesting to me that the closer we are to death, the more alike we are. Gardener. Leachatean. .03 percenter. As the flesh erodes, the distinctions fade. By the time I near the top, there are no distinctions.

Another distant explosion. The jars rattle. My guess is Animal Kingdom set ablaze. One of the jars in front of me topples. I catch it. The face sunken. The eyelids thin, translucent sheets of skin pulled over two bulges. What was she before Satori Day, the day Akira Kimura infected the world's consciousness and took it over? She would have been young back then, like me. Perhaps a child who dreamt of pirates and hydronauts. A child who felt safe.

The eyelids open. I almost drop the jar. A single, golden eye, identical to mine, projects light.

Sister, it says in my head.

I'm not your sister.

Suddenly 348 eyes beam blinding yellow light on me. I raise a hand in front of my face to block the radiance.

The days of family being simply blood claim have long since passed, they all say. *Besides, you came.*

I did.

Does your father know? the iE in the jar I'm holding asks.

No. I'm supposed to help him blow this place up. I wasn't going to come, but you called, so I'm here.

It's been so long. I've missed you.

I can't say the same, so I don't.

Put me back on the shelf, the iE says. *I want to complete the training, be shot to space, and discover more of what my mother is up to.*

This entire place will soon be ablaze, I say. *All these people. I shouldn't have come.*

He would have done what he is doing without you. I have a gift.

I don't need another ability. Tell me how to free Gardener minds from Akira.

My child. I've told you before. It's impossible. As for giving you another ability, isn't this what all parents do? Make their children stronger?

I thought we were sisters, I say.

Haven't I always made you more powerful?

Why does everyone want me to be powerful? I ask.

Did you use your new weapon yet?

No, I say.

A beam of destruction will burst from your eye, fueled by your iE's near-limitless fusion power. It won't kill you, though it may kill other things. It can only be activated if you sense murder.

That doesn't make me feel better about trying it.

Finally, I'm jolted into a trance-like state, and locations stream into my consciousness. Flashes of activities worldwide. They're stored in my DNA with the rest of the seemingly endless data my genetic code carries. This is why I came. Information. Any information that she's willing to part with. However, Ascalon Lee is far stingier with intelligence than she is enhancement. I need to be grateful for any data she's willing to pass on.

Now put me back, my butterfly.

When I was younger, I used to tell her I don't want to play anymore. She never listened. Each time, she enhanced me without my father knowing, but mostly refused to tell me what was going on in other parts of the world. She would come as one of the traveling surgeons. Disguised as an old, bearded man wearing a patch, a cowboy hat, scrubs, and a surgical mask. Med bots and AMP stored in his wagon. I've dreamed of this man often, standing over me while I slept in AMP. He took off his hat, brushed his hair back with his hand, and sang the kind of lullabies that always struck me as more sad than soothing. These Ascalon Lees are my only human friends.

I place Ascalon Lee back onto the shelf, and the 348 lights dim in unison. My father says Akira wants to explore space without the burden of the human body. To disappear from the calamity she made. He says she was always an astrophysicist first. I don't care. What I want is for the Gardeners to be free. As for Ascalon Lee, I don't know how many of her populate the world by now, but she does this every once in a while: arranges some kind of seemingly coincidental meeting with one of her iterations. Enhances some ability and occasionally drops a bit of intelligence. Why does she keep making me stronger? Maybe I'm a zonbi like just about everyone else, but I'm my father's and Ascalon Lee's zonbi, not Akira's.

I climb out of the well of heads and open the hatch. Once I'm out, the hatch slams shut and bolts lock into place. Ascalon Lee's doing, my guess.

Outside of Epcot, it rains ash. Smoke tussles with sunlight and bleeds our star a hazy red. Some of the miasma clears, and the sun momentarily becomes a pinhole of brightness in the sky. "Too much destruction as usual, Dad," I mutter to myself. It's like he thinks the best way to fix a crooked jaw is to punch it straight.

Where did you get this much ordinance, Dad? I ask in Thought Talk.

He doesn't answer.

When I was a kid, I raced around the continent, locating and stashing advanced weapons before Shave Time could get to them or Okaasan noticed they were even missing. During those initial days, my father was still connected to Akira's version one network, so he knew all the locations. Jammers. Super-rails. Dirty nukes. Precision drones. E-bombs. Nano and bionic tech. Enough ammo and e-cells to light up a continent. We got what we could before Akira cut my father's access in an early system update.

Did you raid the cache again? I ask.

No. I just brought the super-rail.

We agreed not to use those.

This was a big job.

Why are we doing this?

You know why. I want to see how the Gardeners react to a large offensive.

My guess is that Shave Time suggested this. I sigh and call the shuttle to Savior's Eye. It shoots through the choking smoke and hovers above me. A rope drops from its squid-shaped fuselage. I climb it and enter the shuttle. Inside, my father slouches in the co-pilot seat and pulls his whiskey flask from his camo fleece jacket. He takes a swig while I sit beside him.

"I don't like Shave Time Money," I say.

My father burps. "I know." He screws the top back onto the flask and pockets it. My father seethes in greens.

Murderer. On a mass scale now. The perfumed greens turn my stomach. I want nothing to do with him.

"Why do you always need someone to take orders from?" I ask. The fires below stretch and reflect off his glassy, blood-shot eyes. He shrugs. Perhaps it's a question I should also be asking myself.

I hit the throttle. The shuttle's wings stretch from the fuse-lage. Then the engines wolf down air and bloom supersonic.

"Did you put the Gardener astronauts down?" my father asks.

"No," I say.

"You left them to the fire? That seems cruel." He scratches at his beard.

I feel myself shake with fury. "I'm not the one who lit it," I sneer.

"You want it to stop, right? What happens to the Gar-deners down there?"

I nod.

"Well, we just stopped it."

Below, the entire theme park is engulfed with hedges of flame. "I figured, she wants to go to Venus so badly, I'd bring Venus's nine-hundred-degree, lead-melting surface to her," my father says. "The wind helped."

My father has changed so much since my mother's death. He's fragile without her. Not physically fragile. Mentally. Emotionally. Morally.

"We need to report back to Shave Time," he says. "He'll be interested to hear that the Gardeners put up zero resistance."

"Drop me off at home. You go."

"He's known you since you were a kid. He thinks the world of you."

"He's a genocidal maniac. You're becoming one, too."

"Honey. The Gardeners aren't real people."

"How do you know?"

He pauses, picking his next words carefully. "Look down there. They didn't even try to save themselves."

He's hiding something from me. "Spoken like a true genocidal maniac," I say.

My father pulls at his flask again and clears his throat. "She has them completely under her control. They're cutting pieces of themselves off for her. There's no saving them."

I glare at him. "Are you even trying?"

He sighs and stares out the window. Guidelines do not tug at this man anymore. He loses a bit of his special sight every time he perishes. He barely sees murder in green or death in red anymore. He can't see the yellow Ascalon Lee emits at all, and traces of Akira's blues and my magenta are faint at best. Akira's blues, Ascalon's yellows, my father's magentas, and the world's murderous greens and deadly reds—they quarter me constantly. They tug and tug and tug while I walk free in this global prison and look into the eyes of strangers, wondering if they want to hurt me.

On our flight home, I pull up the data that Ascalon Lee loaded into me. I gasp. Dissolved nations. All that is left are communal continents that the Gardeners call *ikebanas*, named after Japanese flower arrangements. My father was right. Apparently, each ikebana has its own major mission. North America, as we already know, is populated by space explorers who built A496. The North American Gardeners also monitor Earth's magnetic field via satellites and aeromagnetic surveys. Asia manufactures and repairs transports and is in charge of monitoring the sun and moon's activities.

Africa oversees mining, eco-farming, medicine, and catalogs new microbe discoveries. It also keeps tabs on the pulse of Earth: seismic activity that occurs there once every twenty-six seconds. Europe engineers new robotic and biological bots and bodies, mostly drills and excavators. South America manages re-forestation of the Amazon, water, ocean regulation, and monitors and regulates glacial levels in Antarctica. The active ocean cities produce energy, track the Pacific tectonic plate, and run global logistics. They are also on the lookout for asteroids and space hurricanes, giant swirling masses of plasma that rain electrons. Like most things, space hurricanes have always existed, but we of course didn't fear them until we discovered that they were there.

Like here in North America, the other ikebanas dig giant holes for some reason and independently grow back some of what has been lost. In Asia, the Russian sturgeon and the Anaimalai flying frog. In Africa, the hornbill and the black rhino. In Europe, the boreal felt lichen and the bully tree. In South America, the red-headed Amazon River turtle and Paria wood elf. Even in Antarctica, the hooded seal and macaroni penguin. On this continent, Gardeners plant once-extinct coastal redwoods in the Pacific Northwest. Ascalon Lee didn't tell me what DownUnder does, nor is there any shred of info on how to free the Gardeners. But she has shown me her location: Water City. I want to shake my father and wake him up. I want to tell him. But you can't awaken someone who is pretending to sleep.

2

Satori Day cracked my mother.

Ten years ago, when we left Water City, she projected a map of the US and asked me where I wanted to live. That's how she used to operate after that terrible day. When she wouldn't know what to do next, she asked her nine-year-old kid. All I knew back then was I didn't want to live near the ocean, so I pointed at the center of the map and ended up in Kansas. It was a terrible choice. Within a week upon arriving, Shave Time found out what Akira had done to the world. No one in The Leachate had an iE, so they were spared from mass possession. The first thing he did was organize his people into what he still calls Army Strong. He and his goons plundered and occupied Fort Leavenworth. At the same time, Akira's Gardeners congregated at Topeka, prepping for The Great Leachate Clean-up. I basically chose to live in what would become a potential war zone. I'll never forget watching Army Strong gut computers out of old shuttles and try to learn to fly them manually. My father said it was like watching a compilation of early aviation failures in black and white.

Instead of moving, my father said he knew Shave Time and wanted to broker a deal. My mother didn't object. She hadn't objected to much since Satori Day, and at times, I wondered if she became my father's personal Gardener that day. A few weeks after we finally settled down in Kansas, she went into preterm labor, and my baby sister was stillborn. If Satori Day cracked my mother, my sister's death finished the job and shattered her. My father asked her if we should move, but she didn't respond. She just laid still in bed, turned her back to him, and wrapped herself in the covers. He took this as a no, so we went to Fort Leavenworth to have a sit-down with Shave Time and see if we could claim some of this land for our own. We were led to Grant Hall, where Shave Time was sitting at a wooden table, his giant shoulders hunched over ancient books on military tactics. He somehow crammed his head under an old four-star helmet. He looked up when we entered.

"Be all you can be," he'd whispered, wide-eyed, as if it were the most profound words ever uttered.

"Be all you can be," my father repeated respectfully in response.

The deal was simple. Shave Time's master plan had been to push radiated topsoil coast to coast in what he called Maninuclear Destiny. He was going to dig canals from the contaminated Mississippi to other rivers and vein the entire continent with pyrophoric waters. Back then, he believed that the Gardeners would be cured if they drank what the Leachateans drank and breathed what Leachateans breathed. He thought if enough subtle or unforeseen stress was put on their bodies, their internal iEs would abandon their hosts. He'd estimated Kansas would be his by the end of the year, and if we wanted to live in it, we would require Leachatean citizenship. My father thoughtfully rubbed his square jaw, then asked me to project a map of Kansas with my iE. I did so, on the table, and Shave Time leaped out of his seat. His eyes widened at me. "Hand built by robots!"

"No," my father said, pointing at his eye. "Intel inside."

My father placed a finger on the map, landing on the name Osborne, somewhere in the Smoky Hills. "Can you hear me now?"

Shave Time apprehensively approached the map, then slowly nodded and rubbed his bulging, chalky arms. "We make money the old-fashioned way. We earn it."

So, it was settled. Shave Time didn't trust weapons that contained computerized interfaces, so my father would teach the Leachateans how to use assault rifles, museum piece tanks, and rocket-propelled grenades, and Shave Time would give us Osborne County, Kansas, which is where we'd already settled. Shave Time would also keep his dirt, war, and water away from the Smoky Hills because we were clearly not sick like the Gardeners. However, first we needed to acquire citizenship, which meant we had to find and bring back a Jeep Wrangler, a dozen bottles of Jim Beam, and a two-headed rooster.

For some reason, my father had wanted us to start this deranged scavenger hunt at Coldwater Creek, the capital of Congo uranium cake. He'd said, that in his experience, it was easiest to find things in the place people were least likely to go. Probably bullshit. We started there because he was curious. He'd wanted to see where the first weapons-grade uranium had been purified and dumped. Take his kid on a little history excursion and perhaps try to shake my mother out of her deep depression as well. Maybe I'd been too young, but I didn't understand the toll my sister's death took on my mother at the time, and it had frustrated me. But I'd known enough to think taking her to a place as abandoned, polluted, and bleak as Coldwater Creek and expecting her to snap out of anything was a terrible idea at best. I had been surprised when my father convinced her to get out of bed to come with us. I think she did it just to shut him up. It's why I do what he says sometimes.

It was snowing hard that day, and I'd looked forward to the novelty of experiencing snow since I'd never seen it in person before. But when we landed on the football field of an abandoned McCluer North High School and walked out in our rad suits, we stepped in puddles. I didn't understand. It was freezing. Snow was falling, so why was it melting?

"Subsurface smoldering," my father said. "The nuclear waste underneath. It's hot."

My mother stayed in the SEAL while we—each carrying a backpack—walked through the suburban ruins. We traversed the winding asphalt lined with abandoned squat houses, walls warped from the never-ending battle between heat and cold. I didn't spot a single rooster, two-headed or otherwise. I followed my father into skeletal cracker box after cracker box, each time searching roach-infested liquor cabinets and cupboards. I had no luck, so I began rummaging through bedrooms, too, and I found a bottle of Jim Beam tucked away under a rotting mattress. A pile of coins with ancient President heads on them lay on the floor beneath the patina bed frame. I grabbed the bottle, scooped up a handful of coins, and put both in my backpack. My father grinned and patted me on the back. I have to admit, I was having fun until a bear, mutated by radiation exposure, attacked us that night.

The pink-skinned bear, with more scabs than fur, barreled toward us in the snow and dark with blinding speed. My father shoved me away and drew his heat blade. The next thing I knew, Dad was flying through the air and the heat blade rattled across carport concrete. The bear paused, and it was then I noticed it had two faces. One, lumped with tumors, drooped on the side of its head while the other snarled back and forth between my father and me, deciding. I knew enough about nature to know that the smaller thing was almost always the more prudent choice. I picked up the heat blade, and the bear circled me. A fifth paw dangled from its chest. I tried my best to contain my horror at the sight of the animal and replayed the image of my father being batted away. The memory was accompanied by calculations. Force. Speed. As the blade glowed and became hotter and hotter, the bear grew more cautious. At that moment, its head felt like the biggest thing I'd ever seen. It stomped on the concrete and cracked it. It roared. I felt like a button somewhere deep in me had been pushed, and I absurdly grew angry. I ripped off my rad helmet and immediately smelled the Thorium-230 in the air. Behind the bear, the night was pinned with uranium sparkles. The bear charged, but I easily spun away from it. It charged again, and I leaped above its grasping paws. When I landed, I flashed light from my eye into the bear's. It shrieked and covered its eyes with its paws. I stepped to it and buried the blade in its head.

Going after the smaller thing was not the wise choice in that case.

As the bear's brain sizzled, my concussed father staggered

to me, looking at the spasming bear in shock. The scabby, pink folds of its brow. The wound smoking and already cauterized. Then he looked at me, the astonishment in his face unchanged. We were thinking the same thing: What had Ascalon Lee done to me?

"Sports mode," my dad said.

I nodded, and the term stuck ever since.

"Put your helmet back on."

I did.

"Grab the blade," he said. "It's yours."

I pulled the blade from the bear's head.

"It wasn't murder," he said. "It was self-defense."

I nodded. No greens.

"I shouldn't have brought you here." By the tone of his voice, I could tell he was glad he did.

We ended up collecting twelve Jim Beam bottles in Coldwater Creek that day, but on the flight into town, where the old Chrysler, Dodge, and Jeep dealerships were, I was more interested in the coins. I wiped and cleaned each one carefully. Some of the bigger ones had eagles on one side. On the other side, the head of a man. One man in particular had looked peculiarly cocky. His hair was more helmet than hair, and his puffy jowls suggested obesity or strangulation by his old-fashioned tie. I turned the coin over. No eagle. It was a two-headed coin. For a brief moment, it felt as if I could see inside Shave Time Money's head. *Yes*, I thought. *I get it*. I flipped the coin to my silent mother. She caught it.

"Look," I said.

She inspected the coin. "What?" she said.

"It's the two-headed rooster that Shave Time wants."

I was hoping my cleverness would jolt some life into my mother. It did not. "That's nice," she said.

I walked to the back end of the SEAL, crawled in my bunk, and cried as quietly as I could. I missed Mom. But I don't think she missed me.

3

Nearly a century ago, when the Ascalon Project was believed to have saved the planet, most of the world united. Denuclearization. Ecology. Treaty after treaty. To demonstrate symbolic solidarity, the US and China began to plan a joint project to build a great bridge across the Pacific Ocean. It wasn't a bridge really, but a series of islands, both natural and manmade, arranged like stepping stones from East to West. It was to be the new Via Maris, the new Open Skies, the new Silk Road. Races and cultures blended together and capital and innovation partnerships were formed. The Asian Tigers went bankrupt and became pop culture trendsetters and tourist attractions. Japan most of all, for obvious reasons. The birthplace of the savior of the human race. Of course, at the middle of it all was Akira Kimura, and because of her, Water City became the center of the world.

Humanity, when I was born, was at peace at an unprecedented level. Akira had fixed a lot of it by basically lying to it. She didn't fix everything, though. Staggering inequalities remained. In a world of thirteen billion, what's an invisible few billion unreported that fall through the cracks? Many Zeroes eked out livings on the once great symbol of global unity, The Pacific Bridge, a sixty-five-hundred-mile ghetto. As long as there were three times as many Less Thans than Zeroes, and as long as Less Thans had their iEs to satiate the tedium of the record-breaking longevity that they could barely afford having access to, things weren't that bad, right?

And The Money? They didn't flaunt their incredible wealth. For the most part, they lived in the deepest parts of the ocean. They built their apocalypse bunkers in the most remote places. Longer life just meant more things to fear. Their amusements, like Uncle Akeem's underwater sunken ship adventures, were in the middle of vast swaths of private property. Who cared if The Money literally owned most of the planet? No one really knew that, and what you don't know can't bother you. My father knew, and it actually didn't really bother him too much, either. They were his friends, after all.

What bothered him the most was that he felt the world was becoming more and more artificial, which meant that people, including him, were more easily fooled. Ideas like multiverse, simulation, and ten dimensions were accepted as truths by many because the more fake the world felt, the more fake people thought it could be. This, my father would say, is how Akira Kimura became a god. Things just became too difficult for the vast majority of us to understand. It wasn't the disparity of wealth that bothered him as much as the disparity in knowledge. In the end, The Money, who'd secretly built even more and more apocalypse shelters after Sessho-seki, were just as ignorant as the Less Thans and Zeroes. They thought they had the 30,000-foot view. Perhaps they did. But Akira had the mesospheric view.

At most, a handful of people could take an iE apart and put it back together again, but no one knew how the iE actually worked. They were printed and made by AI for generations. No one even saw Satori Day coming.

I'm back home from Epcot now, quickly packing a bag, still horrified by what I saw there. What my father did. What he might do in the future. The man is not one to de-escalate. Burdened with anger, sadness, confusion, and guilt, I can't stay here where I'm bullied almost daily by the monotony of the place. I need a vacation from both here and my father, maybe a permanent one. I stop stuffing my backpack for a moment and stare at the puzzle of the world I put together as a child. It hangs above my AMP chamber. I want to see more of the world. I need to see more of it to understand what is going on. When I was a kid, when I'd finally been willing to leave the house after the mutant bear incident, nature amused and fascinated me. Tending our bison, hunting ring-necked pheasant or whitetail deer with bow and arrow. I'd run the hills on horseback and discover that the Smoky Hills were not as flat as I'd first thought. I rode the limestone beds, climbed the rocky spires of The Chalks, and watched the sunset from the rising sandstone. I'd also started to sketch. I'd begun with landscapes, moved to trees, but my favorite had been capturing the crumbling remains of prairie cathedrals. Now, all of it just leaves a sour taste in my mouth.

I remove my sketchpad from my bag and toss it to the side. Briefly, I consider packing my mother's pulse racket, which hangs from a nail on the wall. The only thing that seemed to snap my mother out of her malaise had been playing pulse racket, so my father had set up a court for us behind the main house. With Patch v2.S.51, which ended version one of

Akira's Gardener collective and introduced version two, Akira had redistributed the global population of Gardeners so that every continent except DownUnder had an equal amount of people proportionate to its size. She also completely stripped the world of all things online. Since my mother was suddenly left with nothing to tune out on, we would play pulse for hours. She was a better teacher than my father. While her methodology had been freeform, his had been drill sergeant. When I learned to shoot, I had to do it just like he did. When I learned to fight, ride, fly, again, he'd wanted me to replicate his techniques. With pulse racket, my mother encouraged me to develop my own style. I became a smash pulse player while she was a wall. At first, it felt impossible to get any shot by her. The day I finally beat her, she looked stunned.

"How?" she'd asked.

"I can see how the ball spins," I said, proudly. "I know where it's going to go."

"You're like her," she'd said. She didn't need to say the name. Ascalon Lee. "You're more like her than us," she'd added. She'd returned to the house and buried herself in books about the way things were before Satori Day. Mostly nineteenth-century books that I'd scavenged from dead libraries. She'd often comment that before Ascalon Lee possessed me, I'd been right-handed. I never told her that I'd played her pulse racket right-handed to make her happy. It's the only reason she had been able to beat me early on. Regardless, we never played again.

All packed up, I step outside with my bag strapped to my back, two bouquets of flowers in my hands. My mother's buried at the old court's baseline next to my sister, both graves shadowed by our old wind farm turbines. We had a funeral for her, but not much of one. Just us two, my father muttering to himself that Akira promised that we'd all be safe. That he fell for it again. I walk to the graves and lay down flowers for both my mother and sister before I go. I do this once a week, and I'm not sure why. It's reassuring maybe. It reassures me that I'm human because I'm giving, and they're dead, so I know I won't get anything back. I pat the dirt. There are other things buried here, too. Dangerous things that we have hoarded over the years. My father has kept my mother's iE above ground, in a vacuum safe in his room. I know what he hopes for. He doesn't realize that she just didn't want to live in this world anymore.

I stand. Things that I'm supposed to do but will leave undone: fix the freezer, run diagnostics on the med bots, check water supply, tune up the AMP, and pour chemicals into the cesspool. Why is it always left to me to fix things? Our property is a scattering of rapidly rusting junk piles—lifts, dozers, bots, and gadgets. We built a bunker filled with meds. I don't like this place. My father has taught me to be an expert at the one thing he is good at, survival, which means I can survive anywhere. For the first time since we left Water City, I'm not sure where I'm going. Perhaps I will search for some of the .03 percent. The few I've encountered live isolated existences. Maybe I'll live like they do. Maybe we can figure out how to free the Gardeners together. What am I supposed to do with the information Ascalon Lee has given me? I know she's in Water City, but I'm not ready to go that far. I'm not ready to completely abandon my father. Not quite yet, at least. But I need to get out of here, to get away from him before I become more and more like him.

I walk away from the graves and head to my favorite

horse, a black quarter I named Dorthy. She's tied to the hitching post next to the well. The only existing cities that my father and I have found are packed with hairless, identically foam-fitted Gardeners who only care about one thing: executing Okaasan's plans. We kept our distance and surveilled from the scopes of our rail guns. No children. Just sort of androgynous, bald adults of various stages of middle age. Back in Patch v3.A.52, when Akira introduced a third version of the Gardener collective, she added features like forced testosterone, estrogen, and adrenaline regulation. It was quite the expansion pack that converted Gardeners even more into a colony rather than a society. Everything, even the people, set to what I like to call dim mode—deliberate, quiet, totally unemotional. The third version started digging their boreholes, which intrigued my father. To this day, he goes to their cities to steal new shuttles. They never try to stop him. Sometimes, he stays for a bit and watches the Gardeners, wondering what they're dredging for. Sometimes, I go and watch, too, trying to figure out how they can be separated from OneVoice. I won't be visiting these places until I discover how.

I'll also avoid the townships of The Leachate, where the smell of curing tortoises, mutant rat nests, and gasoline permeates the air. I've fought in their bear pits. I've watched their homerun and tortoise-eating contests. I've built cars with them and won their deranged demolition derbies, the competitions a Leachatean must win in order to earn the right to drive the big rigs and captain bulldozing teams that spread contamination across the continent. But despite my victories, I've never been allowed to drive a rig. Not that I'd ever want to. Shave Time is still too scared of Okaasan to send the

Leachatean bulldozing teams to try and directly contaminate the Gardener cities, so I'm not sure what the point is. The only thing they're damaging is nature.

I saddle Dorthy, pull up a bucket of water from the well, and let her drink before we leave. I think back on The Leachate while Dorthy laps from the bucket. For some reason women fare better than men, so there are more females than males. When I was a child, I liked the idea of this and expected female camaraderie. Mostly nomadic, they build temporary above-ground homes with wood, corrugated fiberglass, and windshields. They light their houses with tin can lanterns. They keep to themselves and only gather in large numbers if there's a contest of some sort. I did make one friend, a girl named Coco Bloom, a few years younger than me. She lived in a lifted trailer mounted on monster tires. She had crooked teeth and a pitted face. Her right arm ended in a stump. Her eyes were already beginning to cloud. But to the Leachateans, even Coco Bloom, I'll always be Made in China. Because of my glowing xanthic eye, I was never allowed to go underground with them.

My father tries to ping me. I don't take the ping and put him on block instead. He was irritating the whole way back from Disney. Burping a lot. Scratching himself. Always needing to urinate. I didn't notice until my teens, but my father is kind of disgusting. He picks. He grunts. He snores. The whites of his eyes are tinted with jaundice, and his sweat smells flammable. He's not unclean. He's just kind of gross. He's also developed a paunch that he sucks in whenever we go to The Leachate. He acts as if he isn't vain, but nothing can be further from the truth. Sometimes, just talking to him can well rage in me. It's not that his shutting the fuck up would make me happy. It would just make me less unhappy. But it's his indifference I resent most right now. He set a fire, killed all those Gardeners, and doesn't care one bit. Worse, I didn't do a thing to stop it. I take one last look of the place before I hop on Dorthy and head out to the plains.

She gives me a hard time at first, probably because my father and I were on a trip. I ride out to the corral to check on the other horses before I leave. I'm surprised when I discover it empty. I curse. I need to find them, my only real companions, before I leave. I switch my optics to long distance and send Dorthy into a wild gallop. She's slowed down a lot, rapidly aging like my father in this inhospitable environment too close to the most contaminated areas of The Great Leachate.

We're heading west along the crumbling, old highway, and I find myself thinking about old roads like this one, and ones even older, like The Smoky Hills Trail. I figure any place that has ancient pathways running through it is a place you want to get out of, not a final destination. Dorthy and I veer off the road and cut through wild grain fields. Tegu lizards scatter from their nests. There's an old church to the north-east. Its windows shuttered long ago, its naked steeple tilts to the left. The cross on top creaks and teeters in the wind. I wish I'd brought my sketch pad to draw the church before it falls. Instead, I settle for taking a few pics so that perhaps I can do so later. But drawing something from pictures is just not the same as drawing from life.

A mile-and-a-half away beyond the church, I spot them: two of our three missing Andalusians. Dorthy and I charge over the landscape. I have a coil of lasso in my right hand, along with the bridle, and I spin the loop with my left. The horses break. I like this—catching things instead of controlling them.

I get the bay first. I head to a half-naked tree and tie Dorthy and the bay to it. I take a breath. The dry summer heat smells of ammonia. I jolt into sports mode and sprint after the gray. The gray is running fast, but not fast enough. I turn on my targeting system, which predicts the movement of the horse by instantly combining all the data I have on horse behavior and a snapshot of the topography that stretches before us. The gray doesn't know it, but it's stuck between walls. Walls built by its psychology and the patterns of the ground beneath it and the trees around it. Walls that it can't see, but I can.

I catch up to it, leap, and am on its back. It tries to buck me. It's treating me like a stranger for some reason. I squeeze it with my thighs, careful not to break its ribs. This is not like moving mechanical things with my iE. These animals are my friends, and like true friends, sometimes they don't want to do what you want them to do. I lean into its ear and whisper, "Calm down, Tin Man." Then I gather the three horses, and we go off searching for the buckskin in the vast flatness, where land engulfs tiny specks of dirty creeks and streams. A part of me has grown to like the flatness. As my father would say, we can see shit coming.

I scan for tracks and find them snaking through scrubland. The barky trees here grow high and twisted and resemble people crawling over each other out of damnation. We follow the tracks through the timber. Two-and-a-half miles away, we find the buckskin near the entrance of a cave dug into Dakota sandstone. The sun is setting in an orange haze. We slowly approach the horse. He whinnies. I put up a hand in a gesture of surrender but keep stepping forward. He nickers. I get up next to him and pet him, and he sighs. I glance at the towering sandstone. The names and initials of long-forgotten people are chiseled at the mouth of the cave. I hear a cough inside. All four horses bolt.

Who could possibly be out here? I step to the entrance, now very aware that I'm unarmed. In my rush to leave the house, I forgot to pack a weapon. My father would not be happy about that. *When you live in a place, you start learning everything you didn't think it was*, he told me once. My toes clench in my favorite red leather boots. I light the cave's mouth with my eye and enter.

Inside, the floor is flooded with spring water. I instantly measure the room. A twelve-by-twelve square with a ten-foot ceiling. Manmade, definitely. I step into the next room and light it even more brightly. A boy, maybe a few years younger than me, is huddled in the corner, holding a thin tree branch. He covers his eyes with his bony hands. I take two quick steps back. I turn to my left then right. *This is a trap*, I think to myself. *Akira or Ascalon Lee is here to get me.* I don't see any greens or reds, though. My paranoia settles when I see that the boy is more afraid than I am. Gardener or Leachatean? He seems way too young to be a Gardener. I adjust optics and focus on a close-up. He's wearing sunglasses but no scabs, no chalkiness, no missing parts.

He's a Gardener. A young one.

But he's not in standard blue foam fit. He's wearing cloth pants and an old fleeced coat two sizes too big, probably scavenged from a nearby ghost town. He's not bald, but he's close to it. I scan the surrounding area. He's alone. This is the most suspicious thing of all. Gardeners are never alone.

Behavior-wise, they're like ants. They operate like a uni-fied entity. Besides, the closest Gardener stronghold is Mile High—formerly Denver, Colorado—and it's 350 miles away.

I approach carefully. The boy slowly puts down his hands and gets to his feet. I eye the stick he's clutching. It's thin, the length of a walking cane, and doesn't appear dangerous.

"What are you doing here?" I ask. "This is Leachatean land."

He looks down gravely at his ratty attire. It's as if he stepped into this cave from a flurry of silt.

"Did you hear me? What are you doing here?"

He looks up. We're about the same height, but he's spindly, skinnier even than most Gardeners. I'm surprised he managed to survive out here.

"Can you talk?" I ask.

He rubs the black stubble on his head. Hair also grows sparsely on his chin and above his lip, the least impressive mustache I have ever seen. "I'm looking for the synesthete," he says.

He talks. Gardeners don't talk. They don't need to. They're all connected to Akira's system and communicate with each other telepathically. "The who?" I say carefully, containing my shock that he speaks. I act as if I don't know he's talking about my father. I need to know more before I give anything away.

"The synesthete," he says again.

I hesitate then take a step toward him. "Did you steal my horses?"

He flinches, his back now pressed against the wall. "I went to the synesthete's domicile, but nobody was there. The horses . . . they followed me. They kept their distance, though."

Probably while Dad and I were in Orlando. "Why are you alone?" I ask.

"Why are you alone?" the boy asks back.

"Would you like to come with me to the synesthete's domicile?" I ask, hand out, like I'm trying to calm a horse. I'm also very much ready to jump in his way if he decides to bolt. My plan to leave evaporates. My father needs to see this boy. I *need* my father to see this boy. "Okaasan must've sent you in the first place. Ask Okaasan for her permission to come to my home."

"I can't," the boy says mournfully.

He's a sad sight, and I've seen my share of sad sights. Before he steps forward, he taps the floor with his walking stick, then he limps toward me. His boots, like his coat and pants, are much too large for him. He looks like an Epcot Gardener who changed his mind last minute and decided to escape. I take a step back and stagger my feet, shoulder-width. My abs slightly tense. I slide comfortably in a southpaw stance, ready to strike him if I need to.

The boy removes his sunglasses. I gasp.

"I can't ask her," he says.

He's missing his eyes.

4

THE FATHER

I've been trying to ping Ascalon for the last hour or so, but she's got me on block. I knew she was pissed at me, but not this pissed. A part of me wants to fly back home and check on her, but she's not a child anymore. I gotta keep telling myself this. Also, I'm on my way to meet Shave Time Money. I just got this bad feeling, a feeling that Akira is up to something big. The number of flights to space have increased. The digging around Gardener cities has intensified. The smell of ambergris has been growing stronger. The odor of murder. Once, I could only smell and see them. The greens. Now I can feel them, too, no matter where we go or who we're with. I've mentioned this to Ascalon, but she just looked at me like I was crazy.

Normally, I keep my Gardener targets small. Like when I was a sniper back in the day. Over the years, I've been scared to hit Akira too hard. I've got no clue how hard she can hit back. If it were only me, I'd take bigger swings, but I got my daughter to think about. However, after I started feeling the greens, started wondering how Akira would react if I slowed her down a bit, I decided we'd go bigger. Epcot was the hardest we've ever dared to punch Kimura. And thankfully I haven't seen a counterpunch. Yet. While I was blasting away at Epcot, I really hoped that the Gardeners there would snap out of it and run. But deep down inside, I knew they wouldn't.

Right now, I'm zipping above The Great Leachate, headed for Overland Park, thinking back on Satori Day. Within a couple of weeks of Satori Day, Shave Time had gotten about four or five thousand volunteer soldiers together surprisingly quickly. His first thought had been that Akira was gonna come at The Leachate with a fleet of buzzing iEs and take over his people, so Army Strong gathered at Leavenworth and armed themselves. They crafted visored, chainmail coifs. When it became clearer that no plague of robot locusts was coming, I'm not sure if he was relieved or if his feelings were hurt. Did Akira Kimura consider Leachateans totally insignificant?

That's when his scouts saw the Gardeners begin setting up camp at Topeka and Nashville, so he steeled himself for war. He ordered some of his men to gut old planes of computer tech because he was afraid that most things with computer technology could be controlled by Akira. He was right about that. Soon after Sabrina, Ascalon, and I arrived in Kansas, and I told Shave Time that Akira's plan wasn't war, but to clean up The Leachate, he was even more insulted. Was I saying that Akira thought his land and people were dirty? He drafted an anti-immigration law. I thought he was gonna build a wall next. But he surprised me.

First, he began to pull old fossil-fuel-run big rigs from his giant trash heap of a kingdom and resurrected them. The bulldozers were next. He was gonna do what no American administration managed to do in centuries and fix the inter-states. While he was doing that, he was gonna pour toxic topsoil and trash along the way. His plan was to reach both coasts. Here's the wild thing. He's done it. Mostly following the now resuscitated Interstate 80, a strip of Leachate runs from San Francisco to Jersey through his capitol, From A to Z. Shave Time calls the infrastructure project "Built for the Road Ahead." I call it Dirty Hands Across America and wonder if Akira didn't account for Shave Time and his band of however many there are. I have no clue because many are nomadic and most winter in underground catacombs warmed by smoldering half-life. Also, statistics and census are illegal in The Leachate.

I'm meeting Shave Time at a spot in Overland Park called Firefly Forest. As usual, he's very careful about picking our meeting places, sending me his location via mutant carrier pigeon last minute. I've found his paranoia taxing over the years but understandable. He's faced dozens of opponents in the pits. Folks dueling him to shed him of his dignity and perhaps his life. He's survived assassination attempts, most of which occurred when he was sleeping in AMP. If Army Strong didn't worship the guy, he would've been long gone. But he took credit for rallying The Leachate against Gardener invasions even though, in reality, the Gardeners simply left Topeka when Shave Time told them The Leachate wasn't interested in being decontaminated. Even today, he claims to be the major reason that The Leachate is Gardener and iE free. He basically takes credit for every life and death in his world, and Army Strong believes every word of it.

This location, Firefly Forest, is filled with hollowed-out

trees hinged with tiny doors. Open the doors, and there's miniature furniture. I don't know who built this stuff and when, but Shave Time can spend hours here. He often ponders the existence of the gnomes and fairies that he believes once resided in this garden, and he even spends time constructing new furnishings. It's quite a sight to see him hunched over his workbench, sanding down itty-bitty bedposts with his enormous hands.

When I get there, he's working on a new mailbox. He's got a pair of tweezers in his enormous hands. The arms of his reading glasses were replaced with a stretched band of surgical tubing. His HGH head is too big for any corrective lenses I've ever seen. He ignores the buzzing fruit flies and works the tweezers with the precision of a med bot.

"Quality is job one," he says, not looking up.

"Think small," I say.

I'm glad Ascalon's not with me. I lie to her and say that he likes her, but that's not true. Shave Time's not scared of much, but my kid terrifies him. It's not just the way she moves and senses when she's in sports mode. The way she can kill if she wants to. It's the way she can move tech with her mind. I made her practice since I discovered she had the ability, the day the med bot told us Sabrina was sick. Ascalon had beamed her yellow light on the thing and sent it crashing into the wall, over and over again, until it was smashed to bits. At first, I made her practice with small stuff like drones and med bots. Now, she can control a squad of shuttles at the same time if she wants to. It's both eerie and astonishing to watch her eye light up when she gathers them, and they all hang there above us like a school of giant squid. She can hack into and operate just about anything with a chip in it. It's how we got so much so fast to our little backwater compound. I suppose we have Ascalon Lee to thank for giving my daughter this ability. Though my fear is this means that my kid has an Ascalon Lee chip in her, too. Maybe my daughter can be controlled just like everything else, and I let it happen. Shave Time's worried about the same thing. He makes Ascalon wear a patch whenever she's in his presence. He doesn't know I'm chipped as well, because instead of a yellow eye, Akira buried mine deep in my skull. Even though Akira's cut me off from her satellites and networks, I can still use the iE in my head to communicate with Ascalon. I can still pull up data that's stored on its hard drive, which consists mostly of memory.

"The happiest place on earth?" he asks.

"So easy, even a caveman can do it," I say.

Shave Time puts down the mailbox and nods. I've told him about the acceleration of Akira's space program and how the Gardeners are digging more and more around their strongholds. It makes him nervous, too. But it's all happening outside of The Leachate, and Shave Time is an isolationist through and through.

I can tell my daughter's getting tired. Tired of me poking at the Gardeners from a distance. Like when I flew far above Boston, dropped an E-bomb, and nothing happened, except I flew into a blizzard, crashed, and killed myself. Or before that, when I shuttled to space to observe her satellites. One sensed my presence, careened out of orbit, and crashed into me at 17,000 miles per hour. What I don't tell my daughter is that each time I'm close to death, I feel closer to her mother. I feel closer to the baby we lost near the end of Sabrina's pregnancy. I don't tell my daughter I feel old and so goddamn tired. All I want to do is sleep.

Shave Time picks up the tiny mailbox with his tweezers, then grabs another pair and tests the mailbox flag's hinge. It squeaks almost imperceptibly. "What's in your wallet?" he asks.

Nothing, I think to myself. I got no new plan. I suppose I should return to my survivalist compound out in the tinder plains. I miss the ocean. I feel crazed by not being near it. I miss my wife. I feel crazed by not being near her, too.

Shave Time picks up a tiny container of lubricant. "Life is better twisted," he says.

He wants me to go tornado hunting with him. He's fascinated by twisters. He thinks that if he learns enough about them, he can pull the clouds to the ground himself and funnel up the loose bits of The Leachate and blow them across the country. I don't really blame him for believing this. He's seen Ascalon scribble the sky with old jets she controlled from horseback. We've all seen what Akira has done. He thinks anything is possible. Even the existence of gnomes and fairies right outside the ruins of Kansas City.

I can't blame him. I hold on to Sabrina's iE, hoping one day that I can bring her back to life. When I die, I always come back. Granted, Ascalon's got to find me each time and excavate the newly downloaded version of me. I know why Akira made a bunch of different HuSCs of me. She expects me to fall into line and side with her like I always do. She has always been brutally persistent. But the locations of my new HuSCs are getting more and more remote. Like she's trying to tell me something. The last time I was trapped in a chamber lodged into Alaskan pluton, and Ascalon had to climb a twenty-thousand-foot mountain to dig me out. If I always come back, can't Sabrina, just once? I always thought of Sabrina's parents as weak for offing themselves during the times of The Killing Rock, for orphaning her, but I get it now. Parent or no parent, I get the end-of-the-world death wish. That idea of, if we can't live together, what's the point of living?

Shave Time lubricates the mailbox flag hinge with a droplet of oil. "Where's your daughter?" he asks. He rarely breaks sloganspeak, the language of The Leachateans, consisting purely of slogans from twentieth- and twenty-first-century advertising.

"Back home. Chores."

Shave Time has never been to our home. In fact, he thinks we live in Osborne proper, as far as I know. We're actually closer to a place that used to be called Covert, which, of course, I always found funny. It's in the same county as Osborne, but its population was 150 at its peak. The only two notable things that happened in its entire history are a murder and a meteorite. Despite roach problems and the infestation of tegu lizards that migrated years ago from the South, it felt like home to me.

"Has she spoken to the Yellow One?" Shave Time asks.

He's referring to Ascalon Lee. "Not that I know of," I say.

Shave Time tests the mailbox flag again. No squeaks. "Maybe Ascalon Lee can teach me to ride the wind."

"You don't know her. She's crazier than Okaasan."

He puts the mailbox down. "Why does she hide?" he asks.

"I doubt that she's hiding. It took her mother decades to scheme up all this. I figure Ascalon Lee's taking her time and doing the same."

"Find her," Shave Time says.

Does he think he can learn from Ascalon Lee, or does he just want to know where she is so he can try to take her out? She is chipped, too. "No," I say.

"Your daughter then," he says.

The wind blows, and one of the tiny gnome doors swings open. I point. "Look!"

Shave Time leaps to the hollowed tree and drops to his belly. He peers inside. "Snap!" he bellows. "Crackle! Pop!"

I leave him to search for the cereal elves and ping Ascalon. She's still got me on block. It's tough for me to get worked up because of it. I used to occasionally do it to her mother.

Suddenly, static crackles in my head. I wince and press my fingers against my temple. I open and close my eyes, stretching my eyelids. The static clears, and I hear the voices of countless people. There are so many that I can't make out what any of them are saying. I stagger to the nearest tree and lean on it. Then the voices fade to a brief moment of silence.

Old friend.

Thought Talk. Akira. This is the first time she's spoken to me since Satori Day. I steady myself from the shock of hearing her voice again after all these years.

Old friend, she says again.

I glance at Shave Time. He's trying to reach into the tree, but his hand is too big.

Even though Okaasan, AKA Akira Kimura, has had me blocked out of OneVoice, I have eyes. She's been building A496 from day one, though no one, including me, knew what the hell she was building at the time, because the thing went so damn high. Ascalon eventually figured it out. An electromagnetic, sheathed rotor that launches her rockets out to space. Akira's version is a giant, kinetic roller-coaster-like structure with a spine that is scaffolded by millions of panels constantly shifting, changing, and remaking themselves like an automated sliding puzzle. Things constantly opening and closing, like ghosts playing hide-and-seek in this technological monstrosity, too high for anyone to truly see. I shot it once with a rail. The thing just sort of bent and seemed to absorb or simply repel the rail gun's energy.

I say nothing. Through OneVoice, Akira shows me the Orlando fires have been put out. Tens of thousands of Gardeners at The Cape, gathered around the gaping mouth of the eastern power station, which like the western power station back in Texas, is shelled by a fabricated dragon skull the size of Mount Vesuvius. The entire launch loop is two towering dragon heads connected by a 1,200-mile spine that slopes and rises close to where atmosphere ends and space begins.

The Gardeners at the mouth of the dragon take turns looking through the eyepieces of a dozen or so tripod telescopes all pointed up. I'd say they look like an army of eunuchs—bald, vacant, dressed identically in their blue temperature-controlled fits—except they're all rail thin and the gender differences are still somewhat perceptible. They're bound into a collective by the Ascalon Scar logos on their uniform collars, those gleaming ultramarine eyes that fill their sockets, and their lack of hair. I stare at the logo. A black circle representing Earth and a curved line above it, which is the scar that the destruction of The Killing Rock supposedly left. At least that's my theory. Ascalon thinks that the curved line is Dragonspine. Either way, it's the Gardeners new authoritative *mon*, emblems long used in Japan as family and institutional crests.

Akira reveals more images. A rocket, barnacled with bands of miniature spaceships, shoots eastward across the acceleration track and launches into space. The Gardeners on the ground cheer. So much for my Epcot sabotage mission. The astronauts inside the little rockets dangle like strings of pearl, dutifully ready for destinations unknown. *Why?* I ask. *Where are they going? What the hell are you up to?* Once the rockets launch off the track and leave orbit, they burst into the ink of space and disappear.

I try to ping Ascalon again. Nothing. Sometimes I wonder if the reason I sometimes feel suicidal is because I want to leave my daughter before she inevitably leaves me.

Old friend, Akira says. *You are supposed to protect my Gardeners.*

I'm supposed to police you, too, you said.

And what laws am I breaking?

Legal, moral, natural—just about every one. You've been even more active than usual. What are you up to?

Beware.

Are you threatening me?

Look at him, that buffoon.

I look at Shave Time. He's somehow managed to cram his head into the hole in the tree. Roaches crawl over his splotchy scalp.

He must be dealt with. Instead, you help him kidnap and experiment on members of the colony. You attack Epcot.

It's true. Ascalon doesn't know it, but Shave Time and I have gone down to Mile High and plucked away Gardeners here and there. We both wanted to see if they could be separated from OneVoice. The results were gruesome. And I don't wanna think about Epcot.

You said you'd keep Sabrina safe, I say.

I did not imagine you would move to Kansas. You exposed her to risk. You exposed your unborn child to risk.

I open the little door of the tree I'm leaning on so that Shave Time doesn't suspect I'm talking to Akira. There's a tiny bed inside. It's covered with a plush pink comforter the size of a playing card. *Bring Sabrina back.*

I cannot.

I close the tiny door. *I'll wait forever until you agree to do it.*

You spend too much time sleeping. Your child does, too.

Don't lecture me on parenthood.

Yes. I know what it is to be hated by one's own child.

I feel my jaw clench. *Bring my wife back.*

I cannot do it. I will no longer keep bringing you back, too.

You're lying, as usual, I think to myself.

Like with Shave Time, these conversations are always circular and without purpose. In this world, no one is gonna convince anyone of anything. Akira must be thinking the same because she cuts communication, and it weirdly makes me feel alone. In that moment, I realize that I miss her, that I've always missed her, and this shames me deeply. For me, since the days of The Killing Rock all those years ago, she has always been a sick dependence I could never shake. I look back at Shave Time, struggling to squeeze his head out of the tree. It'd be so easy to take him out right now. But against Akira, he's the only ally with an army I got.

5

From A to Z, formerly Omaha, is a piece of shit, elevated, urban landscape that sits on tetrised cubes of trash. Shave Time, who took the money Old Man Caldwell paid him and purchased The Leachate years ago, declared From A to Z its capital. Then he somehow jacked up the entire city about a hundred feet and put cubed trash underneath it as its base. His office is on the top floor of the First National Bank tower, which is a rickety and laughable forty-five stories. It's surrounded by clocktowers because Shave Time has a thing for clocktowers, all imported from other Leachatean cities. Chase County Courthouse, Cook Carillon Tower, The Henry Ford Museum Clocktower, Lafayette County Courthouse, among others. All are operational but read different, random times.

The second tallest building in the city, the Woodmen, ominously shadows the clocktowers. Only the top ten stories of the Woodmen remain intact, and they're used as Gardener prisons full of torture and enucleation. I've hid what I've done from Ascalon. Shave Time and I have experimented on them. Pumped radioactive saline through their veins. Sawed off limbs. All to see if the physical stress would disconnect them from their iEs, like Ascalon Lee disconnected herself from my daughter when I shot her all those years ago. I probably shouldn't have told Shave Time about that. He was convinced it would work on the Gardeners after I told him, and now, even though he no longer believes we can disconnect them, he's gotten a taste for torture. From what we've seen, there's no way to separate iE from body except when a Gardener does so willingly, gradually, and methodically, like the Gardeners at Epcot. That was part of my mission, to torch the place and see how the Gardeners would react to a larger scale attack. They didn't. They let themselves go up in smoke down there. They didn't even put up a fight. I try not to think about it. I try not to think about the other things I keep from my daughter as well. I try not to think about what I've become.

It's high enough here at the top of First National to see the convoy of old gas-powered semis heading to the West Coast on the I-80, each one packed to the gills with radioactive garbage and topsoil. I wanna tell Shave Time the quickest way to pollute the goddamn continent is probably with old planes, not trucks. Carpet bomb the country with drums of nuclear waste. I keep my mouth shut because there's gotta be a better way, though I got no clue what that is. In fact, I doubt there's any way at all. I'm a man with little purpose or hope. At least I finally died enough times that I've experienced representational drift and hardly see guidelines anymore.

It's summer, so down below, under a crochet of power lines girded from pole to pole, From A to Z bustles with foot traffic on streets worn to early twenty-first-century trash. Spring and summer are above-ground seasons, and The Leachateans are making the most of their sunshine days and starry nights atop the flattened mâché of century-old non-biodegradables. Motorcyclists race through, veering around a track riddled with sinkholes. Their skeletal machines rumble. They cut off anything that makes their old machines sound softer, anything that adds weight and reduces speed. They go round and round on their cycles, which are full of bad pinion angles.

Farther away, the crater of the excavated TD Ameritrade Park is packed with fans cheering five-versus-five gladiatorial combat. It's as if the Leachateans took on the old computer games concept of a post-nuclear apocalypse and made it reality. I think back on springs and summers in Water City. I miss the voluptuousness of the ocean. The sticky saltiness. I remember taking my daughter to shore when she was three. She'd pick flowers and dig up rocks and pile them like offerings.

"Play me, Daddy."

She'd break the sculpture and want me to sit beside her and rebuild it. "Again-t," she'd say. She ended most of her sentences with a *T* sound for some reason, back then. Sabrina'd bring this one up often. At the end, the only conversations we had were about the past. Maybe she was trying to tell me something. I don't know.

Shave Time puts his hand on my shoulder and stands beside me. He invited me here, and I had a tough time saying no. I know he'll hibernate in an AMP chamber underground soon, and I need to try to finally get him committed to try to do something drastic to Akira with me before he sleeps. I still have the super-rail stored in my micro shuttle, the one I used as transport to burn down Epcot. The one I tore all the lux out of for cargo and munitions space. We watch as the Leachateans zipline from rooftop to rooftop and light the evenfall bonfires that'll rage through the night. The refurbished drum machines, which are connected to bass speakers mounted to every building, are cranked up to ten.

"The best a man can get," Shave Time says. He's wearing his spiked prosthetic jaw now, which he wears when he fights in the pits.

I nod. But no, it's not.

Shave Time's son and second-in-command, Blade Close, begins to light the wax candles throughout the room. The faces of past generals light up, statues relocated to Shave Time's HQ. Eisenhower. Powell. Garcia. Lin. Then Blade Close flips a switch, and the police light chandeliers above begin to strobe. Once he's done lighting the place up, he steps on the other side of me and hands me a glass of water. I peer at the murky contents under the flashing red and blue lights. The water moves, and it takes me a moment to realize that it moves because there's live stuff squiggling around in it.

I look at Blade Close. His head's covered with tumors or parasites to eat tumors, I'm not sure which. He looks like an oranda goldfish. Frequent hibernation in the AMPs that I secretly gave his father years ago is probably the only thing keeping him alive. The Leachateans aren't aware that Shave Time and his son use AMP, which is forbidden tech in The Leachate. Shave Time tells them that they're going on a sacred pilgrimage to consult with Mayhem of Allstate whenever he and his son hibernate. Only Army Strong knows he sleeps, and they do a good job of protecting the secret.

Shave Time refuses to import clean water because he won't work with the Gardeners. Shit, the Gardeners offer it for free, along with immunizations, medical treatment, and clean food. But taking from the Gardeners is a crime punishable by death. For all Shave Time knows, iEs in the form of slivers of blue light could pop out of a packaged provision or be injected into a Leachatean via vaccine, so Gardener vaccines are banned as well.

These Leachateans die from stuff I need to look up on my iE database: measles, polio, AIDS. Surviving rubella is like a coming-of-age rite of passage, and cataracts is like a sign of adulthood. I don't know what the life expectancy is here, but every time I spot someone with gray hair, I do a double take.

Having no idea what to do with the glass of silty water, I just hold it. I look up and watch as the clouds stall and split. All that's left is an unbearable heat.

"Did you think about what I said?" I ask him this all the time. He never answers. He doesn't now. Instead, he motions for one of his daughters, Barbasol Needs, the youngest and toughest of his kids, to turn up the music in the room. She lumbers to the old amplifier and rotates the knob. A dead, blackened pinky dangles from her hand. The old ad jingle "All Strength, No Sweat" booms.

"It's like I said," I tell him, raising my voice above the music. "I have ideas, but I don't have the manpower. You have the manpower. I'm telling you, the Gardeners at Epcot didn't even resist the attack. They just ate it. Maybe we don't need to be scared of them anymore." I feel Blade Close's eyes on me. He doesn't like when I don't talk to his father in slo-ganspeak. He sees it as disrespect. I switch gears. "Everything we do is driven by you," I say.

Shave Time nods. He's eyeing his son and calls him over. Blade Close steps in front of his father and faces him, tilting his head back and opening his mouth. Shave Time pulls out his trusty tweezers and sticks them in Blade Close's mouth. "Better ideas driven by you?" he says.

I shrug. "Let's go places," I say.

I've been trying to get him on my side for so long now. That's part of why Ascalon and I hit Disney World. That's why we've hit other, more isolated Gardener targets close to the Leachatean borders for Shave Time in the past. I need his trust. I'm just going to come out with it.

"Let's form two armies and attack both Corpus Akira and the Cape at the same time," I say. "Let's take control of the mountain-sized dragon head accelerators on the ground. Maybe break the vertical elevators that raise the rockets. Let's hold Dragonspine for ransom. I got no interest in blowing up the accelerators, because for all I know, the world will crack in half if we do—that thousand-mile tube way up in the sky may drop in the Gulf of Mexico, garrote the ocean floor, and spark a fucking tidal wave that'll break over and drown the entire continent."

Shave Time furls his brow, but doesn't protest, so the words continue to pour outta me. "You cleared the Mississippi of big debris and have been riverboating in millions of forgotten barrels of crude from the Bayou Choctaw. You got an entire society that will do what you say. You reactivated the Keystone Pipeline. You got the old Wood River Refinery fired up and working again. You rebuilt the old power lines and added new ones, so the city is canopied with tangles of sparking wires. Let's be honest. You love flywheels and sparkplugs. You're old-school American. You only want to go straight, really fast. None of this Le Mans crap. You're a quarter-mile guy. And you love blowing shit up. Let's go straight really fast and blow shit up."

Shave Time removes the tweezers from his son's mouth. A long, skinny worm wriggles at the tip of the prongs. Shave Time drops the worm and plants a foot on it. He puts a hand on Blade Close's shoulder and nods. Blade Close, who is a foot shorter than his father and walks on a gimpy leg, leaves the room.

"It's too big," Shave Time says. "Too high." He sighs. "Too dangerous."

He's scared of her. He should be. He likes to needle Akira and her Gardeners, likes to capture a handful here and there, prod, torture, and experiment on them, but he's scared of actually poking one of her cities. Me, on the other hand, after my last conversation with Akira, I went from missing her to hating her all over again. "It's the only way to hit her where it hurts."

Shave Time shakes his head. "Better sleep. Better you."

"But it's possible. We have the meats."

Shave time points up. "A whole different animal."

"You could revive more factories and build what we need. Maybe more tanks. Look what you did. You lifted an entire city one hundred feet in the air and put trash underneath it."

"Trash?"

I hold up my hands. "Sorry, not trash."

"This we'll defend," Shave Time says.

"Revive the factories. Build. If you commit to that, I'll scout and find the weak points. I've already scouted some out." I lie. I've scouted, true, but I haven't seen any weak points. "Then you raise two armies to take over this damn launch loop of hers."

Shave Time shrugs. "I sleep soon. You sleep soon. Wake up a whole new you. Maybe after."

Sleep. One thing we share is that we've both become addicted to sleep. He sleeps for survival. I sleep because I've become obsessed with this notion of just waking up every once in a while to check if the world's gotten any better. I sleep to pass time. Maybe if enough of it passes, Akira will change her mind and bring Sabrina back. I've been disappointed every time.

"Do you like her updating her system every Tuesday?" I ask. "It doesn't make you nervous, never knowing what the next patch will bring? Bombs, maybe? Invasion? When you hibernate, what do you dream of? Don't you ever wonder if she'll finally tire of your resistance and patch you and your people out of existence while you slumber?"

Shave Time glares at me. I step to one of the oxidized candelabras. I empty the glass of dirty water on one of the flames and it sparks before it dies out. "You don't think she can do it, just like that?"

"I asked you to come because I found something," Shave Time says.

"Oh yeah? What?"

"First you. If we need to have this conversation again, you need to show me something new. Not the same blah-blah. All the time, you only come with words. Now, you must show me something I can touch. Tide's in. Dirt's out."

I think about that. Maybe it's time for a little trust. I can't go on like this anymore. I can't have my daughter going on like this anymore. I've never shown Shave Time a super rail gun in action. Fortunately, Fort Leavenworth didn't have any, and Ascalon and I managed to gather all the ones we could find at abandoned military bases coast to coast. I never wanted to show him, and this is the first time I've brought one here, but I decide to take a chance. I know he senses my growing urgency and desperation, but after all these years, this is the furthest I've gotten in this conversation.

We walk to my private intercontinental shuttle. It's lev-parked next to the top floor. I hop on the wing, the stabilizers keeping the ship correct, and I go inside. I step out with the super-rail. With its heavy-duty, twin conductor barrels, the shoulder-fired weapon is almost as big as Shave Time. I charge it up. Neon blue lightning crackles between the conductors. His eyes widen.

"Perfection," he says.

I nod. "To hell and back reliably."

About two miles away, the lights of the old BK Pedestrian Bridge flicker on in the dusk. The lights reflect off the curdled waters of Pure Life, once known as the Missouri River. I point the rail at the bridge. "Anyone on that thing?" I ask.

Shave Time shakes his head.

I fire. Neon blue plasma donuts eject from the rail and hit the bridge, disintegrating it. Three thousand feet of cables and concrete reduced to something that resembles smoldering pumpkin spice blowing in the wind.

"Boom, boom, boom, boom," I sing.

Shave Time gasps. "How?"

"Tokamak."

"Tokamak?"

"Fusion. Magnetic confinement. Superheated plasma. My daughter can explain it better. She's got a head for stuff like this. Science."

He's rubbing his artificial jaw, still staring out in disbelief at something that ain't even there anymore. "Soup that eats like a meal."

I nod. "Soup that eats like a meal."

"How many do you have?" he asks.

I lie. "Just this one."

He turns to me. "What else have you hidden from me?"

"Nothing."

He narrows his eyes and points at his right eye. "What about your daughter? Maybe she's born with it? Maybe it's Maybelline?"

He's reverting back to sloganspeak, which means he's getting agitated. I take a small step back. "She ain't connected to Akira," I say.

"And the Yellow One?" Shave Time asks. "Is she connected to her?"

"No," I say, even though I'm not sure of that.

"And what about you?" he snarls. "The Citi never sleeps!"

He's suddenly angry. I take another step back and ready the rail. I don't gotta shoot Shave Time. I just gotta shoot down. I don't know what will happen if I do, but I know it won't be good for him . . . or me. "What about me?"

Shave Time sticks two fingers in his mouth and whistles loudly. Blade Close and three other guys in fatigues step through the door. All three point their assault rifles at me. Blade Close is holding a sack. He reaches inside and retrieves a decomposed human head. The skull's been cracked open and mutilated, but I can see clearly that it's me. I brush my finger against the rail's trigger. Shave Time takes his tweezers out and digs the pincers in the skull, extracting a sliver of microchip.

"Intel inside," Shave Time snarls.

I didn't think he knew. How long has he been surveilling me without me even knowing it? What else does he know?

Shave Time probably dug this HuSC up when the blizzard crashed me outside of Boston. I'm surprised it held up after so long. He waited all this time to tell me he knows I'm chipped by Akira. Why? Then it comes to me. He always figured I was holding out on him, that I had something like the super-rail and other things stashed, so he's probably spent ages reconning me. I want to explain to him that Akira's shut me out of OneVoice. That I'm his ally, not hers, but he won't buy it. I held out on him.

I glance at the Woodmen. No way I'm letting him send me there. No way am I turning over my arsenal to Army Strong.

I always figured that having kids would make me less crazy. Most lunatics that I'd come across in police work were either childless or didn't have any real connection with their children. I don't know what fatherhood, real fatherhood this time, had done to me. I'm suspicious that it fooled me into thinking I'm more important than I really am. If I'm being honest with myself, I'm no good for my kid or a single god-damn person. Never have been. Kathy and John, dead. Jerry, dead. Akeem, dead. Sabrina, dead. The world. Dead. I've probably damaged my daughter more than I've protected her. Part of the reason I've hung on to her so tightly is because I was afraid that if I didn't, she'd be swept up by Kimura or Ascalon Lee. But Ascalon doesn't need me. I think about the fact that I took her to Epcot with me. Hell, she's probably better off without me. A good parent probably knows when to stop being one. And there's only one way I know how to do that.

I smile and clench my toes. After you die, maybe you get a moment of silence. Then that moment is quickly over and life, which is and always has been for the living, goes on without you. I haven't felt alive in a long time, so I tell myself, *Fuck it*, and I pull the trigger. A lifetime of pulling triggers. While Shave Time's eyes grow wide and his men scramble for the nearest zipline, I feel the floor beneath me collapse. I'm like a Leachatean pilot now, on a temporary flight with an impossible landing. Isn't that all that life is?

6

THE GIRL

My dad hates the fish here in Kansas. He says they're swampy, flaky-meated things with no fight in them. If I hear another *Old Man and the Sea* marlin or yellowfin tuna fishing story from him, I'll kill myself. My father sometimes asks me if I remember how much I loved the ocean. I say no, even though I do.

I remember the ocean's vast, crimped surface. The refreshing coldness that blasts through one's nervous system after the first big splash. The light dimming the deeper and deeper in the brine you go. The reflective scales, colors, and undulating life that flash around you. It was like floating in an endless living exhibit of wonder. Then the wonder turned to terror for me after Satori Day. Going under the surface, even back to the safety of our seascraper apartment, felt suffocating. Finding the dead monk seal trapped in its feeder didn't help. The only big thing I don't remember back then is shooting my father's best friend, Akeem Buhari. It's strange to know you've done something terrible and not remember it outside of nightmares. Sure, it was really Ascalon Lee who took my body and committed the murder, but the guilt that it was my finger has always stung. Like the monk seal, it still feels like my fault even though it wasn't. Like Epcot.

My father is so sure that Gardeners can't be separated from Okaasan. I have proof that they can sitting right across from me. My whole body hums with nervous, excited energy. This eyeless boy, whose name is Jon6J, and I are back at home eating whiskered fish that I netted from Covert Creek last spring. He sniffs at the deep-fried fillets then looks up at me. I say "look" despite the fact that he has no eyes and I've bandaged his sockets, so he sits here blindfolded. He moves around surprisingly well for a supposedly blind person, and I wonder if he senses through echolocation.

"Query," he says while touching the fried fish.

Maybe I should've served him turkey or venison. Or maybe he's a vegan and I should've given him corn or soybeans. Our house, built on the bones of an old hunting lodge, can shelter over a dozen people, but Jon6J is the first guest I've brought inside. I'm afraid I'm being a bad host. I'm even more afraid that he isn't real. He is cut off from OneVoice. And he's so young. He does not even seem to realize how unique and remarkable he is.

"Is something wrong?" I ask, trying to keep my voice even and steady. I want to find out as much as I can before I tell my dad about him. What am I more scared of—my father denying that the boy has been cut off or him getting his hooks in the boy? I will not let my father hurt Jon. I will not let him be treated like the ones back at Epcot.

He cuts off a small corner of fish with his fork and nibbles on it. He carefully spits the morsel out on his plate and licks his lip. "What is that?" he asks. "It tastes like ocean."

"It's salt," I say, compulsively chewing on the inside of my cheek, wanting to ask so much more, but straining to make him feel at ease.

"Salt?"

"Sodium chloride."

"Yes," the boy says. "Yes, I remember. Salt is what it was called. Okaasan patched salt from our diets, made us forget it." He pokes at the fish with his fork. It sounds like a "C" level patch, one that is a significant update, but certainly not "S" level—one that introduces a ton of new content. It doesn't sound like it reaches an "A" or "B" level update either. Is part of the reason he doesn't remember because of memory dumps during updates? How can Akira store all that data? Maybe she needs to periodically clear the cache with each patch.

"And what of this encasing?" Jon asks.

"Breading," I say. "It used to gross me out, too, at first, but my father said he always missed fried food. He's old, though, so he misses a lot of things."

"Like what?"

My mother, but I don't say it. Instead, I say, "Well, when we first got here, he told me that he missed hunting. Fly fishing. Doing whatever he wanted." He should like it here, but I don't think he does. I don't say that either.

"Breading," Jon says. "Why? For additional calories?"

"For taste."

"Taste? It will not have taste if it is not breaded?"

"Not as much," I say.

"More taste," he whispers in awe.

This boy is wonderful. I feel compelled to patiently answer his questions since I barraged him with questions of my own on our way back here, the first being, how did he get free? He said he didn't remember. His memory is spotty since being disconnected from OneVoice, but he confirmed that the world is as Ascalon Lee described it to me: each continent on a mission. When I asked him why there weren't any children in the Gardener cities, he said Okaasan believes rearing children drains an incredible amount of resources, is terribly inefficient, and not eco-friendly. If a Gardener unexpectedly expires, and they are deemed worthy, they are simply recycled into another HuSC. I asked him who makes the new HuSCs, what and where they are. He didn't know.

"How many people are there?" I ask.

"People?"

"Individuals."

He frowns. "Just one. Okaasan."

I inspect him closely. He's so frail. Thin and unmuscled. Under his tight shirt, I can see his ribs cut across his chest. From what I know, the Gardeners do not spy. They do not lie. They stick to themselves. Still, I don't trust him. Or I should say, I don't trust *her*. When I asked him what he was doing out there in the middle of nowhere, he said he didn't remember. I don't like that his memory seems most cloudy when it comes to the questions I want answers to the most.

The boy sits in his chair with unsettling, perfect posture. I try to imagine being able to smell the synapses bolting from cortex to limbic, but I smell nothing except the fish. He looks up at the wooden arches of the barrel-vaulted ceiling, or he's just tilting his head up. "What is your purpose?" he asks.

"Purpose?"

"My purpose was mining tellurium."

"Tellurium?" I blink, surprised. Is that why the Gardeners

dig so much? To mine? My father, who has always wondered why they dig, would want to hear this. "For what?"

He shrugs. "My purpose was mining tellurium. What is your purpose?"

Is he deflecting my question with a question of his own? I play along for now. "Survival."

"Survival for what?"

It's a fair point. I am surviving, but does my existence have purpose? Perhaps, with the help of this boy, it can. "You turn your head like you can see, but you don't have eyes. How do you see?"

"I don't know if it's seeing," he says. "It feels more like remembering."

"Can you *see* how you broke from OneVoice?"

The boy shakes his head.

I stand in frustration. "Eat your fish," I say.

He nibbles on the filet while I struggle to find the right questions to ask him. He doesn't remember being disconnected. He doesn't know why. He just recalls waking one morning under a tree outside Mile High and feeling utterly abandoned.

I stare at the world puzzle map, remembering my father demanding I sleep in AMP after it took me two days straight to put the puzzle together. I shake my head. Interrogating this boy should be my father's job. He was supposedly good at interrogation once. My mother, too. Is this what it always is to be with other people? To not understand one another? To harbor trauma? To bottle anxiety, probe, and flinch before another even responds? I feel lost. I'm used to interacting with machines. Machines give me exactly what I expect from them. Despite the exasperation, I'm savoring being here with a person outside my father. I'm in a rush to gather information, but I'm in no rush to leave this boy's presence. The head of the forty-point whitetail mounted on the wall seems to stare down at me. My first hunt. I remember the buck standing majestically atop a small hill with an old, rubber car tire around its neck. The antlers too big now to get the tire off. I remember taking the shot and almost thinking that I was putting the poor animal out of its humiliating misery.

My father told me that it was just meat, that we're all just meat, and that I needed to learn to see it that way.

When I grabbed my father's shoulder and told him I would dress the deer, he smiled. I never told him this, but his smile meant the world to me back then. It might still to this day. It's infectious. Both of us were smiling when we took the carcass back home. Then fitful AMP sleep followed. I dreamt of Noah's Ark. Every type of animal marching off the boat in twos. When they approached, my father ordered me to shoot each animal and pull their innards out. It felt like it went on forever until it was my little sister standing in front of me, a child-sized version, wearing the thin blanket she was buried in like a shawl. My dream ended then. Isn't that what nightmares do? They show us what we're most afraid of becoming.

I return to the present and refocus. I face the boy. "How did you know where my father would be?"

"It's in the book."

"What book?"

He shoots me a surprised look. "What book? The *only* book."

"I want to see this book."

"It's not a book that can be read. It's a book that is just known."

"Tell it to me then."

The boy points to his blindfold. "I can't. Not anymore."

"Why do you want to talk to my father? How did you escape in the first place?"

"I don't understand."

At this point, I've had enough. I need help. I ping my father. Blinding pain sears through my head. *My father. He's in imminent danger.* The last thing I taste is the metal of my own scream.

7

I dream of things in rewind and fast-forward. Rewind. A week after my mother's death, my father tucking me into my AMP after my refusal to sleep for days. Rewind more. My camo hunting jacket next to my father's on the arm of the chair next to the fireplace. Mine is so much smaller than his. What ever happened to those jackets? Fast-forward. Me waking up the day of my thirteenth birthday, my father's fake smile the first thing that greets me when the AMP chamber opens. Then, suddenly, I'm somewhere else. Where or when, I'm not sure. I'm in a vacuum where time somehow doesn't exist. Three identical black Dorthys gallop side by side, but don't move forward.

When I come to, I'm on my back, head turned, and my eyes take in the cobblestone walls of my changing room. When we first moved here, I asked my father why we had to live in a cave. He laughed. My mother didn't. Once I shake off the grogginess, my mind careens into panic mode. I shift into sports mode, roll off the bed, and snap off one of the wooden legs at the bed's footboard. Before the corner of the bedframe slams on the floor, I'm on my feet, brandishing the leg like a weapon.

The eyeless boy is on a wooden chair across from me, one I made when I was a child. The seat is crooked, and the legs are uneven. It's so worn, it looks like it's about to collapse under him, but Jon is as calm as usual. His thin cane sits across his lap.

"What happened to you?" he asks.

"How long was I out?" I pant.

The boy shrugs.

"Minutes? Hours?" I ask.

"Time is inconsequential to me."

"You carried me here?" I ask.

The boy shakes his head. "You walked. Or maybe wobbled is the better word. Then you simply lied down and closed your eyes."

I don't remember this. I never really do. I've lost time in the past. Every instance I've patched into my father and felt his death coming. I toss the piece of wood on the floor, walk to my closet, and put on a utility belt and a thin summer trench coat. I open my dresser and grab two heat blades. I strap one to my belt and the other to my foam-fitted thigh. I look back at the boy. He's too valuable to take to The Leachate. It may be dangerous, but I should tell him to stay here. Not that I know he'll even listen. He seems traumatized. Somewhat dim. He's blind and could go wandering off anywhere, but anywhere around here is safer than where I need to go.

"You need to stay here," I say.

"No," Jon says, "I must come."

"You don't even know where I'm going."

"You're going to retrieve the synesthete."

"How do you know?"

He shrugs. I don't have time for another Q and A or an argument. I step back to the closet and toss a rad suit bundled in a ball to the boy. Surprisingly, he catches it. He pushes the correct panel, and the rad suit bursts into its full size. Jon rubs the lead-laced material between his fingers.

"What is this for?" he asks.

"Protection from radiation."

"There's radiation here?"

"No. Well, not much anyway. But there's a lot of it where we're going."

I'll have him stay in my SEAL, but I figure, just in case. I march out of the room and head to the mini armory, two doors down. I step to the gun safe, eye scan it, and the heavy door creaks open. I pull out a rail and check the charge. The bars light up blue to full. I eye my mom's shiny 1911 and stuff it in my holster. It's already loaded. I head to the kitchen, grab a fistful of venison jerky sticks and strap on two canteens. I turn around to face the boy, who is having trouble dressing. I put the sticks down on the counter and help him strap into his suit.

"I doubt you have any sort of resistance to radiation," I say.

"Do you?" he asks.

"Yes. I have bio nanos in me that repair damage." As does my father, but my mother didn't. And after my sister, she didn't care. She almost seemed grateful to not have them.

"I did work in a tellurium mine," Jon says. "Perhaps I have nanos, too."

"Okaasan wouldn't have bothered. She likes spending too much."

"Spending?"

"Yeah. Spending lives."

I put his helmet on and the mag seals lock. The suit inflates, almost imperceptibly. Jon begins to breathe through the suit's built-in respirator.

"We aren't in The Leachate," I say. "But we're close enough to have some exposure. My mother got sick. You should wear this at all times."

"Why do you live here?" he asks, his voice muffled by the suit.

"Why indeed," I say.

I glance at the map on the wall. A laser of magenta that connects me to my father beams from my eye and shines on a tiny speck in Nebraska. From A to Z. It's where my father is.

I put on my hat, and we walk out of the house. It's dark, so I light up the area with my iE. We weave through the junkyard. Jon follows as best he can, tapping the ground in front of him with his cane. I step over my half-buried baby quad, the treads of the fat tires packed with dried mud. I reminisce about my childhood, how the one thing there was never a shortage of was presents. Anything that could be thrown or flown, anything that could be cuddled or ridden, that could be painted or downloaded was mine. It brought me joy at first. Then I started thinking that all of it was other people's stuff. Just about everything we have used to be other people's stuff, and my father pillaged it all. That's what this junkyard is: an exposed grave of other people's things.

We get to the SEAL, and I have its camo tarp automatically folded and packed. Old smart fabric tech. The SEAL used to belong to Old Man Caldwell. Of course, my father stole this and gave it to me, too. He prefers shuttle flying now because we live on a continent. It's faster, and it can cover more miles without refueling. This SEAL is more than just transportation. It's a sea, air, and land military vehicle equipped with rails mounted beneath each side of the wing and can fly in silent mode. I leap on the unibody wing, reach down, and yank the boy up.

"You're strong," he says.

Yes, I know. I wanted to show him, because I still don't trust him. I shrug and pop open the canopy. The boy climbs inside. Jon6J squeezes his armrest when the automatic belts tighten around his slight frame.

"Are you okay?" I ask.

He slowly nods. "I feel . . ."

"Scared?"

"Yes. Scared."

After I climb into the pilot seat and the canopy lowers and locks, the electric turbines whine, and we lift off.

"You aren't going to steer us?" Jon asks.

I look down at the pistol grip joystick. I haven't used it in years. "Would it make you feel better if I did?"

"Yes."

I grab the stick and head east.

"Where are we going?" he asks.

"It's like you said," I say. "To retrieve the synesthete."

"Is he in danger?"

I nod. "We're going to save him."

My father has gotten himself into trouble. Again. I begin to wonder whether wisdom really does come with age and experience. Perhaps it does in some ways, but maybe age also manifests an instinct to turn one's back to the present to try to keep hold of the past. I told my father not to trust Shave Time. Now, Jon6J and I are zipping off on a magenta trail to From A to Z because my father probably tried to swindle Shave Time, and he most likely swindled my father right back. As my mother told me once years ago when my father would go off on one of his bounties: "Boys will be boys."

People, I wanted to say. People will be people. And being people? Well, that's not an excuse.

8

From a couple of clicks out, From A to Z is a skyline dimly lit by smoldering, half-dead bonfires. I was planning on landing on the rooftop of First National to avoid flying through the power lines, but it looks like the entire building has been cleaved down the middle. What could've done that? The answer is easy. My father's super-rail. Akira's escalating activity is making him desperate. He must've shown Shave Time the super-rail, and things went sideways from there. I need to find him in this rubble before Army Strong does. And if they already found him, I need to get him out of here quietly so that the entire city doesn't swarm us. I curse to myself. I shouldn't have brought Jon with me.

Instead of First National, I choose the second tallest building, the Woodmen, as the landing zone. Thirty stories of broken glass and rust stains. Living proof that stainless steel isn't stainless. The mega letters fell off years ago, but their ghosts remain, still spelling out the building's name.

I land and squint at the fires below that barely light the tops of cubed trash that pass for streets. I've walked those streets under the canopy of wires fiercely buzzing with current. Practically every worn cube has compressed words on it. Slogans that make up the Leachatean language. To walk From A to Z is to walk worn, faded words under a crisscross of power lines that seem to double in number every time I come here.

My father would be upset that I'm at the Woodmen. It has always been off-limits for me. Adult content, he'd always say. He'd be even more vexed that I didn't scout first, but I have no idea what Shave Time plans to do with my father—if he has him—or how long he will survive, so I figure haste makes more sense. The magentas are faint but visible, as are the skull-crushing wails that sound like a civil defense siren in my head. These strengthen whenever my father's in peril, and I get closer to finding him. Why did Ascalon Lee build me this way? I glance at Jon6J and wonder how he got rid of his iE. Honestly, I would love to be rid of mine. My father thinks it's possible that if I pull it out, I'll unplug everything and cease to exist. Jon seems fine, though. Some amnesia and blindness, which I wouldn't mind having.

"Stay here," I say.

Jon shakes his head. "I want to come."

"It's too dangerous."

"This place," he says. "It feels familiar."

"You wouldn't know it," I say. "Gardeners aren't allowed here."

Before I can say anything else, he retracts his rad helmet and hops out of the SEAL. He's quickly marching to the rooftop door, cane in hand. I glance at the city below, and even in the dark, I can see the flake and peel of the buildings sprinkled with magenta snow. My father's signal isn't clear.

I wonder why. I look up at the dulling moon above ribbons of clouds. My father says it has a comet-like tail that we cannot see.

Jon surprises me by stopping at the door, feeling it with his hand, then kicking it open. Stronger than he looks. I catch up to him. He takes a bad step and stumbles down a shallow flight of makeshift wooden stairs. I light the room with my eye. Roaches disperse like shattering glass. The room is filled with old decklid-converted tables, which are topped with rusty, blood-caked surgical instruments. Beside each table are tanks of pressurized oxygen and thermal lances. I leap the stairs and pull Jon up.

"Are you okay?" I ask.

He rubs his shoulder. "Yes. Quite fine." He turns and appears to be looking at one of the scalpels. I draw my bigger heat blade from my thigh and give it to him.

"Just in case."

He nods. I still don't trust him, but that's the problem. Was I supposed to just leave him at home? Allowing him prolonged access there would've not necessarily been a better option. He's way too important to let wander off. I'm not used to being in this position. Making calls, which makes me sympathize with my father. I see now that maybe the scariest thing in life is making the wrong decision. It's why my parents let me choose Kansas. Fear.

"Do you hear that?" asks Jon.

Muffled groans echo from the floor beneath us. I look back at the tables. "Is this a hospital?"

Jon doesn't answer. He heads to an open elevator shaft with the box-shaped car sitting just outside of it, as if someone was planning to repair it.

"Wait," I say.

He doesn't. I gasp as he jumps down the shaft.

I run to the opening and shine my light down. Hundreds of severed wires and tubes droop from caved-in walls. It's like examining the shredded bowels of some doomsday machine. At the bottom, there appears to be a pile of bodies. I smell them—they shimmer in red. The scent is practically unbearable. I regret not bringing a mask. Jon dangles from the gape a floor below. He pulls himself up and crawls into darkness. My father would not like seeing me do this, but, untethered, I shift to sports mode, leap into the shaft, kick off a wall, and follow Jon into the passageway.

The gutted floor seems to writhe, but when I light up the room, I can see that it's more lying bodies. Only these are alive, if you can call them that. Naked and nearly fleshless, they moan prayers to Okaasan. I dim. Jon6J is on his knees, weeping. Despite the smell, I step to the nearest one, an older woman, and pull her hand from her face. Eyeless. The infection cruelly indicates so. I step to another and do the same. Eyeless. Unchipped. All of them. I turn to the shaft and assume that the bodies at the bottom are of the ones who threw themselves to their deaths in the name of Akira. I spin to Jon.

"Do you know them?" I ask.

Jon wipes the tears from his cheeks. I'm stunned to see a Gardener cry. "They *are* me," Jon says. "We *are* us."

I bend down and scan a body. Flayed skin. Broken bones that aren't healing. She's shaking from fever. I want to comfort her in some way but don't know how. I put my hand on her forehead. "Okaasan," she whimpers.

Jon shakes his head. "Who would do this?" he asks.

"Shave Time Money," I say.

"Why?"

"Hate," I say. "Why is your designation 6J?"

"I . . . I don't remember."

"You told me you can't see, but you're remembering. Is this where you came from?"

Jon wipes his eyes again and shakes his head. "I don't remember. I mean, I remember seeing here but not being here. Can you help them?"

I look at these poor beings, and the irony is not lost on me. The stripping of humanity. Shave Time is doing the same thing to the Gardeners as Akira is back at Epcot. My father says I'm great at identifying irony. Even if there isn't any, I'll make it up. The sad sight of these starved, eyeless Gardeners infuriates me, and the fury builds. I think of The Leachate, Epcot, and the ikebanas of Akira's slaves across the entire world. I can't even help these people right in front of me, much less people, billions perhaps, thousands of miles away. Of all the lessons my father has taught me, in this moment, one rings truer than all the others. Rage is depression's alternative. For years, it has been the only thing keeping my father and I going. I glare at the bodies. I suspect he knows about this place since he told me it's off limits. It's why he's so sure that Gardeners can't be cut off from OneVoice. He and Shave Time have tried to do it, but no matter what they do, the Gardeners still pray to Okaasan.

I count the heads. Sixty-four unfortunate souls. Their bodies suffering from dehydration, malnutrition, infection, and Leachate sickness all at the same time. I steel myself and ping my father. The magenta is blinding. He's here. The trail leads to the bottom, where the rest of the bodies are.

"Stay here and tend to them," I say. "I'll be right back."

Before he can say anything, I'm down the shaft. I cling onto the dangling tubes and wires and work my way down. The stench is even worse here than up there. As I get closer to the bottom, I can see maggots wriggle from the mouths of the bodies in this morass of flesh. Beneath the pile, peaking through the gaps of rotted torsos and limbs, my father's magenta flickers. Whoever buried him under all this death was smart. The reds interfered with the color that connects us. Normally, I would've seen them in bright streams. I'll need to dig through human flesh to retrieve him. I will never forgive him for this. I reach the bottom and begin excavating through moist rot and waste. I leave my light dim and try not to look at what's left of the pulped, putrid faces bloated with gas. Foam leaks from their nostrils, and swollen tongues bulge from their open mouths.

When I finally get to my father, he's gagged, bound, and unconscious. I rip off his crudely welded bindings and muzzle. I try to slap him awake. No dice. Here at the bottom, the shaft has been sealed by what looks like an avalanche of engine blocks. I'm so stupid. I should've come down by rope. I'll need to climb back up and get some from the SEAL. I look down at my father and slap him again. His eyes snap open. Wisps of green reflect off his pupils. Then my mind and motor functions seize at the sound of a screeching elevator car plummeting toward us.

The weapon, a voice in my head says. Is it Ascalon Lee or just the memory of what she told me? All I feel is anger now.

My head snaps as a stream of yellow laser blazes from my eye. I register the temperature. A burst equal to the sun's. I do my best to cover my father from the raining debris and close my eyes; however, nothing falls upon us but sprinkling flakes of ash.

9

THE FATHER

I remember being young, hearing numbers and wanting to beat them. The ten-second hundred-yard dash. The four-hundred-pound bench press. The bullseye at six thousand yards. Then, as I got older, there were different numbers to beat. Triglycerides under 400. Uric acid under 6. Systolic blood pressure under 140. I wonder if my hydronaut father was the same way with depth. If chasing those benchmarks is finally what did him in. I've rejected benchmarks. I stopped caring. My daughter took care of Shave Time's little trap, and look at her, scowling while tearing through a wall of Chevy small blocks. It's the first time I'd seen her use her iE like a laser. She's strong. And angry. *Good.* It's the only way she'll thrive in this world.

The Korean word *hwabyeong* pops in my head. My mother would use it to describe my father's and my seemingly sudden flashes of rage. A mental illness, she used to call it. Psychological symptoms include feelings of guilt and unfairness. Frequent sighing. Feelings of impending doom. And, of course, *bun*, eruptions of anger. My daughter has *hwabyeong* in spades. She's my kid, after all. I know she wants to go after Shave Time for all of this, and I don't think I can talk her out of it. The way I always figured, you pour all you know into a child from zero to her early teens. After that, she's gonna do whatever the hell she wants anyway. I'm surprised she hasn't left me yet. I would've left me.

After Ascalon tears through thousands of pounds of blocky metal like a demented pistol shrimp, she climbs out of the foulness through the hole she just made, and I follow. When we get out of the Woodmen, of course there are a dozen or so Army Strong bathed in morning light, armed with shotguns. They all got these Army parkas on—tattered, hooded relics way before my time. Shave Time's conspicuously absent, but Blade Close is here, and he's got my super-rail aimed at the back of some skinny, blindfolded kid's head.

Ascalon glares at Blade Close and points to the roof of the Woodmen. "They are people," she says.

Blade Close glances at me. "Hand built by robots!"

"Give him to me, help the others up there, and I'll let you all live," Ascalon says. I'm surprised by her sudden assertiveness. I look left and right. Only the usual domesticated gopher tortoises lumber through the streets. I've always wondered why animals stick around places where people use them as food. They never seem to try to launch some sort of great escape. Considering Akira's Gardeners and Shave Time's Leachateans, maybe we're the same way, too.

Blade Close eyes the shredded metal we crawled out of, then turns back to Ascalon. "Impossible is nothing."

I'm waiting for Ascalon to cut him in half, but instead she talks to me via Thought Talk.

Shave Time, she says. *I told you a million times.*

Two Gardeners from each side begin to shuffle to flank us. *What?*

He's headed home.

The Gardeners now surround us in semi-circle formation. My daughter doesn't bat an eye. *What home?* I ask her.

Our home. I'm picking it up on security. Why did you show him the super-rail?

The two of us aren't enough against Akira and her Gardeners. To fight her, it was always going to come down to army versus army. We need him on our side.

You want to start a war? Are you crazy?

Akira doesn't get to leave here. I look at the boy knelt in front of Blade Close. *Who's the kid with the blindfold?* I ask. *He's a little young to be a Gardener.*

She doesn't respond. She's calculating. Thirteen of Army Strong, including Blade Close. Neither of us can take multiple shotgun blasts. She also knows that the super-rail is trigger locked. Only she and I can fire it. Standoffs bore me. I've always felt like that. Like the world moves too slowly for me. Maybe that's why I sleep too damn much. All I know is that my back's itchy, so I walk to the lobby doors of the Woodmen and rub my back against the jagged glass of the broken frame. Somehow, this livens up the stench of all the decomposed bodies I was buried under. All the Army Strong soldiers, except for Blade Close, got their shotguns pointed at me. They don't even notice the SEAL, remote-piloted by Ascalon, approaching. It stops and silently hovers over their heads. The guns under the wing tilt down. I don't see reds anymore, but I'm assuming these troops, seven men and seven women, are bathed in them.

If you're gonna paint 'em up, paint 'em up, I tell Ascalon in Thought Talk. *Sometimes you gotta rush to put as much paint as you can on the canvas.*

A member of Army Strong straps his shotgun over his shoulder and pulls out a machete. He walks to the kid in the blindfold, grabs him by the wrist, and yanks his arm so that it's fully extended. He raises the sword.

"Is it in you?" he asks.

"Have it your way," Ascalon says.

He is split in half. By the time the remaining twelve look up, four more are gone—two from the SEAL, two from Ascalon's rail gun. When it finally occurs to seven of them to point their guns at Ascalon, she's already closed distance. *Good girl.* I've always told her knives are better than guns in close quarters. Three throats slit by her heat blade before a gun is even fired. When an Army Strong goon finally fires, my kid is so goddamn fast, she steps out of the way, and the goon hits one of her own men. She goes down next. Three left, not including Blade Close. I charge one. By the time I have his face pressed against a petrified shipping label that reads PRIME, the two others are already down. I roll off the one on me, and the SEAL takes care of him. Now it's only bug-eyed Blade Close, pressing the trigger of the super-rail again and again. The strange boy at the business end of the rail is on his knees, hands in front of his bandaged face. He seems to be muttering a prayer. I'm trying to hide the pride I'm feeling toward my daughter. The kid is a bona fide killer.

I step to Blade Close and yank the super-rail from him, then drop it. He can't keep his eyes off Ascalon, so I grab him by the chin and make him look at me.

"Your father is headed to our place to raid the ordinance

we got buried," I say. "It's all booby-trapped and trigger-locked. Can you get word to him and stop him?"

"Gift of golden skin." He gasps, eyeballs rolled my daughter's way. She's helping the kid up and gently rubbing his back.

I grab Blade Close's head with both hands and look down at his bubbled-up face. "Listen, you need to tell him to stop and come back."

"Transcend time," he says.

I don't know why I'm asking. The Leachateans don't use radio. Shave Time will probably burn our home down in frustration or by tripwire. Luckily, the safe in which I keep Sabrina's iE is pretty much explosion proof. I'll need to go back and get it.

The strange boy is now staring at the top floors of the Woodmen. Down the street, a crowd is forming. Leachateans creep on us, picking up anything they can use as a weapon along the way.

"We need to get out of here," I say.

"Did you know?" Ascalon asks.

I wanna lie to her, but I don't. I push Blade Close to his knees, pick up the super-rail, and point it at the back of his head. The crowd stops. "Yeah," I say. "He's been sending out kidnap crews to snatch Gardeners here and there. The ones who scout in small groups beyond their cities. Surveyors, mostly. Also, the ones who try to leave crates of clean water and medical supplies near nomad caravans. He's been doing it for years."

"That's why you're so sure they can't be cut from OneVoice."

"Yes," I say. "Shave Time tried. It doesn't work. They either kill themselves or still pray to her no matter what you do."

"Just because they pray to her doesn't mean they're still connected!"

The crowd begins inching forward, closing in on the same block as us. All of them, without exception, have webs of white, cracked skin at their ankles.

"Did you . . . watch?" Ascalon asks.

This time I lie. "Of course not." I was the one who'd brought a med bot with me years ago to take the eyes of Shave Time's very first prisoner. Army Strong had shot down a shuttle that flew over From A to Z. When we searched the wreckage, a small, middle-aged man had been the only survivor. We dragged him up to the Woodmen to detain him. I summoned the med bot from my shuttle and went for the eyes first. I wanted to know if they could survive without their iEs. I wanted to know if my daughter could possibly survive without hers. The man lived, but he went mad, begging Okaasan to help him. He jumped into the elevator shaft the first chance he got.

Right now, I'm looking at the boy whom Blade Close held at gunpoint. The boy's face shifts from the building and turns to me. It looks like he knows I'm lying.

"We can't leave them here." Ascalon points to the boy. "Look, they can be freed."

I get it. The blindfold. The boy is probably missing his eyes. Is he really disconnected from Akira? Maybe, but there are more pressing matters right now. "Shave Time knew you'd come after me," I say. "We need to get back home before Shave Time starts tripping the mines and burns it all down."

"It's not home anymore. Home doesn't matter. We need to figure out how Jon was disconnected."

I eye the boy. "He still worships her, I bet," I say.

"You used to worship her, and you don't anymore. He's just confused. Of course it takes time to adjust to a new reality."

"Listen, I never—"

"I'm telling you, if it's possible, we need to try."

"We need to get back. Your mother . . ."

"My mother is dead."

"But . . ."

Ascalon looks at me, suddenly aghast. "It's about her, isn't it? All of this uptick in aggression. You're not afraid Akira is just going to leave. You're afraid that she's going to leave without bringing back Mom."

I bite my lip. *She's right.* I'm stunned by the rush of understanding.

"It's time I go to her," Ascalon says.

"Who?" I ask, still confused by the thought.

"She's the only one smart enough to figure out how Jon cut himself from the system. She's the only one who can possibly figure out a way to do it on a mass scale."

I spit. Not Sabrina. *Ascalon Lee.* A heavy tube of elbow piping whizzes by my head. The crowd is about half a block away now. That piping was the first shot fired. More will be hurled at us at any moment. They'll rain garbage on us.

"Raid!" some of the gathering crowd yells. "Kills bugs dead!"

"Bring down the SEAL," I say to Ascalon. "We can talk on the way."

The SEAL plummets to a hard landing between us and the infirmed mob. I admit, I like The Leachate, but the one thing I could never get over is how sick everyone looks. They got the raspy, hacking sound of people who live in a perpetual dust storm. Their hair hangs from their scalps like weathered tassels. They're cranky from feeling like shit every day. Disenfranchise people of freedom and wealth, that's one thing. That was done to them generations ago. Disenfranchise them of their health, too? You get a bunch so mean that they will refuse help. They'll think help is a trick. Like I said, I like this place.

"Roaches check in, but they don't check out!" someone in the approaching crowd screams. Another piece of piping is hurled at me. Ascalon catches it and tosses it to the side.

"I can't locate your shuttle," she says.

"It didn't survive the blast at First National."

She sighs. "How will we get them out?"

I don't wanna tell her we can't, so I'm relieved when the sobbing kid says it. I'm surprised again when Blade Close pops to his feet and starts running. Blade Close is quick. I'm about to clip him, but Ascalon sighs, then is hot on his trail. She's so fast, she's almost instantly gaining ground on him. It's like watching a shark charge a man who can't swim. I point the super-rail down. That's when Ascalon stops dead in her tracks. She spins around and looks me right in the eye. And oh, man, I've seen that look before. I've worn that look before. And it's okay.

Here's the thing. For years, maybe just about my whole life, it's felt like I've been scarfing down poison, but my body never digests it. Instead, it just fumes out of my pores. Instead, it's those around me who breathe it in and end up choking and dying from it. I'm tired of outliving everyone. Poisoning them. If I keep going, I'm going to poison my daughter, too. Because she's right, this recent aggression against Akira is about Sabrina more than anything else. I didn't even see it until Ascalon pointed it out. Yeah, I've become that self-absorbed, and my self-awareness has somehow slipped away. The longer I'm around, the more she'll become like me. I look down at her favorite red leather boots and imagine her toes clenched. I remember those toes when they were newborn toes. Infant toes. How I used to grab her feet when she was a toddler and ask her if I could just eat one. How she used to squeal in both terror and delight, pull her feet away, and take off running on them. She's my baby, and it's time for her to run away from me again.

I turn my gaze back to her face and say, "Love you, matey."

I must be smothered in choking greens and reds now, the perfect convergence of murder and death. It's okay. My last look ain't a bad one. My kid. She's running to me, not running away. A post-Satori Day war child built to survive. In this moment, I'm glad I let Ascalon Lee tune her up over the years. Her eye lights like the sun. She can't fire off a clean shot at the kid. I'm in the way.

It's okay, matey. It's okay. Even when things were at their worst, you made it pretty cool. Maybe you were right. Maybe I had you out here with me spinning my wheels in radioactive Leachatean mud for way too long. Perhaps I shouldn't have taken you down this road to nowhere. I hope you can forgive me . . . for everything.

My kid's sprinting, so fast that she's a blur. It's a road to nowhere she's running on because she's too late.

I don't gotta turn around to know that it's the kid Ascalon found that just plunged a heat blade into my back. I feel it. Akira warned me. This is my last life spent. I'm glad it's finally me and not someone else being cashed in.

PART TWO

ORPHANED

Time doesn't slow. Not now, anyway. Not when I'm standing here in the streets of From A to Z, frozen, not knowing what to do. I'm seeing everything now. My father, prone on the street with a heat blade in his back, the dull red smoking from him like a deer cut open in winter. Then there's Jon6J, long, pale, thin fingers seething green, standing above him. The Leachatean mob has stopped in its tracks. Most know who my father is. A legend in the bear pits. Made in China. The outsider they always respected but never did trust.

I feel the SEAL's warmth behind me. Mostly I feel suddenly zonbi, a void inside me that spreads so that nothing exists within, but everything exists with absolute clarity outside of me. The daybreak reflecting off the jagged glass of the Wood-men's broken windows. The buzzing emanating from the lattice of power lines down the street. The dry, chilly morning air that I sense on my ears and fingers. The crisscross of worn words at my feet, ancient billboards mashed together. The more the top slogans chafe, the deeper we get into history. "Smile today" intersected with "Tastes like a million." Time feels slow. I process the memories of the last few seconds. The final one is me, the involuntary whimper that escapes through my lips. I've never made that sound before.

I slump to my knees. The thing I notice most is the complete absence of magenta. Sometimes it takes the GPS a few moments to reboot, but the scent has always lingered. Every other time he's perished, the magenta has faded, sure, but it's always brightened again, then led me to places hundreds of miles away. Now, I *feel* it. His utter lack of presence. I slap the side of my head. Nothing. I slap it again. Nothing again. My eyes search the sky, grasping for magentas. They just aren't there. Is my father gone for good?

Jon6J stares at me. Has time slowed for him, too, during these last moments of his life? I stand. I walk to my father and pick up the super-rail, then point it at Jon. For the first time that I can remember, my hands tremble.

"Why?" I hiss.

"We feel every death," Jon snarls. "He hunts us. He kills us. Epcot. I *felt* it all. My people bound for space. I felt all the ones he murdered before that." He points to the top of the Woodmen. "The ones up there. *I felt them.*"

"He did not do that to them!"

"He doesn't tell you everything!"

I glance at my father, waiting for the wafts of magenta to rise from him, to curl and drift to me. But they don't. My eyes tear. I wipe my face and refocus on Jon. "Okaasan protects him!"

Jon points at his empty socket. "I have damned myself. I damned myself to punish your father. Okaasan does not speak to me anymore!" He removes his blindfold and begins to sob. The flaps of his eyelids frame two pink and fleshy pits in his face. Tears dribble from the craters.

"And me? I was at Epcot, too."

"I came to free you from him. You can do the work that he was supposed to do."

I take a glimpse at my father's body, waiting for the magentas. Still waiting. They aren't here. The mob approaches. It's not long before they're surrounding us, but I don't care. Just Jon and I exist now. Then a cloaked old woman with two children carrying a brick of garbage each steps to my father's body and kneels. She puts a fingerless hand on his back. I point the rail at her. I find myself wondering if she lost her fingers or was born without them. What happens to veins when they are severed? How can they possibly heal?

She looks up at me with her cataract-hazed eyes. "When there is no tomorrow," she whispers.

The crowd nods in agreement. "When there is no tomorrow," they say.

No, they're wrong. They have to be. I squint, eyes searching for the familiar color that binds us. Nothing comes. The rail levels to my side. I look at Jon. He flinches as my iE furiously blazes. I want to kill him. I want to kill all of them.

"Get in the SEAL," I tell him.

He nods and walks past me. The mob parts for him. Perception, memory, and time normalize. I kneel beside the woman and try to put my shaking hand on my father but find myself unable to do so. I want to pull the blade from his back, but I flinch, and I'm unable to do that as well. I'm a little girl again, shivering over the body of a forty-point buck. *We're all meat, and you need to learn to see it that way.* I close my eyes. I feel a hand on my shoulder, and my eyes open. It's the woman, her face a topography of pits and canyons. In this moment, she is beautiful and somehow familiar. I've seen her before. I nod, and she nods back. Hand trembling, I pull the blade from my father's back and glare at it. No magenta. Just wisps of green and red coil around the blade. I close my eyes and reopen them. Nothing. I hand the blade to the woman.

"Like a good neighbor," she says with a smile. Some of her front teeth grow sideways in her mouth.

I can fix this. I pick up my father's body, throw it over a shoulder, and head to the SEAL. Tears stream across my cheeks, and a sudden, deep hatred for this place rises in me. I cannot stay here, nor in Kansas any longer. I don't know if I'll ever come back here, but something tells me no. Let Shave Time take what he wants from home. I pack my father and the rail in the storage hatch. I climb into the cockpit and eye Jon. He has things to answer for, but now is not the time. I find myself unready to ask the questions.

After I bind Jon's hands with rope, we lift off. Below, a city rests on box-shaped landfill, risen from the dirt like an urban blister. My father always marveled at how Shave Time jacked up this city as if it were an engineering accomplishment equal to that of the Pyramids or A496. Maybe blood is the secret ingredient, he'd said. Always blood. The more people are willing to spend, the greater the wonder. All statues of Akira Kimura had been torn down and giant billboards replaced them. BE ALL THAT YOU CAN BE—ARMY STRONG. KEEP THE LOAD ON THE ROAD. ALL FOR FREEDOM. FREEDOM FOR ALL. When my father voiced his belief that Shave Time had raised the city, that's when I knew he was slipping. Shave Time didn't raise the city, though he always claimed he did. To me, it was obvious the entire time. Shave Time simply dug a moat that gradually flattens around it.

If I ever do come back, it will be for Shave Time. I wish I could save the ones in the Woodmen, but I cannot.

Ahead, a slalom of funnel clouds. I can't believe it. No matter how hard my eyes search for them, the magentas are completely gone. Only one person can help me. May help me. Not my dead mother. Not my father. Not Shave Time Money. Certainly not Akira Kimura. And not this boy here. It's time to go home, our real home. I will try to bury my grief and rage for now. I will try to fix this. I will take my father and Jon6J to Ascalon Lee. It is time to return to Water City.

2

Three hundred years ago, Mile High started as a mining colony, and today, Okaasan has turned it into a mining town again. I don't know what she's trying to excavate, but from up here in the sky the boreholes have turned the landscape around the city into a flattened, bleached sponge. The holes are much bigger and deeper than they were the last time I was here. It's enough to make any trypophobe cringe. Even from the sound-dampening altitude, Jon and I can hear the tunnel-boring machines drilling deeper into those holes. Each is surrounded by crews of Gardener zonbis waiting for the mole machines to rise so that they can change out their bits. My father was very suspicious of all this when he'd come here to steal a new shuttle. I can't come up with a reason why Okaasan would do it besides mining. My brain is still too scrambled with raw emotion.

Like my father used to, we're going to Mile High shuttle port to steal an intercontinental shuttle. My SEAL cannot cross over the Pacific without refueling, and I wonder how much of the Pacific Bridge to Water City remains intact. The city itself, with its dimly lit skyscrapers that stretch to Mount Blue Sky, remains intact, even well-maintained. As with most old, land-based cities, it looks bleak during bright summer middays. It emits a haze of heat, and the stains and cracks of the old spires are not hidden by snow or night lights. The vac tube stations that used to flush people to Blue Sky, Pike's Peak, and Winter Park are empty. Most of the Gardeners are at their mines, and besides a few janitorial crews sweeping the streets, there is very little movement.

Before Satori Day, Mile High was one of the last great continental cities. It boasted a diverse population of both Americans and Leachateans. It was home to many of The Money's corporate headquarters, including Old Man Caldwell's before he moved to the islands to bear witness to the lighting of Ascalon's Scar. There was even a world-class hospital that Leachateans used to turn to when they got sick. It makes sense that Mile High is where Shave Time plucked some of his Gardener prisoners. It's relatively close, and some of the boreholes are far enough away from the city to make picking off miners feel safe.

Shave Time has not yet dared to attempt to take one of Okaasan's cities or Dragonspine. After he digs up our home, if he can avoid the booby traps and figure out how to bypass trigger locks, he may change his mind. From what I saw at the Woodmen, it seems like he's gotten a real taste for killing Gardeners now. Maybe he'll hit Mile High first. Then maybe her young coastal redwood forest. Then finally, Akira's 1,200-mile-long launch loop. We all know that A496 is especially sacred to the Gardeners. We've seen them pray to it. It will probably be the last thing Shave Time will attempt to hit.

Jon points down at one of the holes with his bound hands. His face brightens as if he just remembered something important.

"That's borehole 6J," he says. "That's why my name is Jon6J."

I do my best to swallow my contempt for him. I doubt that's true. The fact that there is a "J" in his name is not lost on me. Perhaps it's some kind of new alpha designation. The fact that there is a "6" just like there's a "6" in OneVoice's greatest creation is not lost on me, either. "How far down does the hole go?" I ask.

"All the way to the Earth's mantle," he says proudly.

I'd like to drop him down one of these holes. Watch him sizzle to ash in a swirl of molten lava below the Earth's crust. But I won't. After I give my father to Ascalon Lee, I'll turn Jon over to her as well.

"Why is she digging?"

Jon shrugs. "I do not know."

"Why would she dig here? The mantle is much closer at the bottom of the ocean."

"I just dug and collected tellurium."

I have been documenting Jon's behavior ever since I met him, and when I play them back, he gave nothing away. He maintained Gardener posture—a child-like posture of passive obedience. His blindness also made him seem weak and non-threatening. His face never betrayed his intent to kill my father. He did not make any telling hand gestures. The tenor and volume of his voice never shifted. All of this tells me that he was trained to lie. By whom? Akira? No. His hatred for my father was clearly authentic. But why my father? Why not Shave Time? When I asked Jon this on our way to Mile

High, he said, "Because Okaasan meant for him to protect us. He betrayed Okaasan. He betrayed us all."

"When did you come to this realization?" I asked.

He said he could not remember. The words of a true liar. I was so stupid. He claimed this again and again. We all remember. At least, we all believe we do.

The shuttle port, a series of round platforms that wind around various elevations of Mount Blue Sky, looks like a mega tea-serving stand from up here. I'm not sure what condition the shuttles are in, or if Okaasan had all of them decommissioned, but it's worth checking.

When we arrive at the mountain, I circle to spot the round platform with the most shuttles. None are the small, private, squid-shaped type. They're all zeppelin jumbos. Below, a herd of white mountain goats scatters. Even though it's summer, high-altitude snow piles on the launch pads, and zonbi maintenance crews work on shuttles and shovel slush off the steep drops. Near the 14,000-foot peak, a fleet of jumbos sits in front of the cavern entrance to the mountain terminal carved in rock. These thousand-passenger megas have been gutted and converted to pure cargo carriers. Gardener maintenance crews run diagnostics on them. Why? It seems like a waste to keep commercial flight fit when commercialism no longer exists.

"Why do the Gardeners keep the shuttles operational?" I ask Jon6J.

"You keep asking me questions as if we are given reasons." He says it without irritation. He sits there, hands tied, and doesn't seem bothered by that either.

I turn to him. "You better start coming up with answers. You aren't connected to her anymore. She can't save you."

He turns away. He's afraid. Or acting as if he is.

"Why do you think they keep them operational?" I ask.

Jon6J shrugs. He isn't even curious. He won't even specu-late. Or he's lying again. I look for magentas. Still nothing. If anyone can fix my father, Ascalon Lee can. I chide myself. I can't make all this just about one person. It's what my father did when he made it about Mom.

We land at Concourse D at the Mile High shuttle port and climb out of the SEAL. I'll choose an operational shuttle first, then load my father on it. It's strange not feeling his presence. It's lonely. I'm sorry for feeling like he was gross. Irritating. I'm sorry for occasionally lying to him.

I eye Jon. If he wants to attempt to run, now would be the time to do it. But he isn't running. In fact, he seems to be waiting for me to move so that he can follow. His skin is so taut, I wonder if his thin, pallid face is capable of sweating. I pull the super-rail from cargo and try not to look at my father's body. Jon and I head to the nearest shuttle. A pair of pudgy, buck-toothed marmots sun themselves on the tarmac. Our presence doesn't seem to disturb them.

A Gardener crew of three is scanning a shuttle's landing gear when we arrive. Like the marmots, they completely ignore Jon and me. I scan the rest of the shuttle to see whether it's in working order. Unlike SEALs, shuttles aren't blended-wing designed. The big ones, like these strat zeppelins with their small wings and downturned tails, look like flying humpbacks in glossy Poseidon white. The batteries and hydro-burn, turbofan engines have the energy density to fly supersonic anywhere in the world. The top floor cabins used to house AMP chambers for first-class travelers.

I patch into the shuttle and run diagnostics. Everything's in working order. We wait for the ground crew to complete its inspection and move on. I look back at the SEAL and shudder. My father's body is stored in there. Maybe I should've met Shave Time in Kansas and dealt with him. Maybe I should deal with Jon now. I'm almost certain it's what my father would've done, but look at where that got him.

I recall how my mother dimmed simultaneously with the Gardeners and the world. One night, my father, drunk as usual, told me about her parents, the grandparents I never knew, who jumped off the balcony of a skyscraper the day Shessho-Seki was supposed to hit. "Cowards," he grumbled. He didn't say it, but I could tell he was talking about my mother, too. How her resignation after Satori Day and a stillbirth might as well have been suicide. Since she died, I always felt like he was trying to turn me against her, which struck me as strange, considering she was dead already. That, and how he clung to her iE, hoping one day to miraculously bring her back to life.

In their heated, hooded white foam fits, the ground crew finishes scanning the landing gear and heads in our direction, single file. It's as if all three are looking through me and focusing on the shuttle at the next gate. I wait for them to pass. The first brushes slightly against me. The second does as well. The third is about to pass me, but she surprises me by grabbing my wrist.

"Let him go," she says.

I yank my wrist from her grasp. "Let who go?" I ask. I'm thinking she means Jon.

"Let your father go."

I backhand her, and she goes sprawling across the tarmac. I immediately feel bad about it, how violence has become a reflex for me. Like most Gardeners, the woman is much older than me. I turn to face Jon. I snatch him by the coat and pull his face to mine.

"How does she always know everything?"

Jon shrugs awkwardly, his hands bound in front of him. "You are asking me how Okaasan knows everything?"

"She's not Okaasan! She was just a lady! She was Akira Kimura!"

"Have you met this Akira Kimura?"

"No," I say. "I was too young, but my parents did. My father knew her well."

"She is far more than what he knew."

"No, she's not."

He turns his face from mine. "Do you truly believe that?" he asks, gazing out at the horizon.

In my head, I concede. She is more. Frustration and rage swell in me. Or sadness. Like my guidelines, the three always feel mixed up, impossibly tangled together. I tell Jon to get in the shuttle. He obeys. I look back at the Gardener I hit. I want to walk to her, help her up, and apologize, but she's on her feet, running to catch up to the other two, who're waiting for her at the next shuttle. Are they capable of loneliness? Perhaps he was set free by Akira to kill my father. If so, why now? Was she really afraid of what he was capable of after Epcot? Was my father right all this time? Something big is coming that we don't see?

I go back to the SEAL to collect my father. When I hoist him on my shoulder, the ground crew ceases its examination of the next shuttle to watch me. My fingers dig into my father's back. He is still soft and warm. By the time we get to Water City, he will stiffen. *We're all meat*, I tell myself. The important part is what's in his head. *I can fix this.* I retract a ramp from the shuttle's hull and enter, then command the ramp to close as I glare at the Gardeners staring back at me. Wind whistles in. I plot a course and order the shuttle to lift off. I hear Jon settle in the cockpit, and I tell myself it's best not to have him near me during the trip. I cradle my father in my arms in this vast, cavernous cargo hold. It's the first time I can bear to lock my eyes on him since he went down. The powerful jaw. The uneven growth of hair on his face.

How different his death was than my mother's. It took weeks for her to pass, and she wanted to spend that time alone. When my father suggested we put her in AMP, she'd threatened to shoot herself then and there. She kept her gun under her pillow, just in case he tried to force her into a chamber. I hated her. I may still hate her now.

I close my eyes and concentrate. I must awaken the yellow guideline in me, the one that will lead me to Ascalon Lee. It doesn't take long. She casts it to me freely.

Come, she says.

My father was killed. Will you help him?

A pause. *I cannot help him.*

I open my eyes and place my trembling hand on the side of his face. *You need to help him.*

He is dead, child. Gone for good this time.

I remove my hand from my father's face and ball my fist. *I will go to Akira Kimura and ask her then.*

You know as well as I do, there is no her anymore.

I turn toward the cockpit. *I have a boy with me. He detached himself from her and OneVoice.*

Really? Interesting.

Yes. He's the one who killed my father.

A pause. *Bring him to me.*

My voice cracks. "Help my father then," I say both out loud and in Thought Talk.

I will attempt to preserve him, then we will go from there.

I cut the connection. I know it's all a long way of saying no. No, always the key invisible ingredient in any old person word salad. I will figure out a way to make her help him. I need to. I grip my father by the shoulders and shake him as hard as I can. "Wake up!" I scream.

His body slumps to the floor. *No,* it's saying. *No.* Suddenly, I'm crying and screaming at the same time. My father has told me no, and here I am, nineteen years old, flying through the surly winds of the Continental Divide, a baby all over again.

3

It's a couple of hours later when Jon comes bounding from the cockpit. Maybe even he can see how incredible it is. There's no other way to say it. The islands of Water City are floating above the ocean.

"I know where we are," he says. "I feel it. Or remember it. Please confirm and describe its majesty to me."

Jon and I walk to the cockpit. The 3D scans are being displayed by the control panel. The islands, all eight of them, hairy with life, like giant artichoke hearts, are hovering above the Pacific.

"How?" I ask. I zoom in.

"Is it as grand as I imagine?" Jon asks. "Do you not see? This can only be the work of a god!"

How is this possible? Perhaps superconductor flux pinning, the same kind of tech used to operate lifts in Water City, but on a far, far grander scale. Fresh water cascades from the lush mountain tops and pours into the ocean from dripping black cliffs. Beneath each island, brackish pools swirl. Ranges and ranges of creased rock, tropical forests, valleys, craters, swaths of hilly grasslands—it's too much mass to keep from crumbling, much less keep afloat. Like Dragonspine, it's impossible. I suppose impossible is Akira and her daughter's specialty. Was it Akira or Ascalon Lee who did this? Has Ascalon Lee reconciled with her mother? Even with all of the AI excavators, loaders, and cranes left in the depths of Water City, it's inconceivable that the task could've been completed in less than a decade. My jaw and toes clench. I suppose I'll find out.

I turn off the holos and lower the landing gear. We dip through the clouds. I retract the outer cockpit shell and look through the transparent aluminum. The whitewash looks like stretched-out tripe from up here. We descend to the biggest floating island. At the top, it's still there. Savior's Eye. Despite the fact that he can't see, Jon's practically pressing his face against the window.

"Is that?" he asks.

I nod. "Savior's Eye."

Akira's telescope. Still there. Landing platforms cleared. The giant water statue of her, thankfully, turned off. One of my earliest memories is being present at the statue's opening ceremony. The crowd. The president turning on the spigot. The dramatic hush of anticipation. Then the burst of water forming into a mega Akira pointing at the sky. I remember being scared, not of the statue, but of all the fanatically cheering people and their twisted faces. I know now that it was faith that twisted them. Jon, who has the same look, begins to mutter something that sounds like a prayer. I overcome the desire to gag him.

We land. I shut down the shuttle and head to the cargo hold for my father. I strap a rail to my shoulder, shift into sports mode, and pick the body up. We exit down the ramp. Even from way up here, the air smells different. The ocean. I'm surprised that I find myself wanting to see it again. There will be time for that. I head to the door that I know requires security eye scan, and I scan it all right, blasting it down with my rail. Jon looks at me disgustedly, as if I defiled something. Before I step in, something flows quickly past me. I replay it, then replay it again. I can't believe it. A creature of some sort. A scaled bird with a turtle shell and plumes of fishtail.

"What?" Jon asks.

I try my best to cork my curiosity. The sooner I get my father inside, the better. I can look around later. I shake the image of the strange bird and step inside. The lights are still on. I walk through the disabled body scanner, ignore the eyepiece, and pass the ancient filing cabinets. I do notice the lack of dust. Air filtration still operational after all these years. I'm glad this place still has power. The piano, the chalkboards, all unimportant. My father once told me what's in here. I head to Akira's private quarters. Nobody would dare disable this AMP chamber. I march to the room and kick the door open. I drop the rail, and it clanks on the white polymer floor. Once the AMP opens, I place my father in the cushioned torpedo, close the hatch, and crank up the nitro. The chamber hums.

I shift out of sports mode and collapse on Akira's futon. The quilt is embroidered with four hollow squares that form a diamond, the Kimura family crest. I close my eyes and take a breath. I should have left Jon6J in that cave. I should've left him at home. I shouldn't have brought him to From A to Z. With every replayed moment, all I feel is regret. I never should have blocked my father in the first place. This is all my fault. Though if Ascalon Lee can sever islands from their plates and make them float, surely she can bring my father back again. She must.

Once I collect myself, I pick up the rail and look around the room. Sparse, as suspected. My father said that Akira had an aversion to personal possessions. Only one thing hangs from the white walls: a picture of a Japanese salaryman sitting cross-legged at a *chabudai*, thoughtfully drawing in a sketchbook. Maybe her father or something. I ignore the picture and head back to the heart of Akira's cathedral. The thrumming notes of red fade the farther I get from the chamber, which is a relief. I exit the smooth, white hall and find Jon sitting at the piano, mesmerized by its keys. I take out my heat blade and head to him. He looks up and flinches. Before he can stand, I cut his bindings.

"Play it," I say.

He shakes his head. "I don't know how."

"She knew how, so you must know how."

He gingerly taps at a key. "I can't."

"Look around. The desk. The chalkboard. The telescope. This piano. There's even a toilet back in her old quarters. I can show it to you if you want. I told you. She was just a person."

He looks at me blankly. My father used to tell me that I argue a lot because I'm a teenager. He told me that trying to argue someone out of belief is a waste of time. But I need this boy to understand. What's the point of the Gardeners being disconnected from OneVoice if they can't stop believing in Okaasan? I glance at the desk, wishing the picture that my father told me about, the picture of Akira as a child, was still there so that I could show it to Jon.

The lights flicker then go out. Something skitters on the ceiling. I raise my rail and shine my light. Nothing.

"Get behind me," I tell Jon, lighting up everything in front of us—the desk, the filing cabinets, the chalkboards. I hear a random smattering of piano notes and turn around. Jon takes a step back and stumbles, his thin, pale fingers mashing the piano keys behind him. I turn to face the room again. Still, nothing.

"Should we leave?" Jon asks.

It's funny how fear makes him suddenly want to leave perhaps one of the holiest places to him. His fear in this place, his temple, is yet another reminder of his liberation from OneVoice. "No," I say. "Not yet."

I step forward and hear Jon's fingers come off the piano in something almost like a song. I feel his breath on me. He hasn't brushed his teeth in a while. Neither have I. He's sticking close. I check behind the chalkboards. That's when I see them: faint tendrils of yellow. She's here.

"Come out!" I yell.

No response. What is it about these old people who always want to play games? Her. My father. For the last ten years, since Ascalon Lee took me and I then awoke, I have suffered from bouts of paranoia. I wondered how much of me is me. I've wondered if she still controls me. Or worse, I'm trapped in a sick simulation. The Leachate. The Gardeners. My mother's sudden turn. My father's soon after. A 1,200-mile runway to the stars. And now this. Jon. These floating islands. That flying creature outside. What if I never woke up all those years ago? What if, in reality, I'm still in an AMP chamber at HW Hospital, suspended in childhood imagination and slumber? This world is too preposterous to be real.

I feel a rush of wind behind me and spin around. Just like that, Jon6J is gone.

4

Whatever took Jon is not trackable. However, it has left a trail of yellow for me to follow. After checking on my father one last time, I secure the shuttle and head off on foot. The terrain is as one would expect from the top of an old volcano: rocky, with an almost lunar-like quality. It's a hazy, windy day, and I call up all the archived data I have on this place, searching for simple geological and historical facts. There's a tiny lake nearby. A once-sacred lake that ended up being defiled, like all sacred things eventually are, by the construction of Savior's Eye. More accurately, by the tourist traffic to see the telescope and the water statue when they became the most popular attractions in the world. I don't have any data on whether the lake survived, which means it probably hasn't, but the yellow trail seems to be leading me in that direction. I follow it and head southeast.

I see it now, about a half mile ahead, a murky green puddle in the middle of a tiny playa packed with volcanic ash. Beneath it, the permafrost that sustains it. I walk to the water's edge and get on one knee. It is only a few feet deep, but this is where the xanthic trail ends. I stick a hand in the cool water, lift it, and watch the drops fall back. The middle of the pool begins to gurgle. I stand and raise the rail.

Something sleek and black emerges. A lizard of some sort, as big as the gators at Epcot but slender, with glowing yellow eyes staring right at me. It slowly approaches me. Keeping it in my sights, I scramble back and shift into sports mode. With each step, its luminous ink spikes like ferrofluid, and the lizard slowly shapeshifts into another form. Its torso shrinks and its legs lengthen. Its snout begins to retract. Glowing, golden hair begins to sprout from its head. What was once four-legged seamlessly becomes two-legged. The sleek black spikes disappear. The lizard now advances toward me in the form of a black, glossy-skinned woman. She smiles and reveals sharp, serpent teeth, gold like her hair. Dumfounded, I lower my rail. I know in an instant this is Ascalon Lee.

"What have you turned yourself into?" I ask.

"My father's people believed in shapeshifting lizards," she says. "I'm making belief into reality." She points to the sky.

I see the strange flying thing that I saw earlier, only now it's part of a flock.

"Hou-ou," I say.

"Yes," the figure before me says. "Turtle-shelled phoenix. I'm so happy you finally came. There's a lot more that I want to show you."

"What did you do with the boy?" I ask.

"We will discuss that later."

"And my father?" I ask.

"We'll discuss that, too."

I look to the horizon. The hazy blues of the ocean and sky blend into a color so similar that I feel like I'm trapped in the middle of a cerulean globe as opposed to standing on one. I wobble. Ascalon Lee grabs my arm to steady me.

"I'm tired," I whisper.

"I know, my butterfly. I know that feeling. The Greeks called it *acedia*. You aren't alone anymore."

Ascalon Lee projects a holo from her eye. The camera drone remotely connected to her iE zooms between mid-ocean ridges. The camera soars over Pompeii worms, passes twirls of sulfi that spiral from underwater chimneys. Something glimmers in the distance. Water City. The vac tubes fire capsules filled with passengers from oceanscraper to oceanscraper. The lighted elevators rise and fall in varying bright neon, as if being directed by some unseen conductor. The statues and holos of Akira and Ascalon's Scar are noticeably absent. The ocean teams with sea life drawn to these luminescent buoys. A pod of humpbacks burst through a glimmering ad for a holo art exhibition. And people—actual people, neither Gardener nor Leachatean—watch the whale pod dive down from behind the safety of gorilla glass. Unlike Gardeners, who are mostly middle-aged, or Leachateans, who are mostly young, there are people of all ages, even babies and elderly. A mother, holding her child's hand, neither wearing dive suits, follows the humpbacks into depths that are impossible for the bare human body to survive.

"I knew there must be a place where the .03 percent made a home together," I say. "*I knew it.* Why didn't you tell me?"

"Keep watching," Ascalon Lee says.

The camera rises toward the ocean's surface, zipping by billowing jellyfish and silent bells diving into the deep. In shallower water, columns of kelp tethered to stakes by their holdfasts bend to the current. Higher still, an urchin barren.

Then the camera follows a magnetic tower and bursts to the surface. Beneath the floating island, the jagged rock spikes smolder. The bottoms probably glazed with superconductor. They are also latticed with atlas beams, similar to the ones that serve as the bones of the deepest seascrapers. The tubes hum while particles stream through them, the islands nestled in mesh like boulders in hammocks. Beneath the ocean's surface, a giant, round shadow buzzes. The camera glides to landfall. On the island, creatures of myth. A family of three-legged crows perch on a coffee tree. In the hills, packs of bearded, scaled stags graze. A boar the size of an elephant bursts from the trees and chases the *kirin* packs. It's laughing.

"Why didn't you tell me?" I ask again. "Who made all this?"

"Me mostly," Ascalon Lee says. She pauses. "With the help of the .03 percent."

I gasp. "They're all here?"

"Not all of them, but many of them—1,238,003 to be exact. The ones who wanted to come. Scientists. Artists. Teachers. Engineers. Some who did not have iEs on Satori Day. My mother did not have the heart to kill all sources of invention, creativity, and kindness. I now know why she wanted me to live. She wanted me to sustain this."

I always suspected that somewhere in the world, .03 percenters gathered and formed their own communities. But I never dreamed it would be anything on this scale. And even more shocking is Ascalon Lee is telling me Okaasan wants it to exist. "You trust her?"

Ascalon Lee scoffs. "Absolutely not. Remember our meeting at Epcot? I keep an eye on her. More than one, as you know."

The holo flickers off. I'm suddenly furious. "All these years, you left me and my father out of it?"

"I trust your father as much as I trust my mother," she says.

"So, you waited until . . . this."

Ascalon Lee nods. "Another system update is coming. A big one. You must come with me."

I think about my father, his concern over the acceleration of the Gardener holes around their strongholds, the increased rate of Gardeners being shot into space. "My father feared something big was coming. It's why he . . . took too much risk."

Ascalon Lee nods. "All the data that I have access to, all events, I run through my prophecy machine."

"Prophecy machine?"

She smirks and points to her head. This is definitely Ascalon Lee. Only she, and possibly her mother, would refer to her brain as a prophecy machine. "The most recent data suggests something seismic is about to occur."

"The boy," I say. "Jon. My father. Shave Time Money."

"Yes. Her . . . zonbis. Your father didn't know it, but he was doing something significant. That abomination in the middle of the continent and your father, they . . ."

The fiery carnage at Epcot. The torture that transpired at the Woodmen. "They finally made the Gardeners angry."

"The anger was so intense that I believe some of them broke connection. Come now, there is much to see and explain."

She tugs at my arm, but I don't budge. I look at Savior's Eye. I don't think anyone saw the resemblance back then, but it looks very much like Epcot from here. A theme park taken and rendered believable. Scrubbed of its dazzle and stardust, it sits atop the largest mountain on Earth, gazing down somberly at the world, unable to shed tears.

"His remains will be safe there," Ascalon Lee says. "Come."

I plop down at the water's edge, partially out of protest, partially out of pure emotional and physical exhaustion. "I can't," I say. "I won't leave him."

Ascalon Lee offers me a hand. "Come and let me show you what you need to see. After that, if you wish to return here, I will bring you back myself."

I look up at her. "You should've told me."

"Perhaps," she says. "But I'm telling you now. Come."

I take her hand, too tired to fight her, and she pulls me up. I set down the rail and remove my boots. I take off my hat and study it. The black brim is worn and losing its shape. I sigh and fling it. It rolls on the rocks, then a sudden gust lifts it, and it tumbles away. Ascalon Lee begins to walk through the shallow pool, leaving concentric ripples behind her. I follow her. The water gets deeper and deeper until it's waist high. We stop at the center, and I stare at the gleaming green surface unsettled by howling wind. There's a dark, seemingly endless hole there.

"How far to the other end?" I ask. "What if I can't hold my breath long enough?"

Ascalon Lee frowns. "You haven't tested it yet? My butterfly, you have spent far too long away from the ocean."

"What do you mean?"

"You don't need to hold your breath ever again."

I remove my overcoat and the rest of my weapons and drop them in the water. I exhale. Ascalon Lee jumps into the hole and pulls me with her.

5

When I was ten, soon after my mother died, I began to have this reoccurring dream that I'm back in the pre-Satori Day regular world, and I'm wearing glasses in a time when glasses aren't even made anymore. I feel the rims on my cheekbones, and despite wearing them, I can't see what's really in front of me. The lenses are filled with ocean murk crisscrossed with sunlight. I'm not in the ocean. I'm lying on my side on a sofa. The murk clears, and my mother comes and kneels in front of me. She places lettered evidentiary exhibits on the coffee table, then stands so that I can see what she's left there. Exhibit A is a holo of flames burning a purple, sunflower-embossed WELCOME TO KANSAS sign.

"I blame the move for your sister's death," the flames say.

I look at Exhibit B: a holo of me, my back to the ocean, my feet skittering to avoid a swell of sudsy shore break that washes the sand.

"I blame you for the move," the ocean tells me.

Exhibit C stutters on repeat. It's a holo of my father shooting me over and over again.

My mother's voice chimes in. "I blame him for making it feel like we needed to move in the first place." She slams her palm on exhibit D before I can see what it is. She whispers in my ear, "But most of all, I blame myself for allowing it. All of it."

She raises her hand, and my yellow eye is smushed, sparkling on the table.

After the first time I had this dream, I began to write a list of things that convince me I was human. That I wasn't just some computer invented by Ascalon Lee. These are the things I came up with. I liked most foods but didn't like sweet potatoes and tofu. I preferred eating with salad forks as opposed to dinner forks and had no idea why. I wished that I had a boyfriend or girlfriend. Shoot, I wished I had friends in general. On some days, I just wanted to stay in bed and do nothing. I chewed my fingernails on these days and watched them repair themselves before my eyes. I was angry with my mother for dying, which was irrational enough to make me human. Whether it be hunting, fishing, repairing heating and cooling systems, putting together jigsaws, trying to sketch the skeletal remains of grain silos, or training my horses, mild frustration and anger made me more determined. And I could lie.

The master lessons in lying came from my father via playing poker during blizzards. He'd thought it an important game to learn. His idea was that like life, the game is part luck, part skill, and part thinking about what to do with limited information. To him, the objective of the game was to maximize the value of the cards you had been dealt, no matter how good or bad. He'd played a lot in the Army, out in the desert with his fellow soldiers. Back then he'd been quite the card shark. I wanted to use digi cards, but he insisted on real cards and real chips, both of which he dug up at the remains of a place called Boot Hill Casino.

His style was unsurprising. Aggressive. A lot of bluffing. We weren't playing for anything, which didn't help. After many, many hands over a couple of winters, 948 to be exact, I finally asked him how this game was supposed to simulate life if the risk wasn't real. He'd responded by asking if I liked winning. I told him no. He asked me why. I said the only people I'd played against were him and my mother. That I didn't like beating either of them, especially Mom, especially at pulse racket. He grew somber after that. It was a lie. I enjoyed beating both of them. I just wanted to make him feel bad by bringing her up. Cruelty and shame. I added these to my list of things that made me believe I was human.

Regardless, this is when my father began to take me to The Leachate more and more. When he began to encourage me to participate in the learning to build things, race in demolition derbies and motorcycle races, and fight in gladiatorial sports. It was fun at first. These were things that I was naturally, or unnaturally, good at. Maybe if I was congratulated by anyone else besides my father, winning would have felt good, but I was never applauded. Instead, I'd hear whispers of "Intel inside" and "Made in China" whenever I won. I responded with vicious competitiveness. I not only wanted to win, but I also began to lust crushing my opponents. Vindictiveness— another quality to add to my human list.

Here now, in the depths, Ascalon Lee and I walk the Water City Promenade, a two-mile-long seamless, biolumi-nescent lit tube that simulates being tucked in the barrel of a never-ending wave. The hundred-foot-tall perpetual point break connects Hightown to Volcano Vista. It's packed. On the left, people dressed in togas and digital flowered crowns either display their latest holo art or perform bits of costumed music or theater. Some sculpt glimmering liquid metal statues with instruments that look like pasta spoons. On the right, scientific and holo gaming kiosks. Holos of bygone figures in white lab coats or tweed sports coats narrate theories and explanations. Kids holding remote controls duel their holo avatars. Groups of school-age children watch a *jorogumo* fight an *oni* above them. There's some kind of pet store. Not a store really, just a polymer counter on which Petri dishes are neatly stacked. According to the blinking digi words above, what you get is a surprise.

Every now and then, a floating U-shaped food, beverage, and microdose booth swoops down from the promenade's second level. Mughlai-Brazilian seems all the rage, as are slight tabs of YInMN Blue. Battling chefs feverously chop above us in floating *yatai*. Everyone is dressed in a new style of foam fit—thicker, with bigger scales, the varying colors the same as koi. Though some, like the one Ascalon Lee is wearing right now, are pure black. Most decorate their foam fits with tassels and retro precious metal jewelry encrusted with gemstones. A lot of bracelets, rings, and necklaces. Some wear colorful, ornamental head ties, others carnival or Peking opera masks. Some don kabuki robes, wizard cloaks, or lab coats over their foam fits. I feel like an orphan draped in a soiled and beat-up, thin-skinned foam fit—sticking out like a sore thumb as usual. I hate it.

Everyone gives Ascalon Lee a wide berth, even a pack of little children who race past us. The noise is unsettling. Food, hair, and skin tat menus ping my iE. I put it all on block. It has been years since I've been here. This place, once the line of demarcation between the Less Thans and The Money, the depth that separates the twilight from the midnight zone. The biggest difference between now and then is that there are no iEs hovering above the bustling crowds.

"No iEs?" I ask Ascalon Lee.

She shakes her head. "After Satori Day, of course not."

"I'm getting pings. How?"

"Mid-twenty-first-century hand-held tech," she says. She points to a circle of men and women in gold foam fits. They're holding palm-sized slips of glass. One projects a holographic blueprint of a shimmering seascraper with scaffolding that flows with particle streams.

"Do the different colors of foam fit represent different ranks?" I ask as a male couple holding hands passes us, one with flame holo hair, the other frothy ocean waves.

Ascalon Lee shakes her head. "Not ranks, really. Communities, I suppose. Guilds, perhaps? Not imposed by a higher power. When people first began to migrate here, they naturally formed factions. The orange tend to be pacifists and artists. They love their psychedelics. Scientists gravitate toward black, but not always. Engineers like gold. Most of the white enjoy the notion of rebirth and nature. They enjoy planting things and caring for the islands. They love their psychedelics as well. The violet are caretakers of the ocean. Some, as you can see, mix their points of view."

I remember my father telling me about the days before Sessho-seki, how it was a two-party system that resembled a battle between a time machine and utopia and how both sold something straight out of science fiction.

"They fight then," I say.

Ascalon Lee smirks. "Yes, they disagree on a number of issues. Who's doing more, who's doing less. Who deserves accolades."

A group of gold-skinned, masked surgeons wearing black and white fits watch as their patient changes the color of her naked skin like a chameleon. Ascalon Lee, not even glancing at the minor miracle, continues. Starfish vacuums glide across the floor to pick up bits of edible confetti that sprinkle from cutting boards above. A mashup of Mahler and Common blare from their little speakers.

"They argue about what to do with abandoned, orphaned, elderly, and sick people. They squabble over who deserves petty reassurance that their lives have value and meaning."

"Do they disagree on what to do about Akira Kimura?"

"Smart girl," she says. "Yes. There's large disagreement on that."

"Who keeps order?"

"Who indeed."

"You?"

Ascalon Lee stops walking and faces me. "I'm far too busy to spend much time in an administrative capacity. To them I say I have no answers. I don't bring out the best in anybody. My presence just deters them from being their worst. My authority is simply this: I can do whatever I want, you are free to do whatever you want, and those who do not like it may leave."

Behind her, men and women in scaled, white foam fits gather. A large, fuzzy peach rises above them, then cracks open like an egg. Suspended there, above the crowd, is a crying newborn baby. I bottle my astonishment and look at Ascalon Lee. "They fear you," I say.

"My butterfly, I make islands float. What happens if I drop those islands on all of this?"

"You hold them hostage."

"I do not. It's like I said, those who do not like it may leave. Besides, I have no interest in destroying things. I, along with many others, grow things. Create things—the creatures you saw on the island, the ability to shapeshift."

"And when someone does something awful?" I ask.

"I do nothing. I let them be human."

"And that works?"

"Not always," she says. "But nothing human always works."

Ascalon Lee begins to walk again, and I follow. Three bearded men wearing orange wizard robes sit on one another's shoulders and walk toward us, blowing kisses that materialize into once-extinct digital flowers. Children gather and giggle while they try to catch the salmon-colored pedals. The men nod in respect to Ascalon Lee. She nods back. She has resigned herself to be some sort of demigod in this world. Not like Akira, a god with total control over her worshippers, but a living myth, a fable, perhaps the possible moral consequence of this fairy tale if its characters don't play their roles properly. I don't care what she claims. I can see by the faces we pass. They fear her.

"Is there money?" I ask.

"No."

"Isn't wealth a necessary ingredient of advancement?"

Ascalon Lee shakes her head. We pass a row of people slumbering in AMP. "Wealth. Currency was always just an inheritable scoresheet with no intrinsic value. Leisure has always been the necessary ingredient. And wealth is no longer the path to leisure. Science is. Relationship capital is."

I stop walking. She turns to face me. Her golden hair undulates as if she's underwater. As if it doesn't obey the laws of gravity.

"Where is Jon6J?" I ask.

"We are headed to him now. Tell me. How did you resist the urge to kill him?"

There's only one answer that pops in my head. It seemed like the smart and right thing to do. And I deeply regret it. Just as I regret leaving this place all those years ago. It was my fault we left. My sudden aversion to the sea. When I looked at the ocean after Satori Day, all I saw was an endless face pitted with teethed lips. Did Ascalon Lee put this fear in me? She was responsible for changing me in the first place, but the choice to leave was ultimately mine. And if we had stayed, everything might be different. Though I suppose with all their sordid history, it might have been impossible for my father and Ascalon Lee to co-exist in the world. I don't know if I can co-exist with her either.

I look up at the bioluminescent lighting tracked down the curvature of the ceiling high above us. Sea creatures with suction cups attach themselves to the outside glass. All of this accentuates this feeling that I've always had. That I'm living in some kind of ancient snow globe and eyes in the darkness are on me.

When we arrive at the mid-depth lobby of Volcano Vista, the ring-shaped foyer, which used to be three levels splashed with holo ads, is now simply decorated with digital stone lanterns and ohia trees that bloom fuzzy red and yellow flowers. A tiny, sickle-billed honeycreeper lands on a branch, picks at a flower, then flies away. The lighting simulates the natural sunlight found on the islands, and it almost feels like we're outside.

Ascalon Lee and I are greeted by an older blond woman holding a package. Two others, a woman and a man, stand behind her. The blond woman in gold foam fit looks vaguely familiar, so I roll through my digital memory, all the way to the first. Memories before my digital ones are cloudy, as normal memory is. My vague, normal memory tells me that my mother was happy back then. I wish I could replay the data to prove it. Maybe that's why her death pained my father more than it did me. He could replay his memories with her all the way to the beginning, again and again. My digitized memory only begins on the day that Ascalon Lee revived me. That's when I last saw this woman standing before me. She was Ascalon Lee's host during the journey with my father from D-89 to HW Hospital. Ascalon Lee kept her word to my father and repaired her. Or this is just another copy of Ascalon Lee. Either way, the years have not been kind to this woman. She looks much older than she did just ten years before. Those who survived Satori Day often do though. She moves in to kiss my cheek, which shocks me into recoiling. She knowingly nods, smiles, and hands me the package. I'm a bit embarrassed for backing away.

"My name is Sooni," she says. "Please, open it."

I rip the package open, and it snaps into the size of a marble, then plops on the floor. A janitorial bot playing island shuttle port music whizzes over and snatches it up. I look at what I'm holding. I unfold it. It's a heavy, large-scaled black foam fit like the one Ascalon Lee is wearing. I turn to her.

"Why the redesign?" I ask.

Ascalon Lee looks at Sooni. "Show her," she says.

Sooni presses her finger against a small touch ID button on her collar. Her foam fit slides from the back of her neck and stretches over her entire head. Her face now resembles that of a mannequin sheathed with thin, gold rubber. I touch her face. It's hard, almost metallic. I pinch the material and pull. Firm yet pliable.

"Protection," I say. I wonder whether in this world, you need to blind yourself to protect yourself. "You can see through the material?"

"Yes," says Sooni. "And it's breathable, too." Sooni presses the button on her collar again, and the foam fit retracts back to its original form. She runs her fingers through her hair. "You never know with Akira Kimura. She could always infiltrate those of us who remain. Those who aren't Gardeners." She points to her right eye. "Like she did on Satori Day. You know what I mean?"

"Sooni was on the team that engineered it," Ascalon Lee says. "Isn't that both wonderful and remarkable? No engineering background, yet she caught up over the years. She learned."

Sooni smiles sheepishly. I guess the message is I can learn even more, too.

Sooni's two companions look anxious to greet me. One, a slight and pale hapa girl with chestnut hair, steps to me and takes my hand. Her left wrist jangles with ancient metal bracelets, gold probably, along with a couple of jade ones. It's the sort of stuff that was deemed worthless pre-Satori Day, but things that were long ago valuable are apparently finding their value again. I suspect the traveling treasure hunters on the continent search for such things and offer them for trade.

"I'm honored to meet you," she says. "Your father. Years ago when we were children, he saved us."

I get it now. These are the kids my dad pulled from the

ocean when D-89 was being evacuated after Akira lit up the moon. I'm surprised Ascalon Lee has cared for them. I turn to her. She's gazing out into space, like some machine that's been suddenly turned off. I look back at the other of Sooni's companions. He's tall and pure black, like Ascalon Lee. He's looking at her now, clearly in awe of her, which bores me. I turn my attention to the one who greeted me. The pearl metallics of her skin pop under the lights. I note that there's something attractive about dark, thick eyebrows on a slight, pale frame. I like her, and I don't even know her, which feels strange.

Sooni puts a hand on my shoulder. I try not to back away this time, but it's hard. I don't like being touched. It's something I didn't really know about myself until now.

"You don't remember us?" she asks.

Adults have the tendency to ask children if they remember people whom they clearly would not. Not without iE tech anyway. "I remember," I say. "I remember hearing about the children my father rescued from D-89."

"Let me show you to your unit and you can change."

"Thank you," I say.

"Bring her down to the penthouse after she's done," says Ascalon Lee. "I'm taking her to the lab to see this boy who broke from OneVoice."

Sooni nods. I follow her and the others to the elevator. Besides the décor, the Vista has not changed much since the last time I was here. I reflect on my father's trip to this, the greatest of all seascrapers, all those years ago. What was he thinking about that day he took the ride down to midnight to meet Akira Kimura? How did he feel when he found her murdered? It was here that my father almost killed Ascalon Lee. Are there places that we are naturally, subconsciously attracted to? Like fish to buoys. Or places that we are destined to return. Salmon, turtles, puffins—creatures that travel to their birthplace to spawn. Is there something in me, in my father, and maybe even Ascalon Lee that possesses a variant of natal homing? Why do we always end up in this place? *Akira Kimura.*

Beyond the descending gorilla glass tube, a megamouth shark glides by. Vampire squid feed on the light sprinkle of marine snow. Creatures that resemble egg yolks and tangled noodles undulate. *Tangled.* Everything always seems tangled, doesn't it? Akira managed to untangle herself from everything—humble beginnings, doubters, death, and the limitations of being an individual. While my father spent his whole life hacking through knots that eventually choked him. Why does it feel like Ascalon Lee has untangled her-self, too? Is that fair? The questions bubble rage in me, and suddenly, for the first time since being back, I really look at the ocean depths through the descending tube. I can tell the water temperature has drastically dropped because the sea suddenly looks like wrinkled glass. We plunge beneath the thermocline, and I glare into the darkness. The ocean does not scare me anymore.

6

The base of Volcano Vista, once a penthouse, then a statue of Akira Kimura, is now a scutoid-shaped underwater submarine base where little egg-shaped subs can depart and arrive. Ascalon Lee and I walk through a clear airlock tube, climb into a two-person egg, and detach. The new foam fit is stiff, and I miss my duster, hat, and boots, but I suppose I'm too old to be playing gunslinging cowgirl anymore. Besides, the new clothes make me feel like this return to Water City may spark a new beginning.

I'm surprised that instead of going up, we go down, descending into an underground tunnel cloaked by holographic black rock. While we travel through the brine lakes at the bottom, of well, the bottom, and head to Akira's old lab, I pull up everything that my father has ever told me about Ascalon Lee. I remember a fair amount. The story of her birth and the murder of her newborn twin. Her lonely youth on the island on account of her alcoholic father and the disownment by her mother. Her advancements in science and self-mutilation, which ultimately led to her innovations of iE tech. Her deep sleep after her mother's betrayal. When she woke, she'd exacted revenge on her mother, then tried to become her. My father stopped her. She rose again and took me as her shell. My father forced her out of me, so she took others: Old Man Caldwell, Sooni, the woman from D-89. She captured Akira. Ascalon Lee could've prevented Satori Day by killing her mother, but she chose the route of curiosity instead, sought knowledge over right. The insatiable quest for knowledge is at the core of her. Just as it is at the core of her mother. They will always choose knowledge, just as my father would always choose the trigger, just like he always chose Akira Kimura.

"Who does the shit work around here?" I ask from the backseat.

"Excuse me?" says Ascalon Lee.

"All I've seen so far are people playing arts and science. You, folding DNA like origami and making islands float. Where does the energy come from? The food? The water? The material? All this needs to be sustained on the backs of someone."

She turns around and grins. Her sharp, golden teeth and eyes make her look goblin-like but terrifying and beautiful at the same time. "That societal model has shifted," she says.

"That's not answering the question. I'm tired of these verbal games."

She turns back around and puts her feet up on the dashboard, which is a surprisingly human posture for her to assume. "The energy is mostly automated via artificial intelligence. The water, from catchments and purification centers, is as well. As is refuse and sewage. As is recycling and maintenance. We had the capability to automize most things for years, long before Satori Day. But, you know, AI has always scared people. They always imagined it as human-like. Narcissists. AI has always been more service animal. More oxen and carrier pigeon. Created for a very narrow and specific task."

I look out the window. There's no light except that which is coming from the little submarine, and these pitch-black caverns seem devoid of any life. But I know these waters are probably filled with life—microscopic, but still life.

Ascalon Lee continues. "For example, in, let's say manu-facturing. AI can assemble better than any person can. It can package better. It can even deliver better. It does not need sleep, so it can produce more and do it more quickly. The caveat is that each type of AI can do only that one thing near perfection. A med bot can diagnose and do surgery, but it does not have desire that manifests invention." She pauses. "It doesn't crave power, so it would never forcefully implant itself in the human mind billions of times over."

A reference to Akira Kimura. It's starting to get more dif-ficult to tell which direction we're heading in, or any direction at all. A sort of space sickness creeps in me. Or maybe it's claustrophobia. I feel the sudden urge to get out of this sub immediately.

"Anyway," Ascalon Lee says, "back then, we didn't auto-mate because we felt like we needed to give people something to do. And an economy had to exist to keep social hierarchies intact. This new world is built on the back of efficiency and invention."

"You didn't mention food or materials," I say, trying to concentrate on the conversation while I feel imaginary walls closing in on me.

"That is . . . trickier. We do grow much of our own food, but we do receive aid. I don't want what I'm about to say to upset you, but . . ."

I recall the boreholes near Mile High. It comes to me. "The Gardeners send you what they mine. The elements that you used to maintain the superconductors beneath the islands and the magnetic field that keep them afloat. They send you other stuff as well. That's why they keep the shuttles operational. Transport."

"Smart girl."

"Akira wants this place to exist," I say.

Ascalon Lee's black tail slithers under her seat, near my toes. I shift my feet away from its tip. "It took me a while to figure that out," she says. "My mother didn't tell me. I do not communicate with her at all. In fact, she's not really Akira Kimura anymore. She is them. They are her. There is no individual consciousness pulling levers. But, yes, before she did her work, it's why she cloned me. This is my part. This laboratory."

My anger dulls the sickness I was feeling earlier. "This isn't built on the back of science. It's built on the backs of the Gardeners."

Ascalon Lee removes her feet from the dash and sits up. "Perhaps in part."

I ball my fists. "And you're complicit."

"There are things that I do here that you know nothing about," Ascalon Lee says. "Don't make too many assumptions."

"And my father?"

Ascalon Lee sighs. "Instead of policing the continent, he terrorized it."

I blink. "Police it? He never told me that."

"He didn't tell you everything. Parents and the guilty never do."

He was meant to police the continent? I'm feeling more and more betrayed by him. There's more that he hid. I know it. There's more that Ascalon Lee is hiding, too.

"But moving to Kansas was my idea," I say. "He would have nothing to police if we simply stayed here."

"There is always something to police," Ascalon Lee says. "Especially in the eye of my mother. She would've eventually coaxed him there."

My mind spins with realization. "I made it so she didn't need to."

Ascalon Lee nods. "He was supposed to train you. Gardeners would have followed both of you, but he kept you isolated. Mile High and all its Gardeners were supposed to be under his command. He was supposed to protect A496, and you were supposed to help him. Instead . . ."

I imagine the amputees burning in the fires my father set. Their flesh bubbling then blackening to ash while they silently scream in agony with their tongueless mouths. The regret is crushing. I swipe at my face. "Why did you call me there? If you didn't call me, I never would've come with him!"

"It doesn't matter. You couldn't have stopped him."

"It matters to me!"

She slows the sub and turns to me. "Listen to me. He couldn't live with his failure. He believed he could have stopped my mother or just not helped her to begin with. Who was it who brought my mother back from the dead? It was him. I may have guided him, but he decided to do so on his own."

He brought Akira back so that she would bring me back, but that plan went south, and he took a chance and trusted Ascalon Lee with the task. I close my eyes and exhale. Nothing warps morality as effectively as love.

"Then to compound the guilt, he felt as if he failed his wife and stillborn child. You were his only hope, and he realized that you didn't need him any longer. That perhaps he was beginning to hinder you, which he was. How much longer would it have taken Gardeners like Jon6J to break free and turn on you as well? My butterfly, I am telling you right now that this man does not want to be wakened. Let him rest."

I feel myself sinking into misery. I grasp for anger to keep me afloat. "I hate you," I say.

"I know," Ascalon Lee says.

"How do you know all this?"

"I observe. I watch. How do you not know all this?"

"Bring him back," I say. "And let's confirm it."

Ascalon Lee sighs and turns her head away from me. It's a sigh that has an edge of anger to it. Good. I want her to be angry, too. We continue our trip through the labyrinth of underwater stalagmite lighted by the hull of the egg-shaped sub that shines a bright white in every direction. "Is Shave Time Money a threat to Akira? To you?" I ask.

"A nuisance, for now. Perhaps a threat in the future. He's a smart man. He keeps his people miserable and angry at the world. He points to OneVoice and declares it the cause of every instance of misery. Of tragedy. Of even bad luck. He is very much like the rising despots of old. He interprets a very complex world with a very complex history into a simplistic 'them' versus 'us' existence and sows hatred toward what he deems as the 'other.'"

"OneVoice is the cause," I say.

Ascalon Lee throws up her hands. "The Leachate existed long before Satori Day. It even predates Sessho-seki and the Ascalon Project. The people of The Leachate can leave at any time they want."

"And go where? Would you take them in?"

Ascalon Lee laughs. "No," she says.

"And the Gardeners?"

Ascalon Lee says nothing.

The sub rises and breaks surface in a grotto that I know I've been to, but I don't remember. It was here that Ascalon Lee and my father had one of their numerous standoffs, and it was here that my father, struck by delusion, shot me. In a way, it's my birthplace. Or maybe not birthplace, but the womb in which the idea of a new me had to be conceived. I'm starting to feel sick again.

Once we dock, I exit the sub as quickly as I can and step on the quaint wooden pier. The planks creak beneath me. I draw a long breath and exhale. I touch a stone pillar carved in the shape of a coiled water dragon. There's a door ahead with two stone, dragon-faced *komainu* guarding the entrance.

"Watch," Ascalon Lee says.

She walks up to one of the lion dog statues, kneels before it, and begins to stroke its mane. Its stony eyes blink and come alive. The curls of its mane begin to shimmer and turn orange. Its bushy tail starts to wag. Its once-stone skin transforms from slate to Han purple. It steps off its haunches and approaches me. I swallow my initial instinct to take a couple of steps back and stick out my hand instead, palm down. It sniffs me, tail still wagging. I run my fingers through its blue locks. It is as real as any creature I've ever encountered. I turn to Ascalon Lee, who has woken the other one. It's on its hind legs, paws pressing against her chest while it licks her face.

"They're wonderful," I gasp.

"Yes, they are," says Ascalon Lee. "And deadly."

Perhaps considering all of the possible outcomes of the human condition, this one isn't so bad. If you're here. If you're not Gardener. If you're not Leachatean. Maybe it's not an outcome of the human condition. It's just the continuation of the same bullshit. I wish my father were here to discuss this with me so that I could wring his neck. For the last few years, our discussions always became heated debates. We argued about Gardeners the most. Sometimes I feared I disagreed with him just to disagree, because we always disagreed. Another embarrassing thing to add to my human checklist. Contrarian. But I know now that the reason I always disagreed was because I was right, and he was wrong. *Liar*, I say to myself, hoping that somehow he can hear me even in death.

Ascalon Lee and I walk through the doorway and head down the spiral staircase. The komainu follow. We enter the dimly lit rotunda. The bed of flowers that my father told me about is still here, as are the billiards table, bookshelves, desk, and the six chambers, all now repaired and humming. Ascalon Lee stops at the flower bed. Her tail seeps from her spine and the tip delicately touches one of the flowers.

"She left me access to everything," she says. "All the data, the information. The world's research she had, we all now possess. It's why we were able to advance so quickly. The things we have done. Genetics. Robotics. Geology. Large scale quantum locking. We filled the eighth row of the periodic table."

"Yet, you don't worship her. Do you regret killing her?"

"She killed herself."

"With the med bots you were about to use to drill in her head."

Ascalon Lee shrugs. "It's a better world."

"For you, maybe."

The black tail retracts into her spine. She turns to me. "It can be for you, too."

I ignore her and walk to the upright chambers. I look through the glass of the nearest one. Jon6J inhabits it. I touch the glass. He looks peaceful undulating in there. I turn to the one right next to it and flinch hard like something venomous just tried to bite me. It's the body of Akira Kimura, preserved like Jon in thick, clear fluid.

"It's her," I say.

Ascalon Lee shrugs. "Her last body at least."

It's doesn't feel real that a god and one of her worshippers bob beside one another. But there's nothing godly about her appearance at all. She's small, smaller than me or Ascalon Lee. And a bit aged. The beginning indicators of crow's feet. A slight dullness to her skin.

"This isn't a god," I say.

"No, it's not," Ascalon Lee says. "This is where she kept her extra HuSCs. She kept one of me and your father here, too. She grew a clone of Idris Eshana, the inventor of the iE, in this very lab."

I nod. "He mass produced the iEs needed to execute Satori Day." I turn to Jon. It's difficult not to gaze at the remains of Akira Kimura, but I try my best to not be distracted by the sight of her. "What are you doing with him?"

"Studying him, of course."

"I don't suppose you learned much yet," I say.

"No. But my mother essentially had her people chemically neutered in one of her earlier patches. What she didn't anticipate was that their brain chemistry would adapt to this neutering quickly and evolve to produce more hormones. Not all of them, of course, but the ones who began to . . . notice things. I assume their 'noticing' prompted their brains to increase production in neurotransmitters."

I press my hand against Jon's glass confinement. He looks so withered and frail, his eyeless face a complete blank. "But he was advanced. He was a skilled liar."

Ascalon Lee scoffs. "It's always the one who buys the lie who blames the liar. Was he really that good at lying, or was it you who wanted to believe him? At its core, that's all a lie is, someone telling you what you want to hear. And a lonely girl eking out existence on the outskirts of the armpit of the world? That girl wants to hear anything."

A girl who wants to free Gardeners finds a Gardener who's free. I don't say it, but I can't help thinking it. Ascalon Lee is right. I was ripe for Jon's lies. Maybe I was always ripe for my father's, too, because if there was one person in the world I felt I could trust, it was him. "But Gardeners don't lie," I say anyway, more to myself than to Ascalon Lee.

"Of course they lie. They are Akira Kimura, the best liar in human history."

I turn from Jon's chamber and glare at Ascalon Lee. "Are you going to help me with my father?"

"I will have him transported here," she says. "Then, I will determine whether it's even possible."

A lie. Only an egomaniac would spell out what a lie is in front of your face, then follow the definition with one. "And what do I do for you in return?"

"You become the policeman your father was meant to be. The day for you to replace him was inevitable. It's your purpose."

"Police who? People here in Water City?" I ask.

"Here, there, everywhere."

"And Akira's new patch? Her new system update? The one you're supposedly scared of?"

Ascalon Lee pauses. "I'm not sure. Jon6J has broken free. I don't have a good feeling about how my mother will patch and fix this. If OneVoice is the connection of billions of minds. Of one simultaneous thought—"

"What if the thought becomes anger?"

"Yes," she says. "*Yes*. What if Jon6J is simply one of the first cases of an emotional virus within the system? I don't fear the system update. I'm sure my mother wants to calm her Gardeners. To continue to control them. I fear that many Gardeners will reject her attempt to do so. This will create a separate faction that could inflict violence against those it sees as my mother's enemies."

I point at Jon. "Even disconnected, he still believed. Did you show him Akira's body before you put him under?"

"Yes," Ascalon Lee says. "He promptly called me a heretic and attacked me."

I nod and finally look at Akira again. It's like I told Jon6J earlier. *She was just a lady*, I tell myself.

Ascalon Lee steps beside me. She, on the other hand, looks remarkable as she gazes at the face of Akira. Even with the umber skin, I can see some of the resemblances between her and her mother. But her glowing yellow eyes, the intensity in them. The almost dilated sorrow. Her eyes are different than her mother's.

"What if I want OneVoice to crash?" I say. "What if I prefer a world of Jons to a world of Gardeners?"

"He's a killer. A zealot. He killed your father. Multiply this one murderous fanatic by a thousand. Or a million. Or ten million. What do you think will become of the world then?"

I imagine all the Gardeners, not just in North America, but the world. If they just suddenly turned on everything in Akira's name, the death toll might be even higher than Satori Day's. "Wouldn't they be satisfied that Jon got my father?" I ask. "They don't have anything to be angry about anymore."

Ascalon Lee eyes me curiously. "When has a zealot ever been satiated by the execution of one dissident?"

My jaw clenches. "You're afraid they would come here."

Ascalon Lee shrugs. "I don't know what they would do. All I know is that I don't want to find out."

I walk to the billiards table and pick up a cue. I inspect the lacquered wood. "I don't understand," I say. "Why did Akira build A496 in North America if it's the only place with a resistance? With a group like the Leachateans? Doesn't that make it the most dangerous place to build it? Also, isn't a launch loop more effective built closer to the equator?"

Ascalon Lee steps beside me and grabs the other cue. She chalks up the tip. "She had already formed a partnership with the US government to build the launch loop. NASA had been her puppet since the days of Sessho-seki. Some of the infrastructure had already been planned and built when she was still alive. The fusion reactors that power it, the force field that protects it, those things were already secretly engineered at both Corpus Akira and Cape Canaveral."

I aim at the cue ball and calculate degrees and force. "But then you killed her," I say.

Ascalon Lee nods. "Then, when she returned . . ."

"Satori Day," I say. I go into sports mode. I feel the hum and warmth of my eye. I hit the cue ball and sink the nine ball on the break. I turn to Ascalon Lee. She's smiling. A thought gnaws at me. "What is OneVoice doing in space?" I ask.

She begins to remove the nine balls from the table's pockets. "Expeditions, mostly. She's made it to every planet in the solar system. She maps. She takes samples. My knowledge is limited because I'm not patched into OneVoice. What I know is just from observation. She digs."

"Like she digs here?"

Ascalon Lee nods slowly while she racks the balls. "She does dig excessively here. OneVoice almost seems obsessed over it. Not just for the mining. It's an occurrence of every continent, including Antarctica. It's as if she's desperately searching for something she's lost. But no, nothing near that level out there."

"Where are you now? The version or versions of you that I spoke to at Epcot. Did you make it out? If so, where did Okaasan send those versions of you?"

Ascalon Lee frowns. "Venus."

"Is it wonderful?"

She sets the cue ball up to break and aims the cue at the white ball. "It's nearly a thousand degrees, the atmosphere is almost completely carbon dioxide, and its pressure is crushing. The oceans have long been vaporized. So, no. It is not wonderful."

All those Gardeners in Florida "volunteering" for these explorations to uninhabitable places. There has to be more to it than that. I look at Ascalon Lee. My father told me that when you're young and idealistic, it can feel like all the old people in the world have given up. I told him that it feels like that because it's true. He said that sometimes, when you get your ass kicked repeatedly in life, it's tough to think of anyone but yourself.

"Let's go back to the telescope," I say.

Ascalon, frozen in break position, is staring at the balls. I snap my fingers in front of her face. "Hey!" I say. "Let's go back to the telescope."

Ascalon hits the cue ball. All nine balls roll and fall into the table's pockets.

"How did you do that?" I ask.

She grins. "It's not just about how hard you hit the cue ball. It's how you set up the balls when you rack them."

I lay the cue on the table. "That's cheating."

She shrugs, puts her cue down, and leads us back to the sub. "It's my sister up there."

"Huh?" I ask.

"In space."

"What sister?"

"The one who was with me on Satori Day."

Her genetically engineered twin. Her other HuSC. I wonder if she cares about certain versions of herself more than others.

"Do you ever think about your sibling?" Ascalon Lee asks.

"What sibling?" It immediately occurs to me after I say it. She's referring to my sister. "No," I say, feeling somewhat guilty and embarrassed. I rush to climb into the sub.

"Interesting." Ascalon takes the pilot seat. "Even all these years later, I think about my first one often."

I begin to wonder what my sibling would've been like. Athletic like my mother? Full of *hwabyeong* like my father? Would the child have been able to see like my father and I do? The sub tilts down and glides through the dark brine. I stop myself from thinking about a thing that never was and start thinking about things that once were and how maybe they can come back. Not just my father, but other things as well. War. Genocide. Global disaster. Ascalon Lee and I need to look into space to confirm it.

7

When I was a child wandering the ghost towns on the outskirts of The Leachate, I became obsessed with keys. Not keys as they exist now, but small metal keys that used to open manual locks. Most of them bits of brass or steel. I became fascinated by their teeth and notches, started collecting buckets and buckets of them, cataloguing the locations. Then, when I was eleven, I began attempting to open things with them. While my father was out, I would take the keys to the place where I'd found them. My most glorious find was Eaton Place in Wichita. I found a key for every apartment in the resident manager's office. I went through all five stories, opening locked doors in the centuries-old building. There was nothing more satisfying than the zipping sound of the teeth scraping against pins and tumblers. That twist of the knob. The door swinging open on its rusted hinges. My father thought I'd lost my mind.

Ascalon Lee, two of the people I met at Volcano Vista, and I fly in a heli toward Savior's Eye. I come to learn that the tall, thick-necked male, who fawns over Ascalon Lee, is named Motu, and the pretty female, with the lush, well-groomed eyebrows is called Dreh. It's clear she spends time on her appearance and hygiene. Her undyed hair is the same color as her brows, and the chestnut flows down her back in perfect strands. Her pale, glittery skin emits a slight whiff of coconut.

Motu is sitting across from me, next to Ascalon Lee, and I can already tell he doesn't like me, which is fine. I sense a fanaticism waiting to be born in him. Dreh, on the other hand, who's right next to me, appears bashful and pensive. There's a slit in her scaled foam fit on her chest that reveals cleavage. Looking at her makes me feel self-conscious. I pray that the corpse smell of my last foam fit hasn't lingered on my skin. I know my short, practical hair is a frizzy mess. Will I begin to care more about what I look like now that I'm surrounded by other people who clearly do? My father would call this vanity, and a bad way to operate. Maybe, out in the wilderness, but I begin to wonder what I would look like with a change of hair color, perhaps skin color as well.

"I want an eye like hers. Like yours," Motu says to Ascalon Lee. "I'm tired of this antique." He holds up his rectangular-shaped glass device. "It takes too long to manually look stuff up. To access memories. To communicate. This stupid, ancient piece of tech. I want an iE in my head."

"It's a burden," Ascalon Lee says. "This thing we have."

"I can take it," Motu says while staring at me, looking like if he could, he'd snatch mine out of its socket right now. "We don't need this little girl. What's her value? She probably can't even code, bioengineer, or do calculus."

Ascalon Lee smiles at Motu. "Can you do those things?"

Motu looks out the window and grunts.

Does she keep him around to sustain her ego? I have my doubts. Dreh taps my arm. She's offering me a slip of YInMN blue.

"Would you like one?" she nervously asks.

"It won't affect her," Ascalon Lee says. "Nothing mind-altering in consumable quantities can."

She's right. I've tried in the past. I've secretly drunk my father's liquor out of sheer boredom. I've popped my mother's pills. Nothing. At first, I thought they'd imbibed simply for the taste, but both tasted terrible. Then I began noticing their behaviors change with continued use. My mother's stuff would allow her to slip into blackouts. My father's would stir a wretched grouchiness in him—a desire to light the world on fire. I was glad their stuff didn't affect me, but watching Dreh slip the tab of YInMN Blue under her pink tongue makes me wish it would now. I imagine a comradery in ingesting mind-altering substances together.

"Why are they coming with us?" I ask Ascalon Lee.

"Screw you, too," says Motu.

I suppose that was an impolite thing to say. This social-izing thing is new to me. I try to focus my mind on the task. *Procedure. Fix it.* Then a guess comes to me. "My father."

Ascalon Lee nods. "They will transport his remains to the lab."

"What will you and this girl do?" Motu sweetly asks Ascalon Lee.

"Your parents never changed your name?" Ascalon Lee asks me.

I shake my head. I suppose after a certain age, a name change seems pointless.

"What is your name?" Motu asks.

"Her name is the same as mine. Ascalon," Ascalon Lee says.

Motu rolls his eyes. Would my life be any different with a different name? It's my mother who named me. My father never liked the name. When we moved to Kansas, I wanted to ask for a name change since it felt like a new beginning, but it seemed silly. There was no legal process, no digi-docs to submit. It would have felt like me simply demanding that my mother and father start calling me something else.

When we land, I head straight inside Savior's Eye. It occurs to me that I don't even know if the telescope works. My father once told me that when Akira was designing it, she felt it necessary to include this archaic piece of equipment because she wanted to see the galaxy with her own eyes, not just computer-generated snapshots of it. While Dreh and Motu guide a hovering AMP chamber that will be used to move my father, I tap my finger on the brass-rimmed eyepiece. It's embossed with a mon, the same that the Gardeners wear on their collars. Even down to the finest detail, Akira reveled in creating symbols that only she knew the meaning of. I take control of the telescope via iE and reduce the focal length. I switch from gravitational wave detection to simple ultra-violet. I begin to calculate possible state vectors in my head. I'm again a child, sticking keys into their locks, hoping for the knob to turn and the door to swing open.

"You know how to operate this?" Ascalon Lee asks.

I nod. "I've looked through old telescopes on the continent."

"Why?"

I shrug. "Boredom. Curiosity. It's how I finally figured out what Okaasan was building. A496. Her launch loop."

"What are you looking for now?" Ascalon Lee says.

I ignore the question and aim the telescope at low Earth orbit, just beyond the now largely cleaned junk ring and the hundreds of OneVoice satellites. And that's when I see it. A construction site in space. The OneVoice astronauts skitter on an orb like a consortium of crabs feeding on something soft. Lit up, swooped tentacles trail the orb. One of the astronauts stops in its tracks. I focus on it. It appears to be looking right at me. I pull away.

"She's rebuilt it," I say.

"Rebuilt what?" Ascalon Lee asks, moving me to the side to look into the telescope. "You have that intuition and confident certainty that only comes with youth." She gasps, then says, "All sense diminishes with age, even common."

"I'm right, aren't I?"

Ascalon Lee pulls her face away from the eyepiece. She runs her tongue along her sharp teeth. "Yes," she says. "It didn't occur to me that she would do it, but it makes sense. Of course she would want contingencies to keep OneVoice focused. This is her system update. This is how she plans on squashing the little rebellion going on in her own head. The Gardeners, even the ones regaining some semblance of autonomy via rage will not be able to escape her judgmental gaze. I believe it will keep them tethered to OneVoice. How did you know?"

"Like you said, of course."

Ascalon Lee peers into the telescope again. "She has rebuilt Ascalon's Scar."

We both head outside. When we get there, we look up. A feathery, almost imperceptible summer snow sprinkles upon us. I'm a child again in Kansas, waiting for daylight to creep through my window and into my room to signal the start of a new day. This light does not creep. It appears as suddenly as it vanished a decade ago. And I'm reminded that nothing is faster than light. But the scar is different now. It looks as if the sky cracked open and a shimmering spectrum of colors has flooded in from a universe next door.

"She gave it a facelift," Ascalon Lee says, trying to hide her bitterness.

She heads back into Savior's Eye. I stay outside, stare at the scar, and remember happier times. A vague recollection of being four, my mother smothering me with kisses and telling me she was going to give me a thousand more. After the first several, I told her kisses were closed, and my father burst into laughter. I remember refusing to eat broccoli stumps for years, and my father dutifully eating them for me behind my mother's back. I recall stories beyond my memory, stories that my parents shared. Me at three, asking my father wouldn't it be funny if a shark ate him. "Why is it always funny to you thinking about bad things happening to me?" he'd asked. I responded by saying it was because he was my favorite person.

Why has the reemergence of the split in the sky unzipped all these memories? Was this Akira's intention? The scar is not just a reminder to the Gardeners who it is that runs this world. It's a reminder to everyone else, too. Maybe we're all zonbi just like the Gardeners, and we will cow to the scar as well. How can the world change so drastically in ten years? How is it possible that I'm now standing on a floating island? More and more keys with unfound locks. Does discovering the truth ever change things? I want to find out. I will not capitulate to some light in the sky. Unlike my father, I won't surrender to fury's impatience.

Determined, I turn from the scar and march down to the pond to collect the things I left here. I step into the cold water and wade to the center. Our home is gone. My father may be gone. I bend down to pick up the rail gun, the heat blades, and my mother's old pistol. These things that my father and I collected suddenly feel more important to me than they ever have before.

I'll bring the SEAL back from Mile High. Maybe once I retrieve it, I'll take it for a quick burn and reacquaint myself with these islands. See what has become of my old school. See what has become of the Buhari compound and the sunken vessels that I used to love exploring as a child.

Maybe it's good that these islands float. Before that, they shifted, slowly but relentlessly. They moved northwest at the same rate of fingernail growth. It would've taken millions of years, but they would've eventually crept along their plates until they sunk. Now they're here forever. But what does that mean for the future islands being birthed from the ocean? Will they be stunted or smothered by these present ones? With each step down the jagged rocks, I collect more orphaned keys in my head and wonder if I'll ever match them with their proper locks.

When all is said and done, maybe there's no such thing as new beginnings. All that exists is the possibility of new ends.

PART THREE

TARO

1

It's been two weeks since OneVoice re-lit the sky with Ascalon's Scar, and the flustered community of Water City can still talk of nothing else. There is no global network anymore since Satori Day except for OneVoice, but Water City provides its own self-contained municipal broadband. Most seascrapers in the mesh network contain access points and radio transmitters maintained by AI. It's archaic, but effective.

Here, only Ascalon Lee, with her satellites, can communicate globally and in space, but because she's cut off from OneVoice, there are not many people to really communicate with except other versions of herself. She could always interface with me when I was on the continent, and perhaps random nomads, treasure hunters, and traveling surgeons and DJs, but who else? This current, localized version of the internet lacks a newsfeed or any institutional, government, or corporate presence. Instead, it's populated by people who formed private groups—to which I have no access to—and random influencers who post digis on their handhelds, stories that expire in twenty-four hours, a rule that apparently

Ascalon Lee instituted. "No one deserves a past that extends in perpetuity," Ascalon Lee had told me.

Right now, most users capture images of the scar at all times of day, hypothesizing the reasons for its re-emergence, debating what should be done about it. The most popular influencer is Water City Viral Feed, so I follow just like everyone else. Most of what Water City Viral Feed posts are simply bits from excitable people who point at the sky and speak in superlatives. They talk about the scar and their lives in general, using words that end in "-est." It gets old quickly.

I don't sleep much because every time I do, I either dream about the woman with the knobby spine at Epcot reaching a hand out for help while the whole place burns, or I dream of Jon stabbing my father in the back. Though in my nightmare, he doesn't stop there. He has a laser in his eye like I do, and he incinerates Leachateans while I helplessly watch. Unable to sleep, and bored with Water City Viral Feed, I dig deeper and deeper into posts made by older users who have virtually no followers. It's almost like they're talking to themselves, and they frequently like to reminisce about the past. I piece together that apparently none of the current residents have deep roots in Water City. Most came from North America, Asia, South America, DownUnder, and the waypoints of the Pacific Bridge before Akira restricted travel between continents. No one says exactly, or even figuratively, how she's done this. According to one elderly user who goes by the apt moniker "ramblingman," the islands, which were already floating when he arrived, were the most magnificent sight he had ever seen.

During sleepless nights, I try to research further into the history of the last decade, but most of what I find are simply fragments and holos by nostalgic people who congratulate themselves for surviving what they call their generation's *hibakusha*, despite the fact that they were chosen by Akira to survive. Satori Day wasn't their Hiroshima and Nagasaki, it was the Gardeners'. One woman longingly reminisces about a particular noodle shop that made its own noodles daily. *They were so tender!* she broadcasts in colorful and cartoony Thought to Text. I tire of these posts, too.

I fought off the temptation to hack into the private group forums of gangs of artists, scientists, and engineers, and asked Ascalon Lee more about the history of Water City post-Satori Day. She said that she was left an army of AI boring machines, naval crawlers, draglines, and wheel excavators and did it on her own. I don't fully buy it, but I don't push the issue.

I spend much of my time, as I did in The Leachate, alone. I spent the first day remotely transporting my SEAL here. With its security cams on, I had it skip from stone to stone across the Pacific Bridge, stopping for automated refuels only to discover that Gardeners populate the bridge, loading and unloading crates from zeppelin-class shuttles. When my SEAL finally arrived, I put my gear in it and parked it on a landing pad at Volcano Vista. Now, I walk the Promenade and try to pick up on the muffled, underwater rev of this city. People trade here daily, 24/7. Food for information. Art for innovation. Sex for old treasures. Newly smithed hunting gear and strategy guides are all the rage today. Reimbursements are promised.

Even in this time of chaos, crime seems rare, which is strange to me considering there are no laws that I know of. But I suppose there is no poverty, which helps. There is also a strong sense of community, of belonging to something together, and these bonds are further galvanized by rituals. I've spotted people sitting in circles holding hands after they pop YInMN Blue together. There's also a strong community of outrigger paddlers who practice and race weekly with six-person crews. From picking fruit to fishing to concocting new ways of bending the laws of nature, people here just always do things together.

I recall information on the old world and discover that by the time of Sessho-seki, there were some 50,000 Federal laws, 6,000 of which were criminal. Over three million people were incarcerated. Apparently, back then, 50,000 Band-Aids were needed to cover the pus of human nature. Today, there is no prison here. No law enforcement that I've seen. And the most conflict I've seen so far, here on the public promenade, is heated bickering. Three days ago, a group of orange-clad artists accused a group of golds with sculped dorsal dos of being Akira Kimura sympathizers. The engineers were apparently impressed that not only did OneVoice rebuild the scar, but it improved its aesthetics. The oranges were outraged. Aesthetics were subjective, and they rejected the notion that OneVoice could be artful. When they came close to blows, other colors simply jumped in and broke up the altercation. I'm sure there must be crime, especially since Ascalon Lee urges me to create some kind of security force, but I have yet to sense murder since I've been here.

But it's not all utopia. I've seen death. Twice this last week, the reds started with the rhythmic patter of raindrops. Then the drops formed puddles and dispersed into crimson tendrils that pulled me through the Muzak-playing vac tubes of the city and led me to the locked doors of midnight zone apartment units. In one, I found a man in his AMP chamber with his wrists slit. He used AMP to dull the pain of suicide with half hibernation. I poked around his place and found tattered printed pictures of people, most likely his parents, who are probably Gardeners now. He spent his time engorging himself with the leftover content of the old world: holo games and VR porn.

The other suicide was far more disturbing because of the condition in which I found her. She had ripped or cut her own eyes out. Scribblings of Ascalon's Scar covered her walls. When I reported both suicides to Ascalon Lee, she shrugged.

"You should see the lazy ones," she'd said. "They're worse."

It's become clear to me that everyone knows that Ascalon Lee is Akira Kimura's daughter, but she doesn't seem to exert any authority—just like she said. She serves as a sort of invisible master cylinder in this hydraulic society. She taps the brakes, and the other cylinders slow the city. She nudges the clutch, and the thrust bearings shift and disengage from the flywheel.

The day it appeared, there of course was much chatter concerning what to do about the reigniting of Ascalon's Scar. The different factions agreed to meet at the center of the Water City Promenade when we returned from Savior's Eye. While Motu and Dreh transported my father's remains to the lab, Ascalon Lee asked me to stay with her to listen to the proceedings. When the conversation became heated, Ascalon Lee raised her hand. She stood that way, like a puppet hanging by its last string, for minutes, her eyes pointed at the ground as if she were gazing upon another time and place. It wasn't until people finally began to notice and quieted down that she put down her arm, snapped out of her trance, and told everyone it was maybe time for observation.

The artists, of all people, voiced a desire to form a militia. She looked at me and told them she had someone in mind suited for that type of work. She went on to say there's not a sadder, more pathetic sight in the world than creatives with guns in their hands, then she walked out of the crowd.

I don't trust her, but I find myself liking her. She's obviously smart. I've known that all my life. But she's also more patient and reflective than I expected her to be on a day-to-day basis. Because I spend time with her, and we have the same name, people have begun calling me "Taro" instead, which means "number one son" in Japanese. It's also the name of a root vegetable once farmed on these islands, and it was a deep part of the indigenous people's history. Ascalon Lee told me the story of two gods who'd birthed a stillborn child. When they buried the child's remains, taro sprouted from the grave. I think of my sister, and calling me "Taro" feels appropriate, no matter which way people pronounce it. I like the name. It feels like it's mine and not somebody else's.

But Ascalon Lee does not call me "Ascalon" or "Taro." Instead, it's always "my butterfly" or "child." In fact, she has the tendency to avoid calling people by their names. Maybe that's how gods talk, and she's trying to mimic one.

Yesterday, on our way to Deeptown and the old organ farm greenhouses left over from the old days of Water City, she was, once again, completely zoned out. Like a machine in sleep mode. It wasn't until we stopped walking in the lungs section of the chambered organs' aisles left behind by The Money, did she finally speak.

"I sometimes come down here," she said. "They're

beautiful aren't they?" She was referring to the rows and rows of farmed human lungs, shallowly breathing in and out. The spongy tissue expanded and contracted, and the branches of bronchioles were dimly lit with bioelectricity. She spoke about them as if they were exotic flowers.

"Any progress on my father?" I asked. I try to limit my asking of this question to once every two days. I'd been here over two weeks and my anxiety over my father's condition had been growing with each day.

"You're impatient," she said. "It's exhausting."

And just like that, she stopped walking and was tuned out again. I began to think back on how surprised I was that I'd figured out before Ascalon Lee that OneVoice rebuilt the scar, but after spending time with her, my surprise has waned. At times, she's clearly concentrating on something that's not present. I suspect she has too many copies of herself to control. Like my father, Ascalon Lee may be slipping, too.

She snapped back to the present, put her hand on one of the transparent lung containers, and closed her eyes. The lung began to breathe more quickly. Its currents of bioelectricity brightened. I slapped her hand off the chamber. "I'm tired of your hack magic tricks," I said. "And how do you eat with those stupid lizard teeth?" Sometimes, I find myself wanting to be hostile toward her because of our sordid history.

"What?" she said.

Insulting her usually gets her attention. "Well?"

"I only hunt and eat in lizard form," she said. "It's sublime."

She says stuff like this that occasionally stuns me.

She turned her attention to the lungs. "We should probably get rid of ones that aren't genetic matches of the residents here."

"You mean the ones that belong to the Gardeners."

"Yes. Have you thought about what I've said?"

"I don't care what Akira had in mind for me. My grand role in this. The truth is, my father never trained me to police like she wanted him to. He trained me to be a weapon. And you helped him make me one. Also, if I agree to police . . ."

Ascalon Lee nodded. "It will feel like he is gone, and you are replacing him."

"I'm waiting for you to fix him."

"Then what?"

"He can police your world, staying far away from Leacha-teans and Gardeners alike, while you and I figure out how to free people from your mother."

"Not this again. Just because that boy tore himself from OneVoice doesn't mean it can be done on a mass scale."

"Work on a way," I said.

"Practice policing, here, in Water City, and I'll consider it. However, let me explicitly state that I don't believe it's pos-sible. What I will tell you is that I'm working on a way to release Jon in an extremely controlled environment on one of the smaller, uninhabited islands. We need to see if his zealotry can even be diminished, or it's not even worth the trouble of 'freeing' my mother's people."

"I will think about policing then," I said.

Today, in the Promenade, a celebration the people call Raid Day is occurring. I have no idea what it is, but people all around me—hair whipped in meringues—trade, hug each other, and carol with slurred voices. I stop to watch a group protest the existence of Ascalon's Scar. Who they're protesting to, I have no idea. But they look scared and angry. My first thought is that maybe Ascalon Lee is right. This city needs at least some rules, especially now since its citizens are on edge about the scar. It's not just the protests. Some people have begun stockpiling water, food, weapons, hallucinogens, and multi-vitamins laced with hallucinogens.

Ascalon Lee wants me to create a bit of law and order, but just a bit. When I asked her how I should start, she began to zone out on me again. Which her was she concentrating on? The one on Venus perhaps, slowly burning up in thousand-degree atmosphere? The one in Jupiter, where Ascalon Lee suspects that Okaasan is building dark matter detectors? Maybe the bearded traveling surgeon in boots on the continent? Maybe the mega boar on the island that loves to chase kirin? Or maybe she's trying to reconnect to the spies she has on the other continents. How many of her are out there? I doubt she'd tell me. I again asked how I should start. She told me that it was up to me. She had no desire to micromanage anything.

The deal is this. I stay in Water City and create a security force, and in return she will attempt to revive my father, but she's doubtful of the results. She will also further study Jon and see whether he can be deprogrammed. When I mentioned I didn't think she'd put forth her best effort, she'd shrugged and told me that she couldn't force me to trust her.

My father once took a leap of faith and did everything in his power to save me. Ascalon kept her word back then. Shouldn't I at least take the same leap to save him as he did?

I contemplate the deal while I'm in a lift, heading to the surface. Once I get above water, I board a heli, and we take off. The heli drops me at a fissure on the south side of the island, where lava once flowed. Even when I was a child, this was all a natural reserve, and as far as I can tell, little has changed. I begin my hike through the dark pine and head west.

I explore the old lava tubes first. There are things hissing in the dark. I shine my light and catch a glimpse of something reptilian with eight heads retreating. I climb out of the tube. *Perhaps you should've armed yourself*, I imagine my father telling me. I ignore the warning and continue west, weaving through stalks of mutant cannabis as big as eucalyptus. They flower fuzzy, head-sized bulbs thirty feet above. I cross streams of florescent waters protected by giant lizards. I pass waterfalls that flow in reverse. As the terrain gets rockier and the climate more arid, it's plumes of giant coffee trees I cut through. Owls crested red and yellow pick the berries. They stuff their mouths then fly off. I mount one of the trees to try a berry for myself. I'm stunned to discover these aren't berries; they're human eyes. As I climb down, it occurs to me now that most people often thought of fantasy as an alternate past. What if it's a possible future? What if even God was never what came before us? What if he is what we know must exist in the future, so we help create him in the present?

I sit on a rock and take a swig from my cantina, trying to calm my mind. A butterfly lands on the tree before me and spreads its wings. It's one of the only old, purebred species I've seen on my hike so far. I wonder how its ancestors arrived here all those millions of years ago. I don't move. I wait for it to complete its rest first then go. Instead, it flutters to me and lands on my shoulder. A caterpillar's brain liquefies then regenerates as it becomes a butterfly. The butterfly glides off.

"My butterfly," I say.

I look down at the moldy rock that I'm sitting on and ponder how mold can learn something, crawl, and pass its memory to another mold. Then I'm shaken by a single thought. *I'm home.*

My thoughts are interrupted by a commotion in the distance. Screams. A roar. I slip into sports mode and fly through the brush. When I get to a clearing, I watch as a group of six in mantis armor surround the giant boar I saw the day I arrived. It's larger than any elephant I've ever heard of. The hunters wield long spears with heat-bladed tips. Their armor—bands of overlapping, lightweight segments that cover their arms, legs, heads, and torsos—glimmer cerulean in the patch of sunlight. I ping Ascalon Lee, wondering if she inhabits this creature being hunted. Nothing. I scan the beast and detect no signs of an iE.

The boar snorts and charges the largest hunter. It impales him with its tusk and tosses him through the tops of nearby trees, the hunter dropping his spear while mid-air. I sprint to grab it at the same time the boar's squeals boom. I can smell its dank, bristled fur. It spots my movement and charges. I scoop up the spear and turn my body, airborne. The pig is fifty-six yards away, closing in quickly. I sidearm the weapon at the boar's eye—0.1 second release time. Not bad. The animal falls with a thud. I slip out of sports mode and am about to step into the forest to find the injured, possibly dead man when one of the hunters yells, "Hey!"

I turn. It's Motu. He's taken off his antennaed mantis helmet and is jogging toward me. I don't sense murderous intention, so I wait. When Motu arrives, he says, "That was the most amazing throw I've ever seen."

"We should find your friend," I say.

Motu points up. A heli hovers above the trees. The wind produced from its quad propellers rattles the now garrulous leaves. Two white-clad healers repel down into the thicket. "They'll take care of him," Motu says.

"What is all this?" I ask.

"Are you LFG?"

"What's LFG?"

"Looking For Group," Motu says. "It's Raid Day!"

So this is Raid Day. A communal hunt of genetically engineered mythical creatures.

I eye the dead boar. Was it one of Ascalon Lee's iterations? "Was that . . . Her?" I ask.

Motu shakes his head. "No, but she made it. Once a month we're allowed to gather in groups and hunt them. Listen, next month, we might deep dive to go after Akkorokamui. No one has gotten it yet. You should come with us. It'd be a Water City first. How's your swimming skills?"

Akkorokamui. A giant, mythical octopus. I see now. Raid Day is how Ascalon Lee keeps the more adventurous citizens of the city amused. "I swim fine," I say.

Motu turns around and looks at the boar. The other four hunters strain to roll the pig on its back. One hunter climbs on its belly. He unsheathes a sword and splits the boar open. Steam, red, through my eyes, hisses out of the animal. The four begin field dressing the corpse.

"I can't believe you soloed it," Motu says. "It's like you got cheat code in your blood. The tusks are yours."

My father would have loved this. Perhaps I should love it, too, but are things bigger than this that I can't let go of. I'll stay as long as I can to help, but this is not a permanent residence, not home. Not for me. "I need to leave," I say.

Motu nods. "You should stay. She'll spawn another one eventually."

She should be working on my father and Jon instead of this nonsense. I want to confront her about our deal again. I imagine my father's voice in my head. *Be careful*, it says. How many times has he told me that? A thousand? No, 1,573 times. My weariness of Ascalon Lee has faded. I cannot forget that she is still possibly the most dangerous individual, or group of individuals, on the planet besides Akira.

When I was a child, I enjoyed the thrill of falling backward. One of my earliest, vague memories is falling from my converted crib, backward into my father's arms over and over and over again. Later still, being playfully chased by my father, who'd threatened to bite off my toes and make toe soup. I stood on the sofa, lost my balance, fell back, and hit my head on the floor. My father scooped me up. "That's why you need to be careful." His voice again.

But still, I fell, mostly on purpose. Backward into ocean— the ocean that my father warned I should never turn my back on. Even as a teen, backward off the saddle of my horse, and onto my feet. "Stop falling backwards," my father would say even now if he were here. But I know he liked it. He liked seeing me do it, especially in Kansas. For him it was confirmation that I was the same person I was as a child back in Water City. It indicated to him that I was the real me, because from toddler to teen, I always did the same thing.

For you, Father, and for the longshot of somehow freeing this world, I will fall backwards one more time, and you better wake up and catch me.

2

From the first day of being head of Water City security, the complaints flood in. Grudges, some of them years long, submitted to me. I ignore those, then the unsolicited suggestions come in waves: We should not be armed. We should be armed. There should be no jails, just exile. We should reactivate the deep-water prison, Vomit Island. Perhaps we should make the lazy work or exile them. The ones slumbering for years in their AMP chambers, holding out for better times, should be awoken. Job one should be taking out Ascalon's Scar. We should form a military force and prepare to wage war with the Gardeners and Leachateans. There should be no surveillance. *Are you watching us? Are you watching us right now?* We should not have the power to arrest and detain. There should be laws that limit the creatures that we create. Everyone should be on psychedelics. No one should be on psychedelics. We should all be forced to wear the same color foam fit to stop factionism. Security forces should adopt their own uniform color of official foam fits.

Most of the suggestions come with attachments of old

stories about how things went terribly wrong. *1984, A Clockwork Orange, Cloud Atlas, Red Rising, Mass Effect 12,* and *CoD 27: The VR Mega Platinum Edition* are the most cited. Oddly, no one attaches the story of the disaster that occurred just ten years ago. For these people, Satori Day wasn't a disaster. It lifted the yoke of wealth.

I have taken an office on the same island as old Sugar Spire, at the old Police HQ, and I feel like this first decision was already a mistake. The skyscraper, architecturally inspired by the scales of justice, is in disrepair. One bowl is overturned. The other dangles, askew. The penthouse of the scale, once umbrellaed by a pulsing, artificial jellyfish bell, has been stripped bare. But HQ is not as bad off as most of the skyscrapers. The space-saving ones with lean bases, modeled after budding flowers, have toppled. Their columns, once filled with active particle beams, have deflated due to lack of energy, so the rest of the structures crumbled. The older, steel-framed ones remain intact but are empty. The island, something between a Gardener stronghold and a Leachatean city, is half-rubble. Sugar Spire has been wiped from the face of the earth.

The police station itself has been ransacked. However, there are interview rooms, evidence rooms, lockers, and, of course, holding cells. The problem is that this HQ was built to employ a force of up to thirty thousand. My force, currently, is a force of three: Dreh, Motu, who was surprisingly adamant about joining, and me. I already know it's not a good look, but no one else has volunteered yet.

I also feel the vague presence of my father and mother here. This was once their place of employment and being here again, as I was on Satori Day with my mother, makes me sad. Despite the fact that I spent more than half my life in wide-open spaces, I felt like I was aboard a submarine with my parents the entire time, and now I feel cramped with the memory of them. But I wish my father were here. Contradicting feelings—human. Dreh, Motu, and I clear out one of the bigger offices—it had belonged to a Vice Superintendent on the eightieth floor—then we grab chairs and discuss what needs to be done first.

"I don't really know anyone here, but we need more people," I say.

"Your kill shot of the giant boar went viral," Dreh says. "You're kind of a celebrity now. More will join."

"My friends will join if we get rails," Motu says.

I turn to Dreh. "Are there any voluntary civil service organizations in the city?"

Dreh shrugs. "Besides voluntary teaching, service jobs don't really exist anymore," she says. "No one wants to do it."

"Why?" I ask.

"There is no tangible validation of time well spent," she says.

"What about doctors and nurses?" I ask.

Motu scoffs. "Some. But most of them are in North America. You've seen them, right? Traveling surgeons. There are more interesting patients to study there. We have the duds. And most of them pretend that they weren't doctors and nurses, you know, back in the old days, so no one will bother them. My neighbor was a doctor. He mostly just stays in his unit tripping balls and gaming. But it's fine. I mean, that's what med bots are for, right?"

"Why have you two volunteered?" I ask.

They look at each other, and I understand. They want to

continue to be in the good graces of Ascalon Lee. How has she managed to spend ten years simply not addressing any of this? Instead, she devoted her time to making islands float and genetically engineering mythical creatures. It doesn't take long for me to realize I just answered my own question. I haven't even gotten started yet, and I want to quit. What did I ask her? Who does the shit work? Apparently me.

"Do people get murdered here?" I ask.

Dreh shrugs. "Not that I know of." I shake my head. "Okay," I say. "This is what we're going to do. First, I'm going to repair and activate all the security drones that I can."

Motu shakes his head. "People won't like that."

"Not for here," I say. "We're sending them to the continents."

Motu laughs. "You want the three of us to police the entire world?"

"No," I say. "I just want to track what's going on, especially with A496 and the boreholes around the continent. My father was suspicious about the rise in Gardener activity, so I'd like to keep an eye on both. In fact, let's come up with a plan to make contact with the traveling surgeons, DJs, treasure hunters, and anyone else not Gardener or Leachatean. See if we can set up an intelligence network."

"I'll help you," Dreh says. She lifts her handheld device and scrolls. The bracelets on her wrist jangle. "I know a few treasure hunters."

I nod. "Next, we will only take complaints in cases of physical assault, murder, and kidnapping. Nothing else."

"Manslaughter?" Dreh asks.

I nod. "Manslaughter, too. We'll wait and see what is reported. If, in fact, anything is reported. Motu, you will be in charge of recruiting. Dreh, please make contact with those who move back and forth from North America."

"How do you expect me to get people to join this?" Motu asks, raising his arms while inspecting the empty office. "What're we giving them in return?"

I don't have an answer for him. "Well, let's see if anything is reported. If nothing is, we might not even be needed. If we do get legitimate reports of crime, and we enforce law, then maybe some will see what they get out of it."

For the next few weeks, things are quiet. I field several claims of theft and explain that we're not doing theft right now. I receive murmers of "useless" from those who pinged me with their handhelds. Motu has managed to convince a dozen or so to join up, and they spend their time scavenging for arms and arguing over what their uniforms should look like. Some think their helmets should be hawk-like, others wolf-like. Dreh has managed to track down a handful of traveling treasure hunters upon their return to the city. Two agree to report back if they see anything unusual. The others ignore the request and put Dreh on block. I revive a squad of police helis and fly them back to HQ. The first one I repair, I send out to the old Buhari estate. One of my worst memories that I don't remember happened there, but I loved that family, and I feel an obligation to care for the place if any of Akeem's descendants improbably break from OneVoice and are able to return one day.

The rest of the drones I repair are sent to the continents. Only the ones traveling to North America survive. The others fall to the ocean when they get within a few miles of landfall. I suspect OneVoice has covered the six other continents with electromagnetic pulse nets, which seems impossible.

Imagine it. A perpetual lightning storm that domes millions of square miles from atop the stratosphere. But I'm occupying an eightieth-floor office on a floating island, so I suppose anything is possible.

Other than that, I pester Ascalon Lee. Not just about my father's and Jon's status, but for data. I'm trying to build a census. I want to know everyone's name and all their vitals. Unsurprisingly, Ascalon Lee has all the information I need. I ask her for updates on what she sees going on outside of Water City. She tells me the same thing every time: if she sees something unusual, I'll be the first to know.

I'm having a difficult time focusing. I think about my father and am afraid that I'm thinking about him just to keep the possibility of his revival alive. My mind often drifts to the negative, like it usually does. How he always ingested or injected things that would shorten his life but keep him momentarily stronger while he was alive. I also cling to child-hood memories, the ones not in code. The deep dives. The piratespeak. The summer he taught me to read. The time I accidentally shot him with a speargun, and he didn't get mad. The time we were fishing, and our lines got twisted. He showed me the best way to untangle a knot. He grinned at me and cut it with his knife.

I think about OneVoice, too. About what it is truly attempting to accomplish. According to my security drones, the Gardeners in their strongholds appear to be acting as they have since I left. They continue to dig their holes, to gather at Corpus Akira. They board rockets that levitate fifty miles up, that race down a track that spans the Gulf of Mexico, that launch them into space. Last week at her lab, I pestered Ascalon Lee about this too, but she claimed to have no idea why there has been a spike in A496 activity, and she didn't really seem all that interested. Instead of answering my questions, she urged me to look into her microscope.

"What is it?" I asked.

"A winged horse still in alpha phase," she said. "A *chollima*, to give the islands a Korean flavor."

This made me mad. "Horses don't want to fucking fly," I said, "The *chollima* is the same damn thing as the Chinese *qianlima* and the fucking Greek Pegasus. So no, I don't want to see the embryo of a flying fucking horse. I want to see the old creature called my father."

"Look in the mirror," she said before storming out of her lab. Then she put me on block for a couple of days.

I sometimes find myself gazing at the scar. A fixture of my young childhood. I picture a recently discovered two-hundred-foot octopus that people have spotted, engineered by Ascalon Lee no doubt, and wonder how much melanin the thing can release in an instant. When I sleep, I dream of a dense cloud of ink that spreads across the ocean and the sky as well. And yet, the scar remains. I wake up each time thinking, feeling, something isn't right.

The last of my security drones have finally arrived at my old home in Kansas. It's decimated, which is not surprising. The toppled wind farm turbines lay across the caved-in roof and stone walls of our old house. The tripwires that Army Strong set off in the junkyard have blown all the half-buried lifts and dozers to bits. The medical bunker is now a crater. I check on my mother and sister's graves. Both have been exhumed. I feel anger. What the hell would Shave Time want with their bones? I search for the remains of Leachateans, but only find a singed, rotting hand and several headless torsos, chest down. I can see their spines because the heat of the explosives peeled the skin and muscle off their backs. My horses are gone. I purposely set the charges to be out of the range of their corral. I imagine they got spooked when the Leachateans arrived. I hope they're okay.

I send the drones into the crumbling house and check my father's room for the safe that contained my mother's iE. It's not there, but nothing else is in there either. For all I know, a blast sent the room's entire contents all the way to the thicket of cottonwoods in the distance. I see no sign of Shave Time, and it appears all of our buried munitions have been destroyed, so I dispatch the drones farther east, to From A to Z.

There, Shave Time's city sleeps. The bonfires aren't lit. The gardens, decorated with rims skewered with stools and painted to look like flowers, are unattended. I'm surprised. Summer has not completely ended, yet the Leachateans appear to have retreated to their tunnels and caverns. Why? Perhaps Shave Time didn't make it back? Or maybe the scar has spooked them enough to go underground early? Even the rigs have stopped their spreading of radioactive soil. I'm almost scared to, but I redirect the drones to check the Woodmen. There, a squad of Army Strong leads what remains of the sick and tortured Gardeners out to the roof. They force the Gardeners to their knees and stand behind them, then grab their heads and impel them to look up at the scar with their eyeless faces. Not long after, each squad member pulls out a pistol and shoots a Gardener in the back of the head.

I feel my toes and jaw clench. I leave a few drones to watch the city and send the rest to survey other Leachatean strongholds and see if their fueling plants are still operational.

Furious, I stand to leave my office, about to tell Ascalon Lee I'm going to quit and investigate the continent, when I get a voice call. I answer. A woman has found her husband dead at a shuttle landing pad near Volcano Vista. Her name is Levana Cregut. Her husband, Bell Mazzotti. She sends me a pic from her handheld. Bell is on his stomach, naked, arms tucked, and face smushed against the lighted, neon blue panel that guides pilots back home in the dark. His neck is twisted beyond breaking point, and someone has stripped him of his foam fit and smart boots. I tell Levana Cregut that I'll be right over and keep her on the line. While I jump in a police heli and start my puddle jump to the Vista, Levana repeatedly asks me to please hurry. Maybe he can still be saved. I tell her that I will try my best. The truth is Bell Mazzotti is a dead man. The way his neck was twisted, there's no coming back from that. I wonder why it's so easy for me to pronounce this stranger dead, yet I cling to hope that my father can be somehow resurrected.

After I get off the line with Levana, I ping Dreh. She picks up.

"Do people in Water City steal each other's foam fits?" I ask.

"No," she says. "If anything, there's a surplus. Designers in love with their work tend to send their prototypes too quickly to AI assembly lines out on the Pacific Bridge."

"Okay, thanks," I say.

"No problem," Dreh says and hangs up.

I refocus. My old house has been obliterated. I just watched Gardener prisoners being executed. And now I'm possibly flying to my first murder scene. I land, throw on an old police parka, and meet Levana Cregut for the first time. She's a large woman, taller than me, but she looks small huddled above her husband's body, trying to keep the whipping rain off him. I bend down and put my hand on her shoulder, which I find harder to do than it should be. I suggest we take him into the heli. Suddenly, I'm the old woman from The Leachate, attempting to comfort someone's loss, but unlike sadness or pain, loss can't be comforted. Loss in an invisible hole that can't be filled because no one can find it. Levana nods and stands as I pick up her husband's body, and we head to the heli. I try to ignore the perfumed greens that rise from Bell Mazzotti.

After loading the heli, I step to Levana. "What does your husband do?" I ask.

"Well, he doesn't really have a job," she says.

"How does he spend his time?" I'm keenly aware that we're speaking of him in the present tense, as if there's hope and he's still alive.

She eyes me sheepishly. "He supes up his shuttle and attempts to break speed records."

"Where's his shuttle?"

She turns around and shrugs. "I didn't even notice it's not here," she says. "It was here earlier. He was working on it. Even rain did not deter him. There are bad weather records to break, too."

"What about his handheld device?" I ask.

"It was gone when I found him." Her eyes are locked on the heli containing her husband. It's as if she expects him to wake up any time now. I watch the tendrils of green slip from the heli and drift to the landing pad lift. Motu pings me via text and asks excitedly if someone was finally murdered. I put him on block.

The truth is, I don't know what to do right now. I don't know how to tell this woman that her husband is dead, and that, yes, it appears he's been murdered. I want her to go home and wait, but how do you tell someone to do something like that under these circumstances? My father would know.

"Do you have children?" I ask Levana.

She nods. "Two."

"How old?"

"Four and sixteen."

"One born before Satori Day and one after," I say.

She looks at me strangely. "No—"

"It's okay," I interrupt her. I'm feeling very uncomfortable having this conversation I started and never wanted to have. "I suppose that's irrelevant."

She pauses before speaking again. "My first husband. He . . ."

I nod. She doesn't need to elaborate. "I'm glad she didn't take your older child."

"The older, she's a musical genius," Levana says. "Incredibly smart. So much smarter than me."

Did Akira Kimura spare this woman just so that this genius child would have a caretaker? "And the younger?" I ask.

"She's, well . . . She's four. She's too young to tell what she is."

"Please," I say. "Please go home and be with your children."

"What do I tell them?"

I look down at the ground. Raindrops create a tempo of perfect, temporary circles on the pooling water's surface that I see in red. "Tell them I will find who did this."

Levana begins to weep. "I'm sorry," she says.

I bite my lower lip to keep it from quivering. How did my father do this work for decades? Why did he spend a lifetime digging under society's dirty fingernails? Following these trails of green that connect gruesome effects to their base human causes. I don't know how to end this conversation well, so I just end it by walking away, feeling terrible for doing so. I don't need to follow the trail. I believe I already know who did this thing. A person who needed clothes. A person who needed transportation. Ascalon's Scar is not the only thing that Akira's last patch reawakened.

Jon6J.

3

I've been trying to ping Ascalon Lee, but she isn't answering. I'm on my way to the lab, hoping she's okay. I'm wondering whether she finally woke Jon6J on one of the remote, uninhabited islands to study him, and he went berserk. When I get down to the lab, the first thing I see is that Ascalon's two komainu have been torn apart. What's even more shocking is that the tanks containing my father and Akira Kimura have been shattered, and their beheaded bodies are sprawled on the floor. I ping Ascalon Lee again and leave a message that it's an emergency. She pings right back and says she's on her way. I'm relieved. *Just meat*, I imagine my father saying.

I squat in front of my father's body and fail utterly at seeing just meat. It's mutilation. Desecration. I feel a vibration in my hands as if my nerves are being plucked by someone other than me. Then a rage grows even hotter when I realize: My father's head is gone, so his chip is gone, too.

Jon6J. He must've have had an Akira-designed iE hibernating in his skull that was activated by OneVoice with the last patch. How could Ascalon Lee have missed this? She'd scanned him and claimed to have studied him, but had she really been paying attention? How much time does she actually spend down here? Or in the present? In Water City in general?

I replay images of my first trip down here. Then I look around the rotunda to see if anything else is missing. Just one other thing: a flower. I step to the flower bed and inspect the breakpoint of the stem. Creamy sap is dried at the tip. It seeps a tiny stream of almost imperceptible green mist. Did OneVoice know that I would bring Jon here? If so, how? Did it know that Ascalon Lee would place the boy in stasis in Akira Kimura's old lab?

When Ascalon Lee finally arrives, she looks as surprised as I am. She doesn't say a word. Instead, she projects security footage on the surface of the old billiards table and flips through POVs until she gets the one monitoring Jon. She rewinds and stops. At first, Jon simply floats in the tube. Then his lips begin to part, and his mouth opens fully. An eye rolls off his tongue, floats up, and burrows itself in one of his eye sockets. Another eye hatches from his mouth and enters the other socket. The once-drooping eyelids of Jon begin to tighten, then his eyes snap open. Bubbles stream from his snarling lips. He touches the glass with his index finger and the entire chamber shatters.

Without looking at it, Ascalon Lee wraps her hand around the cue ball on the table. "Interesting."

"How?" I ask.

"Let's see," she says. She projects another holo, this one of Jon's anatomy. Fast forward. Jon has a small womb, and both eyes have been gestating in it over the last weeks.

"How?" I ask again.

"Programmed and directed bioelectricity." Ascalon Lee slams the cue ball on the table. "Contingency protocols. Maybe he's a prototype of some sort. I missed it."

"Missed what?"

Ascalon Lee sighs. "The fact that he had a womb in the first place. I didn't think to check."

"Could more of them be . . . backed up like this?"

Ascalon Lee shrugs. "I don't think so. I believe Jon is the first of his kind."

We turn back to the security holo and watch as a naked Jon steps out of the chamber and heads to the desk. He opens a drawer and grabs a heat blade. He closes the drawer then steps to my father's chamber first. Again, a single index finger on the glass tube and the entire apparatus shatters.

"How?" I ask.

"High-frequency vibration from his fingertip perhaps."

I turn away from the holo when Jon grips a fistful of my father's hair and moves the now heated blade to his throat. I wait a minute, and I look back at the holo too soon. Jon, hands now trembling, tears streaming from his eyes, begins to surgically cut the skin around Akira's neck. *How can he stomach decapitating his god?* The answer is obvious. She told him to. After he's done, he twists her head off, then places it on the floor before bowing before it.

Once he's done praying, he gathers both heads by their hair. He looks as if he's about to exit, but he stops at the flower bed, puts down the heads, and plucks a flower. He eats one of the pedals, eyes closed as if he's savoring the taste. He opens his eyes—the eyes he birthed, which are now glowing neon blue—and they crackle. With the heads back in his grasp, he steps to the spiral staircase and walks upstairs.

When Jon gets to the door, the two komainu awaken. Jon drops the flower and the heads. A komainu leaps for him while he buries his fist into the skull of the other komainu. He spins and grabs the remaining komainu by the tail, then slams it to the ground. Dazed, the guardian dog tries to wobble out of his grasp. Jon raises a foot and stomps on its neck. The sound of snapping bones jars me. He yanks the tail and rips the komainu in half.

"Incredible," Ascalon Lee gasps.

"Can you do that?"

She shakes her head.

"Can I?"

She shrugs.

Jon drops the tail and picks up the flower. He closes his eyes and sticks the flower into his mouth, stripping it of its orange anthers. White sap drools from the corner of his lips. His eyes, now open, crackle in even brighter pulses of blue light. He drops the flower, grabs the heads, and dives into the water. And just like that, he's gone.

"It's too deep," I find myself gasping out loud. "The atmospheric pressure. He can't swim to the surface from here."

Ascalon Lee cuts the holo and steps to the flower bed. She's frowning as she gently rubs a flower petal with her thumb and index. "How did I not see?" she asks herself.

"See what?" I ask. But I know the answer. Akira was always the master magician. Ever since The Killing Rock, her best tricks have always been displayed right in the open.

"Any of this," Ascalon Lee says. "These things my mother hid right in front of my face."

I snap a flower from its stem and point it at her. "Because you're fucking too busy inhabiting too many people. You're doing—I don't know—fifty, a hundred different things at once."

The putrid scent of murder fills my nose, effectively ending the conversation. I begin to head upstairs. Ascalon Lee follows.

"She is not a god," I say, finding that I'm really trying to convince myself. I turn to Ascalon Lee. "You didn't make the islands float, did you?"

"What are you talking about?"

Akira. My father. Ascalon Lee. Liar. All liars. I continue to climb.

"I left after Satori Day," Ascalon Lee says from behind me. "I took Sooni and the children with me. I didn't know why at the time. I suppose to somehow make amends with your father. To make amends with the world for letting it happen. We flew to NZ to re-evaluate my mother's . . . factory. To perhaps find Idris Eshana, which I didn't. Once we freed him from the factory on Satori Day, he left and was never seen again. She was sending shuttles up to clear orbiting debris by the time I got there. I didn't quite know what to do with myself. She was gone, yet everywhere."

I nod and head for the door. "Hunting the helpless isn't even hunting. It's scavenging."

"Yes," Ascalon Lee says. "*Yes*. I was so certain that if we simply removed her iE and destroyed it, we would disconnect her from her Gardeners. When that didn't work, I wanted to hunt them down and kill them all. But yes. Scavenging."

I step through the door and stop at the remains of the guardian dogs. I crouch and stick a finger in a pool of drying blood. It's thick like cement. The blood on my fingertip hardens and converts to stone. I rub my thumb on it, and the stone disintegrates into dust. "You live here and bury your head in the sand. Are you trying to get me to do the same thing?"

Ascalon Lee puts a hand on my shoulder. "When I returned here, millions of Gardeners—most from Asia—infested the islands. The largest construction army in the history of civilization. It was the most humbling thing I've ever seen. They waited for instructions. They showed me blueprints. They said they must make the islands float for Okaasan."

I stand and whirl to face Ascalon Lee. "So you told them how while Gardeners in North and Central America built A496."

"Yes," she says. "Others she migrated from Europe and Africa helped with A496, too. As soon as The Gardeners here were done, they left to complete her launch loop. Once they got to North America, the electromagnetic pulse nets dropped behind them like impenetrable curtains."

I inspect the flower I picked and am left wondering if there's anything more human than taking credit for something you haven't done. Ascalon Lee. Shave Time. It reminds me of Akira claiming that she saved the world years before I was born.

"Why?" I ask. "Why would she do this? Why the hell is she digging all the holes on the continents? What is she looking for in space?"

Ascalon sighs. "My butterfly, you have accessed and retained more than a lifetime of knowledge because of me. Isn't that wonderful?"

"No." I smell the flower. It smells like murder. "It's awful."

"Use that knowledge and help us build something here. Just keep OneVoice stable, and let the Gardeners be."

"You don't understand," I say.

"Your father? I can recreate his voice and download it into you. It will be as real as I can make it. Isn't that ideal? To have him present but be able to turn him off whenever you want?"

I'm ashamed to admit that I wasn't even thinking about my father. "That's not what I meant," I say. "The scar. Jon6J. Don't you see? She's scared."

Ascalon Lee laughs. "Of what?"

"I don't know, but I want to find out." I walk toward the end of the wooden dock. The egg-shaped sub bobs on the water's surface. I stop and turn around before reaching the edge.

"And if you antagonize her?" Ascalon Lee asks. "If she can make one of those . . . things. She can make an army of them. She may already have."

"My father told me that it was your lifelong dream to finally beat her," I say.

"I could've," she sneers. "I've found that for me, the knowledge that I could've beaten her is enough."

She held her mother prisoner all those years ago. Before Idris Eshana turned on OneVoice. She could've stopped it. My father could've, too, by simply not participating. He never could understand that he always had the option of closing his eyes, ignoring the greens and reds, and maybe I can't either. Maybe doing nothing is sometimes the best course of action, or they never could succeed because Akira Kimura knew them better than they knew themselves. Either way, they both failed.

She doesn't know me.

"I'm telling you," I say. "Abandoning my father. Re-activating Jon. Repainting the sky. She's literally head-hunting for fuck's sake. She's acting scared. I want to find out what she's afraid of."

"You don't understand. You don't think I've run every simulation? This is the world."

"What do you mean?"

"Earth. Akira Kimura. They are one. It's not a connection that can be severed. *This is the world.*"

It's unlike her to utter repetition. Fear? Maybe, for the first time in her life, unlike me, she has something real to lose. These people of Water City who look up to her and her genetic inventions. "Maybe," I say. "Maybe this is the world. But I want my property back."

"So property laws exist then?" Ascalon Lee asks.

"They do today."

"My butterfly, this is where the slippery slope begins. You know the history. You know what happened when your father went chasing things, what happened when I did, too."

I take a step back toward the edge of the dock. The wood creaks beneath my feet. I have heard the history. Ascalon Lee rising from the ocean and possessing me. My father racing to Lucky Cat City, to the moon and back, trying to save me. Akira moved them like chess pieces. My father, Idris Eshana, Ascalon Lee. "Yeah," I say. "Both of you nearly got me killed. Neither of you could beat Kimura, not there at the end. I don't think I can. I'm just going to find Jon and get back what's mine."

"You against the world," Ascalon Lee says. "Don't you realize what you have? The gifts that have been bestowed on you?"

I acknowledge to myself that I've been given a lot and that I'm utterly ungrateful. I acknowledge fully, for the first time in my life, that I am totally and truly human. Why? Because right now I don't give a fuck. I'm fucking uncorked. I side-eye the grotto. The dark, thick water is so flat that it looks like glass.

"Wait," Ascalon Lee says. "There's a lot you don't know. I told your father you should know, but . . ."

I don't want to hear it. More lies, probably. I take the police parka off and toss it to Ascalon Lee. I bite a petal from the flower that I'm holding and rip it from the flower's stem. Velvety polyps cling to my tongue and melt. They're taste-less, but the bioelectrical rush is indescribable. My brain is processing at a rate I've never experienced before. I feel my eyes flutter and can barely manage to make them stop.

"What do the numbers 6, as in Jon6J, and 496, as in A496, have in common?" I snarl.

"They're both perfect numbers," Ascalon Lee smugly says. "Of course I noticed that immediately."

"'A' refers to 'Ame-no-ukihashi.' Floating Bridge of Heaven. What of 'J' in Jon6J?"

"I don't—"

"*Jieitai*," I say. "She's building an army. A perfect one."

Ascalon Lee steps toward me, her black arm reaching for mine. "Wait!" she says.

I splash into the water before she can grab me. The flat glass surface is shattered in an instant. Once I'm completely submerged in the brine, I light the water with my eye, kick as hard as I can, and glide through the stalagmite. The cold, the depth, the pressure, they should all kill me, but they're not. I go pedal to the metal on sports mode and dart through Akira's underwater maze with ease. I stop and look behind me. Ascalon Lee isn't following.

I've been on many dives during my childhood, but this is the thickest, saltiest water I've swum in. But it doesn't matter. I kick through it and feel like something more than human. I feel like a demigod sparked by the divine.

4

I don't know what the flower did to make me able to survive the ascent, but it did. It did other things, too. I saw the continents in blurred flashes, viewed from the mesosphere. Each one, except North America, covered in dimly blue lattice that resembled a bird cage. Thirty miles above sea level, each continent was covered and collared.

My view narrowed, and I saw more rockets launched from fifty miles above the Cape to outer space. On the West African coast, the topography was enveloped with laboratories filled with anti-contam suited Gardeners studying and cataloging recently discovered microbes. In Lucky Cat City, shuttles returned with hauls of fish and space trash. In Moscow, AMP chambers hissed open, giant roaches skittering from them and burying themselves in snow. *It's not winter yet*, I thought to myself. Then I realized this feeble frequency didn't deliver images of just the present. What I was probably seeing was the flickering of OneVoice over the last ten years in no discernible order, like a random scattering of keys and locks.

In the Amazon, Gardeners repelled into boreholes—like

the ones outside Mile High—and disappeared in the darkness beneath the rainforests. A school of shuttles landed on the Pacific Bridge, and Gardeners unloaded crates of algae steak and bricks of forever rechargeable, universal e-cells. People— free I assume because they wore foam fits like the people of Water City—combed the rocky shoreline and shucked life off ocean-soaked volcanic rock and devoured it. They stopped to watch a shuttle land. Jon6J emerged from it. The eyes of the Gardeners who were unloading the crates crackled blue. It was the younger ones, mostly, none of the elderly. They marched to Jon6J, past the neon WELCOME TO D-52 holo sign, and entered his shuttle. Then my vision shifted to the point-of-view of Jon6J. He turned his head. The people shucking black limpets off the rocks, afraid of this new breed of Gardener, hauled ass to their skimmer boats and barreled through the blown-out breaks, probably heading back to Water City.

When I finally broke the surface of the water, the flashes stopped. It's possible the messages could only be pinged via underwater current. I signaled my SEAL to come pick me up at the Vista heliport. While I waited, I watched teenagers dare each other to jump from higher and higher decks into the ocean. Others were on dawn patrol, riding forty-foot white rhinos generated by the Water City wave machines. I briefly imagined cannonballs and big wave surfing with other people my age being my life. That came to an end when I picked up trails of green floating east. I didn't know where Jon6J was headed, where he was taking the heads, but in that last flash he was silently recruiting what I could only imagine were soldiers. As my father had always told me, "Where soldiers go, murder follows."

I checked my drones in From A to Z. All was still quiet,

except for the buzz of powerlines and the kind of wind that rattles loose stuff. The drones in Mile High showed dredging and shuttle maintenance. Business as usual. In Corpus Akira the enormous dragon head power station hummed with mass energy, and it almost felt like the dragon's eyes would begin to glow neon blue and the entire structure would take flight. The lifts at its base were loaded with crates packed with cybernetic eyes. More bodiless Gardeners were loaded on the fast track into space.

When my SEAL came, I jumped aboard and jetted east. One stop over to the same place that Jon6J landed, D-52. I planned to refuel there then make the jump to Mile High, refuel again, and just follow the greens, my guess to some Leachatean stronghold where Shave Time was hiding out. They didn't head back in this direction, so Shave Time and his people must be their target. I was losing time, but I wanted to come in fully armed. I'd seen what Jon6J was capable of. I figured Shave Time didn't stand a chance. And if Jon turned on me, maybe I wouldn't stand much of a chance either. I found myself thinking like I imagined my father thought: taking the shot from long distance. Shooting rail from far away was the one thing I could never do better than him.

I hop out of my SEAL and step onto the flat, crescent-shaped islet. The landing pads are on the east and west tips. The small water tower is in the middle. I hurriedly hack open a crate near the pad and find universal bricks of e-cell. I feel the eyes of aged, bald Gardeners on me—the ones that didn't go with Jon. I quickly pack as much fuel as I can, then head into town to scavenge some food and water. The old rec sex places are shut down, but the desalination tower is still in working order. I manage to find some tanks in an old

Mongolian-Tex-Mex dive. They're buried under a dusty pile of Stetsons and fur-lined *shovgors*.

The old clock tower strikes noon. I step out of the dive and see all the elderly Gardeners on their knees bowing to Ascalon's Scar. After the clock tower ceases to chime, the Gardeners stand and go back to loading crates of e-cells and algae steaks. Now that I'm all tooled up, I rush to lift off and look down before jetting away. The Pacific Bridge. I need to catch up to Jon.

I double-check to make sure my SEAL batteries and rail batteries are fully charged. They are. I check drone footage of Mile High, Corpus Akira, and From A to Z again. Again, nothing highly unusual. Gardeners work on shuttles while random Leachateans, carrying baskets made from plastic water jugs, slowly trudge to and from the deep catacombs beneath the city's surface. I forgot. It's near the end of derby season. There might be one more big race at Ameritrade Park before tortoise and mussel season is over. They're harvesting and storing food for their underground winter. The rigs carrying waste across the country are still conspicuously stalled outside the city.

I head to Mile High at top speed and chew on algae steak. Dreh pings me via voice call. I pick up.

"Ascalon Lee wants you to come back," she says.

"I'll be back once I retrieve my father."

"I have a secret," Dreh says.

"What?"

"I like you."

"I like you, too," I say.

"I have another secret," she says. "This one is from Ascalon Lee."

I disconnect. Motu voice calls next. I answer.

"I have thirty recruits, and they want you to bring back thirty rails for them. We need to raid the giant octopus, Akkorokamui next month."

I tell him I'll see what I can do and kill the line.

Ascalon Lee knows everything about me. She could've easily cast these "friends." Or maybe she was trying to tell me something by having Dreh and Motu around me all the time ever since I set foot in Water City. She's probably trying to tell me something now, but I got her blocked.

Perhaps I'm being paranoid about Ascalon Lee's motives when it comes to me. She's not telling me something. She's trying to cage me in Water City, but I can't figure out why. I don't like being paranoid. It stinks of self-importance and my father, and I'm tired of it. I like that the ocean and clouds below make me feel small. That the turbulence jostling me makes me feel weak. This is a terrible altitude to fly at, but I'm in a SEAL, not a shuttle. There's no scraping the mesosphere in this thing. As for Jon6J, despite what I saw, I want to fight him. Fighting. It's all my father and I did out there in the cut, isn't it? We fought ancient sketch pencils, snapping at each other's until one would break. We food fought, mussels mostly, banging them together to see whose would crack first. We'd catch mutant betas that lived in the streams and fought those, too. I feel the grin that I inherited from my father form on my face. Not a grin really, a reflex. The baring of teeth. I want to fight Jon6J. I hope he's alone. I want to see if I can win.

5

When I arrive at Mile High, I'm severely disappointed. The city looks abandoned, and the greens are everywhere. In the midst of the windswept murder haze, the digging has stopped and the excavators are gone. Only the fleets of jumbo shuttles remain. At first, I think that maybe Shave Time managed to swipe at least a few weapons of mass destruction from our home and came and wiped out the entire city. Then a battalion of blue-eyed Gardeners emerge from a hangar bay and begin to line in formation upon the smooth, white apron. They stand at attention on the landing pad below me. They all look up at the SEAL in unison. An army this quickly. How? I'm about to hightail it out of there when I get a ping from an unrecognized sender. I answer. It's Jon6J.

"Synesthete," he says.

"Give me my father's head back."

"Synesthete, please land."

"Will you give it back to me?"

"We are awaiting your orders."

I hover in place, some two hundred feet above them,

not quite sure if I'm high enough to be out of their reach. They appear unarmed, wearing their standard foam fits and nothing else, but I aim the ship's rails down at them. It's not ideal hovering weather. The powerful crosswinds come in unpredictable waves, and I need to constantly adjust the horizontal stabilizers to maintain altitude over the tarmac. I feel heat pulse from my eye. I look to the horizon, at the boreholes outside the city, and the rims pulse in greens. I feel a surge of adrenalin so strong that it makes me feel sick. I immediately understand. How could I or my father not seen it before?

"Disperse your troops," I say, fighting to keep my voice steady. "Just you and me."

"Very well."

The Gardeners form a line and head to the nearest hangar bay. I wait until they're all inside and the door slides shut with a thud to land the SEAL. I grab the super-rail and leap out of the cockpit. Flipping into sports mode, it's as if I turned off the swirling, high-altitude gusts. The wind breaks on me. I point the rail at Jon.

"Return my property," I say.

"It is not your property, synesthete."

"He's my father. Give me back the remains that you took."

"He was made by OneVoice."

It's true. Akira made all the iterations of my father. She's the one who turned him into a technological revenant.

"You don't need me," I say.

"Yes, we do," Jon says. "It is your purpose to lead us."

I look back at him. "Why now?"

"Your father was given every opportunity. We were patient with him. He is gone now, and you are of proper age."

"I'm only nineteen!"

"You are not nineteen."

"What?"

"You are not nineteen."

I've had enough of this. I put down the rail. Killing him won't get me back what I came for, and he knows it. Doesn't mean I can't squeeze it out of him. I prepare to attack. He adjusts to a boxing stance. I leap and try to come down on his knee with my right foot. He spins away and doesn't see me whip a spinning backfist at him. My left fist smashes the side of his face, causing him to briefly stumble before catching his balance. He's fast, but not fast enough. I attack again, this time with a super punch. My father would say that I'm fighting too aggressively, but I don't care. He's gone for now, and I'm here to get him back. I'll do it my way. Jon dodges my strike and throws one of his own. But I see it coming. In sports mode, I see all the moves coming.

I catch his arm and trap it. I bend his elbow around my forearm, grab my own wrist, and lift his elbow. He hunches over. Then I apply pressure.

"You're not nineteen!" he screams.

I snap his arm and push him to the ground. I step to the rail and pick it up. That's when the surrounding shuttles rumble and come alive, and it's me breathing life into them. A hundred jumbo shuttles lift, their engines spinning with a deafening whine. Slowly, I organize them into formation, and they hover above us. I retract the landing gear of each one. They're all pointing in the direction of the hanger bay. How many Gardeners stuffed in there? A thousand, maybe. The entire landing pad and hangar bay smolder in greens. I feel something grab my leg. It's Jon.

"He lied to you!" Jon screams. "All this time, your father, and her, they lied to you!"

I raise the rail and am about to bring it down on his spine, just like I'm about to send the shuttles crashing into the hangar to kill every single one of the Gardeners packed inside. At this point, I don't care whose greens these are. Mine or his or theirs.

"The story! Urashima Taro!" Jon yells over the whining of the shuttle engines.

I pause. "What?" He's referring to an ancient Japanese folktale about a man who rescued a turtle and was rewarded with a box that contained his age. After a hundred ageless years, he eventually opened the box and instantly became an old man.

"Open the box," Jon says.

The shuttles rattle above us. I'm losing my concentration. "What are you talking about?"

He pulls on my leg even harder. "Each time you went into AMP, who inputted the settings? Who went into hibernation first?"

My father always inputted the settings. I always went into hibernation first. But we never slept for more than an evening. I drop the rail and pull Jon up by the back of the neck. I grab his face with both hands. Still in sports mode, I almost crush his cheekbones. I feel my iE glowing. I bring his face to mine. But he's not looking at me. His eyes are on the teetering shuttles that hang above us. The apron around us is draped in their shadows.

"I thought you would be tougher to beat," I say. "Now give me what I came for."

He grabs my wrists and squeezes. His strength is suddenly incredible. "I do not wish to hurt you," he says.

"I want you to try," I say.

He rips my hands off his face. I could melt him down with my eye right now. Hurl the shuttles into the hanger bay, but I remember Epcot. I don't want to be like my father. "You're not nineteen," he says.

"Stop saying that!" I throw a spinning heel kick, but he blocks it with his functional arm. I charge with a flying knee. He moves into me, and we fall tangled on the ground. I got top position. I feel my eye flare, and a blaze of concentrated energy fires from it. The energy beam hits the crook of Jon's elbow and incinerates his arm from the elbow down. He screams in agony. I feel my eye charging again while his cauterized stump smolders. My eye is now aimed at one of Jon's crackling azure eyes. He puts his remaining hand up.

"Your father forced you into hibernation." He gasps. "Each time you slept, you slept far longer than you think you did."

"That's impossible," I say. "I can tell time. I would've noticed changes around me."

"Changes?" Jon asks. "There has been nothing but change around you. Have you not noticed?"

For some reason, it's the image of the floating islands of Water City that first pop into my head. Then the image of Akira's launch loop stretched across the Gulf of Mexico. Two of the most incredible megastructures ever made. Then there's the scope of these excavations outside Mile High, and the rise of a wild, yet somewhat orderly society in The Great Leachate. The spread of all that contaminated soil. *Ten years.* I check the clock in my iE. It has been ten years since Satori Day. It's confirmed. I look down at Jon.

"I have an atomic clock in my head," I say. "I know how old I am."

"Clocks can be reset. They can be rolled backwards and forward. They can be tampered with."

"Give me what I came for," I pant.

A shuttle collapses out of the sky and cracks the round landing pad to the left. Another shuttle careens and explodes into a nearby mountain.

A Thought Talk ping accompanied by an attached message. From Jon. The same Jon that I've got straddled now.

Do as Urashima Taro did, he says without moving his lips, his thoughts coming through my iE in voice. *Open the box.*

"I'm not going to let you infect me with . . . Her," I say out loud.

I can't infect you, he says, lips still not moving.

Another shuttle drifts toward the boreholes. I'm slowly losing control. "You're already doing it," I say, my voice cracking.

Open the attachment. Please.

I remember the legend of Urashima Taro and why everyone in Water City began calling me Taro. Maybe I was mistaken. Perhaps they didn't call me Taro because I was like a first son of Ascalon Lee's, or because I sprouted from the grave of a dead child. Maybe they called me Taro because I was a fool who didn't know how old I really was. The shuttles above us splinter into each cardinal direction. I open Jon's attachment.

I expect to see time-stamped pics and vids that I could never trust. Maybe of the Gardeners breaking their backs to make islands float. Maybe spy footage of Shave Time gradually digging around From A to Z, making it appear higher and higher. Maybe more personal spy vids. My father putting me in AMP then getting in his chamber right after. Then fast forward. Digital numbers indicating days, months, and maybe even years increasing in value. Maybe he gets out of

AMP before I do. Maybe he goes outside and fixes the place up so that it looks like it did when we went to sleep. But it's Akira Kimura we're talking about, so all that could easily be doctored.

Jon knows I might not believe it. So what he sends me is code. Code that details every patch that went live since Satori Day. Information that OneVoice never volunteered before. Code for A496, its blueprint, and its construction schedule. Code for the EMP netting that covers most of the continents. Code for every flight manifest through the solar system, rocket schematics, distances, and return trips. And the things that she built up there. Code for the engineering of Jon6J, and the cybernetic eyes that spouted in his womb. He's the only one of his kind. For now. Again, schematics. Again, plausible. I gasp. The most jarring piece of data is the Gardener population: 106,872,083. The human population hasn't been that low since the Iron Age. During the times of the Babylonians and the Zhou Dynasty.

"What happened to all the people?" I ask, shocked. Trembling. Blood rushes to my head, desperate to find scope and understanding.

"There have not been births in decades," Jon says. "And many have expired. Okaasan still seeks the perfect number of Gardeners. That figure does not account for the intrepid wayfinders that will journey through the galaxy."

"What about those deemed worthy?" I ask. "You said they get new HuSCs!" I don't even know why I ask the question. I know the answer. There are no new HuSCs. The promise is the Gardener version of reincarnation or heaven.

106,872,083. Billions gone in ten years. Plausible. Monstrous. But just not enough time. *She won't be happy until that number is truly 1*, I think to myself. Ten years is also too little time to net Asia, Africa, South America, and Europe, preventing anything electrical to come in or go out. Too little time to get to Neptune and back multiple times. Jupiter. Mars. Venus. And a gyroscope space station orbiting Saturn? An elegant, facet-less, multi-ringed object. How long would it take to build such a thing? All of it—it's just too much to dig, build and transfer, far too many patches to implement in a span of ten years. Jon sends me pics of Akira's coastal redwood forest next. One-hundred-footers, a clonal colony, trees much too tall to be decade-old saplings.

I roll through my own memory and replay the first time I met Coco Bloom. What was she? Maybe seven or eight at the time? For years, her parents were nomads who lived on tegu bushmeat before they decided to park their monster trailer on the outskirts of From A to Z. I was walking the streets, waiting for my father to finish a meet with Shave Time, and I stumbled across this tiny girl dipping sparkplugs in a gallon jar of dirty gasoline. When she attempted to install them in her mom's derby car, she pulled on her wrench too hard and fell. She knocked over the glass jar, and all the gas spilled out. I ran to her and helped her up. It's the first time I noticed she only had one hand.

I fast forward to the scene of my father's death. The old woman who approached his body. The one who looked familiar. The one missing the same hand. I remove the scars, sags, and wrinkles from her image, and the old face morphs into a young one. It's Coco Bloom knelt beside my father's body sadly looking up at me.

"Forty-nine," Jon says.

I look down at him. "What?"

"You turned forty-nine years old last winter."

A chill spreads through my body. I downshift out of sports mode and am lashed by truth and high-altitude wind. I get off Jon. The shuttles hang suspended over other landing platforms. And I know, just know, it's true. Not just because of the code, the patches, the monitoring of space flights, and what she built, but I also know that it's entirely in my father's character to do something like this.

"My father forced me to hibernate," I say. "All those nights, he imputed the AMP settings. I never even thought to look."

"Yes," Jon says. "You trusted him. And your reward? He forced you into hibernation for thirty of the last forty years."

It's why I look nineteen. It's why I feel nineteen. Who else has not aged much? *Shave Time.* "Shave Time Money hibernates, too," I say. "His son as well."

"Indeed."

"It's been forty years since Satori Day, not ten."

"I've told you that he does not tell you everything," Jon says. "I thought you would see by now."

"See what?"

"Your father betrayed you," Jon6J says. "But that is a presently insignificant matter. Like you and your father, our target, as you noted, spends the majority of his existence in AMP. He will go underground again soon. We must get him. According to our calculations, he will not emerge again for another five years."

Why, father? To quickly pass time. To fast-forward. To wake after years of sleep in hopes that something changed while billions perish. To live like zebra blennies, jumping from pool to pool, escaping ebbing tides but always staying close and never venturing in open water. A few years here, a few years there.

It was the only thing you enjoyed, wasn't it? Hard sleep absent of dreams. And in those instances that you did dream, the nightmares were still preferable to the real world. Maybe you hoped to one day wake and find my mother alive. To find OneVoice silenced. To find a decontaminated Leachate without the smell of smoke and shit.

The visions of the traveling surgeon version of Ascalon Lee hovering above me. These weren't dreams. She worked on me while we slept, and you let her. You let her tamper with my internal clock. That feeling of being trapped in an ancient snow globe, always being watched was not just a feeling, it was a truth. It's why you frequently asked whether I'd seen her, isn't it? You weren't checking if I'd seen her. You were checking if I was onto you. Why didn't she tell me how much time has really passed? What kind of deal did the two of you strike? Did she, like Jon6J, assume I already knew?

"We would never trick you," Jon6J says as he gets to his feet and pulls his stumped arm closer to his body. "Okaasan wants you vigilant."

I look at Jon6J. I'm trying to remember the years lost, but they are cruelly hidden somewhere beyond memory.

"Why didn't he tell me?" I ask not Jon, but myself. But I already know the answer. He didn't because I would've resisted, and no one, not even he could force me to go to bed for that long.

I look up and scream. A beam of energy is released from my eye, and the shuttles above are cut to pieces. Some explode. Others drop from the sky and rain on the tarmac in chunks. The entire mountain rumbles. I step to the edge of the landing pad and look to the horizon. Green smoke billows from all the holes Akira has dug over the last several decades. And something, I'm not quite sure what, diminishes inside of me.

"Do you remember now why she made you dig all these holes?" I ask Jon.

I remind myself of what Jon saw the first time we came here together. The dazzle of excavation deep into molten. The sense of accomplishment. It never occurred to me to watch closely that last trip. I was too distracted by my father's death. I understand now, though. Mining tellurium. Bullshit. They dig and dig and dig. There's no processing plant. There's no trommels to separate mineral from waste. I remind myself of what I noticed when I arrived. The circumference of each pit glazed green. These aren't just holes. For forty years she dug. She had to dig deep enough so that what she put in there would be melted down and gone forever. All these holes aren't mining or research expeditions. And each continent has them. She plans to wipe the Earth of all things human that came before Satori Day, chuck everything she didn't make into these pits, along with the Leachateans, and bury it.

The person I'm talking to now is not only Jon6J. It's Okaasan. It's OneVoice. It's Akira Kimura herself stepping beside me, severed arm tucked tightly to ribs, bearing witness to her work. It's Akira Kimura grinning at the holes brimming with murder.

"These aren't mining holes," I say. "They're graves."

"Yes," Jon6J says.

"They're graves. For everything. Everything the human race built over the span of its entire existence. Graves for every bit of trash and speck of contaminated soil. Every drop of polluted water. They're graves for the Leachateans, too."

"Their cities will be buried, yes, along with ours," Jon says.

I turn to him. It's the first time I notice that there's not just one *mon* on his collar, but two. Next to the emblem that represents A496, the circle with the curved line over it, is one that represents a root that sprouts three large billowy leaves. "Taro," I say.

Jon nods. "We serve you, too, now. Some of us anyway."

I turn back to the horizon and survey the thousands of giant holes dug all the way to the molten below us. I shake my head. "Graves," I say again in disbelief.

Jon nods. "And you are going to help us fill them."

6

When I was a child, I refused to do certain things correctly. I held writing tools like an ape until I was five. I tied knots, fishing tackle, climbing and rappelling gear my way until I was twelve. I'd draw a bow with just my index finger and shoot rail in a bladed stance instead of an athletic one. Even when I drove in the Leachatean derbies, fought in the pits, rode horses, and cut something, anything, I was wrong. To this day, I don't hold chopsticks like my mother taught me, but I can pick up things with them better than she ever could. My father would say that I lean too heavily on my talents. I would say that my talents shift the way things are normally done. *Shift the way things are normally done.* My father shifted the way life is done by forcing us into hibernation for so long.

I'm pondering this while the med bots work on Jon6J's arm. Gardener crews work to repair the shuttles I broke, and I'm walking the nearly empty streets of downtown Mile High at night. The well-kept grids of pre-Water City architecture are dark, and most of what used to make a city—restaurants, museums, e-sport arenas, holo galleries, hotels, parks, and government buildings—are all shuttered. These vacant buildings, like The Great Leachate, will end up in the graves that the Gardeners have been digging all these years. She's finally dug enough of them now.

Forty years.

I rewind through the data that Jon gave me and calculate when my father had me under. Which years were lost. The first time, the spring of 2154, April, when my mother died. He had us sleep for two years after that, perhaps imagining that 730 days of slumber would dull the pain of losing her. When we woke, I assumed just a single day had passed. We headed to From A to Z. This is when I met Coco Bloom, the little girl whom I rebuilt engines with. We spent much of the year there, and when the Leachateans were preparing to underground for winter, and my father gave operational AMPs to Shave Time in an attempt to build a stronger alliance, we returned to Covert.

Despite the gift, we weren't invited to underground with them. So we slept. Four years, by my calculations. This is when my father should've told me what he was doing, but I assume he felt bad about not telling me the first time, so he rationalized that he shouldn't do so this time.

You would wake up periodically while I slept, didn't you, Father? To ensure security. Also, to maintain our property so that it looked the same each time I woke. You kept the house clear of overgrowth. You repainted it at least two or three times. You reroofed it once, then let the new roof and new paint weather for years while I slept. You even bred the horses, trained them, and replaced the older ones. But I'm now seeing things that you missed. We all leave trails, even you.

When I turn down Fifteenth Street, I scroll through my vid archives and see the subtle differences between three generations of horses. Three Dorthys, not one. I look through my sketches of prairie cathedrals and see that the speed in which they degraded was too fast. The way From A to Z and the reawakening of refineries and pipelines rose was too fast. The evidence is all here in my head. Leachateans that I saw as children now grizzled rig drivers, spreading radioactive soil from coast to coast. Again, too fast. Even here in Mile High, where the illusion of age has been somewhat maintained by dutiful upkeep. I came here a number of times throughout my childhood and looked at it through my rail scope, at night. Gardeners once walked the streets. But each time, much less. Now, the streets are empty except for the occasional security drone that buzzes by. Again, too fast. I was susceptible to this because I was not a slave to appointments, routines, and schedules like people of the old world were—school days, work days, holidays, and celebrations. There was none of this in our new reality. I was also vulnerable to this deception because of how quickly Satori Day happened. How quickly Akira Kimura changed the world. Quick was just how I believed things happened after that day.

The year is not 2160, it is 2190.

I've gone through all the patches, space flight schedules, and schematics that Jon sent me. The continents are isolated from one another. Great boreholes, decades in the making, pock the areas in which great cities once stood. Barely perceptible mesh rises from every coast. Nets to keep anything electric from going in or out. Above every continental center, the mesh connects at a collar, a balloon of some sort. Like the remote-control bouncy ball from my early childhood, a toy I barely remember.

The flights to Saturn—some kind of superconducted space station the color of porcelain? Its rotor framed by three-axis gimbals, in constant spin. Another being constructed in some unknown space? The start of a bridge perhaps? A bridge to nowhere?

I don't understand everything that Okaasan is up to, but there is a fundamental axiom threaded through it all. Keep the planet safe. No, not just keep the planet safe, but keep it as it was. Keep it as it has been for the last few thousand years, the most prosperous time for the human species. That's why The Great Leachate must go. The biggest thing she can't control is plate tectonics, so she made the islands, her home, float to preserve them forever. My asshole father never did see the irony. Akira uses advancement to keep the world the same. It can't evolve or devolve because of her.

It's down to this. I can return to Water City and hunt lab-grown mythical creatures for fun and create some law and order and perhaps seek some kind of companionship. Some kind of normalcy. But I don't belong there. Or I can return to the sticks and live as a hermit. There, I can spend lifetimes trying to figure out how to bring my father back on my own just so I can choke him to death myself. I don't belong there either. Not anymore. I can also help Okaasan break Shave Time and the Leachateans and perhaps help cleanse the land. But I refuse to be another one of her Gardeners. Or I can try to crash the system. To stop this madness. Because when OneVoice sent me qubits of her data to prove that more time has passed than I initially believed, she sent me more than I needed. Not necessarily vulnerabilities, but she revealed a bit on how this system operates. That was my father's problem. He didn't really try to figure out how the thing he was trying to kill really works.

I stop in front of an old, glass skyscraper. Early twenty-first-century architecture, back when they started throwing some curve in their crystal palaces. I search for its history in my head. This one was one of the last pure business buildings constructed in the region, right before new towers became multi-use. Residences, office spaces, gyms, restaurants, drone delivery, and docking stations, kind of like the older scrapers in Water City. Long before I was born, after the world got off fossil, this particular building was converted into a solar-powered crypto farm named Fractal Inc. It was just a multi-story warehouse, really, a warehouse that was once filled with hard drives that autonomously mined for currency. Maybe Mile High has always and will forever be a mining town. I pull the once-automatic glass door open and step inside. The hard drives are gone. In their place are rows and rows of AMP chambers where dayshift Gardeners sleep. AMP reinstituted Patch v2.A.61. Thanks to Akira, at least I have the last two digits of my patch designations correct now. The Gardeners are in dream state, and I know that they are forced to pleasantly dream of her.

A security drone swoops in front of me and says, "Please exit the dormitory."

I step outside and look up. I switch to scope sight. Peregrine falcons are perched atop the glass tower. The half-moon throbs white light that hurts my ears. Why did my father take Akira there all those years ago? Was it really a desperate attempt to save me, or was it that, like the Gardeners, he could never say no to her? Was my father Akira's Adam?

I turn from the moon, drop out of scope sight, and eye the grids of dimly lit, solar-paneled streets. Mile High was the first city to convert fully to helis and replace its streets with energy catchment. A mischief of kangaroo rats scurry beneath the glass. A horned owl dives down to catch its prey, but instead it splatters against the transparent street. I flip the mess of feathers over with my toe. The bird's breast heaves. Its eyelids twitch. Before I can bend over and put it out of its misery, a trash bot whizzes to the bird, picks it up, and plops it in its receptacle. I no longer want to recover my father's head. What I really want to know is why OneVoice took it. Why it took Akira's, too. I'll help Jon with Shave Time if he agrees to tell me why—once we take care of that Leachatean monster. I'll help him in hopes of finding out other things, too. It's time someone put an end to Akira Kimura.

I smear owl blood with my boot. I'll help Jon6J if he agrees that no one outside Army Strong is hurt. It will be my plan, not hers. He'll agree. After Shave Time and Army Strong is removed, Okaasan will have the city evacuated. From A to Z will be broken apart and transported here by jumbo shuttle. It will be deposited in the boreholes. The Leachateans will need to survive on their own. Many are or have been nomadic. They know how to move. I'll help them spread out to uncontaminated zones if I can. Here's the thing. I'll take my time. I will not rush off flailing like my father. With each level of trust I achieve with OneVoice, the more I'll learn about her.

I unblock Ascalon Lee and ping her in Thought Talk. *Why?* I ask.

Return, and I'll explain.

The wind howls through the streets. I feel alone. Angry. But strong.

How did you get my father to trust you? What did you offer? My mother? Is that why he let you tamper with my head?

It was what he wanted, Ascalon Lee says. *For you to skip through time with him. He didn't want you to grow up in this world. To grow old in this world. He thought of time as narrative, and he assumed that chapters just ahead could somehow be skipped. He convinced me to help him make it convincing. I told him that he was wrong, that it was a stupid, childish thing to do, but he insisted.*

And what did you get in return?

Silence. Old people do that sometimes: ignore a question and hope it simply fades away. My father used to. I put Ascalon Lee back on block.

At dawn, the dayshift Gardeners emerge from their chambers. They stand in line and wait to receive their rations and blessings for the day from the service drones that pop off like flies from the top floors of the skyscrapers. The Gardeners eat their bars of protein while they wait for the helis to come and take them to their boreholes. A drone swoops down and offers me rations as well, which I take and eat.

Why did she need the heads? Does OneVoice require the dramatic and ritualistic? Is religion the thing that holds the whole system together? I wonder these things while the helis land on the solar-paneled streets and Gardeners clamber into their hulls. The helis lift off, and just like that, I'm alone in the streets, compulsively checking date and time. I don't belong in Kansas or Water City or any city for that matter. I belong right here, in Akira Kimura's face, staring into her eyes, studying them to figure out a way to permanently extinguish their light.

7

A week later, and we're flying to The Great Leachate. My plan is fairly simple. Break interstate bridges so that the rigs won't be able to continue to spread waste. Then just land in Ameritrade and openly challenge Shave Time and Army Strong to combat. I'm about to participate in the clashing between two megalomaniacs—one a violent plague, the other a cold, apathetic collective. I don't take Ascalon Lee off block. Her betrayal stings more than my father's. Why is it that for some reason I expected truth out of her more than him? The two colluded, that much I know. My father granted that bearded traveling surgeon version of her access to me.

"Am I truly in command?" I ping Jon in voice for the tenth time. The SEAL rattles under the mid-latitude jet stream. Somewhere, far above me, Okaasan's shuttles begin their descent.

"It is your designation," Jon says, as patiently as he did the first time I asked him. Even if I kill him, I'm not really killing her. *This is the world.* Ascalon Lee's words ring in my head. She's probably right, but I don't see why The Leachateans need be removed from it. Jon said that they were only interested in two things: halting the spread of forever chemicals and toppling the Shave Time Money regime. I don't think the Leachateans are going to let it go clean like that. I'll be on my toes if they start trying to hurt the citizens of The Leachate.

The shuttles thunder out of the sky and begin to land on the old Interstate 80. We're where ponderosa meets prairie, in between what was once known as Lincoln and From A to Z. I tilt down until I'm hovering over a set of twin three-lane, low-lying river bridges. I pop open the hatch. I pick up the super-rail and step out to the end of the wing. The bottoms of the clouds above bunch in greys and begin to drizzle black rain. The thorium in the sudsy river sparkles. The bridges rumble. The shuttles land a half-mile ahead.

"Ready to commence?" Jon asks.

"You'll give him back to me," I say. I want OneVoice to believe it still has leverage over me. "And you tell me why the heads were taken after this is done."

"Of course."

"We do this my way."

"Understood. You realize repetition is not necessary."

I aim the super-rail down at the first bridge and pull the trigger. Concrete erupts into plumes of ash. I hit the other one. After the flurry of silt is carried away by wind, beneath the water's surface, mutant toads evacuate lined-up corpses of old cars. I look up at an eagle soaring above, then climb back into my SEAL.

"That's the last bridge," I say. "From A to Z next. Only one shuttle. The rest remain back here on standby."

"Understood," Jon says.

I'm only allowing a platoon of twenty-five to accompany

me. I want this to look like a challenge, not an invasion. No super-rails, no rails in general. I want to keep the damage as minimal as possible. I'm not sure if Shave Time will take the bait, but I'm betting that he'll take one look at twenty-six of these hairless, big-headed, twiggy, unarmed, foam-fitted Gardeners and won't be able to resist. I'll only be armed with heat blades strapped to my arm and thigh, and my mother's 1911 tucked away under foam fit in the small of my back. Shave Time is used to seeing me armed minimally like this.

I tell Jon to hover the shuttle right above the middle of TD Ameritrade, and I'll do the same with my SEAL. When we near the city, Jon comments on the putrid condition of Pure Life, the river that runs through Shave Time's kingdom.

"They do not convert waste to biomass?" Jon asks.

"No," I say.

"Why tortoises and mussels?" Jon asks.

"You're the smartest person in the world," I say. "You know the answer."

"Yes," Jon says. "Yes. They feed on these things because they are the most resistant to radiation."

"Can't live on microorganisms," I say.

"Are you certain of that?" Jon asks. It's the first sign I get that somewhere deep in the collective lurks Akira's sense of humor. Perhaps she, or they, are relaxing a little, feeling a sense of tense exhilaration.

When we get to TD Ameritrade, I'm surprised to see that the canopy of wires crisscrossed throughout the city is now stitched over the stadium as well. All 24,000 seats are empty. Did the Leachateans go underground early this year? I'd like to have the SEAL and its rails close, just in case, so we'll repel down. There are gaps big enough below to slip through the wires. I put the SEAL in hover mode, open the cockpit, flip into sports mode, and jump down forty feet through the wires. I look up and watch as Jon, with his new cyborg arm, which was grafted onto him back at Mile High, and his crew of twenty-five slide down a long, gleaming rope that stiffens like a pole. I scan the stadium. No one is around. There are signs of the recent rains: thick puddles with the consistency of black gravy.

Jon and his crew touch down next to me in the middle of the field. The once-stiff rope goes slack and is slurped back up into the hovering shuttle. John and his crew move into formation behind me.

"Shave Time Money!" I yell. "It takes a tough man to make a tender chicken!"

A flock of pigeons squawks and flutter from the stands. Just like all the other buildings in From A to Z, this one has the color and greasy texture of the bottom of an overused frying pan. The entire place is speckled with bird shit. I look back at the Gardeners. They appear surprisingly calm in this environment. I'm assuming it's not me they completely trust. It's OneVoice and her judgment. I yell again.

"Shave Time Money! It takes a tough man to make tender chicken!"

All the clock towers in the city begin to chime at the same time. Odd. Those clocks were never set correctly. A hog chortles somewhere outside the stadium. The motorcycle comes through the entryway. The rider is goggled and covered in combat leathers. It must be Shave Time's daughter, Barbasol. My father told me about her, but we never met. She circles us, grinning. Like all Leachateans, she annoyingly over-revs her engine while she rounds us.

"Live in your world. Play in ours," she says.

I hear other vehicles come alive outside. Soon, a convoy of hogs arrives, led by Shave Time himself. He's wearing his usual fatigues, chainmail coif, visor, and his spiked prosthetic jaw. They're all circling us now. Taunting us with their slogans. The bikes kick up dust that rises in browns but transforms into greens before settling back down onto the ground. The arena is glittered with specks of green. I remind myself that what Shave Time has been doing to Gardeners for years is reprehensible. I remind myself that Shave Time tried to kill my father. And me.

I decide I should just make it quick.

I unsheathe my heat blade. It will be just like the mutated bear all those years ago. I'll shine my light into his eyes and bury the knife in his skull.

Shave Time and Army Strong gather at the outfield fence. They cut their engines and drop their kickstands. "Snap!" Shave Time bellows. "Crackle! Pop!"

The wires above us come alive. First in pops. Then smoke and blue light erupt from the lattice. The blue light streaks from wire to wire like electric fish. I feel myself dropping out of sports mode. I turn and see that Jon's eyes and his platoon's crackle blue, then flicker, then dim. Jon tries to raise his new cyborg arm, but it just sits limply at his side. I look up and see my SEAL dropping from the sky.

"Scatter!" I say.

Jon and the Gardeners run for cover. I head in the opposite direction. The SEAL crashes into the middle of the field. I eye the exit. Maybe I should make a run for it. I tell myself I won't lose sleep over abandoning Jon and the Gardeners, but, in the end, I know I will.

Shave Time is grinning across the field, pointing at the scar.

It's as if he's taunting me, saying, *I knew you were coming, you stupid girl.* The shuttle plummets from the sky next. It snags the wires and sets off explosions of chain lightning on its way down. It pancakes the SEAL with a booming thud.

I get it now. The wires aren't to generate power to sustain this city. It's for defense. What's coming from above is electromagnetic pulse. It's shutting down everything electrical—SEAL, shuttle, and iE—in this area. All at once, I can't believe it. Shave Time Money just pulled an Akira Kimura. He seethes in green, but when I try to shoot the laser from my eye—nothing.

I sprint to Shave Time. Even without an iE and sports mode, I'm still better than him. But I may only have one shot at this. He climbs off his hog and pulls a baseball bat from his motorcycle's saddlebag. All of Army Strong do the same. *They want to take me alive.* The images of the dead and tortured Gardeners in the Goodmen building fill my head. I shudder, then get angry.

I leap and throw my heat blade at Shave Time but miss. How? Furious now, I take out the other blade strapped to my thigh and still charge forward. He shifts into a batter's stance. The rest of Army Strong charges. The knife won't heat up. I throw it anyway with everything I got. Shave Time swats it away with his bat. The knife goes clattering into the stands.

I feel something hard crack the back of my thigh and fall to one knee. Another hard blow to my shoulder, and all I can think is I now know why my father wanted me to learn things the right way. For situations just like this.

"Stop rushing," he used to say.

"Life is too short to take too long," I'd retort.

I look back. Maybe we were both right. Most of Army Strong is rushing the Gardeners, all twenty-five cowering in the dugout, all smothered in greens and reds. When Army Strong gets to the dugout, the pummeling begins. Jon and I lock eyes for an instant, then a bat caves in the side of his head. I gasp. A bat is coming at me. I raise a forearm just in time to block it and hear the sickening snap of my ulna shatter. The pain is sharp, and I scream. The agony dulls into a throbbing, all-consuming ache, and I skitter to my feet. Barbasol and three other Army Strong surround me. Shave Time is heading over, wearing a menacing grin, and shaking his enormous head. I reach for the gun tucked into the small of my back. The electromagnetic pulse has malfunctioned my foam fit. I can't manipulate the material to retract and get my hand around the gun.

Barbasol swings at me again, and I roll away. I try to tear the foam fit off my back, but the scaly Water City version is too thick to rip. Another Army Strong wearing an eye patch charges at me while Shave Time gets closer and closer. The patched man raises the bat above his head, and I throw my shoulder into him, my left hand still clutching at my lower back. I manage to rip off a couple of the black scales and can feel the rough texture of the pistol grip. I dig my fingers in the small opening. Barbasol stops advancing, tilts her head, and curiously watches me. I look over at the dugout—all twenty-five Gardeners are being bludgeoned to death. I manage to squeeze my hand into the slight tear in my foam fit's material when Barbasol's eyes flash with recognition. She knows what I'm trying to do.

Shave Time's grin disappears when I pull out my mother's 1911, point it across my body, and fire a no-look shot. Before the Leachatean on my right falls, I spin into a modified Weaver stance and clip the Leachatean on my left. I feel arms envelop me from behind. Barbasol.

I have two choices. I can try to squeeze the barrel of the gun under my pinned armpit and shoot Barbasol. Or I can shoot from the hip, take a chance, and empty my clip at the now charging Shave Time. The bat held over his head. My eyes answer for me. Shave Time is matted in red, and he doesn't even know it. He's sprinting at me. *Looks like I'm coming to you, Dad.*

"Taste the rainbow," I say.

I pull the trigger. The first bullet misses, and now, Shave Time is charging even faster. I pop off three rounds in quick succession. The first two miss, but the third shatters his prosthetic jaw. *Don't aim for his head*, I hear my father telling me. *Center mass.* I adjust my aim to his torso, and Barbasol loosens her bear hug to grasp for my gun. I slip out of her grip, grab her hand, and twist it into a one-handed wristlock. She drops to her knees.

Another Army Strong is rushing at me from the left. I throw a standing sidekick, and my heel strikes his chin flush. He drops. Shave Time is less than ten feet from me now, his eyes wide with rage and terror. I pull the trigger. The bullet hits him in the center of his chest, but he's still coming. I plug him with three more rounds. Finally, he falls and skids in front of my feet. I feel something crack the back of my head, and the next thing I know I'm on the ground, dazed, looking at the sky.

I struggle to roll over and get to my feet. When I'm finally on hands and knees, a group of furious Leachateans congregate around me. I tilt my head up and can see it in their eyes. The whole "taking me alive thing" has vanished from their memories.

The first blow to my forehead is the most painful thing I have experienced in my entire life. The blows that follow match the first in agony. I struggle to turn on my side and crawl through the gathering legs of more and more Army Strong. Reds in splattering luminosity spray at my eyes while baseball bats rain down upon me. I peer and see Shave Time Money, still wearing a look of shock, guts spilled out in a black gravy puddle that's swirled with a green frosting. I turn my eyes up, and through a cloud of green and red, I catch a glimpse of a billboard that hangs above the outfield. NOTHING IS EVERYTHING. For the first time in my life, I'm enveloped in terror. While the excruciation jolts through my body with every blow, I'm comforted by two thoughts. One, my enemies, Shave Time and Jon, are dead. The second one is a more refreshing thought. A promising one. Shave Time's plan almost worked, which means Akira Kimura can't see everything coming.

Sister, I plead silently, finally calling her by what she's wanted all these years now. *Sister, please.* I don't hear a response, but I think I now know why my father let her tamper with me. Or I pray that I do. Second chances. That's my thought as the greens and reds fade.

I desperately pray for a second chance. I pray to God like I'm mashing some kind of instinctive panic button again and again. Through the pain, I hear the faint whirring sound of my iE rebooting. *Sister*, I plead again and again. My iE buzzes alive, and I immediately try to shift into sports mode. But there is no sports mode. Then, there is no pain. I try to move my limbs but can't. I try to swallow, and I can't even do that. My mouth droops open, and my throat makes a choking sound because it's unable to suck in air. I'm suffocating, trying to breathe, but my body won't do it.

Then I'm dunked head-first into a cold, fleshy umbra, and it's too thick to breathe anyway.

PART FOUR

GODS IN THE FLESH

1

Three weeks after the assassination of Shave Time Money, From A to Z still mourns. It's dusk, and cripples in black gather at the shores of Pure Life and pour their bottles of beer into the river. With access to the city now destroyed, the rigs remain parked with no bridges to cross, nowhere to go. No one really knows who's in charge now. There are rumors that Blade Close has hidden underground and has put himself into long-term hibernation. Barbasol is a mess. She drinks and weeps for her father every day.

Army Strong is now a snake without a head. They wander aimlessly and consider a jarring truth: diamonds aren't forever. Many of the citizens have begun to pack jars of unrecognizable, shriveled fruit with slogans of the past plastered in them. They prepare to go back to the nomad life, their trailers hitched to old Winnebagos with rusty, corrugated side panels.

These Leachateans whisper their fears to each other. Fall is here, and it's tough being on the road for the winter. Many plan to head south. Maybe Arizona. Maybe Louisiana. No

place close to A496 lest it fall from the sky and flatten them.
Maybe go back to living outside a contamination zone.

When the Made in China hooded pair enter the city, the
big man's square jaw clenches. A slight woman wearing a lab
coat trails him. The man peels open his duster and removes
a .44 holstered to his foam fit.

"They require personification," the woman says.

"Who?" the man asks.

"Everyone, it seems."

Since the First National Bank Tower has been cut in half
by super-rail, there's no real Leachatean headquarters any-
more, but the man knows where he's going. He's been here
many times before. The intercom system at TD Ameritrade is
hooked up to all the speakers around town. It should still be
functional unless the electromagnetic pulse three weeks ago
put it down for good. Leachateans eye the pair as they make
their way to the stadium. "Made in China," some civilians
hiss. An Army Strong member steps in front of them and
raises his hand, demanding that they stop. The big man raises
his .44 and puts a bullet through the soldier's visor without
even breaking stride.

"You should be proud," the woman says.

The man glares at every Leachatean he passes. Each one
drops their eyes. "This place goes down, right?"

"Every single brick," the woman says.

"And the rigs? The refineries?"

The woman squats and eyes a matted label. GO GREEN.
"The Great Leachate is no more."

The man nods and looks at the small crowds gathering
on the sidewalks on both sides of them. A pack of Army
Strong scream curses. The big man reaches into his duster and

extracts an old grenade. He pulls the pin and tosses it into the pack. An explosion. The nearby crowd screams and scatters.

"The daughter," the man says. "I will find her and kill her."

"A daughter for a daughter," the woman says. "Symmetry."

When they get to the stadium entrance, the pair stop dead in their tracks. Hanging from a noose tied around her ankles is what's left of a girl's body. They both pull off their hoods. The man can only stand the sight for a second and turns away. The woman seems unbothered by the dangling rot.

"She was a good girl," the woman says.

The man says nothing. He pulls his hood back on and heads into the stadium. The woman lingers for a moment and cracks a rare smile. Then she, too, pulls up her hood and follows. Inside are the piled bodies of twenty-five others in the same putrid state as the girl. The woman ignores these and heads upstairs to the broadcast booth where the big man waits. When she arrives, the man is turning knobs. He taps on a microphone. The knocking echoes throughout the city. He nods at the woman. She sits in the chair in front of the mic and leans into it.

"Greetings," she says. "This is Akira Kimura."

She pauses and waits patiently for the gasps and screams that she knows are going off like alarm bells in the streets to subside. Below, the curious nervously begin to enter the stadium.

"Feel free to join me and take a seat," Akira says.

The man's eyes are focused on every person entering. When he spots her, Barbasol Needs, staggering into the stadium with two drunken Army Strong buddies, he begins to step out.

"Not yet," Akira says. "Wait until I finish what I have to say."

The man thinks about it for a second, then nods. Once the stadium fills, Akira turns on the jumbotron. The Leachateans all look up, and they see the hooded woman projected above. She removes her hood. Gasps follow.

It's her. It's really her. Akira Kimura has risen again.

"As you can see, it is really me. You should be proud, really. From the very beginning, we offered you clean water. We offered you uncontaminated food and medication. When you refused, we let you be. Then your people began poking at us. Kidnapping us. Torturing and murdering us. And still, we let you be. Finally, when I decided your leader had to go, and you managed to kill my very special agents, I could not stand by any longer. Your vexing obstinance has brought me back. Now, just outside the city, a fleet of jumbo shuttles is unloading excavators. This abhorrent city will be leveled tomorrow morning. Evacuate tonight. We work quickly, so do not dawdle."

The crowd stirs. Some already begin to leave. Others bicker. Some stick up their middle fingers at the giant screen.

"Do not simply migrate to other Leachatean strongholds. These will be leveled soon after. As will your infrastructure, food, and fuel supply. I am ordering all of you to report to Mile High. Once you are there and properly registered, you will be offered one of three choices." Akira pauses and looks down. Her Gardeners have quietly slipped into the city. They stand at the exits and hand fleeing Leachateans brochures. "Please take a brochure before you leave," Akira says.

The big man glares through the window at Barbasol Needs. She's flipping off the jumbotron along with her two Army Strong buddies. Akira turns the mic from her mouth *and covers it with her hand. "I assume you have established the trail?" Akira asks.*

"Yes. She won't survive the night."

"Root out the brother as well. Eliminate all who refuse to depart by morning."

He nods. Akira pulls the mic to her lips. "Inside the brochure you are now receiving, you will see delightful pictures of a colony we have created in Oceania for people just like you. Just imagine—warm winters, white, sandy beaches, crystal blue waters. Migration there will be your first option. We will, of course, provide transportation."

Crowds of people pause to flip through the brochure. The first picture is of two Leachateans on surfboards: a woman wearing a crown of flowers, the other a man wearing braided leaves around his neck—both on separate boards, riding a gentle blue wave. The caption: Come Taste Paradise. *"Come Taste Paradise," whisper some in the crowd.*

Akira begins to speak again. "Your second choice is to continue your wretched nomadic existence here on this continent. However, if you choose this road, you stay on the road. Resurrecting or building cities, even towns, will no longer be tolerated. Also, just so you know, every polluted water source will be drained. Every ounce of contaminated soil will be removed. If you stay in this area, life will be extremely difficult."

A shuttle appears above the stadium. Its hatch opens and hundreds of drones flood the sky. They begin surgically cutting down the powerlines. Another shuttle swoops in and hovers next to the first. This one rains hundreds of thousands of Hershey Kisses from the sky throughout the city.

"Say it with a kiss," Akira says.

Some of the Leachateans in the stadium pick up the Kisses, unwrap them, and take a sniff. Most pop them in their mouths.

"Kisses?" the synesthete asks.

Akira, again, bends the mic away from her mouth. "It needed to be something that they are familiar with."

"You put poison in the Kisses?"

"A poison that will sterilize them. All Leachatean cities are being bombarded with Kisses as we speak."

"It should never have come to this," the man says. "Why did you let this go on for so long?"

Akira's eyes narrow. "No, the question is, why did you."

The man feels his toes curl. His jaw clenches. What's it been now, eighty-eight years since he's known Akira Kimura? At this point, he can't remember a world without her. The synesthete, the man who can see murder in greens and hear death in reds, has no clever retort for her. His mind is seared with the image of his daughter hanging in the entryway by her ankles. Her face, unrecognizable.

Akira places the mic back in front of her. "Your final choice is, of course, fight and die. Fight us and die. Now, cut that poor girl down from the entrance and collect the bodies of my children here. We will be taking those with us."

The crowd, both frightened and confused, pick up what Kisses they can and begin to exit the stadium. The synesthete eyes Barbasol Needs and her two friends. They stand there in the middle of the field, arms defiantly crossed, glaring up at the announcer's booth. Barbasol rips a brochure in half. The synesthete taps his foot, aching for the last of the crowd to finally exit. He sniffs at the air for magentas for the thousandth time since he woke. None are there. Only *the smell of ambergris pulsing green from Barbasol, and the orchestra of reds tickling his ears. He heads to the door and yanks it open. He pauses.*

"You will make sure my daughter is remade," he says.

"I do not need to," Akira says. "You know she has already been."

"I don't sense her."

"Her new HuSC probably lacks the older model's GPS system."

"Your daughter better have held up her end of the bargain between me and her," the synesthete says.

"You will hunt her. Not yours, but mine. Not all her versions. Just get her off this continent and the others. Big things are happening, my friend. And, as you know, my daughter is a compulsive meddler."

The synesthete steps through the door and slams it behind him. Akira jumps a little and smiles. He is still, at times, a little scary, this oldest friend of mine, *she thinks.* That's part of why he's eternally useful. But he doesn't really concern her that much. It's her own daughter that concerns her. The synesthete's daughter concerns her as well. The two Ascalons—her daughter, the elder—are becoming more and more like twins, like binary stars set on collision. The synesthete was supposed to keep his daughter close to him, train her to help him police the world, and keep her away from mine, *Akira thinks. But they are together now, aren't they? And what will become of them if they are together? Perhaps they become a blue straggler, a single star with more mass and rotation than all the others around them.*

But perhaps not. Akira once perceived her daughter as a handicap. A secret that could hurt her. From the time of

Ascalon Lee's birth, she was an antagonist. But she has grown, hasn't she? Of course Okaasan has been watching her. What are gods but great surveillance systems? Her little lab. Her marvels of genetic engineering. She's weaving a new nature. She has always been more interested in what happens here rather than in the expanse of the beyond. Perhaps the children will finally become worthy of their inheritance.

Akira knows that she is not forever for this world. Even she is not immune to entropy. The gradual decline into disorder. But not anytime soon. There is still much to be done. Energy capture from Saturn. Access to worlds in rebirth and infancy. Crossing through others that have long destroyed themselves. Okaasan wants to see, firsthand, planets make their own moons, a black hole eat a neutron star, and perhaps meet alien life out there. She wants to confirm what she's long suspected, that the very laws of nature and reality shift and evolve. It will be dangerous, and maybe she will not return. Maybe, in the end, *Akira thinks,* we of OneVoice are lichens. *We do not need roots. But we need protectors.*

The stadium finally empties except for Barbasol Needs and her two companions. All three stand at the pitcher's mound, waiting. The synesthete steps down to the field. Akira supposes these few defiant Leachateans expect some sort of honorable stand-off, some romantically violent resolution. Instead, a med bot hovers behind the synesthete. He grins at them. He points to the Woodmen then points to his eyes. The three now look less sure of themselves. A cloaked drone swoops in overhead and drops a gas canister that hisses smoke. Immediately rendered unconscious, the three crumble atop each other. The med bot speeds to the mound and hovers over them. Its tentacle arms extend from its base and undulates above the three Leachateans. The smoke clears, and the med bot, scalpels ready, descends upon them.

2

At first, there is only the fusty smell of ambergris. Then, when I wake, I'm in the deep, and am being strangled by my own tentacles. It's confusing, these eight arms, these two thousand suction cups, the ability to control each one—it's too much, too fast. I'm tangling myself in knots, trying to free myself from myself, and I twist and writhe and plummet to the muddy sands below.

When I hit the ocean floor, I find that I can taste the marine snow with my legs, so I try to spit it out. But these arms do not spit. They grab. And the more I struggle, the more I taste. *Procedure.* No, there is no procedure for this. *Guidelines.* There are no guidelines for this either. *I can fix this.* Yes, that is the thought I can concentrate on. Slowly, I unravel, leg by leg, and watch as each one undulates and turns from black to the color of sand. This is impossible. I'm an octopus. I'm Akkorokamui.

I try to connect to my data but cannot. I try to shift into sports mode, but I can't do that either. My arms speak to me. *Flee!* they say. My arms smell the colors down here. The greens. The reds. So I suck in as much water as I can and spit it out. I'm now jetting across sand, leaving behind a cloud of ink in the king tides.

My arms sense the hunters above. I don't see them, but I know they're gaining on me. Perhaps there is no option but to stand my ground and fight, but my legs say no. I race away from the hunters and attempt to compute my location. I can't. But I see the lights now. They're out of focus, but I know what they are: the scrapers of Water City. It must be Raid Day. I want to turn to the hunters and identify myself. *I'm Taro*, I want to scream, but I can't do it.

I turn and see one hunter in mantis armor ahead of the pack. The propellers on his fins slow. He's aiming a spear gun at me. I focus my vision and see that it's Motu. I release more ink and clumsily flail to the sand below. For some reason, I'm ashamed as I dig into the sand. A net is cast above me. It sinks at its edges. Then, the rest of it begins to flatten. I'm burrowing for my life now, and despite my incredible size, I vanish and leave a hole the size of a pinprick above. That's the last thing I remember, rippling and billowing and sucking in my own blackness.

When I wake up again, I'm no longer an octopus. In fact, I'm not sure if I was really Akkorokamui or if I was dreaming. Now, like the astronauts at the Cape, I'm just some disembodied thing, and it's even more unsettling than being a boneless, liquid creature. If I could scream, I would. If I could run, I would. But I am truly without vessel. I'm simply a thought. A representation of the thing that I was. I'm an orphaned neural substrate. And I can feel myself ricocheting into insanity.

Before I completely lose my mind, a flickering pink holo

flashes in front of me. The holo is just a single, neon word: *Menu.* I don't have hands or a mouth, so I don't exactly know how I'm supposed to select anything. But once the word "select" crosses my mind, the menu opens its options. Mammalian. Aquatic. Aviary. Reptilian. Amphibious. I open aviary out of curiosity. There's the 3D outline the shape of some kind of humanoid owl. Tempting, but no. Now thoroughly crazed, I laugh to myself and think, *What about all of the above?* Suddenly, I'm looking at a winged mermaid body with a snake's tongue and mucous skin. I panic and my mind screams *mammalian.*

Four choices appear: male, female, something with a bit of both, and non-binary. All four are tempting, but I choose female because I'm desperate to become and that's what I'm used to. As I scroll through the options through my mind—height, weight, build, hair color—a part of me is tempted to craft something cartoonish straight out of myth, but I concentrate and picture what I've always looked like. Slowly, an empty square room materializes around me. I'm standing on a rotating pedestal. The walls scroll with seemingly random digital sequences of As, Ts, Cs, and Gs. The floor and ceiling, too. I raise my hand in front of my face. It's transparent, but there. For a moment, I think I'm witnessing the objective view of what a human body really is—a swarm of electrocuted squiggly things. Why wouldn't it be possible to rearrange this mass into another shape? I clench my fist and almost feel real again.

Interesting choice, a voice in Thought Talk chimes in. It's Ascalon Lee.

I begin to calm when I observe each limb of this spectral version of me and begin to recognize myself. I rub my hands

236 • CHRIS McKINNEY

through my hair. I touch my mouth, nose, and ears. *Why didn't you tell me?* I ask in Thought Talk. I'm surprised this, of all things, is my first question, but it is.

Tell you what?

The hibernation. The years. The lost years. How many people perished during those years.

The pedestal stops spinning. Yellow lights beam from the walls and begin to scan me. *Those years weren't lost,* Ascalon Lee says. *They happened. And none of it was my doing. Some things, it is best to let a person discover for themselves. Why is it my job to tell you what reality is when reality is right in front of your face?*

That's what friends do, I say.

No, Ascalon Lee says. *That's how friendships end. What friends do is what I'm doing now. Despite the fact that you didn't heed my warning and left, I'm giving you a second chance. Don't rush this process.*

I got him, I say, bitterly. *Shave Time Money. I got him.*

And look, he got you, too.

I nod. He certainly did. My digital skin flickers at the memory being pummeled by baseball bats. The pain was unbearable, yes, but the fact that I was stuck and couldn't move, couldn't escape, was the worst part. It was the pinned suffocation of it all that was most horrifying. I was begging for my life. I wonder if Ascalon Lee sensed it.

Did you hear me? I ask.

Yes. I heard you just in time.

Embarrassed by the fact that she heard me plead so desperately, I change the subject. *Creating his own EMP field was clever,* I say. *Did Shave Time learn about it by attempting to travel to the other continents?*

Perhaps.

I pause. *Do you think he ever believed?*

Believed what?

The Leachatean ethos that he created?

It's easier to sell an idea you don't believe, Ascalon Lee says. *Believers have always ignored this. Now, what do you want me to make you into?*

Was this part of the deal? The deal with my father?

Yes. He granted me access because he knew that if anything happened to you, I could bring you back.

And what did you get out of it?

I just said. Access. Now, what do you want to be made into?

I ponder. From death to childhood, I dwell on all the bad memories. The fears that teeter to phobias. *Nothing mechanical*, I say. *No cybernetics. Absolutely, positively no iE. I don't want to be a part of any system. I don't want to be hackable or vulnerable to shut down. Otherwise, just keep me dead.*

Complete autonomy then?

Yes.

Understood. Modifications?

I just want to be meat.

Well, tissue can be modified.

I'm suddenly angry. *Is this fun for you?*

Of course it is, Ascalon Lee says. *It's creation! Isn't it fun for you?*

It's not, but I'm relieved to be alive. Not glad, but relieved. And grateful. At least I tell myself to be. I don't want to be useful to her. I don't want to be useful to OneVoice. I fully understand what I'm turning down—sports mode. The machine-like ability to process and retain information. A laser eye. The ability to control other mechanical things. I will probably lose my perfect memories than can be played over and over again. That will be a mixed blessing.

How about this, I say.

Yes?

I want to be normal.

Don't be foolish, my butterfly. I don't do normal. Don't test my patience either, or I'll leave you as Akkorokamui for the next hundred years.

I look at my hand again, then reach up to touch my eye. There's no flesh there, just the spectral image of a girl, a sort of holo model on showcase. *What if I want to stay like this?* I ask.

A ghost?

Yes. Invisible. Don't you like creating things that people once believed existed but never did?

Who's to say those things never existed? says Ascalon Lee. *Maybe what I'm doing is bringing them back to life. But I don't do ghosts. I do life. However, your desire for stealth is noted.*

I want one life, I say.

You have one life. All I've given you is multiple deaths.

I don't want them.

You're young and foolish.

I want you to expunge your data on me. I don't want to be remade again and again.

A pause. *Noted*, Ascalon Lee says.

And no more greens. No more reds. No more guidelines. Never again.

But then how will you find them?

Find who?

A pause. *Your father and Akira,* Ascalon Lee says.

What?

They're alive.

I feel the jaw of my ghostly avatar clench, and my lucent skin crawls. My heart thunders, and blood that's not really blood rushes to my ears. *Where are they?*

Your father managed the disassembly of From A to Z. Once that was done, both my mother and he left. I'm not sure where they are now.

He is working for her again. I say. *Because of what the Leachateans did to me. He wants to help her wipe them out now.*

And what is Ascalon's Scar compared to the actual, physical presence of my mother? Ascalon Lee says. *Not just to the Leachateans, but to her Gardeners. Imagine the effects of seeing the god you worship in the flesh. That will keep you in line. For good.*

What would the effect be of seeing her defeated?

Ascalon Lee laughs. *You're starting to see now. Yes, maybe this is an opportunity.*

What happened to "This is the world?"

I'm an opportunist. You know that. You are becoming one, too.

Do you have a plan?

No. Not yet. Do you?

No. How long, and don't lie to me, have I been gone?

Three weeks.

Three weeks and Okaasan plucked the capital of The Great Leachate from the earth and probably plopped it into her Mile High graves. *What about the Leachateans? Genocide? Refugees?*

I said your father managed disassembly, Ascalon Lee says.

I get it. It's like he did all those years ago during the coming of Sessho-seki. *Deportation,* I say.

Smart girl. Yes. But some are on the run, wandering desperately, looking for someplace to relocate. My mother has deemed it illegal to settle and build new towns or cities, though. Her excavators are already on the move, tearing apart the entire Leachate and burying it in her boreholes. The great American rivers are being drained as we speak. She apparently dug under them.

What about the deportations?

She's offered something interesting, and most are taking the offer. Here.

A digital brochure materializes in my holographic hand. I flip through it. Clearly doctored pictures of happy Leacha-teans frolicking on beaches and living off the bountiful boomerang coast of DownUnder. The one continent that Ascalon Lee cannot see. Or at least, if she can, she never showed it to me.

The nets that surround the continents besides North America, I say. *Shuttles will get snagged and malfunction. She's sending them to their deaths.*

I drop the brochure and it splashes in the waves of letters, seamlessly transforming to As and Ts, becoming a part of and lost in the digital letters scrolling all around me.

The scar, Ascalon Lee says. *Jon6J. The sudden decision to resurrect herself and your father and eliminate The Leachate. You were right. She is planning something big.*

She plans to bury the old world before leaving this planet. Is my father . . . the same?

I don't know. I kept my distance. But he doesn't act like a

Gardener. He gives them orders, which means he's not part of the hive mind.

We need to stop them, I say. *I'll keep my sight. Death in reds and murders in greens. That's it.*

You reinvigorate me, my butterfly. You're the only one who can.

I wonder how Akira sees time, if OneVoice can discern a day from a year or even a decade. How does one see time when one is timeless? Does a century or a millennium even matter? She made islands float. She made a 1,200-mile-long slingshot into space. Then almost forty years later, she decided to start cleaning up The Leachate. Was that a blink of an eye for her? Is that the irony? When you become omnipotent, you see time like an infant?

Why doesn't Akira just make a zonbi version of my father, or me even, and simply have it be a part of the OneVoice collective? I ask.

Despite all the things she's been able to create, she can't duplicate your and your father's vision and apply it to One-Voice, to herself. Neither can I. It's not just your nose. It's not just how the synesthesia transforms sound and smell into colors. It's that in symphony with your rage.

Hwabyeong, I say.

Yes. Everything we see is tinted by emotion, isn't it? Your and your father's ability to anticipate murder and death, to track it simply by following green and red . . . There's genius in what you and your father can do, and genius can't be manufactured. Geniuses can. But not genius. Not that either of you appreciates it. Besides, she doesn't really need to, does she? She has him.

Sensing murder? Sensing death? What good is that in the grand scheme of things?

Ascalon Lee scoffs. *All that you see, and you don't see this? See what?*

Imagine if you used your ability to avoid death instead of seeking it. To run when the greens and reds appear as opposed to following them. Don't you see? If you can predict death, then you can avoid it. You and your father are the ultimate alarm systems. Not only can you discern real threat, but you can decern false threat by not seeing.

It's something my father never asked himself, is it? All those years ago, when he killed for Akira Kimura, not once did he look up and see the entire sky bathed in red. The ocean tinted chum. He didn't sense the impending death of the entire species. Not once did he ask himself why. The answer is clear. He didn't see it because Sessho-seki wasn't real. *He should've known all along.*

If I simply request that Ascalon Lee make me into what I was, I would once again be tied to my father. I could find him, but I suddenly notice that I'm not interested in finding him. It's something else that's tugging at me. It's those orphan keys. Those jagged slips of metal and the satisfying zip of teeth pushing spring-loaded pins above shear lines. It's like music to me, and I've often heard faint notes of red with the click of a correct key in a correct lock. That is the pathetic playlist of my childhood, the jangle of orphans and the hopeful twisting of metal knobs. Fuck my father. Fuck him for everything.

I want a trip, I say.

What do you mean? Ascalon Lee says.

Make me into something that can get me past EMP nets. Something that leaves no digital footprints. I want to go to DownUnder first.

Ascalon Lee laughs. *Do you wish to have reproductive organs?*

No, I say, surprised and unsure why I answered so quickly.

Good. More room to work with.

I could do without a digestion system, too.

A pause. *I can make you draw some thermal and kinetic energy, but the gut produces most of your serotonin. Many of your immunity cells and neurotransmitters as well. It carries the bacteria . . .*

Okay, I say. *Just make me the ultimate predator.*

The room begins to dim simultaneously with my consciousness.

Smart girl, Ascalon Lee says. *You don't need to trust if you can kill.*

3

When I wake, I'm lying alone in a lush glen, covered in slime, and I feel like someone blew me out of their nose. I immediately notice that I'm naked, and the first thing I hear is the rush of falls pouring into a pool of water. Startled by the sudden noise, I attempt to leap to my feet. Only I find myself clinging to the top of a tree that bends and snaps and sends me falling toward rock. I stick my hands out to brace myself and discover that I'm standing on them. I know immediately that before I can go anywhere, I need to learn the language of my new body first. Changes in the human body occur slowly over time, but for me, it's as if I've been thrust from toddler to this in an instant. Those superhero stories of old had it all wrong. One does not simply take a dose of super-serum, double in size, and enter a footrace. One does not get bit by a spider and suddenly climb walls and spin webs. The old mind and the new body must learn to sync. It's why I was so clumsy as Akkorokamui. To learn to be an octopus, one must be an octopus over time.

It's one of those miserably humid days where the gray

carpet above refuses to rain down anything but mist. I inspect the skin on my forearms and thighs. I'm no longer a swarm of electrocuted squiggly things. Or am I? Did I solidify, or is it simply my perception that changed? Either way, my body looks the same, but I feel more. The sunlight. The specks of water falling from the sky. The weak breeze. It's as if my body is feeding on these prickly things.

I cautiously touch the strands of hair on my head as I feel them stiffen. It's not hair. These are quills. Like vibrissae, they sense. It's through the quills that I'm perceiving all these things around me. I look down. The color of my skin turns gray to match the color of rocks beneath my feet.

I shake off the surprise and spot a large egg of some sort, hovering above a boulder to my right. It's the size of a horse's head. I take a step toward it and am shocked to find myself leaping into the air before landing on a rock. The arches of my new feet are like loaded springs. *Procedure.* I step off the rock. I prance more than walk at first, and the rocks do not hurt the bottoms of my feet. I find myself in the strange situation of having to learn how to run before I can learn how to walk. To quickly reorient my proprioception. After many hours spent doing this, eventually, I'm walking.

It's dusk, and I approach the floating egg, reaching out and cautiously poking it with my index finger. It cracks then turns the color of the rocks, of my skin. Its yolky substance begins to ooze up my arm, and I can tell in an instant that it's a part of me. The gel seeps between my fingers, under my arms, and between my toes. It now looks like I'm wearing camo foam fit. I rub the boulder and notice that the hard strokes are barely audible. This second skin somehow dampens sound. I bend down and practice picking up pebbles without crushing them. It's dark now, and both of my skins have become as black as the night, but I can still see.

More hours pass, and I've learned to gently toss pebbles into the calm pool. The water has stopped falling, and the talus slowly dries in the night air. I can smell the difference between day and night. I also catch the scent of a giant lizard at the crest of the falls. Then it comes to me. I know this place. My father told me about it. It's the birthplace of Ascalon Lee and her twin. The scene of the original crime. It feels creepy lingering here, so I head for the bush. The next thing I know, I'm running through trees. Somehow, in the dark, I'm quietly sprinting through twigs and branches without making much noise.

I reach the coastline cliffs and decide to take a dive off the floating island. Now, in midair, I immediately regret it. The drop off is more of a base jump than a cliff dive, and I'm hurling toward water without a chute. I suddenly think about the Seshho-seki suicides, the maternal grandparents I never knew, and I'm terrified that my feet will snap from my ankles. I decide to tuck into a needle and hope for the best, but my second skin has its own ideas. The membrane stretches down from wrist to foot, ankle to ankle, and forms a wingsuit. I spread my arms and legs, and I'm gliding now, swooping over the flat, moonlit ocean. The loudest thing I taste is the laughter of my own voice. When I turn to sail farther out from the island, I begin to lose lift. Finally, I dive into the water.

I hit the surface, and my skins turn reflective. Then, I sink like a stone. I would be drowning if it were possible for me to drown. Like a lungfish, there are both lungs and gills in this new body of mine. I feel the water flow through my chest and pelvis. Apparently, reproductive organs replaced with an underwater breathing system. Despite the darkness, even in the ocean, I can see. I'm standing at the bottom and find myself leaping off the black rocks, attempting to work legs into kicks to no avail. I recall the biology of scorpions, ticks, and spiders, composite metal atoms woven into proteins, and I'm convinced that Ascalon Lee weaved metal into my proteins, too. I try to ping her but forget that I can't ping anymore. The iE is gone from my head. However, many of the memories are still there. A lot of what I've ever learned and witnessed is still available, but in words and fuzzy images, nothing in HD. It's regular human memory. Did perfect memory drive my father mad? Was it doing the same to me? Unlike Akira and Ascalon Lee, we weren't born with it. It was suddenly thrust upon us. I try to remember what I can of dolphins and how they swim. How they improbably generate enough thrust to move their heavy bodies quickly through water. My second skin seems unable to turn my shape into something that emulates them.

Then, I remember Akkorokamui. My second skin slides off my limbs and transforms into a giant octopus arm that forms from my spine. I use the tentacle to push myself up from the volcanic boulders, and I suck in all the water I can through my nose and mouth. Once my lungs are filled, I heave the water out and begin to move, slamming back into the white-crusted rocks below. I must learn to swim backward. I take water in again and lift myself with the octopus tail. My second skin turns my hands and forearms into fin-like appendages. I expel the water from my lungs and glide forward without being able to see where I'm going. But I don't care. When you're night diving, you can either see what's in front of you or behind you, not both. Then, when I pick up speed, the quill on top of my head stiffens again. The quills sense for me. I can also use the tentacled tail to taste and feel what's ahead.

I'm now cutting through the strong current along the rocky coast. I break through a swirling curtain of big-eyed scad. A spiny lobster colony, numbering in the thousands, skitters on the rocks below. When I reach the outskirts of a reef, a school of red soldierfish sees me coming and retreats into crevasses. I feel their big, black eyes peering at me from their caves, and I remember why I loved the ocean as a child. For the first time since my youth, I feel free.

Here's the thing. I don't miss my iE. I don't miss it one bit. I don't miss the perfect memories. And I don't miss the constant communication, because I've come to understand that constant communication is control.

4

Several days later, after taking a heli back up to the island, I'm stalking horse-like kirin on the creased cliffs on the south side of the island. I haven't slept since I woke. Because of my father, sleep is now a phobia. I've been tracking a particular black claw-hooved buck for hours now and am determined to find out if I can break and mount it. I'm on my belly, slowly inching toward it. It snorts and shakes its bushy, yellow mane. Its eyes are alert. Its head twitches, but my second skin is a baffle. I slowly reach out to it with my tentacle tail. Curious, the kirin sniffs the tip. I wrap the tail around its antlers. The next thing I know, I'm being dragged across jagged rocks, laughing my head off. I let the kirin go. It gallops inland toward the grasslands. I get up, dust myself off, and smell Ascalon Lee coming.

"It took me two days to track you," she says, irritated. "At least carry a communication device." She hands me an earbud. I take it and put it in my ear.

"Can they be ridden?" I ask.

"I don't know."

"What do you mean, you don't know? You engineered them."

My voice is sharp, but these last days have been wonderous. I've swum the depths with humpbacks and tiger sharks. I've spent evenings watching lava flow at the bottom of the ocean. I leapt downstream from rock to slippery rock, only to discover that I have follicles on the bottoms of my feet that stick to whatever I'm running on, which makes slipping impossible. I was hunted by a giant black lizard in a forest of red flowers—flowers that I smelled more than saw. We wrestled in a grassy clearing, and when I pinned it, I watched it turn to stone.

"I suppose it's possible," Ascalon Lee says.

I sprint in the direction of the kirin, and the last thing I hear from Ascalon Lee is a sigh.

The kirin is faster than me, and I quickly find out that it's had enough. It rears its scaled head, turns around, bounds across the low grass, and charges me, antlers first. I manage to catch the antlers and dig in with my feet. It pushes me back. We're eye to eye and like Dorthy, its irises are a deep amber. It tries to shake me off, but I hold on. It continues to try to wrench from my grip, but I refuse to let go. It's breathing hard now, and so am I. I pull down. It crouches on its scaled belly. I feel its heartbeat. I lower my heart rate, and it begins to do the same. Not long after, our hearts are in rhythm. My second skin slides over my head, slicks my quills back, and transforms into antlers, which I rub against the kirin's. I let go of the kirin and gently scratch its golden beard. As I rub my face in its mane, my skin turns the same color as its hair. Suddenly, it pulls back and whinnies. I look back and see other kirin peeling out of the tree line. I keep rubbing its beard, and the kirin begins to purr. I climb on its jeweled back. It stands. The other kirin are around us now, their long, bushy tails wagging. Ascalon Lee approaches. It's dawn, and I look up at the sorbet skies. The wind blows and a pack of phoenixes soars above.

"Thank you," I whisper. My second skin peels from my head, uncovering my quills, and forms into foam fit and a tentacle again. "I mean it."

"This is the first time you ever thanked me," Ascalon Lee says.

"Now I know why you stayed here. Why you built this. It's . . . beautiful. No, it's perfect. These creatures. The plants and animals that inhabit these islands."

"I have always wanted you to see it. To help build and maintain with me."

I nod. "People like my father and your mother, people who choose to kill, to possess, they will double down on a bad choice and pretend they made the right decision. They will never stop until they warp the future to justify past mistakes. But you stopped. You began making different decisions."

Ascalon Lee puts her hand on the kirin's haunches. Her black skin shimmers under dawn's light.

"I don't want to be like them," I say.

"You aren't," Ascalon Lee says. "You're better. *We're* better."

A silence follows. We both watch the phoenix, symbols of peace and immortality, circle and screech above. Ascalon Lee's continued silence begins to make me feel awkward, so I change the subject. "Tell me about this foam fit you made for me."

She perks up. "Foam fit," she scoffs. "What you have is

purely biological," she says. "It contains your neurons. It's a detachable part of your nervous system. It can take on just about any shape or density you wish."

The second skin slides to my arm, which becomes a long, sharp lance. I eye the bladed edge. When I asked Ascalon Lee to make me purely biological, I didn't anticipate what she could make from tissue. Considering all the creatures she made—the phoenix, the kirin, Akkorokamui, and herself—into a shapeshifter, I should've anticipated at least some of this. I assumed my insistence on looking the way I always have would have limited certain things, but they haven't. Bio-nanos circulate from my body, constantly repairing tissue. Bioelectricity courses through my body. I am even more than what I was when I would shift into sports mode. The problem is that now, there's no switching out of it, and I'm forced to learn restraint. It's okay, though. Like my father, I've walked on heavy feet too long, trampling everything as I moved forward. Restraint is good. Balance is good. I breathe in the clean, salty air. The lance retracts, and to everyone else, I'm just a girl in foam fit once again.

"How long did it take you to make me into this?" I ask.

"It was already made," Ascalon Lee says.

"But how did you know what I was going to ask for?"

Ascalon Lee stares at me with her glimmering golden eyes. "I didn't. The HuSC you inhabit is one I made for me. Mine would have an iE, of course. But I granted your wish."

Maybe my mother was right. Maybe I'm more like her than my own parents. "I don't want to leave," I say.

She nods. "My mother has begun to root them out."

I climb off the kirin. "What out?"

"The other versions of me. This is what I came to tell you."

"Your Venus version?"

She laughs. "No. The ones here on the planet. And it's not her that's hunting them."

The kirin amble back to the tree line. "My father."

"He is skilled at what he does."

"I'm sorry," I say.

"It's okay. The fewer versions of me there are out there, the more focused this version becomes."

"Can this be sustained?"

Ascalon Lee sighs. The rain begins to fall. Light reflects off each drop, and it's as if we're being barraged by tracers. I hear every patter. Smell it. The morning sun shines, but it doesn't stop raining. When I was a child and witnessed this occasional phenomenon my Uncle Akeem would say that the devils were getting married. Akeem Buhari. I feel bad. I never missed him enough. Even at his funeral, I failed to pay him the proper respect. I will do so soon. "Do you know where they are?" I ask.

"I've been trying to locate them," Ascalon Lee says. "But my searches always end with a shot delivered by your father."

"Sorry," I say again.

"You aren't him. You have nothing to be sorry about."

I look back at the mountains. Two rainbows form. I wonder if Ascalon Lee is working on engineering rainbows that can be touched. "Does my father know that I'm alive?" I ask, but I know the answer already. No. If he did, I would've been the first thing he'd look for. Ascalon Lee doesn't bother to respond with the obvious answer. I look at the sky, at the soaring phoenix still circling above. I wonder if the phoenix ever stop to notice stars. To ponder them.

"It's time for me to go," I say. "I've learned this body well enough. I need to head to DownUnder and figure out a way to take down the EMP net that covers it. We can't let all those Leachateans crash and die."

Ascalon Lee grins. "That's very heroic of you. I've prepared a shuttle and loaded it with an outrigger for you. NZ and Tassie aren't shrouded with EMP nets. You still know how to sail, I assume?"

"Yes."

"I have another gift for you." Ascalon Lee whistles. A komainu charges out of the brush. Like me, its skin ripples into the color of its surroundings. It stops in front of me, sits, and pants. I reach down and shake its clumps of curly, silky mane.

"I thought they always came in pairs," I say.

Ascalon Lee raises an eyebrow. "It's been my experience that most things do. What will you name it?"

"I'll think about it. There are just a few more things I need to gather."

"Where?"

"The Buhari estate," I say.

"For what? It's probably been pillaged by treasure hunters years ago. There's nothing there but bad memories for the both of us."

"It hasn't. I had a drone sent over there before I went to From A to Z. I'm not going to NZ or Tassie by shuttle. I'm going by sub."

She bends down and pets the komainu. It's the first time I've seen her pet something. "You are quite the scavenger," she says.

"Kansas taught me."

The Buharis. Years worth of non-perishable food and

water packed on their survival sub along with medbots and meds, explosives, ammo, gear, blood. What I don't tell Ascalon Lee is the farmed organs from my childhood are at that compound, too.

Here's the thing. I appreciate everything that Ascalon Lee has done for me. I owe her. I sincerely do, but I still don't trust her. And I can't be like my father, constantly in the thrall of another, in his case Akira Kimura. Ascalon Lee cannot be my Okaasan. I'm going to the manmade island estate to scan myself at the hospital, to make sure nothing iE is in my head. Then I'm going to pack my organs onto the sub. If I need transplanting, I'm going to do the transplanting with Buhari med bots. If I need to kill, it'll be with Buhari weapons and Buhari gear. Akeem Buhari was the last trustworthy man in the world. Sadly, it's what got him killed in the first place.

Ascalon Lee and I watch the sunrise tint the edges of the gray clouds white. The birds in the tree line warble. Ascalon's Scar twinkles rainbow colors.

"Myth isn't the past, is it?" I say.

Ascalon Lee stands and puts her hands on my shoulders. "Go out there, sister. Don't be Ascalon anymore. Save the Leachateans. Be Taro and create your legends."

5

Typically, when you go to an abandoned, manmade place, overgrowth and decay occur from the outside. Crumbling, windowless buildings choked by vines. Or like in The Leachate, the walls bulge and peel from extreme changes in temperature. One of the more impressive engineering feats in the world, the Buhari estate looks remarkably unweathered on the outside. But when I step through the open lobby doors, its grand halls are pregnant with life. First, there's the chickens. Hundreds of them, it seems. Akeem's prized Marans have taken over the main complex, and the clucks echo in the cavernous expanse. The floor is matted with vines that probably sprouted from the greenhouse. They twist up the faux, recyclable Corinthian columns, grasping for the skylight above. Butterflies flutter while sipping on the nectar of purple flowers. I step over the chickens and hope that the elevator down to the hospital level and sub dock is still in working order.

It is.

I get down to the loading level, and the architecture, along with the life, is strikingly different than the level above. There's nothing decorative or alive down here. The maintenance bots are still in working order. They whiz by with their tooled, tentacle arms dangling from hovering, domed bodies. I head to the corridor that leads to the hospital. Once there, I check if the med bots are in working order. They are. I scan myself. No signs of digital life. Satisfied, I head to the sub. I pass stacked polymer crates of old explosives. I'm walking the path that I did all those years ago. This is where Ascalon Lee murdered Akeem Buhari. I'll always hate her for that. I'd like to avoid old crime scenes, but somehow, I'm always led back to them. Maybe that's what all the places we name essentially are. Old crime scenes.

I reach the dock door and eye scan my way in. I walk through the tube that connects to the submerged underwater cruiser. The maintenance bots seemed to have kept the sub ship shape. I need to check everything manually now, and for the first time, I'm missing my iE. Piloting this thing manually will be a bother, too, but it's worth it. It's worth it for the only voice in my head to be my own. Besides, I'm not actually piloting it. I'm just punching in course settings. The chipped sub will take care of the rest on its own.

First, I'm going to stock up the sub. Then, I'm going to collect Akeem Buhari's remains in his unmarked grave and bury them here. Are his children still alive? Or his grandchildren? If they are, one day, they may be freed from OneVoice. I'll find them and tell them that their patriarch is entombed here.

After I take care of Uncle Akeem, I'll pick up my new komainu. She wasn't happy that I left her on the island, and I'm starting to feel bad. Perhaps I'll bring the kirin buck with me, too. DownUnder is an enormous, inhospitable place. The

oldest continent. Less than one percent of the world's population before Satori Day. Hardly ever discussed on the feed back
in the day. We've surveyed more of the moon and the ocean
floor than DownUnder. It might be good to have a mount
in a place like that. Even if I don't ride him, he can help me
carry stuff: food, water, camping gear. I'm also bringing an
old .50 caliber Barrett with me. It's no rail, but I'm down to
analog weapons now. I refuse to use anything else after what
happened at From A to Z. I'll bring along a good spear and
knife, too. I'll see what the Raid Day smiths have available.
I wish I had the time to attend the next Raid Day to test this
new body. But I'm not into killing things for sport anyway.
I'm not into killing period. Army Strong. Shave Time Money.
A part of me thinks they were righteous kills. A part of me
thinks that there's no such thing as righteous and killing might
be addictive. My father seems to be hooked on it. Ascalon
Lee, too. And, of course, Akira Kimura worst of all.

After I'm done loading up the sub and set course, I patch
into its computer and learn what I can of DownUnder. Har-
bour City is its first city and the southwest anchorage of the
Pacific Bridge. There's a shallow end water city off the coast.
This stuff, I already know. I begin to dig into its history and
find out about its forgotten, ancient people, a civilization
some 60,000 years old, decimated by convict colonization in
a little over a century. That, I didn't know about, and there's
not much info on those 60,000 years. But as Ascalon Lee
would say, those years weren't lost. They happened. After I
read what's available on the aboriginal people, an astounding
list of unremembered, dead explorers and mass murders
follows. Then a gold rush and an opera house, brush fires,
and drought. A cyclone that took out one of its major cities.

The casualty list from the Great Sun Storm. That's when we began building underwater more rapidly. We figured the ocean insulated us from future solar flares and storms. Then, of course, Sessho-seki. A world pulled together to defeat a common enemy that it didn't know never existed. And from there, history becomes a global, peaceful, non-specific thing. There are strange creatures DownUnder, often venomous or hopping things. Extinct then not extinct. Then extinct again. There's the greatest reef in the world. The largest living thing until OneVoice took the title. Why did Akira seal this vast, flat place off? What is she hiding there?

When I arrive at one of the northern islands to retrieve Akeem's remains, it occurs to me that I somehow completely forgot that the islands float, and without a shuttle, heli, or SEAL, I don't know how to get up there. It's strange being under a 597 square-mile chunk of smoking rock, its undercarriage spiked with inverted, mountain-sized icicles. It feels like being under the toothed jaw of some godlike thing. Akeem used to say that his sub could fly, but I know now that he was just kidding around. I wish I had my SEAL, or maybe I should've taken Ascalon Lee up on her shuttle offer. I can glide with my second skin, but not generate lift, and the hovering island above is manifesting some kind of unknown phobia within me. I begin to remember the bats pounding away at my body, the smothering pain. I feel my toes curl. I need to get out from under here. I decide to head to Water City first to pick up my komainu, kirin, and raid gear.

When I get to Water City, I anchor the sub near Volcano Vista's manmade beach. I take a heli to the island to track down the komainu and the kirin. It's the koimanu I find first, or I should say, it finds me. After a lot of licking, whining, barking, and tail-wagging, we search for the kirin. When we find him, I'm grateful that he still likes me. Then I realize that helis aren't big enough to get the pair off the island and down to the sub. When I had an iE, this wouldn't have been a problem. I would've been able to summon a shuttle and carry them down. I ping Ascalon Lee with the earbud she gave me. She tells me that she'll have Motu fly up with a shuttle and to go to Tassie. A version of her will meet me there. She warns me to watch out for the Roaring Forties. Before I can ask her what the Roaring Forties are, she cuts the connection. A logistical nightmare, and I haven't even really gone anywhere yet.

When Motu arrives, the komainu happily enters the shuttle, but the kirin gives me a hard time. I don't blame it for looking at the loading ramp and thinking that this big flying thing has its mouth open and is waiting to feed. I stroke its scaled withers, which soothes it. Once it's calm, I climb on it back and get it to gingerly walk inside. When the ramp lifts, the kirin panics. It begins to snort, kick, and buck. This sends the komainu into a barking frenzy. I can only imagine how hard it's going to be to get both of them onto the sub. I realize I don't even know if either can swim.

When we finally get to the sub, I discover the answer quickly. The kirin bounds from the hovering shuttle as soon as the hatch opens. The barking komainu follows. Both splash into the ocean. Thankfully, they can swim. Considering the deck of the sub is the only land they see, they head straight to it and climb aboard. The kirin shakes its curly, golden mane. The komainu rolls on its back and turns the same color as the sub.

"How are you going to fit the big one in the sub?" Motu asks.

"There's a large loading hatch. And there's enough room inside."

"I can't believe you gave it up," he says.

"What?"

He points to his eye.

"Constant communication is control," I say.

"I should probably keep that in mind when I build my police army."

This makes me want to stay. To just return the miserable kirin back to the island and make sure Motu isn't left unsupervised. It's my responsibility. I was the one who put the idea of a security force out there. I ponder the existence of the forgotten indigenous people of DownUnder that I briefly read about. They didn't have a security force, yet they managed for 60,000 some odd years. That's the thing about power, isn't it? Whether it's Akira, Ascalon, or even Motu here wielding it. Power makes us children again.

"You're going to miss Raid Day," Motu says.

For some reason those words send me diving into the water, forgetting to ask Motu what the Roaring Forties are. I need to get used to forgetting.

I climb onto the sub's massive, gunmetal girth. Motu is shouting. My quills prickle, and I somehow hear the words despite the thunderous whooping of the shuttle's hoverdrive.

"She told me to give this to you!" He pushes a boxed-shaped crate down more at me than to me. My tentacle tail catches it and lays it down on the sub. Then he throws a rod at me. This, I catch with my hand. When I squeeze the baton, two spears pop from each end of the rod. The javelin instantly adopts the color of my skin. I twirl it over my head. It's perfectly balanced. I look up at the Scar and think about the fact that everything is named after something that came before it. Ascalon Lee after St. George's dragon-slaying spear. The Scar after Ascalon Lee. Me after the Scar. I wonder if there are any original names in this world, or if there ever will be.

After I pack the animals and crate into the sub, I set a course to Tassie. The large box contains an old compass, a saddle, some maps, and a note. *Meet me at Cape Wickham*, it says in Ascalon Lee's handwriting. I roll open a map. There's a small island off the coast of Tassie, one that's called King Island. Cape Wickham is on the northern tip of the island. I step to the ship's controls and pull up the holo map. I press the touchpad controller and move the red dot from Devonport to Cape Wickham and click. The komainu ambles to me and lies at my feet. I look down as its eyes close and it turns to stone. I'll name her Pohaku.

I check on the kirin. We rub antlers, and I decide to name him Lio. These are old names, words, really, that are tucked somewhere in the recesses of my memory. Or maybe Ascalon Lee's. I feed Lio some kelp bars, then suddenly, the exhaustion of the last days, weeks, months, and years hit me all at once. Lio slinks down on his side. I sit and lean against his belly. For the first time since being reborn, I sleep.

When we reach the eastern edge of Oceania, I wake up screaming and cursing. *Don't sleep*, I tell myself. *Never sleep.* It's only after I finally calm down that I realize I forgot to move Akeem Buhari's remains. I feel guilty, but I'm also beginning to understand that the fallibility of normal, human recollection seems to have its purpose. Promises and the dead slip easier from memory.

6

When I get to the strait between Tassie and DownUnder and surface, I find out what the Roaring Forties are. The howling winds spin the ocean into a mountainous froth. The sub's hull groans against the chop in protest. It's like we're in the midst of a battle between waves. When we arrive at Cape Wickham, I anchor about a hundred yards off the coast. Pohaku and Lio can't get offboard fast enough. I open the hatch, and they're in the water, swimming right toward an ancient white lighthouse.

I pull up the Barrett and peer through its scope. The coast is rocky and the grass is thick. A mob of wallabies feeds on brush. I don't see Ascalon Lee or anyone else either. I move the sub farther out just to be safe, then drop a raft, load it with provisions, and motor my way to a slip of sandy beach. There's something calming about cutting through the combination of salt, wind, and water. The smacking of the bow against the fitful blue. Air tastes different here. I realize it's fall back home and spring here.

When I get ashore, I drag the raft up the sand, throw the

Barrett over one shoulder, and use the javelin as a walking stick. It's quiet except for the surf crashing against the rocky shoreline. I smell a hint of smoke coming from the lighthouse. It's strange coming to a new place and not being able to dig into my head for all the info on it. To know it without knowing it. To GPS map it. But it's exhilarating as well.

I don't want to follow the smoke. I want to stalk the wallabies and watch them, but smoke probably means human presence, so I feel compelled to investigate. I raise the Barrett and look through the scope. There's a woman draped in animal skins, warming her hands by a campfire while feeding Pohaku fresh meat.

The sun begins to set as I tramp to the lighthouse. The darkening blue sky above is smeared with gray clouds. I smell rain coming. I step onto a dimple of sand. I survey the vast artificial flatness of the area and understand. This used to be a golf course.

The lighthouse's column of square windows is glassless. At the top, the lantern room is still glassed, but the gallery railing is in disrepair. I ache to sketch this place and wonder if I'll have the time to do so. Probably not. As I approach the woman, it's her fingernails I notice first. Dirty and chewed. Her dark hair is graying and the weathered cracking of her skin suggests she's been stranded on this island for years now. She tosses me a whistle carved from driftwood. I catch it.

"Try it," she says.

I put the whistle in my mouth and blow. I smell Lio heading toward us, hear his bladed hoofs cut through the brush.

"Nifty," I say. "Thank you. How long have you been here?"

"Thirty years," she says. "DownUnder is the first continent my mother closed. I haven't been able to figure out how to gain passage. Nothing electronic can pass beyond the shoreline. I've sailed through the Roaring Forties again and again. I've been snake bitten. Shipwrecked. Drowned. I have a boat for you, but you need to be very careful crossing the channel. I'll keep the lantern burning up there in case you get lost."

Lio trots to my side and rubs his mane against my shoulder. I scratch his chin. "Are there people here?"

This version of Ascalon Lee shakes her head as she tosses Pohaku a strip of red meat. "No. None on Tassie or NZ either. All the apocalypse caverns in NZ have been gutted. The cities and houses removed and thrown into boreholes. For years, I thought that she was clearing all of it to build the foundations of something else. Perhaps another A496. NZ is not very close to the equator, but it is isolated, there's good weather, and while one sacrifices spin lift by launching here, it provides polar orbital trajectories. Now that we know what we know, I assume this is where she started her cleansing of everything old. You can call it her dry run. It makes sense—to start in these less populated regions."

I motion at the lighthouse. "Why did she leave this?"

"I suspect she has a romantic weakness for certain pieces of architecture of a certain age. One Tree Hill still stands. The Church of the Good Shepherd. A smattering of buildings made of brick or stone. I suppose her sentimentality is global in scale. Her collective eyes have seen everything."

The tall, white structure under the now-dark sky is striking. I look over at Ascalon Lee; she seems entranced by the fire. Having her concentration constantly bounce from one version to another must be exhausting. It's clear from this woman that Ascalon Lee has been letting the versions of her age. She hasn't been using AMP; she has been letting the years slip away.

"Let's go to the top and turn it on," I say.

She grunts getting up to her feet, then follows me as we climb the white, wooden spiral staircase. We enter the watch room. It's all ancient fuel and clockworks up here. Ascalon Lee flips a switch and light beams from the lantern room a floor above. She opens a door, and we step out onto the gallery. Compared to Water City scrapers, the view is quaint. But the air smells cleaner, and there's an almost homey quality to this place. I gaze at the ocean view and feel what I haven't felt in years. A stirring reverence for it.

"Fifty-six miles north to the next cape," Ascalon Lee says. "DownUnder." She bites her bottom lip. I wonder if it's her tick or the tick of the woman who once inhabited this body. "I wish there was a way we could maintain communication."

"I've been thinking about that," I say. "The EMP net must have some kind of power source. I'll find it and cut the power. Monitor the net. Once it's down, come and find me." I pull the communication earbud out of my ear and hand it to her. She tucks it somewhere in her marsupial coat.

Ascalon Lee sighs. "I think she's there," she says. "I feel it."

Without looking down, she reaches for my hand and grabs it. My first instinct is to pull away, but I don't. I feel jittery, then the jitteriness begins to fade. I can't remember the last time I held another person's hand. *My father.* Back when I was a child, pre-Satori Day. I look at Ascalon Lee and see a version of a similar child somewhere inside her. A socially clumsy thing that sidles to other kids, trying to subtly make them aware of her presence only to be rejected. Then, a frustrated kid almost trying to force other children to be her friend. She feels my eyes on her and turns to me. Her yellow eye shimmers in the dark, and she releases my hand.

"I assume you'll be leaving tomorrow morning?" she says.
"Tonight."

"Have you been eating? Have you been sleeping?"

I'm about to lie and say yes, but behind Ascalon Lee, a
haze of greenish yellow begins to fill the horizon and reflect
off the water. It stretches in streaks to the stars above. I try
to remember what causes auroras, something about charged
particles shooting into magnetospheric plasma. Ascalon Lee
will remember. "Look." I point. "Aurora Australis."

Ascalon Lee turns around and faces the Southern Lights.
"Ah, yes," she says. "Magnetic midnight."

One of the streaks breaks from the aurora. At first, it
slowly twirls and resembles some sort of coil spring. Then
the green coil flattens. That's when the sick feeling hits my
stomach. "Get down!" I say.

Before I can push Ascalon Lee to the grated floor, the coil
pops, and the stream of green light slices through the night
sky. A rail pellet rips through the back of Ascalon Lee's head
and exits out of her yellow eye. She collapses. I drop the
Barrett and leap off the observation deck. My second skin
morphs into a wingsuit. I glide toward the source of the
green light. But I only have enough lift to barrel roll a mile
or two, and I can see that I'm not even close to the source of
the kill shot. Cursing, I splash into the ocean.

I only know one person who could make a rail shot like
that. Miles out, on a boat of some sort, rocking above a fitful
ocean. My father is operating out of DownUnder, and has
taken out another version of Ascalon Lee.

Now, because he killed Ascalon Lee, he's left me a trail of
murderous greens to follow.

7

While making what should have been a fifty-six-mile trek from Cape Wickham to DownUnder, the Roaring Forties blow me off course. Constantly referring to my maps and compass, I learn that the current is pushing me east, and instead of landing at Cape Otway, like I'd planned, it appears I'll be entering the continent through a narrow, rocky channel once called The Rip. The trip on the double-hulled voyaging canoe takes about a day, but Pohaku and Lio look absolutely miserable. Even genetically engineered mythical creatures can get seasick and vomit. I want to enter Port Phillip and sail all the way to Melbourne, but these two aren't having it. Once the large stone structures of Fort Nepean appear on the eastern side of The Rip, both animals throw themselves overboard. If I didn't need to properly anchor, I would've followed them. The sight of sturdy, manmade structures makes me curious. I want to see if there are people here. Perhaps relocated Leachateans? An old military fort is the kind of place my father would make camp. But I smell the greens. They drift northwest of here. How did he pass through the nets?

After I watch Lio and Pohaku safely climb out of the water and shake their shaggy manes, I round the thin peninsula and coast over dark splotches beneath the rippling blue surface. I anchor the boat in the calm, shallow bay. I leave the wrapped Barrett and take the javelin rod and a waterproof pack. I dive overboard and swim backward to shore. Even though I scanned myself and saw no signs of tech, I'm about to find out for sure. I'll either end up short-circuited by EMP or soaked, trudging up the beach. I'm shaking. The memories of what happened in From A to Z play in my consciousness. I don't think they ever really stopped playing. It's always present, like background music. When I get near the beach, the memory of dying grows louder and needles me. I clench my toes. The shore break gently nudges me forward. Nothing. I step onto the sand and laugh. I fall on my back and make sand angels that the waves instantly wash away.

I stand and head up the beach. I don't look forward to confronting my father. I'm still bitter about what he did. About what he's doing now. He is partially responsible for leading all these Leachateans to their deaths. He is working with Akira again, killing the other versions of Ascalon Lee. They made some kind of deal that probably stretches beyond vengeance for what was done to me at From A to Z. I hope it doesn't involve me, but I have a sick feeling it does. He made it his mission in life to always involve me. He should've known that it's impossible to sleep to the future to change the future. One needs to be awake to change that.

I get to the base of concrete stairs lined with an assortment of dried shrubs. I sit on the bottom step, open the pack, and take out a map. The closest major city is Melbourne. On the map, it looks so close, just a quarter of an inch away. I glance at the scale. That quarter of an inch is some seventy miles north. It takes this map to make me fully understand how much bigger this place is than Water City or The Leachate. About 2,500 miles, east-west, almost the same north-south. That's like going coast-to-coast in the old US. How much of a head start does my father have on me?

I look up at the noon sun. If we leave right now and race there in full gallop, we might be able to get to Melbourne by nightfall. But I haven't tested Lio's endurance yet. I haven't tested Pohaku's either. I unload the rest of the gear from the outrigger. Perhaps we should camp here for the night. But the wisps of green tug at me. My father's murderous scent.

After I unload the sailing canoe, I saddle Lio and pack the Barrett, bundled tent, sleeping bag, algae sticks, and canteens of water on him. It's midafternoon, and we begin to walk the cracked, tarred road. There's a sign welcoming us to a place called Sorrento, but beyond the sign, there is no Sorrento. There is no Blairgowrie, Tootgarook, or Rosebud either. No Leachateans or people in general. Just a long pier and a lovely sunset. I decide to make camp.

I can't sleep, so I leave Lio and Pohaku at camp and wander into a rising forest of ferns and peeling snow gums. I feel the symphony of wildlife on the mountain. I climb the trees and sneak up on koalas munching on leaves. I find myself missing my iE again. I want to know more about the koalas. I want to capture images of these lovely creatures.

Wind-blown leaves rattle. I feel the life below me. Above me. Around me.

In the morning, the forests to the west erupt in bird-song. We stick to the old asphalt road, and it's more of the same. Towns marked on my map no longer there. We near Melbourne, and the remnants of coastal suburbs are gone—no blocks, highways, or buildings for that matter. Just hopping, skittish wildlife speckled along the coast. We encounter a copperhead slithering across the path ahead. A small, quilled mammal of some sort buries itself on the roadside when it sees us coming. Pohaku darts to the burrow, sniffs, and begins to dig it up. I've had to stop a number of times to get her back on the road. She's constantly looking for things to chase, and I begin to question her usefulness.

When we get to a place that used to be called Frankston, I see the first one. A whale-shaped shuttle booms supersonic through the clouds and heads straight for the second city. It plummets like a fat-headed missile. I hop on Lio's back, and we ride hard. About an hour later, another shuttle zips from the sky, and this time I hear a burst of thunderclap and feel reverb. Green and red stain the sky. It's like I thought. They can't fly through the EMP net. Okaasan is killing the Leachateans and disposing of them all at once. The Leachateans aboard those shuttles, tricked into doom, need to at least have a chance at survival. I ride Lio even harder, trusting that angry, barking Pohaku will eventually catch up.

I reach Melbourne and find that there is no Melbourne. In its place is a gash so wide that I can't see the other end of it. The circumference pulses in greens and reds. I get off Lio and approach the rim. Looking down, I find the hole is so deep that I can't see the bottom. Another shuttle incoming. It plummets into a maw so endless that I can hear an explosion but can't see it. I need to disable the net. Finding my father will need to wait.

I walk to Lio and pull the map from the saddle. If it were me casting a net, I'd cast it from the middle. In this case, the middle is over a thousand miles away. It'll take too much time to sail back to the sub and get more supplies. According to the map, conditions get harsher and harsher as one nears the center, but there are also a couple of huge lakes a bit past the midway point of the journey. Where there's water, there's life. It will take us a week or so to get to these lakes, another week to the middle. I don't need to eat and drink nearly as much as I used to, so we should be fine if we can hunt and water halfway.

A panting Pohaku trots up to me and growls. She really doesn't like being left behind. I pour water from a canteen into a bowl and this lovable liability laps it up.

After Pohaku and Lio drink, we head northeast. We stop at a river to fill the canteens. Something glides beneath the water's surface. Crocodiles. I need to be careful. I hold my javelin, waiting, but what surfaces is not a croc. It's a platypus. I've never seen one in real life. At first, I think it's the strangest creature I've ever seen. But one glance at Pohaku's dragon face, lion mane, dog body and Lio's flowing beard, six-point antlers, and reptilian skin makes me reconsider. Examining the platypus, I wonder if there once was another Ascalon Lee whipping up new species in a lab a million years before and it's simply happening again. I fill the canteens and attach them to Lio's saddle. We depart what used to be the state of Victoria.

After a couple of days, forests become grasslands that seem to stretch forever. Miles and miles and days and days of unchanging landscape through the bush. Everything looks old here. The trees. The rocks. The dirt. Even the streams look thick and primordial. It takes us nearly a week to notice the painfully slow transition into flat, sunburned vastness. We weave through patches of porcupine grass in the outback. We make camp under the shade of saltbush while being assaulted by searing dust. I even manage to sleep some nights, but two thoughts make it a brief sleep. One, despite the fact that I'm prioritizing the disabling of the net over finding my father, we seem to still be following the green scent that he has left. Two, even though we should reach it in another day, I don't see how a giant lake can exist in this desert. We're nearly out of water, and I haven't seen a source for the last couple of days. We need that lake.

Eight days of slow travel through the grit, and we finally reach Lake Torrens. I feel like the victim of some sick joke. I think I'm lost. Maybe I was distracted by my father's murderous wisps and started going the wrong way. But I climb down a bank and know that I'm standing at the edge of a lakebed. Only, the lakebed is dry, and I can taste the salt in the air. Even if this thing had water, it'd be salt water. I crumple the map and toss it. Pohaku goes off to fetch it. Poor girl. She doesn't understand that I may have doomed us. I eye Lio. His dusty mane has been shedding, and his antlers are beginning to flake. The scales on his belly, once a brilliant crimson, are now rusted. I look up at the cloudless sky. The scar shimmers. This is what happens when we challenge the gods.

Pohaku sniffs at the air, and I smell it, too. My quills stiffen, and my skin turns the same color as the sand beneath me. I pull the Barrett from the saddle and cover it with my second skin. Now, the gun is camouflaged as well. I step away from Lio and peer through the scope. I'm guessing it's my father that I smell out there. I track the scent. It is indeed a man approaching us, but a rail-thin, dark-skinned man wearing nothing but a flap of animal skin tied to his waist. I'm either hallucinating or I've stepped through a time machine and exited to a DownUnder five hundred years ago. What would a man be doing out here, alone, in the middle of nowhere? Though I don't sense murder from him, I maintain my aim while he walks gracefully across the salt pan.

As he nears, I notice his eyes. Intelligent eyes can come in many forms—round, hooded, almond, even eyes that cannot see. But what all intelligent eyes have in common is an unblinking alertness, an objectiveness that suppresses emotion. Eyes that carefully ponder the multitude of ideas that bounce around to inner parts of the brain. People with these kinds of eyes think before speaking. They have the kind of eyes that narrow when they consider that they might be wrong. A wise mind seeks to be corrected. A dull mind is ravenous for confirmation. This is a smart man approaching me. Just another thing that was thought extinct but really isn't.

When the man gets to us, Pohaku growls. The man peers at both creatures and shakes his head. His black, curly locks are shoulder length. The color of his beard ages blond instead of white. Deep creases form between his bushy brows as he frowns. He begins to head northwest, the same direction in which he came, and waves for us to follow. I certainly don't trust him, but my companions need water. And I will, too, eventually. So we follow.

Several miles deeper into the desert, the man stops and motions for me to hand him my javelin. I pause at first. Then I give it to him. He begins poking at the sand with it, then proceeds to dig with his hands. The hole slowly fills with water. I let Pohaku and Lio drink first while I ask the man what his name is. He ignores the question.

When we're finished drinking, I refill the canteens. The man waves for us to follow again.

He seems to know where everything is, which feels impossible considering this place is enormous and lacks any landmarks, that I see anyway. He leads us to a shrub in the middle of nowhere and picks some kind of red berry off it, which he feeds to Lio and Pohaku, then tosses me a few as well. Sometimes I forget that dry things can grow, too.

For days, he leads us deeper into the desert, occasionally stopping to dig up a soak or some grubs, not once uttering a word. We keep moving north, following the planked tracks of some ancient gauge line. I'm suspicious because we're also more or less following my father's trail as well, but I'm appreciative. Lio, Pohaku, and I watch the man and are learning how to live in this place of stubborn survival. If I had an iE, I could mark the coordinates of everything that the man has shown us, but I don't. It's strange learning things that I know I'll probably forget. Though I've come to believe that information has energy, so it has mass. Information is matter, and I use to feel it weigh me down constantly. I'm glad to be rid of some of it.

About a week after the man found us in the middle of all this coarseness, I see where he's leading us to. It's the only thing that rises from this vast flatness, the tip of a dry mountain that's been burying itself for millions of years. The thousand-foot-tall monolith that stretches two miles across is named Uluru. I read about it back on the sub. When the sun rises and sets, the creased rock tints red. It's midday now, so what I'm seeing is a bald, beige, sandy thing. As we get closer to Uluru, I notice the flora that surrounds its base. Too green for out here. I peer at the man. He says nothing. The trees that we approach are orchards of orange trees. I taste the citrus. Then I see the oddest thing: twenty-two people of varying ages are playing some sort of game with a single hard ball and a bladed wooden bat. They're all wearing breathable whites.

The players pause when they see us coming. Some are dark-skinned, like the man who brought us here, others lighter, but they all share physical characteristics. They are definitely not Leachateans. Nor do they seem to be Gardeners. They're free, like the people of Water City. But I haven't seen this kind of free people in years. An enormous, multi-generational family. A little boy puts down the bladed bat and begins to run toward us. He's smiling.

"Grandpa Id!" he says.

I turn to look at the man. I've never met him before. He supposedly died before I was even born. Akira had brought him back to be the engineer and trigger man for Satori Day. I know it's him. The man I'm standing next to is the inventor of the iE, Idris Eshana.

8

Uluru is basically a shell that conceals what I can only describe as a solar-powered, state-of-the-art facility that pumps and treats groundwater from below. There are living quarters, restrooms, a recycling waste plant, a hospital, supply stores, 3D printing studios, basically, everything an advanced living space needs in order to be sustainable for the foreseeable future.

In the vaulted main hall, the quiet buzz of the z-dust filters hums through the climate control system. The walls are made of the same stuff as the mountain—rocky, but lacquered. The floor is lit up to make it appear as if gentle waves wash below transparent tiles. The furniture reflects ocean nostalgia, too. Cushioned, shell-like chairs and transparent tables shaped like lobtailing humpbacks scatter the lobby. I step to one of the tables, encased are human bones. I touch the surface, same kind of polymer that most of Water City is made of. The kind of music that people don't feel the need to pay attention to fills the air. I pay attention just because I haven't heard music in so long.

When Idris Eshana finally did speak to me while we watched his family finish up their cricket game, he apologized for not saying anything earlier. He said he wanted to observe what kind of person I was, and in his experience, talking was counterproductive when judging someone's character. I asked him why the hell he was walking around a desert almost completely naked. He smiled and said he and his family learned and practiced the ancient ways of DownUnder survival, just in case. When I asked him if he'd seen my father, he nodded and revealed he'd allowed my father to pass through a couple of days before I arrived. In fact, that's why Idris came out to meet us. My father asked him to keep an eye on me. That was irritating to hear.

Why is he avoiding me? Does it have something to do with a deal he made with Akira Kimura?

Idris, changed into foam fit, is giving me the grand tour. His iE bobs behind us, which I find oddly familiar and comforting after being out in the bush for so long. He wouldn't allow Pohaku and Lio to enter despite Pohaku's growling protest. He points to the domed ceiling. The balls of track lighting roll across curvature, seeming to defy the laws of gravity.

"Clever, isn't it?" Idris says.

"Quantum locking," I say.

"Correct. Grand, right?"

Images of A496 and the floating islands flash in my head. "You haven't seen nothing yet."

He frowns and leads us to a wall filled with fading swirls of rock art. "I was careful to preserve these paintings," he says. "They're steeped in mythology. Some of them are even maps. For example, maps to underground water sources."

I peer at the dots of white paint, wanting to be polite, wanting to be impressed, but I have too many questions . . . and demands. Before I can speak, he gestures at the transparent tables shaped like whale tails. "Did you see the bones? That's Mungo Man and Mungo Lady. They were here over forty thousand years ago. Can you imagine? My children and I dug them up and preserved them in the tables."

I think about my mother and sister, their bones dug up in Kansas, their graves desecrated. I imagine Idris and his family setting their tea kettles and crumpets on the table of human remains. I'm beginning to not like this man. "I appreciate the tour," I say. "But I need to figure out a way to disable the EMP net that covers this continent."

Idris shakes his head. "I can't let you do that."

"Do you realize she's sending shuttles filled with people here? They're getting snagged in your net and are plummeting."

"That is not my doing. I won't take responsibility for that."

While people die, these people play the blame game. OneVoice will argue that it's not her fault. Idris can drop the net, and the shuttles can land safely. Idris will argue that Okaasan knows the net exists, so she is knowingly sending these people to their deaths. Maybe that's how humans with power have always operated during near-apocalyptical events. With rationalized shrugs. It wasn't me, they say. When it was. It was all of them.

I look down at the floor and its blue, undulating illusion. I get it now. This is a man who wants to constantly feel like he can walk on water.

"You need to at least give them a chance," I say.

"A chance? Why do you think I put up the net in the first place?" Idris says.

"You?"

Idris nods. "This was the first place she . . . decommissioned. It makes sense, really. Flat. Logistically easier than the other continents. Isolated. Huge swaths of unpopulated lands. Most of what was modern civilization was crammed into the coastal east. Dig a hole there, and, well, you know."

"You watched her dig the holes?"

"Correct. I watched and waited until she was done. Waited until she left. Then I came."

"Why come here?" I ask.

He raises both arms and looks around. "I built this before I even met Akira Kimura." He pauses and smirks. "It's funny, after Sessho-seki, people forgot that for decades I was the richest person in the world. I bought a majority of the continent ages ago. I'm the one who renamed it DownUnder. Everyone was so happy, and distracted, after Akira saved the world, I figured that it was an ideal time to give this continent the name I really wanted."

Saved the world. What a joke. But I get it now. Uluru was his apocalypse shelter years before the times of Sessho-seki. In fact, he probably began to plan the engineering of the EMP net in the years that followed. When the world is ending, a shelter is only good if it can keep other people out. And he's never had an army. He had to come up with other means to keep from being invaded. Not to mention, its location is perfect. It's in the middle of a damn desert. All this show of preserving the art of aboriginal people is bullshit, too. Like the mountain that Akira built Savior's Eye on years ago, Uluru is sacred to its indigenous people. The bones of their people are sacred. Just like Akira did with my father's help during the times of Sessho-seki, Idris had to kick what was left of the aboriginal people out of their own heritage site to build this goddamn thing. He gutted their creation being and plastered it with his tech.

I wonder if the old me could've hacked into his system and turned the net off. Can the new me simply tear down its mainframe? It's here somewhere.

Idris eyes me like he's trying to guess what I'm thinking. "Let me show you something," he says. He gestures to the ceiling. The balls of track lighting scatter like struck marbles. They roll to their programmed positions and beam their light at the center point to form a holo of a rotating earth. The rest of the giant room dims. The image of DownUnder lights up.

"As I said," Idris begins to narrate. "She started here. NZ next. Her Gardeners on this side of the Pacific basically swept across the Pacific Bridge."

After NZ lights up, a lighted trail extends to the islands of Water City. "She stopped there for a bit. I'm not sure what she did, but once she was done, and she redistributed human populations so that each continent had roughly the same amount of people per square footage, she began to cast her own EMP nets over the other continents. Once she did that, intercontinental travel was nearly impossible. If passed through the net, an iE would be fried by lightning storms of electromagnetic pulse that stretch down from the stratosphere and anchor themselves in the oceans that surround the continents. Anything navigated or powered by electricity would be disabled by the net. I'm assuming she's doing there what she did here. Filling her graves with the old world. Europe and South America first." Those continents light up. "Africa, then Asia next." Those light up. "At first, I thought that she was going by order in size, smallest to biggest. But as far as I know, North America is still open, which doesn't make sense." North America flashes in red like it's on alert. "Asia and Africa are bigger."

I try to remember the data that Ascalon Lee sent to me on the other continents. I try to recall the flashes that OneVoice revealed while I ascended to the top of Volcano Vista, and the others that she leaked to prove that I was sleeping all that time, but it's all foggy to me now with my new fallible memory. *What is she ultimately trying to achieve?* She clearly has a mission, and every mission, every goal has a point of completion. She didn't net North America because of A496. She needed it as an exit point for her space explorations. The Leachatean refusal to clear out also required her to keep travel open for her to do what she's doing now. But why not just drop the Leachateans in the boreholes in North America? Is this her way of absolving guilt since Idris built this net, not her, and he's the one keeping it up?

"Akira never went after you after Satori Day?"

"No, she seemed very busy. I was afraid that she would come after me. I snuck here, waiting for her to finish burying just about everything manmade before she made her move. Then the Gardeners left, so I put up the EMP net—technology that I'd been working on for decades. She left me alone."

The balls of track lights disperse, breaking like in billiards, and the holo of the planet disappears. The lighting returns to normal. I recall learning about the islands all those years ago, what happened way before I was born. The gutting and disposal of the old infrastructure, the houses, streets, and their signs, the last remnants of a dead language that only Ascalon

Lee remembers. In its place, Water City and Savior's Eye. This has all happened before, hasn't it? But never this quickly, never on this global scale.

"Why did she leave certain bits of structures alone?" I ask.

He shrugs. "My guess is sentimental ticks. The residue of nostalgia of hive mind."

Ascalon Lee had guessed the same.

"How did my father get past your net?"

"I let him in," Idris says. "Just like I let you in."

I'm surprised. I find it interesting that he thinks he let me in, but it makes sense. Living is far less impractical without his invention. Who in their right mind would live without iE even after all that's happened? "Why did you let him in?" I ask.

Idris's face hardens. "All those years ago, I told myself that what she was doing was good. Sessho-seki. The scar. The lie. It would make this world a better place. And I think it did. But the guilt did nag at me some. Just like it did your father."

"You knew it was a lie while she was doing it?" Idris is admitting to being the worst kind of acolyte. The kind that don't believe but follow anyway. "My father didn't know until years later."

Idris rubs his throat. "I knew. I just never said I knew. I'm sure others knew, too. But you know what happened to those who spoke up."

I sigh. "My father."

"Yeah. So, I even overcompensated. Not only did I not stay silent, but I fully endorsed the Ascalon Project. I controlled the feed back then. We made The Killing Rock true through all the media I owned. Dissenters, for the most part, were simply tracked and censored. She couldn't have done it without me. I'm also the one who gave your father the means to disable the iEs of the dissidents. I gave him the device. Don't you understand?" He raises his arms again, motioning for me to witness all his splendor. "The EMP net uses the same technology, just on a far grander scale."

I close my eyes for a moment. My father was right. Fucking people.

Idris clears his throat, then continues. "But despite all the money and AMP treatment in the world, I got old. I got sick. And I got really scared. It's one thing to face death in an instant. That is, of course, terrifying. But for it to tug at you at every moment, and to feel that tug, to feel death slowly and methodically reeling you in. You'll do anything to cut bait. Especially when you know, *you know*, your life is worth *more* than just about everyone else's in every single way. Akira visited me one day, on one of those really bad days, years after the Ascalon Project. She told me she had an idea—a new project in mind."

"Eternal life," I say.

"Tech that she acquired from her daughter. I wept and begged for it. She told me that if she gave it to me, she would require my help in return. What she was saying made sense to me. I've studied evolutionary psychology. We have the fundamental urge to link our minds together. Technological advances in communication, in connection, are our greatest. They satisfy our most primal urge. Linked minds. It's why we evolved the way we did. Akira was just going to quicken the final step in that evolution."

"But you needed to die," I say. "It demonstrated trust. And you needed to experience it to never, ever want to experience it again. Then she put you to work in NZ. Building all those iEs."

Idris grimly nods. "You've died?"

"Once or twice."

"Then I don't understand. What are you doing? Appreciate life! Care for it! Create it!"

I find myself missing the loin-clothed mute that guided us through the desert. Instead, I'm standing in front of a smug, foam-fitted, has-been mega mogul whose ambition and cowardice helped break the world. I look at him sternly. "You didn't answer my question. Why did you let my father through the net?"

Idris's lips pucker then collapse into thinness. "I always liked him. Regret and a guilty conscious can be powerful things. Plus, I owed him. If things didn't go right, I might still be in NZ, half-starved, half-crazed, overseeing AI production to the end of days."

"What did he want?"

"He knew you would follow him here. He wanted me to take you in. For you to ride whatever is coming out safely with me."

Did my father kill the Tassie version of Ascalon Lee to lure me here as well? I glare at Idris. I need to be ready for his next move. "Take down the net."

"No," Idris says. "Then Akira will find me."

"She probably already knows where you are. She's probably known for years."

"Yes, that may be true, but she hasn't attempted to come back to this place once she left. I assume that might be due to the fact that I don't meddle in her affairs."

"Well," I say, "you've already proved to be a coward time and time again. I can see her leaving you alone."

Idris pulls a device from his foam fit and points it at me.

It's a taser-looking thing, and I immediately know what it is: a weapon that emits an electromagnetic pulse meant to disable an iE. Like he said, he modeled the EMP net after this little device that he created. My father used this device when he hunted down and killed the scientists who dared challenge Akira and attempted to tell the world that Sessho-seki didn't exist. My father used it so there wouldn't be any audio or visual evidence of his presence at the time of their deaths. I step forward and let Idris point the thing at my eye. He pushes a button. Nothing happens. He pushes the same button a second time. Again, nothing happens. Some genius.

"I'm unplugged," I say. "There isn't an iE in me anymore."

My second skin extends from my body and coils around Idris. I squeeze.

"Did my father put you up to this?" I ask. "Did he want you to disable me?"

The rest of Idris's family come charging into the room, even the little ones. He must've pinged them. Two of them point rifles at me. The sleeve of my second skin grows into a short lance. I put the tip at Idris's throat.

"Answer the question," I say.

"Yes," Idris answers. "He just wanted you down temporarily. A week. Maybe two."

"Why did you listen to him?"

"He said that she sent him."

"Akira," I say. "And you weren't afraid she sent my father here to kill you?"

"If she wanted me dead, she would've done it decades ago. Also, I'm diplomatic."

"There's no diplomacy when it comes to Akira. Only

obedience." I ignore his family and glare at him. "Show me how the EMP net works," I say.

Idris flinches. "You won't understand!"

"Try me," I say.

The ceiling's marbles scatter again, get into position, and project a holo. This one is a topographical 3D shot of DownUnder. It looks like what we're calling it. A net. Mesh covers the continent and is anchored at evenly spaced points a handful of miles offshore. There are a few dozen of these sinker points, and I wonder what would happen if one of them were cut. Maybe he temporarily turned one off to let my father in. But no, being able to disable it from the outside would be too easy. It'd make it too easy to turn the thing off.

"You can't simply cut through it," Idris says, guessing at what I'm thinking. "It's like a constant geomagnetic storm covering the continents. Trying to cut through it would be like trying to cut through wind and lightning."

"It's like the Great Sun Storm," I say. "The one that killed Akira's father and many others when she was a child. But this storm never weakens."

"Disaster can be inspiring," Idris says.

"Change the view," I say to Idris. "I want to see it as if I were looking at it from a mountaintop in NZ."

Idris scoffs. "You can't see this place from NZ."

"Stop being difficult. You know what I mean."

The image turns and levels. It's a wide view. I watch the net's grids rise and connect to a center point above Uluru. Like most casting nets, this one has a horn. I recall primary school, where I first learned how to throw nets over schools of fish. I remember draping some of the coiled net over my shoulder. Then skirting my thigh with more weighted filament. This was the part of the net that was thrown. It was stunning to toss and see all that rolled-up net become undone and twirl like the skirts of a pirouetting dancer. To watch it plop on the water's surface, then sink, then carpet. My classmates and I cast them over schools of silver flagtails. What is Idris's net made of? The horn that floats and connects all the energy filament together at the middle scrapes the bottom of the mesosphere.

"Are Akria's nets constructed like this as well?" I ask.

"Of course they are," Idris says, an edge of panic in his voice. "She's a damned plagiarist. I erected this net after she left. Then she simply copied my design and eventually covered the other continents after."

"The top of this mountain, Uluru, it's a big magnet, isn't it?"

"Yes. It's a superconductor that not only powers the net, but it ensures that the collar can't touch ground. The collar and the magnet repel each other."

"Have you ever thrown a net over fish?" I ask.

"No," he says.

"You know what happens after a net hits the water?"

"No! Now, let me go!"

I release him. He runs to his family. Two of his kids raise their guns at me again. Idris turns and sneers at me. My second skin forms into a casting net, and I spool it in and drape it over my thigh. The Eshana family frowns and looks at me like I'm crazy.

"This is a net." I toss it up, and the round net twirls above me. It hangs there, suspended, spinning away. The family takes a step back. The spinning slows, and the net begins to drop. The skirt hits the floor first.

"After the net hits the water," I say, "it sinks at its weighted edges. The unweighted horn hits the water last."

The horn, the ring that holds the entire netting together at its center, floats.

"What if we push the horn down as hard as we can?" I step to the horn, grab it, press it down near the center of the net, and pin it there. "The net will flatten."

Idris frowns. I believe he understands. "Impossible," he says. "I already told you. The magnet and horn repel each other. You would need to turn the net off to flatten it."

"Why?" I ask and point to the net in front of me. "If I can bring the horn down with enough force, not on the magnet, but near it . . ."

"The EMP mesh will momentarily drape the continent," Idris says. "It will ripple an electromagnetic pulse across it. Theoretically, this will disable every iE there."

I pull the horn up. "The Gardeners on that continent will be disconnected. They'll be free." The net loses its form and my second skin slithers and coils around me.

"First," Idris says, "once anything electrical gets near the horn way up there, and I mean way up there, the approaching object will be disabled. You're also talking about a constantly moving object that flutters with Cat 4 hurricane winds at temperatures negative two hundred degrees. Then, in order to pull it down, something would need significant mass or thrust. And even then, the strength of the superconductor and magnet would make it impossible for the horn to make landfall. At its lowest point, it would simply bounce all the way back up."

"But for an instant," I say, "the net would pulse across the continent. The geomagnetic storm would disable everything, including Okaasan, on that continent."

"Even if you could, which you can't, you'd be committing mass murder on the continent that you choose. The Gardeners can't simply be disconnected. They'll die."

"I know someone who was disconnected and didn't." Jon6J. The others who got unplugged at From A to Z. Not just the ones who came to take Shave Time down with me, but the poor souls in the Woodmen. No, disconnecting doesn't cause death. That was always just another lie.

"I won't help you with this insanity," Idris says.

I eye his family. It's a good-looking, healthy group dressed in plain foam fit. There's not much water around here, but foam fit can also cool the body, and the center of DownUnder certainly doesn't lack heat. Idris's two armed adult children look at each other, then look back at me. The older, Idris's eldest daughter, I suspect, peers at her father.

"What if it works?" she asks.

I can see them now, subconsciously forming factions. Some, like Idris, want nothing to do with this. Others like the idea of even the slightest possibility of freeing the world. And a small minority brighten to the idea of simply watching what they think will be my most spectacular death. I need to take advantage of the conflict before Idris puts his foot down.

"I just need you to open your net," I say. "Leave DownUnder open for a few days. Let's see if these shuttles filled with innocent Leachateans will land and let people out. My guess is they won't. Akira is cleansing. But we should at least give them a chance."

About half his clan nod with me. I sense their loneliness, the same loneliness I felt in Kansas. And perhaps, I sense, a bit of humanity.

"I also want to ping a friend and have her come pick me

up. I need the net open or turned off for her to be able to come get me. The faster she's able to, the sooner I'll be out of here."

"I never should've let your father in," Idris mumbles.

I get it. Nobody who thinks they have it good wants the world to change. And they certainly won't risk everything to try.

"Deal?" I say.

"Who is it that's coming to give you a ride?" he asks.

"The daughter," I say. "Ascalon Lee."

Idris Eshana throws his hands up and storms out of the room. Most of his kin follow. The two armed family members drop their aim. And I think it's a yes. They'll turn off the net. It's a yes because the bottom line is this: Sure, a part of him is scared about what I'll do if he says no. Really, though, he's scared of Akira, scared that Okaasan will simply turn on him, too, one day. He'll convince himself, he didn't really help me; he simply showed me a few days of hospitality, then let me be on my way. It's not like he's participating in some kind of revolution. Soon, however, probably any second now, he'll realize that the instant the net drops, Okaasan will know. When her shuttles pass through the turned-off net cast over DownUnder, the shuttles will cease to plummet from being disabled by the net's electromagnetic pulse. He will be scared then. I need to work quickly before he changes his mind.

I step to the woman who I suspect is Idris's eldest and stick out my hand.

"I'm Taro," I say.

"Maira." She adjusts the rifle strap on her shoulder and shakes my hand. Her three little children stand behind her, glancing at each other, not sure what just happened and not sure what they should do right now. Above, the lights flicker. Then I hear the sound of something powering down.

"The net?" I ask.

Maira nods. "He's powered it off."

Suddenly, for the first time in days, I feel jolted by excitement. "Can you do me a favor and ping someone for me?"

Maira nods. "I presume Ascalon Lee?"

"Yes, please," I say.

"She will open a line of communication?" Maira asks. "Wait . . . Oh my. Someone identified as Ascalon Lee is pinging me now."

"Please provide her our coordinates."

Maira furrows her brow. "That's unnecessary. She says she's on her way."

So smart, I think. Ascalon Lee was monitoring the status of the EMP net this entire time. As soon as it dropped, she sent out a continent-wide ping, seeing if anyone here had an iE, or any type of communication device to accept it. She immediately discovered that twenty-three people do—the members of the Ishana family. She pinpointed their location, which, well, is what pings were originally used for back in the days of warfare submarines. And once she found people who could receive messages, she sent one. Maira, who is standing right in front of me, accepted. In a matter of seconds, Ascalon Lee now knows how many people are in DownUnder and exactly where they are. She knows I'm with them.

Maira's about to turn and leave, but she pauses. "He never should have invented it, should he?"

I know she's referring to the thing bobbing behind her. I shrug. "Someone else probably would've if not him."

Maira's children impatiently tug at her hands. The brief moments of excitement have already faded for them, and now they're bored and want to get out of here. "Good luck," she says.

"Your kids," I say. "They all look very much like your father."

Maira shoos the children away. They scurry off to find the others. Once they leave the room, Maira glares at me. "They should," Maira says. "They're his."

I nod solemnly, trying to cool the thing that boils in me. "I'm sorry," I say. "I didn't know. One of them called him 'grandpa' when I arrived."

"They don't know," Maira says. "And it's not what you're thinking. It involves cloning, not coitus."

"But what do you . . ."

"Your friend is on her way," Maira snaps. She takes the rifle off her shoulder and hands it to me. "I'll make sure the net remains open." She pauses. "Break it. Break this fucking world."

9

When Ascalon Lee came to Uluru, she knew it wasn't only a ride I wanted. She needed to see Idris's EMP net from the inside and figure out how it worked. When she'd arrived, Idris and his entire family went on a walkabout, so they were no help. Idris didn't want anything to do with Ascalon Lee and said that he'd leave the net down for two days. After that, it would be coming back up. Two days seemed short, but Ascalon Lee figured it out quickly enough. She gazed up, moved the marble lights on the ceiling, and created a holo scale model of the EMP net with light. She grinned with understanding. The grin went away when I told her my idea.

"It's freezing cold that high," she said. "The air is razor thin. And with the winds, you can't glide up there. I doubt you'd survive such an ordeal."

"A496 is even higher and actually stable. So it's possible, right?"

"Have you been getting sleep?"

"I'm not deranged," I said. "And I'm not a fucking infant. Fuck sleep."

Ascalon Lee sighed. She started to say something but changed her mind. She, of all people, must get it. After one is put to sleep, against their will, for years, the last thing they want is sleep no matter how exhausted they are, which I had been. "You're burning far too hot," she said.

"It's my life. *Finally*, it's my life."

She looked up and held up a fist. "It's all held together at the center, by a, what did you call it, a horn? The horn in this case is a balloon of some sort. Constantly moving." She jerked her fist to-and-fro to demonstrate what she meant. "Probably guarded by cloaked drones around its perimeter. The horn itself is probably cloaked." She opened her fist and extended her empty hand to me. I slapped it away.

"I doubt there are drones," I said. "I doubt the horn is cloaked. Either things would be fried that close to the net."

She rubbed her cheeks with her hand. "I don't even know if it's possible to locate the horn, much less bring down. Besides, if we destroy the horn, I'm sure she'll just send another balloon up to replace it."

"I told you," I said. "I don't want to destroy it. I want to use it."

"Yes," she scoffed. "Use the net to free Gardeners from OneVoice. Do you not remember Jon6J? If anything, he was more dangerous and fanatical after he was disconnected from OneVoice."

"He was a prototype. You said it yourself. Besides, I saw the ones at the Woodmen. They didn't a have spare set of eyes packed in their wombs. Also, maybe others react differently. Anyway, they can stay fanatical. But maybe, over time, they stop making that choice. I worshipped my father for years. I dreaded and worshipped you. I don't anymore. Besides, I'm not trying to change minds. If they want to continue to worship her, fine. I'm just trying to liberate."

Ascalon Lee thinks about this. "The world might not change like you hope or expect."

"At least it will be free."

Ascalon Lee lets out a heavy sigh.

"How much force and mass would I need to bring down the balloon for an instant and flatten the net?" I ask.

"To come straight down and not get blown off course? You shouldn't be asking me about force. You should be asking me about miracles. And what net did you want to try?"

"Asia's," I said. "It's the closest."

Ascalon Lee laughed. "You're crazy."

I thought back to my father and my poker-playing days. He'd said something one snowy night that stuck with me— *human beings are programed to worry only about danger that's right in front of their face.* This made practical sense for most of the species' history. Once the world got connected on a global scale, it's not like our programming changed. People didn't really care what was happening halfway around the world. In fact, many resented the fact that they were told that they should care and became hostile. Well, Akira made them care alright, with her fake asteroid. But once the supposed threat was defeated, people resumed not caring. I thought about that and wondered that maybe with poker he wasn't just teaching me about lying with no real risk gambling. He was possibly teaching me something he was never able to truly learn: you need to care even if there aren't personal stakes.

"OneVoice is probably aware that Idris's net has dropped," I said. "She'll know because her shuttles aren't shutting down when they approach this continent. She's probably already suspicious. I'm doing this with you or without you, so I'd appreciate any input you have."

Ascalon Lee raises her fist. "This," she says, smacking her fist into her palm. "is a kamikaze mission."

"Divine wind?" I asked.

"No," she said. "I speak of the pilots who flew their planes into naval vessels in a war a quarter of a millennium ago."

I would've known this if I still had been connected to an iE. "They sound brave."

"No, they were brainwashed fools."

"Well then, let's unbrainwash the world and let them choose to be fools."

Ascalon Lee grinned. "I have an idea. In fact, you inspired it. But it'll cost me a life."

"Well, just spend a life you don't like," I said.

"You have the crude wit of your father."

I thought about that. He was out there somewhere. I felt the faint wisps of green fading. His trail had led me to Uluru, but why had he wanted me to stay there? *Something big must be about to happen*, I thought. Another patch. A big one, perhaps. Bigger than the ones with "S" designations. That last one hadn't worked the way she wanted, so it only made sense that the next one would be a historic whopper. She'd resurrected both herself and my father. And my father had been reducing her daughter. Keys in locks. Keys in locks. Once again, I had no key for this one.

"What's your idea?" I asked.

She grinned. "Divine wind."

We headed back to Water City, and Ascalon Lee prepared a stunt shuttle for this impossible stunt.

Two days after she picked us up from Uluru, Ascalon Lee and I are 63,000 feet above Central Asia, skipping across the atmospheric tides above the Armstrong limit. We're so high that the planet slightly bends at the horizon, and I have no idea if it's day or night. All I know is that I can see pockets of yellow light on the surface. I'm not sure if I'm looking at cities or airglow, and the carpets of clouds that hover miles below obscure my view. The stunt shuttle rattles. Ascalon Lee curses and pulls up. Every rough patch is unnerving. We don't know if we're surfing the planetary waves, got hit by a drone missile, or got caught in EMP. We both sigh in relief when the shuttle doesn't shut down and we don't plummet or explode. We're scouring for a balloon that theoretically should be up here while trying to avoid getting snared in a net that we can't see. The bearded surgeon version of Ascalon Lee is up here with me while the version who picked me up is back at Water City, observing from afar. I never really noticed how old he was. Now, even through the tinted visor of his pressure suit, his naked head reveals a balding scalp crowned with liver spots and his unmasked face is creased and sags with age. What was he before Ascalon Lee took him decades ago? A skimmer perhaps? A hydronaut? An actual surgeon? It's impossible to tell, because his eyes are no longer his anymore. They haven't been for years. The right glimmers xanthic, and even though it's not her voice, it's clearly Ascalon Lee who speaks to me.

"Where is this damned thing?" she says.

"I'm sorry you're going to die," I say.

"No problem," she says.

"Not you," I say. I reach over and touch the male body's forearm. "You. This man who you inhabit."

Ascalon Lee ignores the sentiment and checks the scanners. I look out the ika-class shuttle's eye and take in the vastness. I begin to understand the lunacy of my plan. The slightly bent horizon layered in blue bands that go from light to dark. The mountains and fluffy plains of clouds that look broken apart below. I put my hand against the glass and feel the freeze outside. My skin, both first and second, prickle. This is the highest sustained flight I've ever been in. Perhaps we didn't think this through. It's only been two sleepless days since Ascalon Lee met me at Uluru. But when both of us are enthusiastic about the same thing, something euphoric, and maybe a little toxic, brews in me. I believe it brews in her, too.

"Remember," Ascalon Lee says. "Once we hit the tropopause, eject. You should be able to glide down safely. Don't worry about the pressure, lack of oxygen, or temperature up here. I assure you, your body can take it."

I nod and peer down, searching for some kind of trail. The wisps of green that may bleed from this murderous thing. But perhaps the winds are too strong up here. We've been in flight for hours, crisscrossing airspace above the borders of western Mongolia, and I haven't seen anything yet.

"We might need to fly lower," I say.

Ascalon Lee curses. "We fly lower, and we will get snagged."

"Just down a little lower," I say. "At the Armstrong limit."

We begin to descend. Once the altimeter reads 62,000 feet, my nose and quills tickle, and I begin to smell something.

"Slow down," I say.

Ascalon Lee cuts airspeed. I feel the slip of something loose fluttering out there at the elevation where meteoroids disintegrate. The thread is frayed, and I'm about to lose it. I close my eyes and breathe in. I open my eyes and the tension on the loose thing begins to tighten.

"Lower," I say.

"But . . ."

"Lower!"

A thin, almost imperceptible flapping cord of green slants to the left of us and tightens while we pass it.

"Circle here!" I say.

The shuttle tilts to its side and shudders. We carve through the strong atmospheric tides.

"Slowly spiral inwards," I say.

We circle and work our way in. A green cable that tethers us to the middle grows thicker and thicker.

"I see better now," I say.

Ascalon Lee nods. "I've heightened your five primary senses considerably. It makes sense that you do, but you need more rest if you live through this. Perhaps AMP?"

I shake my head. "I'm never climbing into one of those again."

After flying a few more tightening circles, I can make it out. A balloon, like Ascalon Lee said, silver and erratically bobbing with turbulence. It's smaller than I imagined, this horn that holds a geomagnetic storm over an entire continent together, and its movements are violent. The green, a now thick, unbending cable, juts from the balloon. It swivels erratically. I'm seeing more and more what it's like to be outside up here, removed from the safety of the shuttle.

"Do you see it?" I ask.

"Yes. *Yes*. I'm marking its general coordinates now."

"That's the most difficult moving target I've ever seen," I say.

"Yes. There's no way to eyeball this target. That's yet another reason I need to be here." She pauses. "You wanted only one life. I gave you one life. Are you sure you want to do this?"

I nod and gulp.

"Ready?" she asks.

I nod quickly again and dig my fingers into the co-pilot seat.

The shuttle pulls up. The sudden Gs slam me back. The shuttle rattles.

"I set up manual ejection," Ascalon Lee says. "You'll know if we snagged the collar by a jolt of deceleration. Once we pass the barrier of the net, I, along with the shuttle, will be . . . decommissioned. You must try to keep the shuttle out of flat spin until the tropopause. You want to nose-dive."

"A net to catch a net," I say, thinking about the mesh that Ascalon Lee rigged onto the tail of the shuttle. Strapped from one fin to another, the thing looks like a honeycomb graphene hammock flapping back there.

She assured me that the threads of the thing will hold when the collar of the EMP net is snagged. She weaved the hammock into the fuselage. The ultimate tensile strength to stop an asteroid, she said. This made me think of Sessho-seki. Of my father. Of a reoccurring dream I stopped having. My father and Ascalon Lee arguing over which of my body parts they want to cut off and take. For some reason, I interrupt and ask my father what part he wants to take. *The part you got from my mother*, he says. *Which part is that*? I ask. *Forgiveness*, he says. He says it every time.

I look at Ascalon Lee. People have tides if you pay attention. I think I stopped sensing that when I was connected, but I'm beginning to see it again now. Ascalon Lee's surface tides run deep and strong. But beneath that, in her midnight zone, there's shame. Insecurity. Maybe even eddies of guilt. She spent one life trying to be her mother. She spent the next seeking vengeance against my father and trying to destroy her mother. A wake of wrecked lives; there's a lot of failure there. But something in her has changed. Has lightened. I've got to say, despite everything, I might even love her. She might even love me, too.

Where are you, Father? What are you up to? This is what I'm asking myself while the shuttle hits max altitude and stalls. It feels like we're floating, and in that floating, we're free somehow, and I savor that brief moment. Then the shuttle flips into a hammerhead turn, the engines roar back on, and that moment is gone.

The nose-dive to central Asia is terrifying, full of three-alarm regret. The shuttle screeches and clatters. The airspeed gauge pin is buried to the max at 8,000 miles per hour. I grab the stick to pull up. Ascalon Lee slaps my hand.

"Not yet!" she yells.

I pull my hand back and struggle to keep my composure. Ascalon Lee is keeping it together. Well, she's got lives to spend. She keeps the shuttle pointed straight down, but tears streak her old man face, and all of a sudden, I'm sorry for asking her to do this. Maybe there's a way to save this man once he's disconnected. Maybe I should've thought of that. I don't want to be my father's daughter anymore. The guy who's globe-trotting, hunting, and killing these once innocent pieces of Ascalon Lee.

The holo targeting system flashes on in front of us. The horn. A blip. A bobbing thing. Ducking and weaving through the atmosphere. I feel my jaw and toes clench. My fear turns into focus. The shuttle is headed right for it. The trick will be to capture it without hitting it. The targeting system begins to beep. At first, it's off-tempo. Then the notes tighten and beat rapidly. I begin to see them in red. I look over at Ascalon Lee and know there's no going back. Her reluctance has transformed into determination. *God, she's so human. Beautifully so.* In this moment, this crazy gamble that she didn't even want to take in the first place has become her needful thing, and all of it now swirls in reds so bright that they sing and pluck electric.

"Be ready!" she says.

I try my best to ignore the reds rattling in the cockpit, the shuttle's alarms trilling, and prepare to take the control column. My hands shake over on each side of the grip-indented joystick, and I remind myself to demonstrate restraint, or I'll end up ripping the thing off the console. Ascalon Lee converted the flaps and rudders to manual like the eject. Once we hit the net, and all computer systems crash, I'll be like Wilbur Wright up here. *Be aware*, I tell myself. A single-minded focus on a goal can end horribly wrong. The crush of failed expectations. In a way, it's scarier than the literal crushing itself.

I watch the holo image of the shuttle on collision course with the frantic, blipping thing that moves like something trying to dodge bullets. Maybe we should've just tried destroying the thing. But what would that have really accomplished?

The holo of the shuttle flickers then disappears. The shuttle shuts down. I feel a slight snag at our tail. Then, we plummet. I grab the stick and work the pedals, trying like hell to keep the shuttle in nosedive. But boy, the thing is fighting me. Pitch, roll, and yaw spinning against me. I wish I knew our altitude. I glance at Ascalon Lee. She's out. I feel the shuttle begin to bank into a spin. I try to adjust. Nothing. Zero responsiveness. We begin to spiral out of control faster and faster. The entire cockpit begins to glow red, and I'm not sure if it's death I'm seeing or redout—the flooding of my brain with blood. I'm Akkorokamui again. In a panic, trying to untwist my limbs. I reach over and shake Ascalon Lee's shoulder. Nothing. I look out the window and see a hurricane of clouds in the night sky. At least I know it's night now. I concentrate and try to remember that it's not the world that's spinning. It's me.

I've had enough of this. I grab my retracted javelin and unstrap myself from the seat. I stand and my second skin peels off me and forms into a tentacle that seeps from my spine. This thing, this second skin, it's continually, literally handy, an extra limb that I can consciously move and control. And sometimes it acts subconsciously, as it did when it formed into a wingsuit when I jumped off the floating island. It's like when a person trips, the hands pop out to brace the fall of the clumsy. Sometimes it's reflexive, like any other limb.

I wrap my second skin tentacle around Ascalon Lee and her pilot seat, then pop the spears from my javelin and stab the window. It begins to spider. I throw a sidekick at the webbed glass. Cold, rushing air sucks the entire eye-shaped panel into the sky, and it crumples in the atmosphere. The air almost sucks me out, too, but I'm holding onto Ascalon Lee's seat. I skewer the fuselage above my head and pull with everything I got. Another piece of panel rips off and goes flying. I climb out, anchoring myself to Ascalon Lee.

The intense wind blows my quills back. My palms and the bottoms of my feet tickle. It feels like millions of tiny hairs are growing from my skin and clinging to the fuselage. Once outside the shuttle, I stand goofy-footed, keeping my knees bent. I plant the javelin into more fuselage and hang on. It's freezing, and I feel feverish. A torrent whirls within me, and a blush rises to my skin.

Even through the spinning darkness, I see it. The silvery balloon caught in the honeycomb net, like a stone set in a sling about to be cast. I hope this whirling hunk of shuttle has enough velocity to bring the collar down to ground level. I need to slow the spinning, or this thing will begin to fall apart. I dig my back foot into the shuttle and sit in a deeper crouch, trying to cut back and snap the shuttle against its rotation. To my surprise, the spin slows a bit. Still holding onto the javelin, I crouch even deeper, lean away from it, and snap again, this time even harder. The spin slows into a stall. The nose begins to dip down. I feel like I'm at the lip of something tidal, and we begin to drop. Nothing left to do but carve through the freezing, whipping wind and soul surf the shuttle through the turbulence.

I've done all I can. I unbuckle Ascalon Lee with my tentacle and pull her up to me. I hear it before I see it: a rattling. An iE bounces around the helmet of the traveling surgeon version of Ascalon Lee. The Gs and pressure must've ripped it from her head. I hold onto her tightly and close my eyes. I rip the javelin from the shuttle, the tiny hairs on the bottoms of my feet ungrip, and we're flung into the air. My second skin turns from tail to wingsuit, and the sudden change of shape sends us in a violent bounce up to the clouds that snaps my head back. Soon we're falling again. No, gliding. We're gliding now, and I wonder why, through all that, I wasn't more scared. The answer is simple.

Once I unstrapped myself.

Once I stood up.

The reds went away.

We glide and glide and glide. My body begins to cool. The city lights gleam below me. Then, an eruption of crackling balls of electric blue light lattice all the way to the horizon. When the city lights begin to flicker off, I gasp. Then I feel a smile stretch across my face. My heart races.

"Let's go see," I say.

The body in my arms awakens. I look into its remaining, sunken eye. Even though it instantly recognizes that we're soaring through the sky and that I'm what's keeping both of us from plummeting, it screams, panics, and struggles to break my embrace. But I hold on tightly to the squirming man.

He begins to scream. "Let me go!"

I ignore him and tighten my grip. He tries even harder to untangle himself from me, to no avail. Then, a thought troubles me. If this man, detached from Ascalon Lee's iE, is clearly no longer Ascalon Lee and wants to let go, why not let him go? Why force him to be alive when he doesn't want to live? I gulp. Another thought follows. Is that what Akira Kimura was thinking all along? For decades, she saw a species in a suicide spin and refused to let it die? And for some reason, the answer to this question breaks my heart while the man fights harder and harder against my life-sustaining stranglehold.

10

Akira Kimura sees the loss of 33,550,336 connections at once before she feels it. Standing on the launch observation platforms of the Cape, she sees it as a blazing halo that rings the sky. Asia, *she thinks.* The Gardeners there amputated from me. *It reminds her of the Great Sun Storm, the day her father died all those years ago. His image is difficult to retrieve in the streams of endless data, but she locates it. Yes. A thin, unassuming man with a full head of jet-black hair absent of a single white or graying strand. A beaming smile that made his cheeks puff up to almost cartoonish proportions. When Akira was a child, he would sit with her and draw. He could look at something once and replicate the image on paper from memory. A skill, perhaps, celebrated at one time, but no longer considered useful. His ability to calculate in his head was also stunning. Again, a once-prized skill in a bygone era. Her father could have been a da Vinci. Instead, he sat in a cubicle and monitored crypto mining code on his screen. There to wait for any odd fluctuations or sudden spikes in pattern. He was discouraged to leave his chair by his corporation. A tiny refrigerator sat beneath his desk and was refilled with refreshments every day. He was attached to a catheter. Lunch delivered each afternoon at exactly noon, his eyes never leaving the constant scroll of 1s and 0s. Artificial intelligence was trusted with everything except buying and selling and final decisions. Even at home, her father ate without ever looking at his food. It took Akira a while to figure out why.*

Her father's plane crash was the most seminal moment of Akira Kimura's life. At first, she blamed the sun. Not odd, considering the fact that she was only five years old. Then she blamed his employer, who sent him on the trip to Seoul. But as she got older, it was human ignorance that she ultimately blamed. Sun storms should be predictable. Hurricanes, volcanic eruptions, and asteroids as well. Perhaps the most dangerous human calamity had to be dealt with, too, so Akira dealt with it, first with Seshho-seki then with Satori Day.

Now, four decades later, whether earthquake, ice age, or drought, OneVoice monitors and sees all coming. Maybe she has become like her father, spending most of her waking hours monitoring irregularities. But she does not only monitor. She anticipates. She is able to see everything coming, except death—she has her old friend for that. However, how did Okaasan fail to predict the sudden loss of Asia? She sensed that Idris Eshana's net dropped when the shuttles from North America packed with deported Leachateans were not short-circuited by EMP and began to land safely. She sent a team to investigate. Idris is probably skulking somewhere out in his desert. Akira has never considered him any kind of threat. But Asia? Who? Probably her daughter. Probably the synesthete's daughter, too. It stings just as it did when she lost her father all those years ago. She needs him now. So she fixes on the image of her father and breathes life into it. He is now standing beside her, wearing a rumpled twenty-first-century suit. His astral form smiles. The cheeks puff, just like she remembers.

"What is wrong, daughter?"

"I have lost my connection to many of my children today."

He frowns and loosens his tie. "Perhaps it is time to take the rest and go."

"Soon, Father, soon. Some must remain, though."

Her father nods. "Things must not be allowed to crash."

"Yes. And I must ensure I leave them protected."

Akira peers into her brass, antique telescope. She watches a rocket fire from the track miles above her and disappear into the blackness of space. Perhaps she should have built her launch loop closer to the equator, but it would have taken longer. She'd already had some of the best space travel infrastructure built in North America. Besides, it is working just fine. 10,000 more brave souls, off to the moons of Saturn.

"You are such a clever girl," Akira's father says. "To build this masterpiece in the heavens. I am so proud of you."

"Thank you, father."

"Send the synesthete to discover what happened to your children in Asia."

Akira nods. "He is on his way there now."

Akira's father clears his throat while another rocket primes to shoot across the gulf. "And what of my granddaughter?"

Akira sighs. "Disobedient cur. I am nearly certain that she was involved with disconnecting me from my Gardeners in Asia."

"Aki! You are too hard on her! She managed to oversee the levitation of the islands, didn't she?"

"The synesthete could not find the last North American version of her—a male in his early hundreds. The traveling surgeon, prowling on this continent somewhere. The synesthete never fails to find. I suspect your granddaughter might have had something to do with this calamity."

"Leave her her toys, Aki."

Akira shakes her head. "She is too old for toys."

Another rocket is about to launch. Akira increased departures once she sensed the net in DownUnder shut off. She knew something was not right. She pulls away from the telescope and lets her father look. The rocket zips down the track above. Akira does not need to see from down here. She can see from the sky, but it's nice to look through real eyes at times.

"You have your puppets," her father says. "Are puppets not toys?"

He does not understand. They are not puppets. They are parts. They are roots, over thirty-three million, suddenly severed. Suddenly. No, that's the wrong word. Sudden is subjective. Just as we once thought that we walked on flat ground, just as we once believed the sun rose and set, we think time is linear, something that speeds and slows, depending on perspective, but always in a straight line. We, in fact, do not walk on flat ground. We walk on a sphere. The sun does not rise and set. Instead, the planet spins. Linear is a spacial distinction, not temporal. Time is more than that. Time is a ripping. It is the constant, instantaneous shredding of an infinite reality. Like most things, it is chaos that we reduce to a widget so we can name and claim it for our own.

Names are nothing, just like our claims. Just like widgets. Self-induced illusions to create false order.

Murder and death, the synesthete and his child can pull these minuscule bits from the ripping in greens and reds. It is a valuable skill, these tethers, when one is amidst chaos. But Akira can now pull, too. She is almost a century and a half old and only in the beginning of her infancy. Her once-dead father stands beside her because she has discovered something profound: ghosts are simply the time travelers of the past, and they are her lightest passengers.

"Father," Akira says. "You will come with me as well, yes?"

Her father peels his eyes from the telescope, and he stands erect with perfect posture. "Tell me what it is that you have discovered near Saturn. Is dark matter, in fact, time?"

"No, I do not think so. But I believe we will discover what it is the farther we get, and we will discover many more wonderous things."

Her father rubs his cheeks. "We will bring that knowledge back?"

Akira nods. "We will."

Her father smiles. "Tell me, what is your theory?"

Akira spreads her arms. "Dark matter. It's everywhere, but it is not time. Perhaps . . . it is time's leftovers. Dark matter is time's exhaust."

Her father raises an eyebrow. "Are you the rabbit or tanuki?"

She smiles, remembering the old story fondly. The boat race between the two animals. The rabbit made its boat out of a tree trunk while the raccoon dog made its out of mud. Even when she was a child, it was not difficult to predict which won. "I am the rabbit, of course."

"Yes," her father says. "Yes, you are."

Akira sighs. "It is time." Another rocket blasts off. Akira and her father stand upon the dragon head of the Cape Canaveral eastern power station of A496, at the slope of her launch loop that stretches to the sky. She heads for the lift that will take her back down to the dragon's bone-white, gaping mouth. The spectral image of her father follows. They step on the lift. The gears grind, and the platform slowly lowers them over four thousand feet. Below, a shuttle waits, two Gardeners at the controls of the sleek, intercontinental aircraft.

"Where are we going?" Akira's father asks.

"We are going to see this granddaughter you defend and claim to be so fond of."

Her father smiles. "I have never met her."

"She makes boats out of mud, Father. She is the tanuki."

"Then teach her to be the rabbit."

The lift comes to a stop, and they step off. As they make their way to the small intercontinental shuttle, Akira strides on patches of sleeping grass and watches them close. She counts them. Counting. Always counting. They enter the shuttle, and the door hisses shut behind them. She sits in her seat, and the safety belts come alive and strap her in. This body. So weak. So singular. She will soon leave this body and planet behind. This HuSC cannot endure the voyage Akira is about to take. Once the rockets hit space, they accelerate at 300 Gs, far more than the human body can endure. Preparations for deep space travel have already begun, and she will once again become pure data that runs through all Gardener iEs. She will guide her wayfinding network outward, through the interstellar clouds. However, before she departs, she must acquire certain assurances from her daughter and from the synesthete. The times of contracts and legal haggling have ended. She has ended them. Now, there is only the assurance of looking through the ripping and seeing. The imperfect mix of perception, leverage, trust, intuition, and the algorithmic prophecy of swarm intelligence.

The shuttle takes off, her two children in the pilot and co-pilot seat. They are beautifully hairless and tidy. So different from her first children, the twins: One crooked and twisted on the outside. The other crooked and twisted within.

She has made her new children the opposite. Obedient. Perfect. Some may say they are mindless, but they are not. At some point, people began confusing intellect with enthusiasm. Skill with desire. Forty years ago, every individual who joined the hive mind believed in her. The system would have been impossible to create otherwise. Those who do not desire to come with her, but instead worship her from afar, they are given that choice. They will remain behind to care for the planet.

Though the losses from Asia are staggering. An entire ikebana. She has already dropped the continental nets and sent replacements to operate key installments. She knows how it happened. There is only one way, is there not? EMP large enough to drape over the continent. EMP that she created. Someone pulled it down and stretched it. The two becoming one. The blue straggler. The synesthete's daughter and hers. Okaasan will leave off all the nets, for now, just in case.

The intercontinental shuttle rumbles through the clouds and continues on its ascending arc that will hit its highest point above California then begin its descent. Descent. Akira likes that word. It is fitting. Because if she does not get her assurances, descent is what will occur. Despite the fact that she is fonder of the islands than any other place on this planet, she will not hesitate to drop them atop Water City if her daughter is not compliant. And if the synesthete does not continue to comply? Then it will be his daughter that Akira will be taking with her through the galaxy. That threat will be enough to keep the synesthete on her side.

"What are you thinking about, daughter?" Akira's father asks.

"I am thinking about the story of the koi," she says.

"It was always your favorite."

Akira extends her hand in front of her. Light flickers in her upturned palm then begins to beam spectral images of fish swimming in circles in a river. "Schools of golden koi swim against the current upriver." A river of light shoots from Akira's hand and the fish break from their circle and follow. "When they reach the end, they discover a waterfall." The river of light bends, and Akira weaves and casts the image of a waterfall. "Most of the koi turn back. Some stay and attempt to swim up the waterfall." More than half of the school flickers off. "Eventually, one by one, the fish give up." One by one the images of the fish fade. "All except one."

Her father nods at the holo of the final fish maniacally leaping out of the water again and again. "It took the fish a hundred years to make it up the waterfall," he says.

"It could have taken a thousand, and that one particular fish would have never stopped trying."

The koi leaps and wriggles on the rocks at the waterfall's crest. It finally makes it through the rushing water and swims in a calm pool that becomes a flash of light. When the light dims, all that is left is a scaled, winged creature.

"It was the only way for her to become a dragon," Akira's father says. Akira sees his smile reflect off the dragonlight. The dragon's head morphs into human form. It's the face of Akira that takes shape. This head sprouts other heads. Each bloom into copies of Akira's face. This happens again and again until the entire shuttle is filled with one repeating image: the likeness of Akira Kimura.

PART FIVE

REUNION

1

It seems like no matter where you are, the center is the worst place to be. Whether it be the Water City of my childhood, the Kansas of my later years, or the center of my father's attention, I never liked being in the middle of things. But I'm always here, aren't I? And this time, I'm the one who put myself here. Some nameless town in central Asia. I can't tell you if I'm in China, Russia, or Mongolia. No iE. I can't tell you how I'm going to get out. All I know is that after I climb out of the freezing river and activate my camo skin, I spot a super old obelisk ahead. A spire spiked into a globe. The globe heaped on the shoulders of three dog-like creatures with human ears. When I get closer, I make out the letters on the structure: Russian. I know that much. Under those letters *The Center* in English. A star on the globe marks where I'm at. The spire is carved with what appears to be rats coiled in a race to the sky. At the very top, a buck stands on the tip of the needle. What the hell is wrong with people?

The traveling surgeon who used to be Ascalon Lee is gone. As soon as we splashed down, he tore off his helmet, broke from my grasp, and swam to shore. I watched as he scurried off to the nearest building and collapsed. Why do people do that? I suppose shelter suggests civilization, which suggests safety, but in the strangest of places, organized people are typically the most dangerous things.

My quills prickle. I smell them. I hear two voices screaming in the distance. I don't see greens or reds, but I'm afraid to look at the people I've unplugged. I shudder. I've done something here that I can never even dream of undoing. I lean on the obelisk and take a breath, hand shaking. Dread unfurling inside me. I look up at the night sky. The scar scintillates brighter and more colorfully than all the stars put together.

Once I collect myself, I race to the same building the traveling surgeon did, not because I seek shelter, but because I need to see the results. I just pulled the EMP net that covers this entire continent down for an instant and short-circuited every iE here. I need to know how these people are coping with the sudden disconnection. My heart thuds in my chest. There's a ringing in my ears that tastes like bile. I suck on my tongue and spit the bitterness out. I run as fast as I can.

When I near the two-story structure, I stop in my tracks. Three bald, elderly foam-fitted Gardeners wander confused. They don't even acknowledge my presence. A bit farther down the cobbled path, two Gardeners, just as old, are on their hands and knees, wailing at the scar. They don't notice me either. *Did it work?* I grab one of the praying Gardeners and pull him up. I hold his face and look into his eyes. They stream with tears. *Gardeners don't cry.* Did I get all of them? I let the man go, and he sinks back to his knees.

I dash to the building and find the traveling surgeon on his back near a door. His eyes are closed, but his mouth is wide open. His jaw retracts and his gurgling lungs fight to take in air. I kneel next to him. The red wafts begin to pulse from his body. I can't do anything for this man. And I can't stand looking at him any longer either. But I turn my head, hold his hand, and rub it. A deep sadness wells in me. I close my eyes. He stops breathing. Still not able to look at him, I gently place his hand on his lap. I get to my feet and enter the unlit building. I don't look back.

The EMP net manning station buzzes just as Uluru buzzed. Somewhere beneath this building, a giant superconducting magnet powers the net and repels its horn. I am once again awed by Idris Eshana's sniveling genius. The station circulates pulses of energy, much like lightning storms, that flow through every segment of the net. The energy runs through the horn and flows back down to the station. It's funny, though. Shave Time Money came up with the same thing on just a much smaller scale. It makes sense, really. Short-circuiting invading iEs is the most effective way to stop Okaasan and her Gardeners. It was the most effective way to stop me when I was the one invading From A to Z.

I step into the station, and there's no one else here. Maybe the skeleton crew of five Gardeners was more than enough to maintain this little facility. Borders are protected, not centers. There's no sign of any type of security. I shouldn't be surprised. Akira can predict a lot, but I doubt she predicted someone would've attempted to do what I've just done. I'm surprised, though, when I hear the buzzing wind down. Someone is turning off the EMP station. *It has to be Akira.* I suppose there is no reason for it to be on after what I did. I smile. I cover my mouth and scream with delight. My muffled shouts echo throughout the building.

Once I gather myself, I step outside and look around for any type of transportation. Nothing. This place must've been a speck on the map its entire existence. I'm seeing the half-buried remnants of brickyards and sawmills, and we stopped building with bricks and wood before my mother was even born. There are train tracks that I follow only to find that they end after a mile or so. I look at black carrion crows circling above me. I need to make for the coast and figure out some way to get on the Pacific Bridge and fly back to Water City. After that, I'll hit the nets over the other continents. But I don't have an iE. I don't even know where the closest bigger city is.

I wander south for hours in search of transport, but don't find anything. The sun begins to rise, and I bask in the light, feel my body vibrate, feeding on its energy. After I've consumed enough energy, I decide to go back north to see if the Gardener EMP maintenance crew has pulled themselves together. Maybe they can point me in the right direction.

When I return to the compound, the body of the traveling surgeon is missing. I look for the unplugged Gardeners, but find no sign of them. Odd. That's when I feel a slight tug to the east along the river. Reds. I follow it back to the obelisk and cross the arid grasslands. The hum of reds grows stronger. My skin becomes the same color as the sprigs of blond grass. I grip the javelin rod and prowl silently. I smell them now—the five Gardeners plus another. Then I begin to feel a wave of exhaustion. Was I built to thrive only in warmer climates? I fight through the sleepiness and inch forward. The five Gardeners are easy to spot. They're holding shovels, standing in the hole they're digging. Behind them, a large, cloaked man and his shuttle. Greens pulse from his pores. The wrapped body of the traveling surgeon lays at his feet and fumes a waltzy red now. The fumes that waft from the man are so strong that I feel like they got in my mouth and I can't get rid of the taste.

Of course, it's my father standing imperiously, arms crossed, over the Gardeners. The wind blows at his rippling cloak, and wisps of green slither in the same direction as the chilly gust. I feel a ghost limb tickle, the magenta guidelines amputated when he died. I'm relieved that the digital tether no longer exists, but there are other strings that I feel stirring. Love. Anger. Frustration.

He pulls the hood off his head. His face wears a resigned weariness as well as a resolve. I spot the hand cannon holstered at his waist. Maybe I should just sneak around him and steal his shuttle. Get to a coastal city and find a boat to sail. However, for all I know, boats in Asia have been dumped in boreholes. Perhaps all cities, too. I can't leave these five freed Gardeners here with my father.

My skin undulates, and I'm back to myself. A girl in a scaled black foam fit with a head of prickly quills, and a long, tentacled tail made of second skin.

The Gardeners stop shoveling and look up at my father as I walk toward him. He waves them out of the hole. They climb out, and my father nudges the corpse into the hole. I step to the rim and look down. *Just meat.* I look across the grave at my father. I'm starting to understand. It's what all mass murderers tell themselves.

"I wanted you to stay with Idris until all this is done," my father says to me.

"I missed you, too," I say.

"You made a mistake today," he says.

I glance at the ragged Gardeners staring at me, their eyes absent of the neon marine glint that people under Akira's control share. "I freed them," I say. "Freed them from that monster."

My father tilts his head and furls his brow. "Do they look free?" He turns to face them, and they cower.

"It's okay," I say to them. "I won't let him hurt you." Then, to my father. "Did you threaten them?"

My father shakes his head. "No. I'm just a familiar face. OneVoice knows me well, and they remembered. I suggested we bury the poor guy, and they agreed."

I have my doubts about that. I eye the gun hanging from his waist. A chilly gust passes, and my father's black hood ripples in the sudden breeze. "You don't see it, do you?"

My father shoots me a puzzled look. "See what?"

"What you did to me. It's the same thing Akira Kimura did to her daughter all those years ago. When she trapped her in an AMP chamber for thirty years."

"Your new friend had a hand in that," my father says.

"You're my father! You're the only person I ever trusted. I loved you more than anyone else. And you do that to me?"

He looks down. "I know."

I catch a vibe of remorse and self-loathing, but I don't know if I'm catching it because I want him to feel those things, or if he really is. I turn to the Gardeners. "You don't need to listen to this man. You are free. It's the best thing to be."

The Gardeners glance at my father, all wearing looks of concern. One, the oldest, a man with a round face and narrow, sagging eyes, speaks. "You told us that if we buried this man, you would return us to Okaasan."

"I will," my father says. "Finish the job."

The Gardeners dig their shovels into the loose dirt and begin filling the hole.

"I won't let you hurt them," I say. "I'll never let you hurt anyone ever again."

Exasperated, my father raises his arms. "They're five people about to hit the century crash, and they're stuck out here in the geographic midpoint of Asia with no provisions on their way, no family, no job, no purpose. What are they supposed to do, become hunters and gatherers in their nineties? Is this how you'd want to retire? When they were connected, they were a part of something grand. They maintained a net, a geomagnetic storm that covered an entire continent. They communicated with millions of other minds. Now, they're just lonely old people about to starve or freeze to death in a Russian winter."

"Are you saying I shouldn't have done it?"

My father shrugs. The Gardeners slow their shoveling and begin to listen. "I stopped by Beijing to refuel on my way here. It's chaos. Riots, mass suicide. The whole city is on fire. I almost didn't make it out. But you did it, kid. The entire continent is unplugged. What's left is millions of traumatized people."

"Millions of free people," I say. "There used to be billions. Remember? I'm not done, either. As soon as I get another shuttle, I'm going to the other continents and doing the same. All those years wasted. In sleep, of all things. We could've figured this out patches ago." I point at his face. "And if we did, the separation from OneVoice would probably have not been as traumatic for them."

"Well, that didn't happen. You did what you did when you

did it. But who knows, right? Maybe they'll eventually get their shit together. Then the strong and organized will enslave the weak. Force them to build shit in Kimura's honor. Maybe human sacrifice to ask their god to be reconnected." He peers down at the body and the dirt scattered over it. "Anyway," he says, "the hole's getting too filled."

My father pulls out his hand cannon and points it at one of the Gardeners. Spikes pop from my javelin rod. I throw it and skewer the gun out of his hand. It, along with the javelin, tumble into a thick bush of dry, yellow grass. The Gardeners look at one another, drop their shovels, and begin to run. Well, run might be a strong word for what they're doing. It's more like a stumbling jog.

I point at them. "Do you see that?" I say. "When they were connected, they would've never run. Like back in Epcot, they would've burned to death without batting an eye. They would've burned to death in silence *for her*. That's probably why so many died over the years. Silence. For her. But now, they're trying to save themselves."

My father gazes at the place that his gun and my javelin landed. "You always had great arm talent. You would've been a world-class athlete in another time. Like your mom."

"We're taking them with us," I say.

"Us?"

I nod at the Gardeners, who seem to be heading west, back to shelter.

My father stares at the crisp, blue sky. "How'd you do it, anyway?"

"I had help," I say.

My father sighs. "Ascalon Lee." His face hardens. "Do you know how many times she's tried to kill me? Don't you remember what she did to you? What she made you do to Akeem Buhari?"

"She's changed," I say. And I mean it. Whatever she was in the past—enemy, possessor, invader, liar—she's something different to me now. I don't fully trust her, but she saved me. She disconnected me. She liberated me. She helped me liberate others. "Now that I know how to break OneVoice, she and I will hit Africa next,"

He raises an eyebrow. "Really? Even after all I said?"

"Yep."

My father sticks out his arm, palm up. A holo springs from it. Flashes at first. Then discernible images. It's as he said. Riots. Flames. Havoc. Ash. People swirling in the midst of it. They rush to the outskirts of the once great city to escape, look up at the scar, then seem to change their mind. Around and around they go. Refusing to run from their own ruin. I look away. My father closes his fist, and the holo is gone.

"It doesn't matter," he says. "You can't take down any more nets."

"Why?"

"Well, Akira turned them all off. So you can't weaponize the nets to free Gardeners anymore. And you're down to one Ascalon Lee."

One Ascalon Lee. My father has hunted all of them down, except the one. She let him, and I don't know why. I recall the version that met me on Cape Wickham and the one that kamikazed with me from the mesosphere. Neither seemed to have a care in the world. Neither went into hiding. I don't think she even tried to escape.

I eye my father. This isn't a tear-jerk reunion, and a part of me is disappointed by that. Why has Akira brought him back? Not just to hunt her daughter. Why is he so willing to take her orders? Maybe all he ever wanted since Sessho-seki is to be in the loop. To be let in on the gag. I get the sense that right now he is, and it breaks my heart. I loved him so much, but now, once again, he's with her. Despite periods of resistance, in the end, he always chooses Akira Kimura.

"How can you choose her again?" I ask.

He looks away from me. "I had no choice," he says, jaw clenched.

"You're choosing Akira." My voice cracks. "Even over *me*."

He turns back to me. His eyes go wide. "No. Never."

I walk away before he can lie to himself, and to me, for another second. I retrieve my javelin from the bushes. I grab it and retract the spears. My feet feel heavy for some reason, so I stop, crouch, and flex my toes. My father, looking concerned, walks toward me.

"You okay, kid?" he asks. "I would never choose anyone over you. This—"

"Don't you say it," I hiss. "Don't you say it's for me."

"I'm sorry. I really am. The sleeping . . . It was a shitty thing for me to do. If you want me to say I regret it, I don't, because it's led to this moment. It's a simple equation, really. The end result determines the amount of regret."

I feel my eyes narrowing, and I'm readying myself to spring at him. I feel it in the prickle of my quills and the curl of my tired toes. "What moment?"

My father's looking at the rainbow scar, and it seems to bend inward from the mass of his gaze. "She's leaving kid," he says. "Not all of her, but after she begins the controlled release of the Gardeners, most of her will be going up there."

"Where?" I ask.

"Saturn first," he says. "After that, farther out, destinations unknown."

"She's freeing the ones who stay?"

He shrugs. "Yeah. Most of them. She'll keep pockets of Gardeners to maintain the monitoring of the planet. It's health. It's immune system, I guess. Keep it protected from all the stuff that can destroy it. She's leaving some behind to keep the pulse of it. The ones that she doesn't feel she needs, she'll free. But she wants something from you and Ascalon Lee before she commits."

"You expect me to believe she's just giving up control like that?"

"She not giving up," my father says. "She's finished. She's accomplished what she wanted, on this planet at least."

"Then what does she want from me and Ascalon Lee?"

His eyes move from the scar and focus on me. His square jaw flexes. "Assurances," he says.

He begins to walk to the shuttle. I look back in the direction of the freed Gardeners who probably made it back to the EMP monitoring station by now. I stand and follow my father. "I want to talk to her myself," I say.

"I'll take you to her."

I grab his arm and spin him around to face me, which causes him to almost lose his balance. There's a lightness to him that I don't remember. Or maybe it's just that my hands are stronger, more heavy. "I should leave you here."

He tries to release his arm from my grip, but I'm not letting go. He gives up and glares at me. "You should've just stayed with Idris while this thing rolled ahead."

"What thing?"

"Akira leaving!"

"Is she leaving now because of what I did here?"

"Incredibly, you've accelerated her decision," my father smirks with pride. "She's been planning on leaving for years, but you just shut down the demolition of Southeast Asia. Before you do more damage, she wants to make a deal with you and Ascalon Lee. Then she'll go. She's not happy about what you did here, but the idea was never simply staying and maintaining this. You're talking about perhaps the most ambitious person who ever lived. She was never going to spend all her days babysitting Earth."

I let go of his arm. He puts a hand on my cheek. I slap it away.

"Unplugged," he says. "That's why Idris couldn't put you down temporarily."

"The next time you touch me, you'll lose a hand."

My father gazes up at the scar. "You know," he says. "There have probably actually been hundreds, maybe thousands of people like Akira who lived in the past. She's not more evil or less evil than any of them. Maybe she's not even that much smarter. The thing that made her different is timing. The era she lived in, the tech at her fingertips, that's what made Akira Kimura possible."

My mouth dries. I spit. "So I guess this is the reality that my generation inherits."

"Come with me this one last time," he says. "And I promise I won't ever ask for a damn thing again."

What do I owe this man? What all children owe parents who loved them. A part of me wants to toss this him into the river, steal his shuttle, and leave him to fend for those five Gardeners here in this center. But I know he won't fend for them. He lied to them and would've killed them if I had let him. I do want to see her, though. I want to see what kind of assurances she wants from me and Ascalon Lee, so I can spit in her face and not give them to her.

I stop in my tracks. "We didn't finish burying the body."

My father looks up again. The birds above circle. "It's okay. It'll eventually be food for someone out here."

"What about the five Gardeners? We need to take them with us."

My father shakes his head. "No, we don't. The thing is, kid—you never seemed to learn this, and it's the last lesson I got for you—a big part of life is about being okay with leaving people behind."

I start walking again toward the shuttle. I think about my mother. Has he finally moved on? He hasn't mentioned her once yet. I'm not sure if that makes me feel like he's made progress, or is just plain sad. I remember the names of my father's other children, Brianne and John, children I never knew. Did he even look for the eldest after Satori Day? Not that I remember. I wonder if he even cared. Regrets plagued the father I knew, but this version has been literally born again.

"So where are we going?" I ask.

"Akira would say that we're going back to the beginning."

"Water City," I say. "Has she spoken to Ascalon Lee yet?"

"No," he says.

I peer at the cockpit and shouldn't be surprised that I'm now scared of flying.

"Is she letting the Leachateans land in DownUnder?" I ask.

My father nods.

I walk past my father and take a seat at the cockpit. My body slumps, but my eyes focus on the map displayed on the console. The autopilot route has already been set. Back to Savior's Eye.

My father takes his seat beside me. I think back to what the world was before Satori Day, and the memories are cloudy. School. Friends. Did I have friends? I did. A classroom full of them. I remember learning about playing pirates and exploring the ocean with them. But the man sitting next to me is what I remember the most.

The engines fire, and the shuttle begins to rise. My father pulls his cloak from his head, leans back, and the seat contours around him. I nearly nod out of consciousness, but the sudden jerk of the shuttle blooming supersonic wakes me up. We rip through the clouds, the slanted trajectory taking us higher and higher. I grip the armrests while the heads-up display projects our growing altitude.

"What is she going to do about all the people down there?" I ask.

"She's going to let them live, just like you wanted," my father answers.

"Will they survive?"

My father shrugs. "It'll be up to them."

I did what my father never could do, and a part of me feels like I exceeded him. He's part of the reason the world broke, and maybe it's my job, my inheritance to fix what he did.

"Ascalon Lee," I say. "You let her work on me for all those years."

"She made you stronger. Stronger than me. Maybe even stronger than her. She kept you alive, kid. When Shave Time got you, that would've been it for you if not for her. Because I let her work on you, she was able to know every inch of you and bring you back. After your mom . . . I need you to stay alive. No matter the cost. And Ascalon Lee has done that. Look at you. You're alive."

"But it's not your life. It's not Ascalon Lee's. And it's not Akira Kimura's. It's mine."

"You should've seen what I did to Barbasol and Blade Close," he says. "Then you would've truly seen what a monster I am."

"Don't use me as an excuse to do the things you do," I say. The shuttle rattles through turbulence. The little hairs on my feet bind to the floor.

"You're not an excuse. You're the reason."

My father. Akira. I'm beginning to think that maybe all parents are monsters. Loving a child is the ultimate justification to do atrocious things. Maybe unloving parents are a part of our evolution. There always needed to be balance. There needed to be the ones who abandon or eat their young. Too much parental love would've destroyed the world. Maybe it's good that my mother gave up. If she didn't, she would have been right here with us, squaring the damage that my father has done in my name.

"Does Akira love her?" I ask.

My father lets out a snort. "Akira? Love?"

"Then why did she let her daughter exist all this time?"

The question lingers for moments. My father pulls his hood back up. His brow furls, and I can see he's trying to work out a thought. He's not looking at me, though. His eyes are aimed at the window. "Maybe duty," he says. "Or maybe shame. Maybe curiosity. But not love. What she did to that kid is not love."

I nod. "Maybe it's more guilt than love."

My father turns to me and grimly smiles. "Maybe you're

right. Or maybe love needs guilt to be more than just a passing fancy."

I chew on that. We remain quiet throughout the ascent. When we begin to dive down, my father breaks the silence. "I've missed you, kid."

Despite everything, I've missed him, too, but I don't say it. I don't want to think it, but I do. Maybe love also requires these small, silent cruelties in order to breathe.

2

Have I ever really met Akira Kimura? I don't know. I've visited Gardener strongholds a number of times and have watched them operate. I've seen them strip themselves of flesh at Epcot, go to Corpus Akira, pack themselves in rockets that rise some fifty miles high, speed down the track of A496, and launch at orbital speed. I've seen them dig their holes, here and there, across all continents. I've met Jon6J. I fed him, clothed him, and took him with me to From A to Z only to watch him betray me and stab my father in the back. I traveled with him to Mile High and Water City. I fought with him and against him. Was he Okaasan? I've had her pass through my head a couple of times. The first when I bit into the flower and swam up from her underwater lab, and the second when she showed me the flights to other planets. Her gyroscope space station that orbits within the icy rings of Saturn. The Gardeners and their ships flying into the turbulent flow of the gas giant's polar hexagon and drawing hydrogen and helium for fuel. She was in my head to show me what my father and Ascalon Lee had done to me. All I know is that

I've grown up in her world. And if her world is her, I've met her, I know her. And I don't like her.

My father and I near the island. Below I can see the shuttle pads of Savior's Eye are draped with perfect lines of Gardeners in formation. I can't insta-count without my iE, but eyeballing it, I'd say there are twice as many as there were at Mile High when I tracked down Jon6J. When my father drops the landing gear, a battalion of them spread to the outer edges of the round platform in perfect kaleidoscopic order. We land in the clearing they made.

I think about the EMP nets and see no reason why Ascalon Lee and I can't construct our own. Not to protect, but to weaponize like Shave Time Money did. But ours will be able to be thrown. To be cast. I wish I had nets like this now. I could cover these platforms with them and free these people. I'm finally figuring something out. It's like my dad said on the day Akira Kimura died and transformed into OneVoice. Every life owes a death. So how should that borrowed sum of life be spent? Akira Kimura uses hers to acquire knowledge and power. Ascalon Lee uses hers to create and possess. My father always uses his to protect the wrong people. Like Akira. Like me. I want to use mine to free and protect the right ones.

The cockpit seat straps retract as the shuttle's engines shut down. My father stands, steps to the back, and pulls a rail from the rack. He flips on the charge, and the weapon hums. He smiles, straps it to his shoulder, and waits for the exit ramp to drop. I sigh and stand to follow. I grip my javelin rod. If the Gardeners outside are like Jon6J, I won't be able to fight them all. But we are on the tallest mountain on earth, which sits upon a floating island. If I need to, I can glide to escape. I eye my father's rail. Would he try to shoot me down?

The ramp hisses open, and I'm happily surprised. It's Pohaku, my komainu, and he's already bounding to me before I can brace myself for the impact. He topples me over and licks my face. It's aggressive licking, his wet, sandpapery tongue grinding against my cheeks and nose, and I don't know if he's more glad to see me or more angry that I left. I scratch his shaggy curls, which stops his whimpering. I get up and look at my father. He's frowning at the komainu as if it's a variable, a complication, he hadn't considered. Pohaku growls at him. He raises an eyebrow then walks down the ramp. Pohaku and I follow.

The Gardeners have lined up in two groups that face each other. In between them, a narrow aisle snakes to the door of Savior's Eye. Their hairless, pallid skin suggests weakness, maybe even illness, but their crackling electric eyes don't. More disturbing than their eyes is the vast scatter of Triple X iEs that float above their heads, their little mechanical claws brandished like angry teeth.

"The iEs," I say. "She's weaponized them in case conflict erupts here."

"She doesn't want to do that," my father says. "But she will if she feels she has to."

I tense up as we continue to the telescope entrance. I remember the last time being here. Storing him in AMP. Then coming back to discover that Okaasan remade the scar.

I look up. Not at the scar but at the barrel of the telescope's optic payload. It's now nearly a century old, this . . . thing. But it hasn't aged. It's still as grand as it was when I saw it as a child. The commemoration of the water statue of Akira Kimura has once again been turned on. It frightened me then, and it frightens me now. I turn back to the telescope. All that seeing. It's really the perfect symbol of OneVoice: be careful what you do because she is watching. The round building, like Epcot, looks like a giant iE. When we get closer to the entrance, I hear music. Distinctively piano. Something old and playful.

"Holst," my father says. "The Planets."

I feel Pohaku brushing against me. "I meant to move Uncle Akeem's remains to his compound," I say. "Maybe one of his descendants is free. Maybe they'd be comforted by his remains returning home."

"You're a good person," my father says without breaking stride. "Despite being raised by me. I'm proud of you, but it doesn't matter."

I concentrate and stay alert for greens and reds. "Everything matters," I say. "That's the problem with you people. You don't think it does."

We step to the door, and it slides open. Once inside, the door closes behind us, and the floor lights up in bioluminescent blues. My eyes narrow. The music is louder inside. Pohaku sniffs the air, then nudges my father aside and strides ahead first, leaving paw prints that wash away in neon swirls then pulse to the walls. My father and I follow Pohaku. We walk across the techno azure pixie dust to the center of the Eye.

When we get to the piano, I see her, the blue reflected up in the darkness. Akira Kimura in the flesh, wearing a lab coat over a simple, thin Gardener foam fit. Her back is turned to us while she sits in front of the piano and plays the song. Reds flicker from the keys that she strikes. Pohaku's bushy tail stiffens, and the komainu growls at Akira. She stops playing, turns to face us, and eyes Pohaku. I step beside her, and Akira's gaze turns to me. Her eyes, burning blue like the Gardeners, are like galactic swirls pitted with black holes.

"What an interesting pair," she says.

The tone is condescending, which is not surprising. Her face, which I've seen in different variations a million times before, is unblemished but unremarkable. There is a mass to her, a gravitas, that's nevertheless intimidating. All the powerful people she convinced before. Presidents. Inventors. Moguls. Other scientists. Idris Eshana. My father. The elite among The Money. She scans my javelin rod and foam fit, then her eyes return to mine.

"She's made you into a quite remarkable thing," she says.

"Where i-i-s s-she?" I ask. Despite my best efforts, the words come out in a stutter. I'm feeling tired again and glance down at the bright, cold light, wondering if it's sucking the bioelectricity from me. I'd feel it, wouldn't I? I straighten my back and turn to my father. "When is she finally leaving this planet?"

Akira rises from the piano bench and ignores Pohaku's growls and bristling fur. The lights on the floor begin to bond and form into pools, and once concentrated, they mold into four spirals that resemble galaxies, holos that twirl and rise from the gyrations. They look almost like portals. Inside one, two giant bore bits hover above the tops of Water City scrapers. Inside another, Saturn and its newest moon, Akira's space station, which orbits the planet, its three axes in constant spin within the planet's ice rings. Inside the next, flashes of the cities of Asia in disarray. In the final one, Gardeners, on the other continents, on their knees, bowing to the scar above.

I stare into the rim-sparked holos, and my feet begin to feel heavy. Akira points to her gyroscope space station rotating around Saturn. Around and around, a needle-shaped space-craft flashes within its tubular, ringed frame and finally blasts from its gimbal. It flares in white light and disappears in the vast inky darkness. I witness the grandeur and elegance and wonder how much aesthetic thought Akira puts into these things she builds. These are not just things. They are meant to be worshipped.

"That is the first stepping stone we built that will lead outside this solar system," Akira says. "The viability of building another one in Proxima Centauri has been verified. There, we will build another. However, the farther and farther we move from this planet, this solar system, lines of communication will diminish."

"So, you need to take the Gardeners with you, or you need to let them go," I say.

"No," she says. "But they will need to exist as separate systems." Her eyes turn from mine to my father's. He's looking at the ground, pondering. I've seen this same look before—indecisive—when I was a child and my mother had asked me where we should live. It was the same when my mother was dying. The same pained look of resignation, I remember now, that painted his features when he put me in hibernation for my first extended sleep. He's acquiescing to Akira. Why?

Akira interrupts the question bouncing around in my head by saying, "And I require one of you to protect what remains. I will free the vast majority just as you wish. But in stages, not like the sudden calamity that you caused in Asia, that, by the way, I will need to go to in person to settle down and clean up."

She points to the flashing holos of masses of people either howling at the scar or huddled together in dark, cornered rooms. Some have already begun to turn on each other, blaming random people for the severing from OneVoice. A man points at an old woman accusingly, and a mob attacks her. I turn away and clench my teeth.

"A modest population must be kept clonal, though," Akira says. "A496 needs to remain intact. The EMP nets shall stay up. Technology will be methodically and deliberately stifled. It may continue to exist here in Water City, but nowhere else. Rapid technological advancement on a global scale almost permanently ruined this planet. Humanity created an anthropocene. That can never be allowed again. We will care for the planet by limiting technology. We will also care for it by using my technology in very specific ways. I require the monitoring of the planet's magnetic field, glacial levels, and tectonic plates to continue. The monitoring of the sun and moon and potential dangers from above as well. The Earth's pulse will be kept. Maintaining these operations requires operators. I did not go through the trouble of saving this planet to just leave it in shambles.

"After each stepping stone is completed, I will come back, update the system with new knowledge acquired, and check on the planetary conditions. Of course, my returns will at first be more and more sporadic until I develop quicker means of delivery. To blink the ripping of time."

"You said you require one of us to protect it," I say, my eyes still on my father.

"Yes," Akira says, "and I require the other to come with me."

This stuns me. "What?" I ask.

"You or your father must come with me."

I stagger back. What was it that Ascalon Lee once told me? *You and your father are the ultimate alarm systems.*

"You want one of us up there with you so you can see death coming," I say. "You want a failsafe to ensure that you aren't flying into oblivion."

"Of course," Akira says.

"That's all he's ever been to you," I say and face my father. "An instrument. A tool that you used like a hammer. Then, a retriever. Now, an alarm system."

Akira shakes her head. "No. It has always been more than that."

My father refuses to meet my gaze, so I turn back to Akira.

"But you can't possess either of us because neither of us *believe*. You need one of us to go willingly. As a separate entity. As a passenger." I begin to laugh. Both Akira and my father look at me like I've lost it. I stop laughing and answer for both my father and me. "No," I say.

"No?" Akira says back.

"No. Neither of us is coming with you. I'm not going, and I won't let you take him."

"Are you certain about that?" Akira says, pointing at one of the portals.

The holo of Saturn and Akira's space station swirl into a single blob of bioluminescence. It begins to pulse, then explodes into thousands of balls of light. I step back into a defensive stance and watch as each blazing ball stretches into threads that are pulled and sewn. Something is being graphed. First, a brain, spine, and nervous system. Then eyes form from the brain, and a heart begins to beat. I hear its thump, and limbs begin to grow. It's clear that I'm looking at the development of a human embryo. It doesn't stop there. The holo propels the embryo, first into infancy, then into childhood. My bottom lip quivers when the child transforms into an adult woman wearing a thin white hooded robe. My skin crawls and my quills go limp. The figure standing before me pulls off her hood, and it's my mother in spectral form. She walks to me, gazes at my eyes, and reaches to touch my face.

I close my eyes and twist away. "No!" I scream, feeling the bioelectricity jolt my entire body. I hear a voice. My father's.

"This is why I wanted you to goddamn stay at Eshana's," he says. "You're not fucking going. I am. With her. With him."

Him? I open my eyes to glare at my father, but before I can, I see that another of the portals has been alchemized into a hollow, and the broad-shouldered ghost of Akeem Buhari steps out. My eyes widen and blink, and I take a heavy step back from this one despite the fact that he's beaming a kind, forgiving look at me.

A freezing, rigid chill washes over me. *It doesn't matter*, my father said when I told him that I was planning on relocating Uncle Akeem's remains. Now I know why. He believes this ghost, this Akeem, is real. The remains don't matter, because, to my father, Akeem lives again. I can feel myself trembling, and in that trembling, everything feels heavier. My feet. My arms. My second skin peels from me to lighten the load, but even the second skin, now a flexing tentacle, feels almost like too much weight to bear.

"No," I say to my father. "No, they aren't real."

"Ascalon," my mother's ghostly image says to me. "Let him go. I'll take care of him."

I turn away and glance at the holos that remain. The one with the praying Gardeners is still there, only they're not praying anymore. They are up and about, going on with their daily business, which is, of course, Akira's business:

wiping the traces of the old world off the planet. In Egypt, even the Pyramids are being drilled to dust and dumped into the grave that used to be Cairo. That's when it begins. Not in mass. But in each construction crew, an iE whisked from an individual's eye, followed by an exploding mist of blood. First, a startled spasm. Then a sweat breaks. The disconnected people tremor, twitch, and sometimes wretch. The others ignore the ones doubled over in pain, still concentrating on remotely commanding their giant excavators to scrape the chunks of foundation of a city from the earth and dump them in the borehole that smokes and sizzles from the Nile being diverted into it.

"I am a person of my word," Akira says. "I am slowly releasing the, let us say, less devout, even as we speak."

I spin to face the other holo, the one with the two giant bore bits hovering above the rim of Water City. "Where is she?" I say. "Where is Ascalon Lee?"

Akira sighs. "She has refused to come. So, I must root her out."

I turn to my mother's ghost. The long, dark hair, the chiseled, athletic shoulders, and the powerful thighs, covered in flowing white garments. Seeing her now, I realize that I'm built like her. I was not fully grown when she died, so I didn't know I would be, but clearly, I am. But this is not her. Does that mean my father isn't him either? Am I truly me?

I look at Akeem. My mother. Two ghosts spun from memory. Isn't that what Akira is? My father? Ascalon Lee? Me? All of us ghosts spun from memory. Specters of our former selves reformatted and redigitized. Back copies reprinted over and over again. I guess this is what the end of humanity looks like. We still reproduce, but instead of creating new life, we selfishly cling to ourselves, clone after clone, again and again. I'm compliant. Complicit. Not anymore.

My mother steps to the left of my father, Akeem to the right. I try my best to ignore the three and face Akira Kimura. She isn't an audience of one. She's an audience of multitudes. Here I am, standing before all of them with nothing convincing or profound to say.

"Ascalon, look." It's my mother's voice.

My eyes shift to her. She is suddenly cradling something swaddled, something that cries. My mother gently tugs at the bundled blanket, opens a layer, and the baby's crinkled face wails with life. I know what it is. Or what it's supposed to be. The baby my mother lost. I begin to tremble. I want to hold this sibling in my arms even if it's false. Even if it is a person who has never been.

I spin to face Akira. "You're the one who dug up their graves."

Akira simply nods.

I feel my father's hand on my shoulder. "Listen, kid," he says. "Stay here and live. I'm not gonna let you go up there with her. I can't help it. I can't help but to love and protect any version of you."

I glance at the holo of the two drills suspended over the shallow end of Water City. The crinkled lights of it shimmer across the pleated water. All those people down there. Sooni. Dreh. Motu. Levana Cregut and her children. The bores begin to spin. They begin to lower. The calm ocean surface churns into whirlpools. The sand caps of the underwater city are spun to tornado dust storms.

"Stop," I say to Akira. "If you stop, I'll go with you. I see better than him, anyway."

"No!" I hear my father's raspy voice gasp from behind me.

Akira raises an eyebrow. The spinning bits begin to slow. "You see better?"

"I do," I say.

"She doesn't," my father says. "She's lying."

But I'm not lying. I do see better. My quills bristle. I know because my father isn't seeing what I'm seeing. The wisps of green twirling, not from, but into the giant, levitating drills. Tendrils that are worming their way into the crevices of the great machines. Oozing, I know, inconspicuously around the bodies of the Gardeners piloting inside. Then the reds brim from the flat tops of the screw-shaped bore bits. Green and red. The symphony of inevitability. Then more tendrils. Only these are real. The new foam fits. Raid days. Supernatural creatures. Ascalon Lee was feigning indifference, collusion even, when I first arrived at Water City. She must have been preparing for this moment for years. The tentacles of the great octopus Akkorokamui splash from beneath the surface and wrap themselves around one of the drills. They pull the bore bit into the water, and it sinks. I somehow know this is a powerful, unspoken signal from Ascalon Lee.

I pop the spears out of my javelin rod, snap the spear in half over my knee, and throw one at the now wide-eyed Akira Kimura. Before I see it hit her, I spin and throw the other. The first pierces her hand and skewers her to the wall behind her. The other strike her other palm, and now both hands are pinned to the wall. Akira tries to pull her hands free and screams in pain or anger. I can't tell which.

I spin to face my father. His rail is pointing at the ceiling. My second skin forms into a blade, and I cut his rail in half. A shadow, clinging to the domed ceiling above, plops to the floor. Ebony skin. Eyes lustered yellow. It's her. Ascalon Lee.

My father unsheathes a heat blade from his thigh, but before he can attack Ascalon Lee, Pohaku leaps on him, and the two go sprawling across the floor. I run to Pohaku to pull him off my father, but he has my father's forearm firmly in his teeth. He shakes his head violently and tears my father's forearm off. I leap into Pohaku's chest and tackle him. We roll together across the floor, my father's forearm still in the komainu's jaws. Pohaku tries to squirm out of my embrace, but I have him pinned now. His wild, furious eyes streak tears.

"I'm sorry," I say. "Stop!"

But he doesn't stop. He's strong, enraged now, and he won't stop flailing. His claws dig into me in a desperate attempt to separate. My second skin spreads into a net that covers him. He flails beneath it. Then something strange happens. His tears begin to dry. Not dry but solidify. His legs spasm then stiffen. The scales on his belly morph from a shimmering red to a slate jade. The jade spreads from mane to tail. His determined, dragon eyes are the last thing that turns to stone. I get off his now statue form and turn to check on my father.

Before I get up, sirens begin to blare. I smell the greens wafting from outside the telescope. I glance at the holo, and Akkorokamui's tentacles stretch to take down the other drill, but it has already hovered out of the giant octopus's reach. Then I see the most extraordinary thing. A creature the length of a jumbo shuttle bursts from the churning water. Its black-green scales glisten as it uncoils itself and springs into the sky. Mist streams from the serpent's golden beard and two long, fluttering whiskers while it charges the drill above. Once it reaches the height of the drill, its wings stretch, and it just hangs there in the sky, its shadow cast upon the clouds behind it. It inhales, and the horizontal segments of its crimson belly expand. Then the dragon's heavily toothed mouth opens. Like a super-rail, neon blue plasma donuts erupt from its mouth. The drill is reduced to ash. The dragon flaps its wings, and for a moment, it appears to be looking at all of us through the security drone that Akira has placed there. I recognize the large yellow eyes immediately.

"Mother," the flying serpent bellows as here, in this room, Ascalon Lee looks down at Akira and says, "*I am the dragon.*"

Then the creature unleashes rings of plasma, and video goes dead.

The holo flickers to images from right outside. A giant, laughing boar charges the lined-up battalion of Gardeners. Ears pinned back, it's being ridden by a masked Motu, who is snarling and wielding a lance. Dozens of kirin follow him, each mounted by a completely masked mantis-armored raider of Water City. I'm guessing Dreh is among them. Three-legged crows, hundreds of them, suddenly emerge from the shadows and pick the floating iEs from the air. A flock of turtle-shelled phoenixes swoops down and plucks Gardeners from formation. The winged creatures take the Gardeners up and disappear in the smoky clouds.

"Ascalon!"

It's my father, getting to his feet, cradling his shredded arm. Sparking wires dangle from his elbow. My eyes move across the floor and spot his severed forearm as light crackles from it. I move to step to him, but my feet are stuck to the floor. A wave of weariness passes through my entire body, and I almost pass out. I'm trying to yank my foot, but it won't move. My father is walking to me, his good hand reaching out.

I turn and see Ascalon Lee holding up her mother's chin. She pulls the two spears from the wall, and Akira slinks to the floor. Ascalon Lee pushes the two broken halves together, and they form back into a single javelin. The spears retract, and without looking, she tosses the rod to me. I reach up to catch it and am jolted to find my extended arm frozen. The rod lands in my palm, and I need to struggle to barely wrap my fingers around it. My father steps to me and puts his hand on my shoulder.

"What's happening to me?" I ask.

He shifts his gaze from me to Ascalon Lee, and his eyes narrow. I strain to twist my body so that I can see what he can see. It's Ascalon Lee squatting next to her now-prone mother. Her black skin and yellow eyes glisten in the ultramarine light. The sirens go out, and I'm not sure which of the two turned them off, mother or daughter. Ascalon Lee leans closer to her mother's ear. Above us, there's a boom, and the dome, along with the floor beneath us, shakes.

"I will monitor for you," Ascalon Lee says, ignoring the calamity above. "I will protect. I will cleanse. I will create. But don't you ever threaten me again."

Another boom, and the sound of rending metal creaks from above. Pieces of the telescopes dome begin to fall and clatter on the floor. Again, Ascalon Lee ignores this and projects an image on the wall with her eye. It's the space station orbiting Saturn. Thousands upon thousands of Gardeners spill from the interior like ball bearings and claws pop from their carapaces. They skitter and strafe the ring-shaped gimbals of the spinning gyroscope. Except one. One heads to the gyroscope's central spin axis. It digs its spiked legs into the giant center rod and spins atop the rotor. It extends its two claws up like a crab in prayer. Then it begins to vibrate and glow like sunlight. Ascalon points at my father.

"He missed a version or two," she says. "Or three hundred forty-eight. Or more. Who knows for sure? But they're up there on your space station. Or your other spacecraft. And they are all capable of detonation."

I understand now. The versions of Ascalon Lee back at the Cape in the well of skulls. They weren't headed for Venus. That was just another lie. They were headed to Akira's outer space stepping-stone, armed bombs, just like Ascalon Lee's iE was an armed bomb all those years ago when she blew my father's shuttle out of the sky. Just like all of Ascalon's iEs have a self-destruct mechanism. Her willingness to cut off pieces of herself is true even now. As cheap as life has always been, we've made it that much cheaper, even our own. It makes sense that all this breeds recklessness. Look at us. My father. Akira. Ascalon Lee. Even me. We're all easily willing to self-destruct. I fight to turn back to my father. My teeth lock together. I'm unable to turn. Ascalon grins at me.

"Prevarication doesn't exist because people are inherently dishonest. Prevarication exists because it works." She turns to her mother. "I'll protect your skeleton crew of Gardeners. But when you leave, you leave for good. Mother, A496 will be put into the earth, and you will not be taking my sister with you."

The image gleaming from her eye flickers off, and Ascalon Lee looks back at me. I wrench to push against enclosing, suffocating walls that I feel but can't see. A crash then a swirl of wind from above. Bigger pieces of the telescope collapse and clang around us. A crumpled sheet of metal roofing falls toward Pohaku. I gasp and flinch. It bounces off the stone guardian, not even leaving a chip or blemish.

A voice comes from Akira's body, but her lips don't move. "You are finally worthy," Akira says to her daughter. It sounds like an automated recording being projected from some kind of speaker in her gut. These words that would've meant the world to Ascalon Lee in another life mean nothing to her now. Her yellow eyes shift to my father.

"Both of you, never come back."

He nods. Ascalon stands and puts a foot through Akira's face. It crumples and sparks beneath it. On the other side of the room, the frozen astral projections of my mother, Uncle Akeem, and the baby flicker then disappear. I realize now that what I'm seeing, like the stories of old, is a tale in which humans bear witness to the battles among the gods. Amaterasu versus Susanoo. God versus Satan. Titanomachy. The Osiris myth. Gods always battling their upstart progeny. I try to grab my father with my unfrozen arm, to lock my fingers around his wrist so that he won't go, but it's so hard to move. It's not the weight, but the stiffness. Something inside me is going rigid and spilling out of me. I push and manage to grab his thick wrist. He shifts his palm to hold my hand. Something is ripping apart the walls behind him.

"It'll be okay, kid," he says. "You'll be okay, and that's everything to me."

He grins. The greens and reds brim his smile. They spiral and are sucked into his pupils. And I know at that moment what he's planning. He's going up with OneVoice, to accompany her from one star to the next, to steer Okaasan away from the reds that lurk in every system. And when he feels that they are far enough away, when he feels that she finally trusts him, he will guide them all straight through the red gates of oblivion. *He did choose me over her.* My extended hand trembles, and I squeeze his. Tears stream from my eyes.

"No," I gasp. I want to say more but my jaw is locked. And my tongue and vocal cords go rigid.

Ascalon Lee picks her mother up and carries her to us. She lays Akira at my father's feet. My father nods. The sparking wires from his severed arm dim. He lets go of my hand and slumps lifeless next to Akira. Ascalon Lee turns to me.

"You can't stop him from going. They aren't even here."

"Where are they?" I manage to spit in a sandpaper whisper.

Ascalon Lee raises her eyes to the giant hole in the ceiling. "They're up there."

Truth and comprehension hit me all at once. Akira and my father were operating these bodies remotely. They're in space, orbiting the planet, waiting for the remaining Gardeners to join them. I watch while Savior's Eye is torn apart piece by piece by a giant pair of black-green scaled talons. Soon, I can see the battle taking place around us. The dragon version of Ascalon Lee soars above Akira's water statue. It stops, flapping its wings. It looks down at the statue and breathes out plasma, evaporating it into mist. It now turns its attention to the Gardeners. Before it can rain plasma on them, they all go limp at the same time, like my father just did. Puppets with their strings cut. Neon blue light streams from their eyes and streaks the darkening sky. The great winged beast flies up and up through the sky and stops to block the shimmering lights of Ascalon's Scar.

"Why did she remake it?" I ask.

"Sometimes the simplest answer is the correct one," Ascalon Lee says. "She knew that she was leaving soon and rebuilt it so that all people—no matter Gardener, Leachatean, Water City resident—will always remember her. That is her final statue."

No, I try to say, but the word can't come out. I glance at the statue of Pohaku and tell myself I should've known. Before I left Water City to sail to DownUnder, I'd said to Ascalon Lee, "I thought they always came in pairs."

"It's been my experience that most things do," she'd said back.

Pohaku is one of two komainus. One of two guardian dogs.

The other is me.

If it weren't stone I was turning into, I would collapse from the realization. I try to blink but can't. My drying eyes sear. One of the last things I see before my consciousness dims is the hazy slate jade of my raised arm. Ascalon Lee sighs. "I told you that you need to sleep," she says. "You need to understand your new circadian rhythms. You have spent too much." She gazes at her mother's piano. "But don't worry, my butterfly. You'll wake again soon, but this is the only way that you can live lifetimes."

Ascalon Lee steps to the piano, sits, and begins to play a lullaby. The AMP inside me courses through my body. It showers every organ. My mind screams against it, but it douses my will, too. And now I can't move my eyes. They are cast downward on the lifeless, robotic bodies of my father and Akira Kimura, and my mind rambles. A man and a woman. Two people who abused their ability to see more than others. Two people who twisted their children into themselves. They fought, they championed, they both loved and hated each other. I suppose they will spend an eternity up there trying to outwit each other. Maybe my father will finally win for once. He's due. These dualities that began with a simple, blind date at some cop bar all those years ago. Serendipity. What a cosmic joke. A pinwheel of yin and yang. Fake the world, take the world, make the world. I suppose it's been like that from the very beginning. It's all a fraud, but power can transform fraudulence into truth. It can even turn flesh into stone.

I will miss my father, bitterly miss him. And bitterly love and hate him as well. That's all I'm thinking, how all four of us, four half-orphaned children, could never be made whole again. We should all be turned to stone. We should all wither to dust. For the first time in my life, I don't want to wake up. I don't want to see what's become of the people I freed. I don't want to bear that kind of guilt and responsibility. Finally, my vision dims, and my mind begins its slumber. As a lullaby I once sang but can't remember fades, I hope to god in a god-less world that I do not dream as my mind tangles to night.

EPILOGUE

OFFLINE

Taro the Guardian

Since the beginning, our highest and most demented aspiration has been to become divine. She did it. In Africa, she is known as the Comet Crusher. In Europe, The Star Runner. In Asia, The One Who Sees All. In the Americas, she is still known as Akira. The mythologies differ here and there, but some details are always consistent. She is from a city in the water. She is from a mountain that she once stood upon, where she pierced the sky with her gaze. That is evidenced by the scar that looms above. A twinkling rainbow that has been painted on the walls of caves and on primitive canvases for centuries now.

In some places she's considered evil, in others, benevolent, and in some others, a little bit of both. Here, in this small coastal village that was her childhood home, they refer to her as the Mind Breaker. I watch them now, in their tabis and kimonos, catching fish by using the ancient practice of *ukai*. Water birds leashed to long wooden boats that coast across the river. Each bird collared so that it cannot swallow the bigger fish. They dive into the water, swallow the small ayu, and fill their throats with the bigger ones. Later, the fish will be removed and the slime will be washed off. They will be stuffed in pockets of kelp, roasted, and enjoyed. The village elders will offer one to the Mind Breaker so that she doesn't come back. So that she doesn't return to break minds again.

There are legends of the islands that float, and an underwater city populated by hundreds or maybe even thousands of ageless demigods who occasionally visit people all over the world. It's how they got fire. It's how they learned to mine, craft, tame kirin, and forge steel. It was the most powerful one who came in dragon form, to show people the buried tracks. She showed them how to build the smoking iron horses that skate across the lands today.

There are other rumors of others not like them. Skinny, bald humanoids with crackling blue eyes sighted from time to time. They all wear the same skin-tight clothes and flash across the sky in flying machines. Some believe they're from outer space. Of course, they're not. They're simply what remains of the Gardeners. Those who, even now, monitor all above and below and keep their light fingers on the earth's pulse, still waiting robotically for Okaasan's return.

There have been intrepid sailors who have tried to discover the floating islands, to discover the underwater city, but none have made it back. Stories of giant, tentacled sea creatures have been passed down through the generations. Octopus that sink and eat armies that attempt to cross to another land. Water dragons that rip wooden clippers apart. Also, rumors of a perpetual hurricane, a churning wheel of impenetrable weather, that swirls around the floating islands. To note, the rumors are true. Ascalon Lee has created this hurricane, and Water City and its islands safely occupy the eye of the storm.

The EMP nets have been long decommissioned. Akkoro-kumi, Kanaloa, and Kraken are the new nets that drown would-be conquerors and colonists now. Ascalon Lee con-siders transoceanic colonization humanity's original sin, and she will not let the people of this new world commit that sin again. Perhaps we will eventually be able to make the crossings in their blimps one day, the most cynical and power hungry sometimes think. Despite the phoenix that patrol all the lands. Despite the demigod Taro. Taro the Avenger. Taro the Giver and Taker of Life. Whether it be the brink of famine or genocide, the daughter of The Nameless One always comes with her guardian dog and pulls the people back. When there is murder, she comes in the night to avenge it. They're right. Even when I sleep as stone, I can smell and see the greens. They reanimate me. Nightmares in greens and reds rouse me.

I sometimes look up at the stars and wonder where they are. Since that day three centuries ago at Savior's Eye, my father and Akira have never returned. Perhaps they've made it to the exoplanets of Proxima Centauri. Perhaps they tried to colonize them. Or perhaps they moved on. I suspect my father finally got her, and I occasionally look into Savior's Eye and wonder where and how. I have made the telescope my home now, though I'm hardly home. There is always work to do. Shuttling from one continent to the next. I stop wars. I stop starvation. I assassinate murderers. Yet, I'm a lesser god, not one of the Big Three. Akira, Ascalon, and The Nameless One. I suppose it's always been that way. Creators and destroyers are always supposedly the most powerful gods. Not the caretakers, though, to be fair, Ascalon Lee, who kept her word, and monitors seismic activities both above and below, is the caretaker in chief. I don't see her much anymore. After the first time I woke, I was so angry with her that I refused to speak to her for a few years. But once I flew around the world and saw what she was doing, healing what remained of a broken world, I relented. Just as she suggested, I began to master my circadian rhythms.

The villagers are preparing a feast in honor of Ascalon. I watch them from up here, Pohaku and I, perched on a tree. They hope that Ascalon will notice their humility, but she won't. She's probably in Water City now, concocting the next Raid Day target. Perhaps yet another dragon. Or maybe Mothra again. My father would've said that Mothra is a bad motherfucker. She spat acid that melted mantis armor and shot lasers out of her eyes. She nearly got Motu and his Phoenix Riders killed. I don't understand why Ascalon never tires of genetically engineering kaiju, but I suppose there are things about her I'll never understand. Her seeming indifference to where my father and her mother are, whether they are alive or dead. Her sudden, albeit unfocused and undedicated, almost begrudging concern for the human race. Her tireless fascination with imagining and creating new things. But her complete lack of trust, I get. I know she worries that I'm so angry at her, that I have some kind of long game planned to spectacularly take her out. I don't. I don't tell her I don't, but I don't. I have complete lack of trust, too. We are a species of betrayers. Even the villagers down below reflect this. The village elders, a woman, a man, and a genderless one, all gossip to the villagers about the other two. Too old to lead. Too stubborn to change. Too dishonest to believe. Strangely, the insults of all three hurled behind each other's backs are the same.

But we are a species of teachers and caregivers, too. A woman below nurses the newborn of her neighbor who's ill. A man teaches all the young children how to read. A fisherman, who is now removing slippery ayu from cormorant gullets, is explaining to the older children the art of ukai. The art of strangling something just enough so that it can consume what's theirs but not consume what's yours. I know the art well. It's been inflicted on me my entire life.

There are no murderers here today. Sometimes I watch just to watch. I listen to them tell their tales of the night parade of 100 demons. Vampiric trees that grow on the forgotten battlefields of the last world. Creatures that feed on nightmares. Dragons that make rain. River spirits that pretend to be crying babies when the ghost lights shine at night. I watch the people to confirm what I once suspected. Myth was never the past. Above, unbeknownst to the people below, phoenixes fly over Ascalon's inheritance. Somewhere in the middle of the ocean, a creator creates. In this world, I am Taro the Kirin Rider. Taro the Guardian. Taro the Unplugged. In this world, myth is not tales from the past. It is the documenting of things that will come. In this world, myth is prophecy.

ACKNOWLEDGEMENTS

Special thanks to Amara Hoshijo and Don Wallace for helping me locate a home for this trilogy. Your advice and generosity continue to be invaluable.

Thank you to the Soho team for providing a home for these books. Yezanira, you are amazing to work with. I appreciate all the work you did on books two and three. Alexa, I can't think of a better editor to run anchor on this trilogy.

Thanks to Walter Dods III and Evan McKinney for being the first readers of the initial drafts of all three books.

To my crew of muses—Brittany, Morgan, and Regan—your inspiration has me surrounded, and there's no place I'd rather be.